Gin & Tonic
and Cucumber

Gin & Tonic and Cucumber

by RAFAËLE GERMAIN

translated by DAWN M. CORNELIO

McArthur & Company

Toronto

First published in Canada in 2009 by
McArthur & Company
322 King St. West, Suite 402
Toronto, ON
M5V 1J2
www.mcarthur-co.com

Library and Archives Canada Cataloguing in Publication

Germain, Rafaële, 1976-
[Gin tonic et concombre. English]
Gin & tonic and cucumber / Rafaële Germain ;
translated by Dawn Cornelio.

Translation of: Gin tonic et concombre.
ISBN 978-1-55278-774-8

I. Cornelio, Dawn II. Title.

PS8589 R4739 G5613 2009 C843'.6 C2009-901049-6

Cover illustration by Maud Gauthier
Text design by Tania Craan

Printed in Canada by Webcom

10 9 8 7 6 5 4 3 2 1

For my boys

To: Fred
From: Marine Vandale
Subject: Test

Is this working?

To: Marine
From: Frédéric Vandale
Subject: Technological triumph

Yes, it's working. And it even makes a nice little musical sound when your message comes in – it's like a good omen wrapped in a little ping. It's a happy sound. It makes me wonder how I managed without Internet access for the two years I've been here.

To: Fred
From: Marine Vandale
Subject: Cyber dependence

By becoming a squatter at the cyber café downstairs from you, if I'm not mistaken. Now you just have to be careful not to get addicted to the Internet, because, I'd like to remind you, you've been pretending to be a fancy Parisian for the last two years, just so you could produce a timeless masterpiece – and I don't think I've even seen the first page yet.

To: Marine
From: Frédéric Vandale
Subject: Cyber killjoy

When did you become a cyber watchdog? But you're right. Work, concentrate, keep my eye on the glorious literary horizon. What are you up to?

To: Fred
From: Marine Vandale
Subject: Tinnitus

I'm trying to get back the use of my right eardrum after spending something like eight hours on the phone with *Maman* trying
to explain to her how her cell phone works and that even if
Christophe is super nice and extremely well groomed, I'm not
exactly planning on having a baby with him before the end of
the week.

To: Marine
From: Frédéric Vandale
Subject: Information

You're still seeing Christophe? Because I seem to recall a rather
recent phone conversation where you said that Christophe was
closer to the door than your bed.

To: Fred
From: Marine Vandale
Subject: Re: Information

Yeah, well, we kind of managed to get a little closer to the bed
the day before yesterday. Do I really need to explain or can we
just agree that you've heard this song before?

To: Marine
From: Frédéric Vandale
Subject: Refrain

Let me guess: Christophe's not so bad after all, and even if it's
not passion with a capital P, he's nice and he's cute and why
should you throw in the towel at the least little annoyance,
you're not twenty anymore, you have to make a bit of an effort
in love, just like in life, and by the way, who am I to talk?

To: Fred
From: Marine Vandale
Subject: Right on key

Perfect. You got it all right.

To: Marine
From: Frédéric Vandale
Subject: False note

Okay, but what happened to my little sister – the one who dreamed of passion with a capital P and love that made her head spin?

To: Fred
From: Marine Vandale
Subject: Denial

She's hiding her head in the sand and she'd really appreciate it if you'd do what other polite people do, and pretend you didn't notice. Speaking of polite people, gotta go, the boys are waiting for me. You think I'm ridiculous, don't you?

To: Marine
From: Frédéric Vandale
Subject: Re: Denial

I love you.
:)

Chapter 1

"The gentlemen are waiting for you in the booth, ma'am."
Once again, I wondered why Olivier insisted on calling
me ma'am. Maybe it was because he'd been a maître d' for
so long, but I always wanted to say something like, "Come
on, Olivier, let's stop kidding ourselves. I may indeed be
thirty-two years old, but I have a hard time myself believing I'm an adult, so let's drop the ma'am." And as far as
the guys being gentlemen, I had doubts on that score, too.

I began the interminable and frustrating process of
removing my winter gear (coat, scarf, toque and mittens
– where can you put your toque and mittens? The scarf,
everyone knows, goes nicely into one sleeve of your
down jacket. But, if you put your toque and mitts in the
uselessly small pockets of your coat, there's a good
chance at least one of them will end up on the ground,
in the mud, between an umbrella forgotten last fall, and
some old regular customer's espadrilles. So, you stuff
them into your handbag, knowing very well that two
minutes later, when you're trying to carve out a path
through the labyrinth of small tables, a pink mitten,
shoved in between your toque, wallet, planner and eight
unused tubes of lipstick, will go flying into some distin-
guished diner's stew. Oops.)

The guys are already waving at me wildly from the back
booth, as if I could miss them, as if there was a chance I'd
forget they'd been there at noon every day, for at least five
years, at the same table, *in the same seats.* Laurent was nodding hello, while next to him, Julien, his eyes open wide,
was nodding his head as if to say, "Bravo, eh." Laurent must

have told him everything, I thought. I should have expected it.

I scooted along in front of them to my seat, opposite Laurent. I looked at his cute little face, which I still call a cute little face, even if, well, at forty you have more of a handsome face than a cute little face. We've known each other for almost ten years now, ten years during which I'd seen his face almost every day – I'd even slept beside him, every night for five years. I was always happy to see him again. Laurent was my personal proof that love never completely disappears, that even when you know everything about love with someone, when you think you've drunk the cup dry, there's still something there. I gave him a big smile and stroked his earlobe.

"Hello, Loulou!"

"Hey, good going, champ! You're back together!"

"Oh, cut it out, I'm happy…" I tried to seem convinced – a dangerous strategy in front of these four eyes that knew me by heart and usually knew better than I did, and *before* I did, what I was thinking. But I was happy. I wasn't ecstatic, but I was happy. It's not like I'd never thought about what I was doing. I'd acted like a girl: I'd made lists, I'd hedged, I'd spent hours on the phone with my sister Élodie (the bad advice queen), I'd even tried "to listen to myself," like Julien used to say (easier said than done, for me – I was born indecisive and every assertion I'd ever made had been followed by "yes, but" or "unless." It was very confusing to listen to me – even for me.) By following the most roundabout path possible, I'd arrived at the conclusion that the seven months I'd spent with Christophe had been wonderful ones and the one and only thing I could complain about was that I wasn't   completely,   hysterically, we're-the-only-ones-in-the-world-and-it's-wonderful in love with him. But (and there was always a "but") I really liked him a lot. I felt good with him. And for the month we'd been apart, I'd missed him. Perhaps I was just afraid of being alone. It was something to consider – but I let the boys worry about that kind of thing and, as a matter of fact, they were making me a list of things to consider, like it was a matter of life or death.

"But it wasn't working!" said Laurent.

"You're one to talk!" said Julien.

"So are you!"

"You're one to talk" is the phrase most regularly heard at the core of our group. We usually answered with a scowl and a little "humph," or, in Julien's case, with a sort of indignant whine. This being said, I was right. They were in no position to judge, stuck as they both were in half-satisfying relationships. I wondered if anyone in the restaurant, or even in the whole city, had a completely satisfying or intoxicating relationship, or if the very concept of shared true love was nothing but a huge, rather mean joke whose only purpose was to make us feel pathetic with our approximate love that all too often seemed like a compromise.

"We ordered you a glass of white wine," Julien said, with a kind of compassion I found a little insulting. "I think you'll need it."

I felt like telling them it wasn't like I'd just found out I had a serious, fast-moving disease. Quite the opposite. We should have been in high spirits, filled with vigorous and romantic optimism, believing in happy tomorrows, seeing a rosy future, in other words, doing what normal people do when they decide to bet on love.

"Little Christophe is cute for sure," said Julien, who was about six inches shorter than Christophe. "He's got a bit of a rough side I wouldn't mind getting a taste of…"

Laurent raised his arm in protest, looking vaguely disgusted. "Okay, what did I say about that kind of mental image? Not good, Julien, not good. Embrace your sexuality, but keep it in your head, okay? I've still got an empty stomach here."

"Yeah, I'm hungry, too," said Julien. "Where's Jeff?"

"Jeff hadn't come home yet when I left this morning."
Both their faces looked astonished, offended even. "My,
my, my…" said Julien, and as I looked at him I couldn't
help thinking again that it was a waste that such a handsome man wasn't interested in girls. When he wasn't
making effeminate gestures on purpose, he certainly did-
n't look gay (except maybe for the excessively bright shirts
he insisted on wearing under bubblegum pink or cobalt
blue sweaters, claiming to be an ardent follower of
Stéphane Rousseau and calling us colorphobes when we
implied that his lovely pink pants could lead to a misun-
derstanding). His immense blue eyes were almost hypnotic
– and, at nearly forty, he barely looked a day over thirty.
Girls often flirted with him, which elated him and upset
Laurent, who found this irony of fate highly unjust. One
night, a young man who was convinced he was gay by his
aristocratic manners and choice of cocktail (a strawberry
daiquiri – "Why not a blow job?" Jeff had said) came on to
the poor guy pretty strong. The *coup de grâce* came when
the handsome young man had said to Laurent, in a deliciously lusty way, that he'd always had a soft spot "for
handsome bald men." Laurent, whose hair was really
beginning to thin, almost cried. He went home, upset,
swearing he'd soon dazzle us with his ultra-virile look. He
showed up at the restaurant the next day wearing a toque.

Julien looked at his watch. "So, then, we'll wait for him
another fifteen minutes and then we'll order, okay? I'm
gonna need another drink." He gave the server an incomprehensible hand signal, which to her alone, obviously
meant a scotch. "And while we're waiting, Marine, you can
tell us what was going on in that head of yours. Because, if
I remember correctly, we debriefed for quite a while about
Christophe."

"We debriefed about Carole and Mathias, too, and I'd
like to point out that you're both still with them, too. So,
be quiet, okay?"

"It's not the same thing," said Laurent.

"Right. It's not the same. You were free, Marine! You'd made your move, you could have gone on to something else. Enjoy being single! You know how much fun it is to be single? You know what I'd do, if I were sing…"

"Mental image…" said Laurent.

"Okay, okay. What I mean is that you managed to do what we can't, and now you've just dug yourself deeper into this relationship."

"All right, but first, I'd appreciate it a bit if you'd be just a little encouraging and stopped talking about this relationship as if it were a swamp. And then, give me a break with your moaning and sighing. If you were that unhappy with your girlfriends…"

"Boyfriend," Julien corrected.

"Whatever." Unlike Julien, Mathias was so effeminate that I had a hard time talking about him in masculine terms. "If you were that unhappy, you'd leave them."

"It's not that easy," said Laurent. "I can't do that to her."

"But you can keep leading her on."

"I'm not leading her on…"

"You're wasting her time. Christ, she's thirty-eight years old, Laurent." Laurent hit his head against the wall. I could understand his distress, at least partly. I liked Carole – she was a lawyer, a little stiff around the edges, but pretty funny and remarkably brilliant. But after accumulating a series of pretty pointless relationships with men who were scared silly of commitment and fatherhood, she'd become a kind of caricature of the nearly-forty-year-old woman panicking at the idea that she still doesn't have kids. It was hard to blame her, and I knew very well that if I was a little ill at ease around Carole it was because I saw in her one of my possible futures and that really upset me. She was frantically – and I do mean frantically – looking for a father for her children. And as far as Laurent was concerned, he planned on becoming a father just as he much as he planned on impaling himself on a cactus.

He let out a little moan, his face still turned towards the wall. "Errrrh… why can't I go out with a twenty-two-year-old girl like all the other guys my age who want to make people believe they're still young? I'd feel so gooooood…"

"Oh, bullshit!"

"What, even you're going out with a younger man!"

"Christophe is eight months younger than I am. Not nineteen years younger."

"Meow…" remarked Julien.

Laurent turned to him, looking tired. "Meow?"

"Yes. Meow. Thirty-one-year-old bums are nice. He must have a nice ass, eh?" And he waited for me to answer. "Come on, Marine, come on. Just a couple of details… to make your friend Julien happy. A six pack? Hot pecs? Give us a little something at least!"

"If you ask her what his cock is like," Laurent said, "I'll throw up in your scotch."

I started to laugh. They'd been acting exactly the same way since I'd introduced them to each other eight years ago. I had just barely started seeing Laurent, and Julien was the accountant who'd helped me out when I decided to leave my job as an artist at the advertising agency and start my own business. Jeff's the one who recommended him to me. ("He's great," he said. "And plus he doesn't think like an accountant.") I didn't see what was so reassuring about that, but in the end it made sense to me. As remarkably professional and competent as he was, Julien had an astounding frivolous streak that did him absolutely no professional harm.

He and Laurent were almost always fighting, hid absolutely nothing from each other, regularly told each other off, and were inseparable. Sometimes, I secretly wished Laurent would show up some noontime, with or without his toque, and admit he'd been repressing his homosexuality before throwing himself at Julien who'd then throw his own arms around him. On the other hand, Julien always hoped Laurent and I would get back together.

"You're perfect for each other," he was always telling us. "When are you going to find someone you get along with so well?" It was a good question, one I even asked myself a little too often, and that I still hadn't found a good answer for. I didn't get along with Christophe as well – and I hadn't gotten along as well with all the other men who had passed through my life since Laurent. But I kept on hoping. I kept telling myself, more or less confidently, that it takes a long time to get to know someone that well, that it's a matter of melding yourselves together, and that it doesn't happen in the blink of an eye, so I had to give what I had with Christophe a chance. I wanted to believe.

"Maybe not even twenty-two," Laurent said to no one in particular. "Maybe just twenty-five or twenty-six. They don't want kids yet at twenty-five... do they?"

"No, they want puppies." Jeff slipped gracefully in next to me in the booth. "Sorry, gang. I got a little hung up."

"Hung up?" I asked. "You sure did – I'd like to remind you that you weren't even home at nine this morning. You could have called at least. You know I worry." I'd been living with Jeff for three years. When Laurent and I broke up, he'd invited me to come stay with him, while I "waited to see." Three years later, I still hadn't found what I was waiting for, but we made excellent roommates. The apartment was huge and we knew each other well enough to put up with each other more than passably. I'd met him at university – I was eighteen, he was twenty-three. He wasn't exactly handsome, but there was something about him. He gave off good vibes, as my mother said, and he had a charm about him that had only increased with time – a grave injustice in my opinion, since I'd long ago realized time wasn't on my side.

He was living with a thirty-one-year-old woman when

I met him, and I was seeing a man who was ten years older than me (but at the time, it seemed like two or three centuries to me). We'd talk laughingly about our sugar daddy and sugar mama, and I think we both knew things wouldn't last with them very long. Since then, he'd been drifting along from woman to woman and I'd gone from Laurent to not much.

"You're one to talk," he answered me. "Would you like to tell me what Christophe was doing in my kitchen in boxers this morning at 10 a.m.?"

"Ooohhh… Christophe in boxers…" sighed Julien, which immediately caused a look of disgust to spread across Laurent's face.

"Oh. He hadn't left yet?"

"No he hadn't left yet. He was eating cereal, reading the newspaper and playing with the cat." Jeff leaned on his forearms and turned to me. "Do you want to tell me what you were thinking? I mean… You know I like him Marine, but didn't we settle this affair already? You know there's nothing to be gained here. Wouldn't you like to try something constructive sometime?" I couldn't get mad at Jeff. For three years, I'd been accumulating the kind of short, incredible relationships that are great at twenty, but start getting a little old when you're thirty. Older men, married men, guys terrified at the idea of commitment, still younger ones who want to marry me after two weeks, the emotionally deficient, the overly independent.

"Does he know you slept with his best friend after you broke up?"

"Jeff!!!"

"What? They didn't know?"

I barely had time to give him a less-than-threatening glare when Laurent, who, three years after our break-up, still couldn't tolerate the idea that I had a sex life, shouted, "Good job, eh!" and Julien started clapping his hands, as excited as he always was when something even a little out of place happened.

"We'd broken up!" I whined. And besides, Patrick isn't Christophe's best friend." I said weakly. "They're colleagues."

"Together again," Jeff pointed out.

"No…"

"No, it's true. Not together when Patrick is with his girlfriend. It's true."

I thought Julien was going to burst with joy. I raised my hand in front of Laurent before he had time to shout "Good job!" again and then I put my head down on the table.

"Okay," said Julien. "I couldn't be any prouder of you than I am right now. You know if you were a guy, we'd think you were really cool?"

"But, since I'm a girl, you think I'm the biggest slut in town?"

"No," said Julien. "No way. It's true that's what we would think, if we didn't love you. But, we love you."

"Thanks guys. That really makes me feel better."

I smiled mockingly. But it really was true. It did make me feel better. I felt better knowing they were there, almost every day, and that I had the privilege of being enveloped by their warm, solid friendship. I knew all three of them so well, and I loved them just as they were, with their many bad qualities and all their precious good ones. I also knew they loved me in the same way and that with them I could be who I was, who I wanted to be, without ever worrying about them judging me. (In fact, to be precise, we spent most of our time laughing about our shortcomings and judging each other mutually – so much so that I'd once declared that all four of us, somewhere between our spleen and our pancreas, had an extra organ, the judgment organ. But I would never ask any one of the three of them to change his deepest nature, nor to alter what made him a unique, completely strange, magnificent and irreplaceable person.)

As for my girlfriends, they judged. And my mother, well she was the Supreme Court. She judged my actions and my inclinations, my decisions and my convictions, but only because "she loved me." I often told my mother that if I heard "I'm only telling you this for your own good" one more time, I'd rip off my own arm and beat myself with it till I lost consciousness, but it was in vain (my mother was no dummy and she knew that I'd always put off ripping off an arm in favor of sighing and rolling my eyes, which didn't scare her at all – with three daughters, she'd seen worse).

"Ooh," said Julien. "Isn't that your friend Flavie over there?"

I turned around. Asking if it was my friend Flavie, now that we're talking about her, was like standing in front of the Eiffel Tower and asking "Is this the Eiffel Tower?" Even if you'd only ever glimpsed Flavie once in your life, you'd remember her. She was a six-foot-tall, very loud French woman, with a red mane that hung to her waist, a somewhat excessively regal carriage (she always came in with her head held so high and her step so light I was often afraid that she'd trip over someone smaller than her just because she hadn't seen them from up there) and a style that was all her own. She always wore huge, colorful skirts and, in wintertime, a heavy mustard yellow or fuchsia coat and a strange green felt hat with roses, or perhaps a scarlet wool hat with white and blue pompoms.

"*Allô*, my darling!" she shouted covering a chair next to me with all of that height and the folds of her green cape. "*Allôôôô!* Oh, I'm so happy to see you. I'm so exhausted! So exhausted!" It sounded like exhausTED when she said it. Flavie was always "exhausted." Because of her job, because of the weather, because of the men in her life or the fact that there were no men in her life, it never really mattered.

"What's going on?" I asked her as the boys exchanged amused looks. Jeff gave her a big smile – I knew he liked her. Old Jeff wasn't afraid of anything.

"What's going on? Oh… Oh! Hi, boys!" she said brightly, as if she'd just noticed they were there. She offered them a hand gloved in a stuffed mouse then turned back to me as if they ceased to exist.

"Oh, I can't TAKE Guillaume anymore – he hit me up again for five hundred dollars (she didn't pronounce it like 'five hundredollars,' but she articulated 'five-hundred-dollars' very distinctly) for his rent, shit, who can't pay their own rent at twenty-five?"

"Hold on… you're back with Guillaume?"

"No! Well… A little. Maybe. Crap, Marine, he's the only guy that can bring me to orgasm every time in less than twenty seconds. And I mean *vaginally*, remember." Out of the corner of my eye, I saw Jeff and Laurent exchange an impressed look as if they'd just seen a nice pass, while Julien whispered "*vaginally?*" in Laurent's ear.

"Yeah, but, Flavie… you've gotten rid of him five times and you keep taking him back. You like playing with yoyos?"

"But, shit, Marine, I can't stand being alone! Since Thierry left, I'm so lonely!"

"Thierry left a month ago."

"A month is a looooong time! You know how old I am? I'm thirty-three, Marine, I have to think about my family! And my children!"

"You've got children?" Laurent asked naively.

Flavie got that patient look people use when they have to deal with a simple-minded person. "No, I don't have any children. I'm talking about my future children. If I had children, I sure wouldn't be sitting here now, throwing my back out of line on this crappy chair…" She wiggled back and forth, sighing heartbreakingly, like she was really in pain. I almost laughed when Julien got up to offer her his seat at the banquette, telling her it was no problem, that he wouldn't mind sitting on the chair for a few minutes.

"You're so cute," Flavie answered with a smile verging on flirty. "But I'm not staying."

She still ended up staying a good half-hour, just to feel sorry for herself about her own life, her future children's lives, and even my life, which I found just a tiny bit insulting.

"Shit, Marine. We're not twenty anymore, you know?"

"I know we're not twenty anymore. I feel it every morning after, believe me."

"What I think is that it isn't exactly hilarious to be back on the market at our age." She pointed over her shoulder with her thumb. "Have you seen what's out there? Have you seen the assholes out there?"

In protest, Laurent and Jeff muttered, "Hey."

"And you're not doing yourself any favors, sweetie. You think guys get turned on by girls that spend all their time with other guys? Not that I have anything against you guys, you're cute as anything and, compared to the wide range of idiots we usually meet, you're not bad at all." I held back a smile and watched the guys out of the corner of my eye as they tried to figure out if they should be insulted or flattered. "This is no way to find yourself a man, Marine."

And there it was. It was one of my mother's favorite lines, too. And she was so desperate for me to find a boyfriend that she'd gone so far as encouraging me to go out to Lovers in a miniskirt and fishnet stockings, with a couple of girlfriends – preferably ones who were not too pretty – in order to tip the scales in my favor. "You're sure not going to find someone if you spend your evenings cooking dinner with your ex and a gay guy," she'd say. "I love Julien, he's great, and you know I have nothing against homosexuals, but Marine, you're not going to get any kids out of the deal. Why don't you go out a little more? You could call Sarah or Caroline."

"Sarah or Caroline?"

"Yeah, you know, they lived one street over from us when you were little."

"*Maman*, the last time I saw them, I think we watched an episode of *Candy* together. I wouldn't recognize them if I tripped over them."

"Okay, but it would be good for you to go out with girl-friends! Do you really think a guy's going to dare come up to a girl who's always with other guys?"

So I'd tell her, with a weariness that was reaching astro-nomical proportions, that that was just the point – I didn't want to have anything to do with a guy who was too cow-ardly to come up to girl just because she was with other men. "A bit of virility, and some self-confidence," I'd say. "A real guy, with balls and everything." My mother would shake her head sadly, and I know for a fact that deep down inside she was saying, "This poor child is going to end up all alone with her ideas about greatness and balls." Then she'd turn her attention to my younger sisters who, at twenty-three and twenty-five years old, were not yet lost causes and might even beat me by giving her what she was asking for more and more hysterically: her first grandchild. "I'm sixty-two years old, Marine! You're father's sixty-nine. We'd like to see them grow up at least…" she'd say to me in a pitiful and resigned voice as if they were both ninety-five and had pacemakers.

I had, naively certainly, thought that she'd relax when she found out I was seeing Christophe, but exactly the opposite happened, and even though I'd only been seeing him for eight months, she figured we should already have three children, a golden retriever, and a mortgage on a house in Laval, preferably only two blocks from her. She called me every week asking when I was "going to bring her" Christophe, but I would always put it off, thinking it was because Christophe didn't deserve such a thing, but to tell the truth, I hadn't introduced anyone to my parents since Laurent, and I was secretly afraid that I didn't love Christophe enough, and I more or less consciously feared that my mother would notice. But, if my mother realized I had a boyfriend that I wasn't crazy about or ready to have children with, not only would I hear about it till the end of time, I would also have to take a hard look at certain things that I preferred to not glance at, or consider from a distance, or even see at all.

"Well," Flavie sighed. "Do what you want. But you can't say I didn't warn you, eh, if you're still alone at forty."

"Yeah, well, that's just the thing…"

"What's just the thing?" She sat up straight on her chair. "Did you meet someone? Did she meet someone?" Now she was talking to the boys, looking almost panic-stricken. I knew her well enough to be sure that having a friend who was single was essential for her. She was looking at me like I'd betrayed her.

"She's back with Christophe," said Julien.

"Are you kidding me?" Flavie asked.

"Jesus, would just one of you like to encourage me? I'd like to remind you you're supposed to support me unconditionally."

"Speak for yourself," said Flavie. "Shit, Marine! What about passion? Do you really just want to settle? You know what happens to people who settle?"

I knew her answer by heart and said it before she could: "They dry up on the inside?"

"Yes, exactly. They dry up on the inside."

"I'm not settling with Christophe. I wouldn't be with him if I was. I'm terrified of settling, Flavie." Honestly, I wasn't really settling. Our relationship could even be turbulent. It's just that I wasn't sure. But, okay, I was never sure. I wasn't even sure I'd ever be sure, which really depressed me, but at the same time, people who were

always sure of everything depressed me, too. I thought
that at least my doubts were honest.

Flavie shrugged her shoulders. "And, hey, didn't you
spend last week screwing his best friend?"

"We'd broken up!"

"The whole week?" asked Julien. "Me-ow!"

"Okay," said Laurent, looking discouraged, "what's
with the meowing?"

"What, what's with the meowing? Meowww, that's all.
It's just that I would have liked to spend the week screwing a guy like Patrick, too."

"Barf! Barf!"

Flavie didn't hide her annoyance as she looked at them,
and she pinched her nose between her eyebrows as if she
had a headache, then she turned resolutely towards me,
all but turning her back on Laurent and Julien.

"Okay. Listen. You know what you and I are going to
do? We're going to go eat and you're going to explain what
you're doing with Christophe. I want you to convince me,
sweetie."

So do I, I felt like saying.

"Do you think Patrick told him about you two?"

"Okay, Flavie, my beauty," said Jeff. "There are some
things about male psychology I'm going to have to explain
to you. Patrick wouldn't mention it even if Christophe
caught him in the act!"

Flavie raised her eyebrows and crossed her arms. "Hold
on, handsome. You can't really think you've got anything
to teach *me* about male psychology." She was half smiling,
and I was thinking she might like Jeff. Now he crossed his
arms and looked happy – he liked his fake arguments with
Flavie – but she raised one hand.

"Some other time, honey. I have to go," she said. She
slowly stood, unfurling six full feet of green wool. We all
looked up. "Call me, sweetie. I'm not letting you off that
easy, you know."

"Believe me, I know."

"Okay, I'm out of here, I have a meeting at the zoo. They've got an HIV-positive monkey, I'm going to have a look. Does anyone know a professional Santa Claus? I'm looking for one for next week's show." She didn't even wait for us to answer. She'd known for a long time that most of her questions ("You wouldn't happen to have a Hassidic cousin, would you? I'm looking for a man who's half Hassidic, half true-blue Québecois" or "Do you know where Satanists hang out in Montreal?") would be met generally with nothing but empty, unsettled looks, and then she was off in a green and red whirl.

"Wow," said Jeff. "What a woman!"

"That's for sure."

"Invite her over for dinner sometime. Okay?"

"I don't mind, but…" I fell silent as the server placed two dozen oysters on the table. "… you know she's completely nuts."

"That's obvious!" He swallowed an oyster. "But she's great, too. As another girl who's afraid of settling, you should understand."

"Sure, I understand." I smiled at Jeff. If I were a man, I thought, I'd dream of someone as literally extraordinary as Flavie. "Okay, I'll invite her over. But, Casanova, where were you yesterday?"

"Me? Nowhere. At a girl's. You guys don't know her." He looked evasive, played my glass. Julien scowled and crossed his arms. "You were at Marie-Lune's, weren't you?"

"Yeah," Jeff said. "What do you want to drink? 'Cause I think I'm going to need a bottle of wine all to myself."

Marie-Lune was a girl my sister's age, as pretty and charming as anything, but she was so stupid and air-headed it had amazed us for years. Sometimes I suspected Jeff loved her deep down, though he had a hard time admitting he liked being with this young woman, who was certainly sweet and kind, even if she was short on brains.

"And what gives you the right to talk about me?" I shouted. "You sit there and laugh at me because I'm with Christophe again..."

"I'm not with Marie-Lune again."

"Seems to me..."

"Lucky... Did you have a good night?" asked Laurent, who'd been wanting to leave Carole for a woman who was not only younger, but also less demanding, and he was trying to convince himself that happiness and intellectual stimulation didn't necessarily go hand in hand. I was close to believing he might be right, after all.

"A good night?" Jeff repeated. "Uh, um... yeah... it was okay. Nice."

"I can't *believe* you're with Marie-Lune again," I repeated.

"You think I can believe that you're with Christophe again?!"

"I can't believe either one of you," said Julien.

"Hey! You're one to talk!" Jeff and I spoke almost simultaneously. Laurent giggled into his glass and all four of us started to laugh. Jeff, still smiling, rubbed his face.

"Jesus, we're tough to please..."

"Oh, it's not that bad!" I said. I was still laughing and so were the boys. I didn't give up. "At least we're trying. That's why we're not as tough to please as that..."

"Yeah, maybe," Julien admitted. "While we're waiting, a bottle of wine might help to..." He raised his head, his attention suddenly attracted by someone or something outside the restaurant. "Oooh... this *is* going to be tough!"

"Oh boy..." said Laurent. "Who is it exactly? But before you tell us, do we really want to know?"

"It's your man," Julien said to me.

That's when I asked one of the stupidest questions of my life: "Which one?" The words were barely out of my mouth when I realized how ridiculous I was: first, I thought my three men were already with me. Then, I had the very unpleasant idea that it was Patrick and that he might be with his girlfriend, and that I wanted to melt into the banquette. Finally, I thought it must be Christophe, and I thought I was pitiful.

"Which one…" I repeated through clenched teeth. Jeff and Laurent looked at me as if I were a bit of a moron, but Julien leaned towards me, his eyes shining and his smile saucy.

"Doctor Gabriel Champagne is in the house."

To: Fred
From: Marine Vandale
Subject: Insomnia

Do you think I screwed up by getting back together with Christophe?

To: Marine
From: Frédéric Vandale
Subject: Survival Instinct

If you don't mind, I think it would be wiser for me to keep silent on that question, because I have a strong feeling that no matter what I answer, I risk having my nose rubbed in it in the not too distant future. Instead, why don't you tell me what brought on this particular concern?

To: Fred
From: Marine Vandale
Subject: Nice and easy

Have I ever mentioned Gabriel Champagne, the handsome doctor who often eats at the same restaurant as us?

To: Marine
From: Frédéric Vandale
Subject: Soft Pedal

You're not seriously telling me you've already met someone else? Because, I don't know, Marine, but suddenly, I'm feeling a little tired of this.

To: Fred
From: Marine Vandale
Subject: Glory to the human body

What if I tell you he is the most handsome specimen of a gen-
tleman I've seen in a long time? That he has black hair that you
just want to run your fingers through, eyes as blue as the
Naples sky at night, and the smile of a man who wears his
charm like a second skin?

To: Marine
From: Frédéric Vandale
Subject: Una notte à Napoli

Have you ever even been to Naples?

To: Fred
From: Marine Vandale
Subject: Trivial Matters

You're very nice, but don't bug me with geographical details.

To: Marine
From: Frédéric Vandale
Subject: The heart of the matter

All right. Who is this Mr. Champagne? And, what kind of doctor is he anyway?

To: Fred
From: Marine Vandale
Subject: Saviour of humanity

We're not too sure about that. The server is the one who told
us he's a doctor. So, it's pretty vague, he could be saving lives in

cardiology or doing root canals on the Rive-Sud. Personally, I like to imagine he's a doctor without borders.

To: Marine
From: Frédéric Vandale
Subject: The doctor's borders

....

I don't want to get bogged down in details, but have you had any contact with the doc?

To: Fred
From: Marine Vandale
Subject: Full Contact

....

First of all, I've already exchanged a couple of non-verbal hellos with him – you know, I nod my head with a twinkle in my eye, and last week Julien pointed out to him he'd dropped his scarf. So, we're not far from an extended conversation. And I'm sparing you the details of all the smiles I've gotten which translate to say "We don't know each other, but I recognize you, because desire needs no words."

To: Marine
From: Frédéric Vandale
Subject: Re: Full Contact

....

So you've never spoken to him, eh?

To: Fred
From: Marine
Subject: RE: Full Contact

....

No. No, not a word.

To: Marine
From: Frédéric Vandale
Subject: The doc comes out of the bag

You're telling me you're sitting in front of your computer at four in the morning because you've got a crush on a doctor, but nobody knows if he's really a doctor, because no one's talked to him? And what about poor Christophe in all this?

To: Fred
From: Marine
Subject: Bad faith

I'd like to remind you that as far as poor Christophe is concerned, you were one of the first ones to tell me to send him packing. So, spare me the compassion for him, I haven't gotten any sleep. And since we got back together, the boys have been showering me with doubtful looks, and you've been sending me uncertain emails. So, none of you are helping.

To: Marine
From: Frédéric Vandale
Subject: Sharing the blame

Okay, maybe. But do you think you're doing yourself any favors? And, I really don't want to play devil's advocate, but my solid life experience is telling me that when a girl starts fantasizing about a stranger, whether he's a doctor without borders or a winner of the Nobel Peace Prize, it might be a sign she's not 100% satisfied with her relationship.

To: Fred
From: Marine
Subject: Re: Nobel Prize for insight

What do you think is keeping me up at four in the morning in the first place? I know all that, Fred. And I really like Christophe, and I know better than anyone that butterflies in your stomach don't last. So, I keep trying to tell myself all this might be normal, and that it's just healthy to melt with desire over strangers, especially when their eyes are as blue as the Aegean. And no, I've never been to Greece.

To: Fred
From: Marine
Subject: (none)

....

You just keep on dreaming, don't you?

To: Fred
From: Marine
Subject: Re: (none)

....

I know. I can't stop.

:)

Chapter 2

Christophe was asleep, lying on his back, one hand across his chest. I gently got free, trying not to wake him when I slipped my left leg out from between his. I looked at him for a second and, like always, I thought he was cute. I didn't think he was handsome, like Julien was, but I thought he was cute. Adorable. He had big brown, laughing eyes, a childlike mouth and two beauty marks on his face, one on his right cheekbone and the other on his left temple; they were almost as elegant as the ones aristocrats used to paint on their faces.

Our clothes were scattered all over, everywhere, and it gave the room a friendly look I liked. I got up slowly, stumbled over his shoes, colorful Puma runners, and over a tee-shirt of his lying on the floor – the kind that looks old even when it's new, with the logo of a band that had probably broken up by the time Christophe was born – how did I end up with a hippie?

Night was starting to fall and I wondered what we were going to do. A movie, undoubtedly, and some homemade pasta. We'd been out late last night and the night before, and I knew he was looking forward to a quiet evening as much as I was. I briefly thought I'd rather be alone, so I could sit in Jeff's old chair and channel surf without thinking twice about watching five reruns of *Law and Order* in a row.

I looked towards Christophe again. He looked so young. I almost jumped on the bed to wake him up and stretch out against his soft skin – I know he would have laughed, and we would have talked a little, all tangled up together, before we got up. But I turned back towards the door. I knew he was capable of sleeping another half-hour and I planned to make the most of it.

My room opened onto the huge room we used as a dining room, a living room, an office for Jeff, and a drawing room for me, and which in turn opened onto the kitchen. I closed the door extra carefully, and hadn't even taken one step before I noticed Jeff, sitting at the table, his nose pointedly stuck in book, holding out a shirt for me.

"Fuuuuck," I muttered. I hesitated a couple of ridiculous seconds, then, with rather awkward steps, crossed the distance that separated us, finally took the shirt from him, and tried to slip it on as quickly as possible.

"What are you doing here?" I mumbled, trying to find the left sleeve. It was one of his shirts and it hung almost halfway down my thighs. With his nose still in his book – barely a half-inch from the pages – he said, "I live here? In case you don't remember?"

"Mmmm. Okay. All right."

Finally, he raised his eyes and looked at me with a smile. "A bathrobe? A tee-shirt? No? You weren't in the mood?"

"I like being naked when I'm all alone."

"Look, if you really insist, I'm totally ready to live with the fact that you walk around naked all day long. Even and especially when I'm not here. But, still…"

"Weren't you supposed to be in Québec?"

"Yep, till four o'clock today."

"I thought you were coming back Friday."

"Today is Friday."

"Ahhhh…" I laughed at myself and sat down hard on a chair opposite Jeff. Then, a rather unpleasant thought ran through my head. "Oh God, how long have you been here?"

"Exactly long enough," Jeff answered with a smile. "I got home just at the right time."

I covered my face with my hands. Jeff and I may well know each other inside and out, but it was still a little uncomfortable. "Soooorrrrry."

"Now, now." He smiled at me. He was speaking in a low voice, too, and I figured he didn't want to wake up Christophe either. He got up without making a sound and gestured towards the kitchen. "You want a drink? A little gin and tonic? I have cucumbers."

"I don't follow you…"

"Gin & tonic and cucumbers. Very, very good. And very summery, too. My new remedy for the gray of winter."

"Whatever." Jeff loved inventing new cocktails. He went into the kitchen, stepping around the counter on the dining-room side that served as a bar.

"Maybe you'd like something more substantial? To relax after all that… er… exercise?" He had his forearms leaning on the counter and laughed as he looked at me.

"Okay… Sorry. I got my days mixed up."

"At least your door was closed."

"At least we weren't on the counter."

He pulled his arms off the counter like he'd just been stung. "Oh, Marine…! Have you ever…?" He pointed to the counter then waved his hands around. "No, never mind, I'd rather not know. Really."

"All right, you know you look a lot like Laurent right now. You okay, you little hypocrite?"

He started to laugh, with his head thrown back – normally there would have been a big burst of laughter, but he was careful. I was laughing, too, and I was thinking about my mother and Flavie. It was true that I never felt as good as when I was with my boys, and it was equally true that this was absurd.

He got busy behind the counter, while I picked up the book he was reading, Jonathon Littell's *The Kindly Ones*, a thick slab of a book that had been mistreated by its first reader – me (I was tough on books). Jeff and I had an informal book club – one of us bought a book, read it, and inevitably passed it on to the other. We had almost exactly the same taste, and neither one of us remembered if this had always been the case or if it was due to living together and getting to know each other inside and out that we'd developed similar sensibilities.

I read a few lines, and then, with my chin still resting on my right hand, I looked up towards Jeff, as he approached me carrying a glass full of beautiful slices of cucumber. "I feel like I'm in the movie *Cocktail.*"

"Hey, no jokes, or else I'm getting out my Hawaiian shirts and my Beach Boys albums."

"Really?! That would be soooooo cooooool."

He laughed and came and sat down next to me. "You okay?" he asked in that undeniably sincere voice that only those who know us inside and out can use.

"Of course, I'm fine." I nodded my head towards my room. "I'm really fine." Jeff seemed to doubt what I said, and I suddenly understood. "Oh my God, you talked to my brother!"

"You can't sleep at four in the morning!" said Jeff. "You ask ridiculous questions. Of course I'm worried."

I raised my fist in a ridiculous gesture of protest. "Stupid, fucking Frédéric…"

We both laughed. "You know," I said to him, "I still haven't written to Fred about you're being back with Marie-Lune."

"I'm not…" He looked discouraged. "Okay. Whatever. I don't know. I don't know."

There was a moment of awkward silence. The cat, who, as usual was sleeping in a fruit bowl, got up, stretched, and came over to rub his face on Jeff's chin.

"Do you think we should be deliriously happy because we're in love?" I asked. "Do you think that, somewhere, there are normal people who are so crazy about their

boyfriend or their girlfriend they just can't get over how
lucky they are and have never even noticed handsome
doctors who eat in the same restaurant they do?"

"I think you ask way too many questions, Marine." He
smiled at me and kissed me on the forehead, and I almost
felt like asking him to teach me about certainty, to tell me
how to wake up one morning without asking any more
questions. He got up quietly to answer the ringing telephone, all the while grasping my neck gently. How could
such a Colossus be so gentle? A triumph of self-control, I
said to myself. If I were him, I would have demolished
armoires and smashed door frames just by moving
around my own apartment.

"Hey," Jeff said. "Hmmm? What do you, *what do you
mean*? I've been telling you for a week and a half I was
supposed to come back today!… It is Friday. Christ, have
any of you ever seen a calendar in your life?" He started
laughing. That was Laurent, all right. He had received
quite an inheritance when his father – who'd made a for-
tune in the aluminum business in Saguenay – died, and
he hardly ever worked anymore (for this reason, we
would tell him he was "independently wealthy," and he
would shout back, "I am NOT independently wealthy!").
He was satisfied with producing, more or less biennially,
funny, brilliant documentaries that won him substantial
success with both critics and the unfortunately limited
population that enjoys that kind of movie. This left him
free about six months every year, and he spent the time
daydreaming, pursuing projects that would never materialize, not knowing what day of the week it was, and very
calmly developing his next documentary (he'd been
working for a while on something he called a road movie
about travelling all the way up rue Saint-Laurent in order
to see the city's history through its main street).

Jeff kept on talking and laughing with Laurent for a
few minutes more, then he handed me the phone.

"Hi, Loulou!"

"How are you?"

"How are you?"

"I'm okay. Helllloooo…!"

"Helllloooo…" Jeff rolled his eyes and grabbed his book with one hand. Every day, Laurent and I had this interminable, useless conversation that other girls usually had with their mothers. Carole hated it, and I could understand her. We said hello a thousand times, found out how the other was, even though we'd been together the day before, gave running commentary on the TV shows we were watching, talked in depth about our work schedules (quite a ridiculous concept given the fact that I ran my own business and that when Laurent wasn't filming, even he would forget what a schedule was), dissected each of our little worries ("I think I have a boo-boo on my elbow…"), gave detailed reports of what we saw from our windows ("Ooof, there's a guy getting killed in front of the house"), and generally exchanged what extremely close people exchanged – laughter, little stories, troubles, even moments of silence on the phone.

"What are you dooooooing?" in the voice he used when he didn't want to know what I was doing, but rather what he could be doing himself, in case there was a chance I'd suggest some simple activity like a homemade meal.

"We're having a gin and tonic," I whispered.

"Lucky stiffs… did he put in cucumbers?"

"Hey, now, does everyone know about cucumbers except me?"

"Cucumbers are great. Julien thinks they're very practical, he says you can put them on your eyes if they ever get puffy."

"Julien's an idiot."

"Sometimes he is, yeah." He was whispering, too.

"Laurent, why are you whispering?"

"Errr… Why are you whispering?"

I couldn't help laughing. "You know you're an idiot, right?"

"Maybe." Still whispering. "But… why are *you* whispering?"

"Christophe's sleeping. We don't want to wake him up."

"Oh…" I could feel he was disappointed. Laurent liked Christophe, he'd actually met him before me, by chance once when he was with Jeff. We'd all been together several times since, but I could see that Laurent wasn't the same when Christophe was there, and I couldn't blame him, that's the weight exes have to bear when they stay friends – I wasn't completely at ease around Carole either. It was undoubtedly due to the fact that we both knew for sure that our current, and future, boyfriends and girlfriends would always have a distrusting eye for this other person, this "ex" who took up so much space in our lives.

"You want to come over?" I asked.

"No… no, it's okay. Carole's coming over."

"Whatever you want, Loulou."

We talked fifteen minutes, then I hung up, not without confirming our date for noon the next day. I was going to sit back down next to Jeff when Christophe came out of the bedroom. More sensible than me, he was wearing boxers and a tee-shirt. He saw me first, shot me a big smile, which I returned, then went over towards Jeff with a big "Hey!" They'd been working together for several years and liked each other a lot.

"Hey, you stud," said Jeff, slapping hands with him (the high-five is an inexplicable, unnerving habit). Christophe smiled, came over and put his arms around me and kissed my neck. He had what I called an extraordinary "ease of being." His movements were supple and graceful, his decisions seemed to be made organically and, as far as I could see, he wasn't familiar with adversity or the exaggerated, useless introspection that characterized so many other affluent young people I knew (including myself, I had to admit). He gave off a kind of purity, and I wondered if it was because he was a stranger to heartbreak and had never questioned himself. Maybe an easy life had some charm to it after all.

"Did I sleep long?" Christophe asked, yawning and scratching his head. His dark hair formed charming, undisciplined peaks, and, once again, I thought he was cute. Despite his thirty-one years, the teenager he'd been was never far off. He still surfaced in some of his gestures, in his constantly moving body, in his animated face. This all infused him with a strange, sensual grace. Next to him, Jeff looked like a rock, or a statue, something serene made from stone. I understood what girls saw in him, especially young ones who were twenty or twenty-five; they were attracted to this tall man like a magnet. You could tell he could pick you up with one arm and that his chest was solid, strong and reassuring. I liked having him in the apartment with me. I called him my Shrek and fell asleep peacefully knowing he was in the next room.

"Gin and tonic?" he asked Christophe.

"Maybe just a scotch."

He went around to the other side of the counter, too, stopping to stroke the cat, who'd gone back to the fruit bowl and was sound asleep, all curled around a lemon, then he started searching through the liquor cabinet trying, amidst the countless bottles, to find the one he wanted. It was a tough job. Along with the expected vodka, rum, gin, scotch and tequila, which were along the left-hand side in high rotation where bottles were quickly replaced, we also had triple sec (for Margaritas), Bailey's (given to Jeff by one of his aunts), crème de menthe (for when my mother came over), Frangelico (for desserts), Godet (a disgusting white-chocolate liqueur Jeff used to ice certain cakes), grappa, Campari and Ricard, Jagermeister (which no one remembered

buying or receiving), Amaretto (for Marie-Lune's
Amaretto sours, Sambuca (for Julien's Sambuca coffees), the bottom of a bottle of Grand Marnier (that no
one even dared to look at since Jeff and I had almost
finished the bottle one night, only to wake up the next
morning with the distinct impression we'd been pick-
led), bourbon (which we'd impulsively purchased two
years ago when we decided to stage the Mardi Gras
parade in the house), ginger ale (why? why?) and even
the dregs of a bottle of banana liqueur, whose very presence in our home was certainly less worrisome than the
fact that almost all of it had been consumed.

"You're not looking so great..." Christophe said, laughing and holding out two bottles of single malt. Jeff pointed
at one, arbitrarily, I think, since he wasn't much of scotch
drinker. He was pouring himself a glass when the phone
rang.

"Madame Vandale!" Jeff answered joyfully. He adored
my mother, primarily, I believe, because he could spend
hours on the phone with her, lamenting over the poor job
I was doing managing my love life and exchanging recipe
ideas. I often told him that my mother brought out the
sister-in-law in him and he didn't protest too much. They
talked for a few minutes, as I stood next to Christophe,
playing distractedly with his hair while he read a magazine
he and Jeff had written for. I listened to Jeff's sympathetic
comments about the way my two sisters were wasting
their time, each in her own way, and about Ricardo's
cooking, "It's not really that good, Madame Vandale. Stop
thinking everything you see on TV is good." (Good luck,
I thought. My mother had spent the last forty years living
in a kitchen with the TV always on. You might as well ask
a Carmelite to question the existence of God.)

"Whenever you want," he finally said. "Monday? Okay,
we'll talk. "Ciao! Ciao!" I turned around to take the phone,
but Jeff was already hanging it up.

"Hey! Didn't she want to talk to me?" Christophe was cracking up.

"Well, no," Jeff said. "She just needed my gremolata recipe."

I looked discouraged, making Christophe laugh twice as hard. "Yes, yes. Very funny." But I was smiling, too. "I'm going to go get dressed, okay? Your shirts are scratchy, Jeff."

"I told you you could stay naked."

"Yeah, yeah…"

I hadn't taken a single step towards the bedroom yet when the cat, who had an all-consuming, jealous passion for me, got up and stretched around his lemon. "Come on, Claude François!" He jumped lightly down from the counter and trotted over to me with his nose turned towards my face as if he was expecting something, con-gratulations, encouragement, food, who knows.

"Claude François?" asked Christophe. Jeff and I rarely called the cat by his name, which was a little on the long side. Most of the time, "cat" did quite nicely. But, now and then, when it was a matter of proving his loyalty to one or the other of us, we got out the heavy artillery.

"His fur is the same color as Claude François' hair," Jeff explained.

"And he's off-key when he meows," I added. "I swear. He's off-key."

"Come here, Claude François!" said Jeff now, adding the normal little kisses people inexplicably offer animals when they want to get them to come to them. Not only did the cat not turn around, he wound himself around my feet.

"Hmmpf," said Jeff, raising his glass to him. "Cheers, old man. I would have done the same thing. She really is a lot cuter than I am."

"No, *Maman*. No, I'm not bringing Christophe over… because he's working that night. Yes, well, I couldn't have known, could I? *Maman*... Laurent? Why do you want me to talk to Laurent about it? *Maman*, Laurent and I haven't been together for three years. I'm with Christophe now. No. No, I'm not bringing Christophe. *Maman!*"

Phone conversations with my mother often gave me the impression I was in a particularly perverse labyrinth, and when we were on the phone together, I felt like Astérix and Obélix in *The Twelve Labors of Astérix* when they're stuck in the insane asylum and all the directions everyone gives them to get out keep leading them back to the same spot.

"*Maman*," I finally said, "I'm going to hang up now, because my hand is completely frozen and I'm at my meeting, okay? But don't worry, I'll be there next week. No. No. *Maman*. No. I'm not bringing Christophe. Bye, *Maman*." I hung up and stopped right in the middle of the sidewalk to catch my breath. A man passing by who'd heard my final words looked at me laughing.

"I feel your pain," he said. Evidently, I wasn't the only one who had a mother who really should have opened a matchmaking business. I smiled at the man and climbed the steps leading to my studio. Strictly speaking, I didn't really have a meeting, but I was at the point where I would have claimed a sudden attack of malaria in order to hang up. And my hand was frozen. Really.

The door was unlocked, a sign my younger sister was already there. She came three afternoons a week to return phone calls, place orders and look after minor problems – I'd hired her last year when she'd lost her job and I got tired of getting six calls a week from my mother telling me it didn't make sense for me not to show "a little more solidarity for my poor little sister." I didn't really need her, since I did my drawings by myself, and often at home, and the studio served more as a warehouse, and occasionally as a gallery. But okay. I would have paid someone night and day if that's what it would have taken to get my mother off my back.

"Élodie?" I called. Silence. The studio, a big loft with white-painted brick filled with countless rolls and piles of paper, and a variety of other objects I'd been accumulating for years and had been threatening to sort for at least as long, seemed empty. No one at the drawing table, or at the desk.

"Élodie, Christ!" The bathroom door finally opened and a little blond head, in tears, appeared. I was going to add something else, but she raised one hand and made her famous pitiful face – the one she'd been working on since she was four and our other sister Ariane would take her dolls. Now that she was twenty-five, she had it down perfectly: it was a mix of big, sad, blue eyes, a little pout and a chin that was just barely quivering.

The miracle was that she still managed to soften up our father and a few other naive men. But I didn't fall for it anymore, in any case, not since the night I was babysitting both of them and Élodie convinced me Ariane had yanked out a hunk of her hair though Frédéric had seen her cut it off herself, all to get permission to watch *Robin Hood* instead of *Beauty and the Beast* (a topic of unending debate between Élodie and Ariane, who, seventeen years later, still fought about which was the most edifying movie). I was fifteen then and still stupid enough to be proud that, despite the fact that Frédéric was eighteen, I was the one my parents left in charge of my little sisters. A dubious choice, undoubtedly, since, exasperated by their schemes, I decided to put in the tape of *The Silence of the Lambs*. Ariane cried for three days and never touched another piece of meat and I think Élodie was sixteen when she stopped believing Hannibal Lecter was spying on her from her closet.

I let out a long sigh. "Okay, what's wrong?"

Élodie gave a little whine and came towards me with her arms out like a child looking to be consoled.

"Élo," I said, "I've been here for five minutes. I know it

would be quite surprising if a rival illustrator came to secretly steal the plates for the next book, but getting my computer stolen because my little sister is bawling in the bathroom isn't high on my list of priorities."

She sniffed and looked at me like I'd slapped her. Then she tried to look noble, but really she just looked resigned as she said, "Stop picking on me!"

"Élodie..." I used a gentler tone, because I knew that even if my sister was often unbearable and a spoiled baby, she was sincere about her troubles, as pointless as they may be. "My work is here. My whole life is on my computer. And I'm happy to have you working here..." I stopped to think. "... most of the time. But you have to show an employee's responsibility, I don't have to tell you that, do I? And just because I'm your sister doesn't mean you can fuck the dog like that... You know how much it costs me to..."

"Okay, okay. I don't need the How-Much-It-Costs Speech again!" And she raised an indignant hand. At twenty-five, there was still a mystery to the way she could command such authority as she assumed an air of completely unjustified indignation, like the kind you see in little kids who've been caught red-handed. She started to sob tragically. She made me almost want to laugh, sometimes, and even if she exasperated me often, she also made me melt. Frédéric had yelled when he found out I'd hired her part-time, screaming I'd go bankrupt and probably destroy the fragile family balance through a possible attempted *sistercide.*

"Well," I said to her. "You want to tell me what's wrong?"

She looked up at me with huge blue eyes where I was supposed to see all the sadness in the world. Instead, what I saw was a freighter of manipulation and several gallons of self-pity. "Élodie. What's wrong?"

"It's Félix."

"Félix who?"

"Félix, my boyfriend!"

"Élodie, I've never heard of Félix. Two weeks ago you were going out with a cameraman named Charles-Antoine."

She moaned even louder. Élodie dreamed of becoming an actress and sometimes worked as an extra on different TV series or in music videos, and sometimes even in movies, when Laurent managed to get her a small contract. Since then, she'd fallen into the habit of developing crushes on all the cute little technicians who worked behind the camera, guys who were more or less young and funny, rather charming little bums I would have fallen for at her age, too. But they truly were charming little bums and they never stayed long. Élodie chalked it up to their "immaturity" and their "fear of commitment." Personally, I took it for a solid, healthy appetite for pleasure and above all for an unfortunate but predictable reaction to Élodie's great longing – she was trying to find a boyfriend with the same urgency as someone having an asthma attack tried to catch their breath.

"Félix!" she repeated. "Félix! I told you about him, I'm sure! Besides, you know him, he used to go out with Ariane!"

"Now you're going out with Ariane's exes?" I thought it was ridiculous and markedly depressing, but I remembered that if I was going to sleep with my exes' best friends, Élodie could certainly do what she wanted with our sister's exes. "Some family," I thought nonetheless. "Which one of her exes? The little cute one with the dreadlocks? The one who looked kind of crunchy granola?"

"Um… have you ever seen Ariane with a guy who DIDN'T look crunchy granola?" She was right. Since she'd discovered the band Harmonium at summer camp when she was twelve, Ariane had immersed herself in a pseudo-hippie culture whose principles would have made even

Laure Waridel go pale. She was a vegetarian, she would walk miles (never in leather shoes, of course) to find a fair-trade, organic product, she lived in a co-op, was an anti-globalist and volunteered on organic farms in the summer, had traveled several times to South America to help build schools in seriously underprivileged areas, played the lute, knew all the Cowboys Fringants songs by heart, and, despite her gentleness, could make anyone feel guilty after talking to them for just two minutes. I often said being Ariane must be a full-time job: waking up every morning trying to open your heart wide enough to provide a home for immense, universal passion, though it would never be enough, and always believing and wanting to comfort the whole world. Sometimes, I was jealous of her, too, when I thought about the absolute certainty she had, and the pure, straight line she saw stretching out before her. Since forever, certainties and straight lines worried me sick. So I'd go back to my doubts and my crooked path while Ariane went to protest the destruction of a silo.

"Anyway," said Élodie with a sniffle. "It doesn't matter. It's over."

"Come on, now." My words were so lacking in conviction that I was sure Élodie would notice, but she kept on going, with the same pitiful and outraged tone (it was quite a feat. As far as tones go, she was like an expert tightrope walker): "And everything was going really great, besides! Really great! But he stopped calling meeeeeeee!!! I left him a message and told him to screw off, so now he's really not going to call me!"

She opened her eyes wide and buried her head in my chest – good idea, I thought, at least she won't see me laugh.

"Élodie. Seriously. You have to stop. Don't you know you're getting worse and worse?"

"You're one to talk! As if you've had any interesting

boyfriends since Laurent! If I had a guy like Laurent in my life, I'd never, never leave him!"

I almost said that as neurotic as they both were, she and Laurent would have never survived together more than twenty minutes, but I held back. Inexplicably, Élodie saw herself as a woman with remarkable self-confidence, the archetype of a modern, liberated woman. No need to burst her bubble just yet, I said to myself. Easy does it.

"I looooove him!"

"No. No, you don't love him!"

"I can't be alone anymore, Marine."

"Ooh." She seemed so sincere, poor little thing, and this time there was so much real pain in her eyes that I put my arms back around her. I knew for a fact that she'd get over it by the end of the week, but I was sad for my little sister because of how bad she felt about not sharing her life with someone.

She was crying on my shoulder and I could smell her sweet perfume, the product she put in her hair every morning before she straightened it. Her mascara's going to leave a spot on my sweater, I thought. She was always perfectly made up; she wore clingy little sweaters and sparkly earrings. She even had a new laugh that she'd let ring like a thousand little bells every time a man, any man, said something even remotely funny, and a wide-eyed look she'd give when she wanted him to feel like his story was *fascinating*. She worked incredibly hard in the futile, touching hope of being liked, of always being liked more. And she missed her goal every time, exactly because, in my opinion, she tried too hard, because she thought she understood what men were looking for when she couldn't see past her own nose – in fact, she couldn't see past the advice for idiots she found in all the women's magazines she always had her nose in.

We're all in the same boat, I thought, as I rocked my little sister and she continued to snivel. I didn't think I was any smarter than her, really. I thought about Flavie, too, as flamboyant as she was, so seemingly free, but she was looking for the same thing as us. *L'amour, toujours l'amour.* You couldn't stay mad at someone who dreamed of being loved unconditionally.

I tapped Élodie on the back. "Anyway, chicky, the show must go on."

"The show? You draw little pictures, for Chrissake!"

I started to laugh and gently wiped away one of her tears, as it tried to carve out a little path between her sparkling eye shadow and her foundation.

"Somebody called you," she said sniffling. "A guy who didn't sound like he was calling for business."

"Christophe?"

"No... no, hang on..." She leaned over the desk and had to stack up a bunch of magazines before she found what she was looking for. "Here it is. Patrick."

Julien was standing in front of the big mirror in my bedroom, straightening the collar on his saffron yellow shirt. A nice colour, in my opinion, but I would have liked it better if it wasn't competing with a sapphire blue jacket and fuchsia pants.

"Do you think I look like Stéphan Bureau?"

"Sorry?"

"Maybe the blue jacket is a little too much with the yellow shirt?" He looked at himself in the mirror, tugging on the shirt collar again. It's a good thing he's still thin, I thought, because he'd almost look like a clown if he had any belly at all. But he really did look good. He wouldn't last two seconds in a tavern or on a construction site, but he looked good.

"I don't know, Julien. I think Stéphan Bureau is cute, if that helps at all."

"Yeah, but he goes a little overboard with colour, don't

you think? I saw him in a restaurant the other day and he looked like a rainbow with glasses."

"He doesn't wear glasses anymore."

"Whatever. He's got mental glasses, as far as I'm concerned. It's like the guy who does sports on the RDI news. He shaved his moustache about fifteen years ago, I think, but he still has a mental moustache. You know what I mean?"

The worst thing was that I did understand. "You look great, Ju."

He smiled and winked at me. Sometimes I wanted to take his eyes and turn them into beautiful marbles, they were so blue, like the ocean in *The Blue Lagoon*.

"So?" he said.

"So what?"

"So so! You tell me Patrick called you and then you don't say anything else! I think that deserves a couple of 'so's'! Did you call him back?"

"No! No, I didn't call him back! Be serious!"

I'd spent the last week and a half at Christophe's so Jeff's brother could use my room while he was in town. We'd gotten along perfectly. It was a short enough period of time, of course, but I could appreciate the simplicity of our relationship, Christophe's accessibility and frankness, since he, unlike me, didn't talk on several levels all at once. He was clever, he loved life, he knew what he wanted, and really liked me, it was no more complicated than that.

"Um... and why does it have to be complicated, anyway?" asked Julien. It's a good question. A very good question, even.

"You're right," I answered. "You couldn't be more right." I started to laugh. "I'm such an idiot..." I felt like I'd just discovered something – nothing impressive, not America, but something, nonetheless. Julien was right: not only did I consider that logically, inevitably even, love *had* to be complicated, but part of me liked the idea – it undoubtedly reassured me because it excused a good number of my romantic failures.

Julien turned towards me and gave me his little wise, mysterious smile, the one he saved for important statements or the times he felt he was going to offer what he called "one of his great truths," and he put a hand on my shoulder.

"Life's short, Marine. Have you ever thought about all the time you've wasted on pointless questions?"

"Heeey!" I felt insulted, but mostly I was aware that he was right again and that there was something humiliating about getting straight talk from someone in fuchsia pants, since from a moral point of view he was not exactly the Dali Lama, but also because he lived his life with absolute, disconcerting ease, as if it was the simplest thing in the world. I thought about Laurent, Flavie, my sisters, and I wondered why, exactly, we turned our existences into a full-time job, requiring thought, work, debate, unending doubts, and at least eight freight loads of indecision. As for Julien, he rolled merrily along, politely laughing at those of us who insisted on taking the road less traveled, the more thankless road, in the hopes (completely unjustified in his opinion) that it would lead us to a Nirvana never to be found by those, like him, who happily chose the way paved with the roses of happiness and simplicity.

"It can be simple," he added. "You're allowed."

I gave him a little poke in the chest. "You're about to form a cult, aren't you?"

"Yes, ma'am!" He raised his hands in a position that look liked Shiva. "The cult of pleasure and..."

"Okay, that's enough. Poor man's Stéphan Bureau. We're late."

"His hands were still in his Shiva position when we went into Le Lulli, our regular bar, where Christophe was supposed to meet us later. Laurent and Jeff were sitting at the bar, laughing.

"Why are we here again?" I asked Julien.

"Because it's good for you to get out a little. At your age, spending every evening in your living room reinventing the world is tough. Let's have some optimism!"

"You really should have been a G.O."

"I know."

I didn't like bars much. Neither did Laurent, really, but sometimes we gave in to Julien. Le Lulli had turned out to be a good compromise: it was a nice, calm place, which suited us perfectly, and the bartender, a tall Australian of Chinese origin, spoiled Julien.

"Hi, Andrew," I said, coming up to the bar.

"Hey, Marine!" He said "Marine" with an English accent and I felt like I was an elite soldier in the American army. "A glass of white wine?"

"Yes, please."

"Oh, Andrew..." sighed Julien, leaning on the bar. "You know what would make me happy?"

"You told him I was straight, didn't you?" Andrew asked me in English. I shrugged my shoulders and turned towards the boys to give Laurent a little kiss on the forehead. A girl who must have been a foot taller than me and weighed twenty pounds less went by. Jeff looked at her, she stopped, looking ravishing in a way I found exaggerated, wrapped her arms around him then leaned in to whisper something and, I think, gave his ear a little lick. She stood up, flashed a smile that said everything and kept going. I tapped Jeff on the shoulder and laughed, while Laurent kept busy banging his head against the bar.

"Hoooowww do you do that? Jeff, you have to tell me." He turned towards me. "Did you see? Did you seeeeeee?"

"I saw."

"Dude, that was hot," said Andrew, making Laurent start banging his head on the counter again, and making Jeff burst out laughing.

"And just who was that?" Julien asked.

"Her name's Delphine."

"How old is she?" It was like Laurent was being martyred. It was pretty funny.

"I dunno. Twenty-five, twenty-six?" As he followed the conversation, Andrew barely had the time to slide a coaster down the bar, just to the spot where Laurent immediately banged his head.

"Forget it," said Jeff. "I swear it's better with Carole. Really. Delphine's pretty, and she's charming, too, but… she's not the brightest bulb in the box, if you know what I mean."

Laurent moaned something.

"What did he say?"

"All the more reason."

"Cut it out," Jeff said. "You'd be bored silly. You wouldn't be happy with a girl like her. Girls who aren't too bright are a vocation. They're not for everybody."

Laurent raised his head and grabbed Laurent by the shirt. "Teach me. I want to be your disciple. Please."

"You think he's cut out for it?" Jeff asked Andrew, who in turn looked dubious. Everyone laughed. It was friendly and relaxed, a nice little Wednesday night out. I don't know how it happened, but I think Julien saw something brewing, and said, "Hey, I'm going to start thinking he's following us around. Since when does he hang out here?" and "Oh fuck," then I saw Gabriel Champagne, oozing charm and casualness, coming up to me and, out of the corner of my eye, I saw Christophe coming into the bar, just as Laurent, looking at me way too intently whispered, "Okay, don't look now, but Patrick just came in and he's heading this way."

To: Fred
From: Marine Vandale
Subject: Vaudeville

....

You know that scene in British farces where everybody's in the
same room – the wife, her husband and his lover, and suddenly
another character pops out from behind the sofa just to make
the situation even more complex and ridiculous?

To: Marine
From: Frédéric Vandale
Subject: Déjà vu

....

Let me guess: either you unexpectedly decided to give everything up to write a thesis on British farces, or you managed to
get yourself into the same kind of situation and, honestly, I
have to say it doesn't surprise me much.

To: Fred
From: Marine Vandale
Subject: Diagnosis

....

Let's say you have a girlfriend and that by some unfortunate
twist of fate you find out that, while you two had been broken
up, she had, as they say, gotten friendly with your best friend.

To: Marine
From: Frédéric Vandale
Subject: Professional Opinion

....

Do you want a sincere opinion or should I make up something
to help you see the bright side?

To: Fred
From: Marine Vandale
Subject: Facing things head on

Don't sugar coat it.

To: Marine
From: Frédéric Vandale
Subject: The hard truth

Marine, that was a pretty stupid thing. I know Montreal isn't
Mexico City as far as population goes, but couldn't you have
cast your net a little wider than Christophe's close friends?
Now, I'm not saying that most guys wouldn't do exactly the
same thing you did if they had the chance, but, as you know,
basing your ideas of sexual morality on men's behavior may
not be the brightest choice.

To: Fred
From: Marine Vandale
Subject: Paging Simone de Beauvoir

Why does it always seem like if I were a man, not only would
my life be easier, but 90% of the things I do would seem pretty
funny, but now it's just downright pathetic.

To: Marine
From: Frédéric Vandale
Subject: Tragi-comedy

Take it easy there, little sister, you're not exactly *la dame aux
camellias*. And honestly, from where I'm standing, it's not
exactly tragic, it's more like burlesque.

To: Fred
From: Marine Vandale
Subject: Re: Tragi-comedy

....

You know what the Queen of Burlesque thinks? Because honestly, Fred, this whole mess really isn't funny anymore, and I'm one useless relationship away from being the thirty-two-year-old girl moaning about the fact that the sky was bluer when she was twenty-five and now all she can see ahead of her are thick clouds hanging over a hopeless horizon.

To: Marine
From: Frédéric Vandale
Subject: Take it easy

....

Okay, get yourself a glass of wine, put a nice happy song on the stereo, snuggle with the cat, think about a sunny beach and roll up your sleeves, Marinette. I won't let you become a hopeless case.

To: Fred
From: Marine Vandale
Subject: Emergency measures

....

I've already had the glass of wine, the bottle, actually, Jeff is going to throw himself out the window if he hears another Jack Johnson guitar chord, Claude François' neck is now bald from my blowing my nose on it, and sunny beaches are only nice if I've got a man by my side.

To: Marine
From: Frédéric Vandale
Subject: Re: Emergency measures

....

What about your sleeves? Did you try rolling up your sleeves?

To: Fred
From: Marine Vandale
Subject: RE: Emergency measures

....

Yeah. It helps. A little. But that may just be because it was your idea. ☺

To: Fred
From: Marine Vandale
Subject: Vaudeville punch line

....

So how does the story of the guy behind the sofa end?

To: Fred
From: Marine Vandale
Subject: Bad vaudeville show

....

I'll tell you later, okay? And it's too bad for Jeff, but I'm putting Jack Johnson back on, and this time I'm pushing repeat, and I'm gonna knock back his last bottle of wine. I don't want to tell you on an empty stomach, it's all too ridiculous.

To: Marine
From: Frédéric Vandale
Subject: Re: Bad vaudeville show

....

I'm not going anywhere. I'm just going to make myself some popcorn and then I'll be here waiting for the rest.

    :)

Chapter 3

Days later, Julien was still repeating that the whole situation had looked just like a scene in a movie. Personally, I couldn't see what was movielike about it at all, since, after the initial shock which a movie would have emphasized, it would have showed me looking at the doctor first and giving him a beautiful, innocent smile, unaware of the chaos about to be unleashed, then looking a little disconcerted as I noticed Christophe, and then looking completely horrified as I saw Patrick come in. Then there would be a superfast, fantastic scene with an elegant series of deep, deadly remarks, looks that bounced from one person to the next, the perplexed faces of Jeff, Julien and Laurent watching everything, and reflecting the audience's own faces.

Instead of all that, what we got was a completely absurd and disorderly opening shot, first because it took me at least one minute too long to figure out exactly what was going on, and then because even when everything was clear and I was forced to admit we were blissfully careening towards quite an unpleasant situation, I kept smiling stupidly at the doctor, unable to detach my gaze from his laughing eyes (which, upon closer observation, turned out to look nothing like the sky in Naples or the Aegean Sea, though they did look like Tuscan valleys or Irish moors, in other words they were green, so while my boyfriend was about to crash into my recent lover who happened to be his best friend, I was mentally searching for a natural entity that would do Gabriel Champagne's eyes justice).

But the superfast, fantastic scene we would have gotten in a movie was replaced by an interminable lapse of time where no one seemed to understand anything. It was so bad Julien thought it would be a good idea to jump in, but that meant Jeff then thought he should jump in, by trying to hold him back and force him to be quiet. There followed an unbearable brouhaha – lacking all the rhythm of the movie's superfast, fantastic scene – where people were all talking at the same time: Laurent was trying to get Delphine's attention; Andrew was furiously serving shooters to calm everyone down (this was a very, very bad idea. How can a bartender not know that the drunker people are, the more stupid they are?); the doctor didn't know what was going on; I was trying to reassure Christophe, who couldn't process the whole thing, and hold Patrick back, too, although I really wanted to make mincemeat out of him; and Jeff was doing his best to get us all to settle down.

I finally ended up sitting at the bar, completely, and I do mean completely, stunned by my own stupidity, while the boys consoled me and Andrew brought me one vodka-lemon after another, which, at the time, made me very relaxed and radiant, but transformed a morning after that was bound to be tough into a real nightmare. I was in my bed, in my underwear, with a big jug of water and a pail by my nightstand. I still had to hand it to Jeff: even drunk, he knew how to take care of his roomie. Ever since, I'd been harassing the boys so I could understand exactly what had happened that night at Le Lulli, including what I'd said and what I could have said to save my relationship with Christophe, and maybe even an ounce of my dignity.

"If you ask me to tell you once more," Julien said, "I'm going to eat my fist, get it? I'm going to put my fist in my mouth and chew it until you go away."

"I'm not going anywhere. Chew away, but tell me."

Julien turned towards Jeff: "Kill me. Kill me now."

"Hey. I have to live with her. So don't complain."

"Laurent?" pleaded Julien.

"I didn't see anything. I was looking at the long and lovely Delphine." Laurent had been reveling in the whole situation for days. He'd seen everything, of course, since, while Andrew was practically throwing shooters in everyone's face, and Jeff was playing referee and Julien, who couldn't resist the prospect of a juicy scene, was kicking up shit as they say, Laurent was simply hoping there wouldn't be a fight, which would have made him uncomfortable and possibly force him to get involved – the thing he feared most of all. Since then he'd been pretending to be the boy who hadn't seen anything, but, knowing him like I did, I knew he'd seen everything and was making me suffer, because he found the whole situation somewhat ridiculous and pointless (and, in those brief moments when I was clear-headed, I had to admit he was right) and because, like every minor situation where he had nothing to lose or to gain, the thing seemed to be of very, very limited interest to him.

"Julien," I said threateningly. I took a sip of wine without taking my eyes off of him. It was a useless ploy: all four of us knew that Julien loved to keep going over this kind of story, usually *ad nauseam*, and that he was making us beg just for fun of it.

"Okay, okay, okay… But Laurent's going to have to help me with the details."

"I didn't see anything!" said Laurent. Beside me, Jeff, looking downright tired, signaled to the server to bring him another drink.

We all agreed about one thing: the first person we'd

noticed was Gabriel. Well, Jeff hadn't noticed anyone; he was busy ordering an old-fashioned cocktail from Andrew, who was busy listening to his directions. But Laurent and Julien saw the same thing I did: Gabriel Champagne was coming towards me with a smile that could melt the Earth's remaining glaciers.

Behind me, I'd heard Julien say, "Hey, I'm going to start thinking he's following us around. Since when does he hang out here?" and I'd turned around to face the handsome doctor. His path was clear and, just like Julien, he must have been thinking, Hey, I'm going to start thinking they're following me around. But he seemed to think the whole thing was charming and – or was this my own unhealthy need to believe miracles were still possible? had I gotten that contaminated by romantic comedies? – he seemed sincerely glad to see me and during those few pure, beautiful seconds before Christophe and Patrick came in, I wasn't thinking anything, because it isn't true that people think about something when time stands still, they don't think about anything, or maybe they just think about the color of the wall in front of them or the last book they read or the song that's playing.

I didn't even enjoy the moment, I didn't even say to myself, "This handsome man I've been happily fantasizing about for months is coming over to talk to me and I didn't even expect it," and there he was in front of me, his hands in the pockets of his jeans, wearing a white shirt and a tweed vest (all these details were collected by Julien – personally, I didn't see anything but his eyes and his smile).

"Hello," he said, still smiling. "We seem to run into each other a lot, I think…" He might have added something else, but I could already hear Julien saying "Oh fuck" and I noticed Christophe coming towards me, and then Laurent's face was just centimeters from my own, announcing Patrick's arrival.

"Is it a habit of yours not to call anyone back, or is it just me?" Patrick asked.

"Hmmm? What are you talking about?" I laughed in a remarkably idiotic way, as if I thought stupidity could erase everything, and that Patrick would reply by saying he was joking and then everyone would go home happy and innocent.

"I called you twenty times, Marine."

"What? No..." And the same stupid laugh again. I heard Julien mutter, "This is too good to be true," then Andrew and Jeff simultaneously yelled "Shut up!" and "*Ta gueule!*"

"Um, you called Marine?" Christophe asked.

Patrick seemed not to hear. "I can't stop thinking about you," he said. And, beside me I could almost feel Julien's orgasm.

"*You're* thinking about *her*?" Christophe asked. He'd finally turned back towards me. "Is there something I'm not understanding?"

"Andrew," Jeff said, without taking his eyes off Christophe. "Give us a couple of vodka shooters, okay?"

We were all quiet for a moment, and I could have sworn I heard each one of us ask what to say next. Patrick is the one who finally spoke. He seemed to wake up and, still without taking his eyes off of me, he asked me: "Hang on... You're back together?"

I'd read some place that when little babies get too much external simulation, they often fall asleep and the phenomenon is called the shutdown reflex. In a nutshell: too much information, I'm closing up the shop. That night, I'd closed up the shop as I raised my face towards Gabriel Champagne, whose eyes were officially green, who'd ended up in the middle of this ridiculous situation and who obviously didn't have a clue what was going on.

He looked at Patrick, then at Christophe, then at Julien chirping between the two of them as if it were his problem, then finally he looked back at me.

He looked at me with a smile, hardly a question on his face, and it occurred to me that he must find the situation more amusing than anything else. I remember starting to open my mouth as if I were going to say something (exactly what, no one knows: "Hi, here's my boyfriend and his best friend that I, gulp, slept with while we were on a break" or "Hi, I thought your eyes were blue" or, better still, "Please, get me out of here"), then I remember his gaze, again, and his smile which by now had changed into a charming half-laugh, it all seemed to say he found everything very funny and who could blame him. He nodded good-bye, then turned away. I watched him get lost in the crowd, then the gentle shutdown reflex was over and the outside world invaded me once again, in the form of two men insistently repeating my name as they visibly waited for me to provide an explanation, and rightly so.

"Poor Christophe," said Jeff, shaking his head. "Really…" He turned to me with the same reproachful look he'd been using on me for days.

"Stop looking at me like that!" I hid my face in my hands, and I felt him take me by the shoulders. At least, beneath the reproachful look, there was a vast expanse of affection that had characterized our relationship since we'd met. I also suspected he felt a little compassion for the apparently inexhaustible ability I had to get myself into inextricable and quite undesirable situations. Usually it was pretty funny, but this time there was someone suffering a lot more than I was, and it was my fault, and it wasn't really funny at all.

"What are you going to do?" asked Laurent. It must have been the fortieth time he'd asked me the same question, which, though I thought it was completely stupid, was the only valid one to ask, given the situation.

"I don't know what I'm going to do…" I answered, exasperated. Besides, what could I do? Christophe had walked out after he figured out what had happened. I'd caught up to him on the sidewalk to stupidly say, "But we weren't together when it happened!" in such a pitiful voice that I felt like sitting down in one of the recycling bins scattered around and waiting for the next collection. Christophe just looked at me, visibly upset by my own bad faith.

"Do you want to tell me it's all Patrick's fault, too, while you're at it?" I didn't flinch under the insult – how could I anyway? He was right on all counts, and to be perfectly honest with myself, I had thought of that same ridiculous, useless sentence. I'd wanted to say something, undoubtedly some depressing platitude, but Christophe put up his hand. "Look," he said. "I can't have this conversation right now, okay? Good-bye." And I'd let him go.

I'd gone back into the bar, beside myself and with every intention of executing Patrick that very moment, but he was happy just to look at me strangely and say "Hey, no one twisted your arm."

"Shit, no, no one twisted my arm, but did someone twist your arm to get you to come here for Chrissake?" I was fuming. Obviously, it was easier to blame someone else.

"I didn't see Christophe there," he'd said, by way of an excuse. He looked upset too, and this gave me a nasty sense of pleasure. "You could have called me back, you know. I don't know how many messages I left you. You could've just called to tell me you were back with Christophe. Is that too much to ask?"

"Touché," said Julien, and I would have hit him over the head with a barstool if Jeff hadn't stepped in.

"Yeah, but no, but he was right," said Julien. "And, if I remember right, I told you to call him back, didn't I?"

"Okay, Julien?" said Jeff. "You're not helping. You're

really not helping."

"But I'm right."

"I said, 'You're not helping!'"

Julien let out a gloomy little "Pfffff" and seemed to concentrate on his plate of smoked salmon. He hated it when we downplayed any role he may have played in a story, and under normal circumstances this would have made me laugh. We could never tell a story about something that had happened, even five years ago, without Julien speaking up to remind us about the joke he'd come up with, the shrewd remark he'd made or, if there was nothing else, the color of the shirt he'd been wearing that day.

"Listen," I said. "Can we all just agree I was bloody stupid?"

"Yes," said all three boys together.

"That I got what I deserve…"

"Yes."

"That Patrick could have done a better job, too…" Silence. "You're supposed to say 'Yes' there." Laurent made a little face, Julien seemed to hesitate, and Jeff said, "Face facts, Marine. You screwed up. You didn't think about anybody else or about the consequences of what you were doing."

"Ohhh… I know…"

"And maybe one option is to stop feeling sorry for yourself?" suggested Laurent.

"You're one to talk!" Laurent was the king of self-pity, for him it was a sport, or a religion. Nobody felt sorry for themselves as sensually as Laurent.

"Um, these days, we can all talk, Marine."

"Okay, okay…"

"And, just so you know, if I did, it would be about something else than this same fucking story."

"Okay, I get it." I took a drink of wine while the boys sighed in a way that was just ever so slightly exaggerated.

"I thought we could talk about Gabriel instead, what do you think? Like, we could analyze the chances I still have talking to him again for something besides medical reasons?" Laurent started laughing, Jeff looked like he suddenly had a very painful stiff neck, and, opposite me, Julien raised an arm, shouting, "We're going to need another bottle over here." When we left the restaurant, an hour and a half later, we were still talking about Gabriel and my misadventures. Going his own way, Julien shouted "You owe us one, Marine Vandale," over the snowdrifts on the sidewalk.

The wolf's paw stretched towards the red hood in a menacing way. I looked at the sheet for a couple of seconds, the wolf's mouth was half open in an unpleasant smile, the little girl's hood had slipped down to her shoulders, revealing her disheveled hair. I erased the paw, for the tenth time at least. I didn't want a threatening-looking wolf, I wanted a wolf that was attractive-looking, but just a little unsettling. It was a thin line, and I hadn't found it yet. I had a pretty good feeling that no one would look for it, or even notice it, but I was certain I wouldn't be able to hand in the illustration until I found the right balance. I was happy with the mouth, though. I dug through my colored pencils – I was doing this project in pastels, and I took out the one I was using for the cape, an absolutely adorable periwinkle blue that made me want to go out and pick wild flowers.

It was a nice idea: a French children's author had written five alternative little red riding hoods. A little blue riding hood, a little pink riding hood, and so on. And the little girl's personality changed with the color of her hood. The blue one was a daydreamer, the green one was interested in ecology. The plaid riding hood was particularly confused. It required pretty conventional drawing, but the stories were well written, and I like the universe they described, the mysterious forest – both beautiful and terrifying, the sly, perverse wolf, the old-fashioned charm of the grandmother's house.

I'd been working hard since I wasn't seeing Christophe anymore – I hadn't heard from him for a week and a half, despite my calling incessantly at first then little by little less insistently, and my stopping over at his place three times unannounced. He wouldn't answer the phone or the door, and I didn't dare call his friends, despite Julien's advice when he said Christophe would have seen this as a sign of courage and true love. I thought maybe he'd gone away, to his mother's or the North Shore or New York, where he often hid out when he wanted peace and quiet. That's where he'd gone the first time we'd broken up, while I'd stayed here, in his best friend's arms.

For three or four days, I'd been trying not to think about all this – to not think too much at all, really. First of all I could only do it out loud and the boys were collectively burnt out, then I'd even managed to confuse myself, and, once again, I didn't know what I wanted. But I never knew what I wanted, so I was used to that; with me it was a permanent state that I'd even brag about when I'd been drinking a little and thought it was romantic and bohemian.

I had huge, vague ideas about what I wanted happiness to look like; I collected inside images of passionate love and deep intimacy, places visited with a man I was crazy in love with – images of freedom and love. But as for concrete, everyday life, I'd have to think about that some more. And in real life, the world where Christophe and everyone else lived, I was unable to make a decision, maybe I was a coward, or afraid to make a mistake, maybe I was lazy. When I was in a good mood, I'd tell myself it was out of love for my ideals, and sometimes I'd even believe it.

But now, I thought I was downright awful, but, this

being said, it wasn't enough to provoke a sudden attack of certainty and the ability to make a decision. I didn't even know if I was trying to get in touch with Christophe because I loved him or because I felt guilty – this kind of confusion is not as uncommon as people think, but it's lousy nonetheless. So I dove into work, drawing wolves and enchanted forests and thinking about my childhood.

Next to me, Laurent was drawing little stick people around one of my sketches. He was hunched over the drawing table, inexplicably concentrating, as if he was accomplishing some highly technical work, when all that was really coming out of the tip of his pencil were little stickmen greeting little stickwomen, or standing next to little stickdogs. They were all smiling, even the dogs, and the women seemed to each have a single hair covering their scalp and falling over their shoulders on each side. In two minutes, he's going to draw a smiley face sun, I said to myself.

"You okay, Michael-Angelo?" I looked at him with a smile. He didn't look up, concentrating as he was on his masterpiece, but he extended one arm to jiggle his empty glass. I went over towards the little fridge in the back of the studio where I always kept a couple of bottles of water and white wine.

"Creating is thirsty work," Laurent explained.

"That's true." When I got back over to where he was, the paper was adorned with a smiling yellow and orange sun, looking happy to shine upon all the little stickpeople. I looked at Laurent, who was now looking back at me.

"You know what the worst thing is?" he asked.

"What?"

"I tried my best." He gave a little laugh. Then I laughed and leaned on one of his shoulders.

"We'll keep it," I said. "We'll stick it to the fridge with a magnet."

"Pfff… keep it up and I'll make a black blob and say it's

a snowstorm."

"Hey, I used to do that when I was little."

"I know. Everybody I know who has kids has like eight ugly scribbles on their fridge or their office wall that their kids drew and said they were snowstorms."

"I think it's cute. One of my friend's daughters is smarter than that; she says it's a snowstorm on a lake."

"I can't stand it."

"Stop saying you can't stand anything that has to do with kids."

"I can't stand it."

"I can't stand you."

"Maybe."

He'd stop by my studio once in a while when he knew I was there, to have a glass of wine, talk a little, or even just spend an hour snoring softly on the old gray sofa (Had it always been gray? Didn't it used to be white? Now, that was a disconcerting question). I knew he only stopped by when he was feeling sad or having doubts. He said he could find answers in the quiet whiteness of the big room and in drawing a bit, but I knew my presence is what calmed him down, not because I was calm or peaceful or even quiet, but because I knew him so perfectly that he didn't have to be anything at all except himself with me. I knew it because his presence relaxed me too, it was a break, a vacation, "the next best thing to being alone," we used to say, paraphrasing Seinfeld and thinking we were clever.

"Everything okay with Carole?" I asked him. I knew something, somewhere, wasn't really okay, and I also knew he'd never answer.

"Mmmm."

"Mmmm?"

"Yeah, yeah, everything's okay." He said in the tone reserved for people who are annoying – he didn't make much of an effort to be polite around me anymore.

"Did she bring up children again?"

"Is there any wine left?" He'd finished his glass. I gave him a little smile, stroked his earlobe and poured him another glass.

"Do you love her, Loulou?"

"What?" Laurent had a strange and complicated relationship with love – he'd never told me he loved me, he'd never told anyone that. Sometimes I had the impression he had a hard time recognizing the signs of love in him. He shrugged, looking contrite, and I knew he wasn't going to answer.

"You going to your parents' tonight?"

"Yep, it's Élodie's birthday. You want to come?"

"Um. We're not a couple anymore."

"Yeah, I know."

He walked around my drawing table, and came to lean over my shoulder to look at the one I was working on, and some others that were further along. "Riding Hood looks like you."

"Come on. She's ten!"

"Errr…"

"Come on, now." Guys always said I looked like I was about sixteen. It was pretty flattering. But I thought ten was a little exaggerated, not to mention vaguely worrisome.

"I'm telling you. The shape of the eyes, the little mouth, that tuft of hair. You going to make her blond?"

"No. A redhead."

"Give me a break! Everyone knows she's a blond, it doesn't matter if her riding hood is red or green or blue."

"Okay, okay. I was going to give her blond hair."

"See? You drew yourself."

I shrugged and came around to lean on the drawing table next to him. In the illustration he was looking at, the little girl was smiling, had her hands folded, and was in awe of the wolf's teeth, though he looked ridiculous in the grandmother's nightcap. I peered at it for a moment, and then I thought to myself that Laurent wasn't completely wrong. Quite an interesting slip, I thought.

"Which big bad wolf are you afraid of, Marine?"

I followed the little path of expertly unmatched stones leading up to the house. My father, who'd become obsessed with household chores since he'd retired, had visibly shoveled the entrance at least a couple of dozen times throughout the day: it had been snowing since the morning, but the walkway was impeccable, no trace of a single flake, and, on each side, little piles of shoveled snow had been tossed behind the halogen lights illuminating the house. There must have been at least forty of them, whose job, winter and summer alike, was to spotlight the masterpiece of insignificant architecture and nondescript landscaping that was the house I grew up in. It was a touching effort, I had to admit, but given that all the houses on the street looked alike and all the gardens had been laid out by the same very moderately talented land-scape architect, one had to wonder why some of the homeowners felt the need to light up their domains as if they were the chateau of Versailles.

At the door, like always, I counted to five after I rang the bell: at four, true to form, my mother yelled, "Raymond! Door!" – you could hear her all the way to the sidewalk. My father finally opened up, wearing the nice smile he always prepared for a guest even before seeing them.

"Marine!" he said, opening his arms. "Marine." He'd often repeat names, to show us, and prove to himself, I think, that he wasn't "as forgetful as your mother thinks." I stood on tiptoe as I tried to bend around his belly to hug him. He'd quit smoking at least fifteen years before, but for me, he always smelled like a mixture of tobacco and Old Spice, which reminded me of my childhood.

"Hi, *Papa.*" He looked at me with the same smile and

was about to say something when my mother came over, an oven mitt in one hand, a spatula in the other, saying at least twenty things at once, taking my coat, telling me about my cousin Samuel's being promoted to section manager (I had no idea what the section was – the last time I'd seen Samuel, he was thirteen and dreamed of becoming a Game Boy champ) and pointing me towards the hors d'oeuvres in the living room.

I gave my father a little tap on the shoulder, he'd already given up on trying to get a word in, and I headed towards the living room, where Élodie was smoking a cigarette, looking singularly bored, next to Ariane, who was nibbling on a celery stalk.

"How's it going?" I asked. Élodie went "Pfff" like a world-weary teenager, while Ariane raised her celery towards me. "I'm stocking up," she said. "It's really the only thing I'm going to be able to eat, *Maman* puts meat in everything."

"Yep. You still Saint Vegetarian?"

"Vegan," she corrected with a smile. Ariane knew that Frédéric and I had always made fun of her crazy green activism. She got up, multicolored striped leggings, red Converse runners, a short, brown corduroy skirt, a huge virgin wool sweater and her blond dreads pulled back in a purple scarf.

"How are you, Big Sister?"

"Great. How about you, Little Sister Saint?"

"Okay." She smelled of patchouli.

"How come you never call me Little Sister Saint?" asked Élodie.

"Well…" Ariane and I both answered at once, and then we started to laugh. My father came in with cold beers for Élodie and me, and a glass of vegetable juice for Ariane, but she refused it and made a face: it was full of sodium, she may as well go lick a block of salt.

"I gotta go back to the kitchen," he said. "Your mother

needs her assistant."

"I'll go, *Papa*," said Ariane.

"No, no, you sisters stay together. It makes me happy."

I wondered if the girls also figured he preferred not to stay with us because even though he loved us like crazy, the professional trucker he'd been had never really learned how to talk to his daughters, strange, laughing little people who, when they became teenagers, turned into creatures he found quite unsettling.

"Happy birthday," I said to Élodie.

"Pffff."

"Hey, now. What's wrong with you?"

Ariane looked at me and made a discouraged gesture, and Élodie caught it out of the corner of her eye.

"That's right," she shouted. "Go ahead and be smart. Go ahead and laugh, you're only twenty-three, I'm going to be twenty-six tomorrow and I don't have a boyfriend. My life is over." She said it with so much conviction that I couldn't help giggling.

"As for you, drop dead, okay?"

I laughed even harder. She seemed sincerely outraged and, knowing her like I did, I'm sure she was. Next to me, Ariane was looking at her in equally sincere disbelief.

"Élo…" I said. "Look at me. I'm six years older than you and I couldn't be farther from having a boyfriend myself. But I've never thought it means my life is over." Did I really believe what I was saying? No matter, though, I know I should have seen Ariane sooner – she was looking at me with her eyes open wide and trying to discreetly point to the kitchen. When I finally noticed, I barely had enough time to turn around when I saw my mother, her oven mitt still on her hand, screaming (at least that's what it seemed like to me at the time. Later on, Ariane tried to convince me she was speaking normally, but I had a distinct memory of a particularly shrill scream): "What do you mean, YOU DON'T HAVE A BOYFRIEND ANYMORE?" There followed the usually cacophony, topped off by the usual, "You so should have stayed with Laurent," with the whole thing punctuated with justified bursts of laughter from my sisters, gentle pats on the back from my father, as he lovingly repeated "you don't need a man to be a great daughter, Ariane. Um…, Élo… Marine. Marine."

As always my mother was overly upset by a situation she didn't understand the half of. Élodie finally started to relax and even when my mother's famous, inedible salmon steaks in cheese sauce arrived on the table, she didn't stop smiling. At least, I thought to myself, I found a way to make her laugh on her birthday. She laughed, fluttering her perfectly made-up eyelashes, and she nudged me with her elbow: "You're right after all, twenty-six isn't that bad!" while Ariane tried to keep up her strength by downing kilos of mashed potatoes that she undoubtedly would have thrown back up if she'd known how much butter my mother had put in them.

"Jeff," I whispered. His room was dark and I could hear light snoring. "Jeff," I repeated louder.

"Hmmm?" I saw a shape sit up in the bed. "What time is it?"

"It's not even midnight."

"Mmmm."

"Are you alone?" With Jeff you never knew.

"What? Yes. I'm alone."

I covered the space between the door and the bed in two steps and lay down in bed next to him.

"Do you think my life is over?"

"Mmmm?"

Then I did what I hate to do most in the world: I started crying, like a little girl, over things that, in broad daylight, didn't seem worth tears. Jeff rolled over and put one of his strong arms around me, pulling me into the big spoon formed by his body. He didn't say anything. I think he fell asleep while I was still crying because I thought I was stupid and pitiful. At about one in the morning, he woke up with a start and asked my neck, "You okay?"

"No." I didn't want to apologize; I didn't even want to get up. Then, the idea that my roommate's arms were the only thing standing between me and a deep but ridiculous depression made me start crying again.

"It'll be all right," he said, half-heartedly stroking the leg of my jeans.

Of course it will, I thought. It will be all right. It always was in the end. I rolled over. I could make out his face a few inches from my own. And, more than ever, the queen of screw-ups that I was wanted desperately to screw up again.

To: Fred
From: Marine Vandale
Subject: The misery of the rich

What is your position exactly on spoiled, grown-up girls who had it easy but still find a way to complain about life when it surprises them again with its sneaky imperfection?

To: Marine
From: Frédéric Vandale
Subject: Field experience

I'd like to remind you I have three sisters. So I'm pretty familiar with overexaggerated complaining. What's going on?

To: Fred
From: Marine Vandale
Subject: Shameful assumption

Who said I was talking about myself?

To: Marine
From: Frédéric Vandale
Subject: Field experience

Listen, I don't want to seem like I'm bragging about knowing how to read between the lines, but, I ask again, do we really need to play hide-and-seek here? Because it seems to me we could save time, and a lot of pixels too, if we just got down to the nitty-gritty.

To: Fred
From: Marine Vandale
Subject: Gift of clairvoyance

You could at least have been nice enough to kid around a little, and let me believe, just for a nanosecond or two, that you thought I was talking about Élodie, who, by the way, just had a birthday and remarked about twenty times that the phone kept on ringing, but it was never her brother on the other end of the line. I don't want to tell you what to think, but I'd take that as a veiled reproach.

To: Marine
From: Frédéric Vandale
Subject: Unworthy brother

....

Shit. Do you think if I tell her I was up to my neck in creativity and that metaphors were shooting from my fingers at a furious rhythm, and that I had a duty as an author to get them down on paper, everything will be okay?

To: Fred
From: Marine
Subject: Re: Unworthy brother

....

Are you kidding?

To: Marine
From: Frédéric Vandale
Subject: RE: Unworthy brother

....

A guy can dream can't he? I know, I have to call her, apologize profusely, and promise her a dream vacation when she comes here to visit.

To: Fred
From: Marine Vandale
Subject: Pauper's wages

....

Somehow you think I pay her enough to afford a ticket to Paris?

To: Marine
From: Frédéric Vandale
Subject: Clear-headed

Of course not. And somehow you think I'd invite Élodie to come here for a week if I thought she'd come? I'm not that stupid.

To: Fred
From: Marine Vandale
Subject: Girl power

Okay, you scribbler. She's unbearable, but she's still my little sister, and she's not doing too great these days either. So, be kind and show some brotherly love.

To: Marine
From: Frédéric Vandale
Subject: Big brother to the rescue

I get it, I get it. And you must know I'm a font of brotherly love, which brings me to ask you why the spoiled little girl has so much to complain about.

To: Fred
From: Marine Vandale
Subject: Image of an old maid

The complaint is directly linked to the fact that I artfully managed to find a way to ruin two relationships at once and to scare off a man who has all the beauty of the Irish moors in his eyes. From which I draw the following conclusion: I'm thirty-two years and I'm going to live out the rest of my days alone, with a stuffed Claude François by my side.

To: Marine
From: Frédéric Vandale
Subject: Taxidermy

The cat or the singer?

To: Fred
From: Martine Vandale
Subject: Re: Taxidermy

You're an ass.

To: Marine
From: Frédéric Vandale
Subject: Lighten up

Lighten up a little, Marinette. Plus, you can't be mad at me for not taking you too seriously, for lots of nice, sweet reasons, like, you're a great girl, and cute, too, and despite my best efforts, I can't imagine you and a ridiculous, stuffed singer in such a moronic future.

To: Fred
From: Marine Vandale
Subject: Re: Lighten up

Well, you see, I can't lighten up anymore, and to tell you the whole story, and I don't know how I'll be able to again. And I can't put things in perspective and I feel ugly and alone, and even more ugly cause I feel ugly, so I shouldn't complain. So, it's a vicious circle of a lousy mood, a lack of confidence and all that, and, if you remember, that's the perfect recipe for screwing up.

To: Marine
From: Frédéric Vandale
Subject: Suzy Screw-Up

....

Oh, no. What did you do?

To: Fred
From: Marine Vandale
Subject: even Suzy would be ashamed

....

You haven't spoken to Jeff, by any chance, have you? I'm just asking here, no special reason.

To: Marine
From: Frédéric Vandale
Subject: (none)

....

Oh no. Oh no, no, no. Marine, what did you do?

To: Fred
From: Marine Vandale
Subject: (none)

....

Shit, I gotta go. He just came home. I'll tell you later. You won't judge me, will you?

To: Marine
From: Frédéric Vandale
Subject: DETAILS!

....

You're not going to ditch me like that, are you?

To: Marine
From: Frédéric Vandale
Subject: You dirty rat

....

I can't believe you ditched me like that.

:)

Chapter 4

"My God," I said out loud when I heard the key in the lock. I abruptly shut off the computer and jumped up to go stand in front of the door like an idiot. We hadn't seen each other since last night, and I was… I was a lot of things. I was sad and confused and disconcerted and embarrassed – but above all, I was terrified. I'd spent the day feeling like I was surrounded by a cloud of fetid, tenacious fear that I'd have a hard time defining, but could feel distinctly. The fear of losing Jeff, fear that things I thought were eternal would change, a bit of all that, but I really didn't know. And I hoped that Jeff, on the other side of the door, could help me.

"Well now!" said Julien as he came in. "Do you always stand in the entryway like a silly goose, or were you just in a particular hurry to see me?"

"Stupid jerk!" I was ridiculously angry at him. For scaring me, for not being able to make my fear go away. Quickly, he took off his coat – a big white down Kanuk with a fur collar that was a little too flirty for my taste – and underneath he was wearing red jeans and a magenta shirt under a purple tee-shirt, which all gave me a headache.

"I came as soon as I heard," he said, as he went to the kitchen to make himself a drink, happy just to give me a quick pat on the shoulder. He's at least going to tell me how he found out, I thought, but no. He was bustling around behind the counter, like a whirlwind of daringly mixed colours that the cat's eyes contemplated from the fruit bowl.

"How about a banana daiquiri?" he asked, thereby revealing the answer to the mystery of the banana cream liqueur.

"I'll have a glass of wine, Ju. But don't you hold back."

He quickly served me a glass and went back to his concoction which already looked like a blinding headache. He was getting on my nerves intensely and I was getting more and more terrified because I still had no answers and Jeff would probably be home any minute, to find me wearing boxers and a camisole in the kitchen with a brightly coloured clown drinking lethal cocktails, but above all without any answers.

"Julien," I finally said, holding down one of his hands.

"What?"

"What are you doing?"

"Making a banana daiquiri."

"Christ, Julien."

He put at least twelve shots of rum in the mixer then stopped. "Jeff called me, so I came."

"What did he tell you?"

"He didn't tell me anything. He just said you probably needed company."

I was ready to start crying, out of an angry sadness and out of affection for Jeff, who was still thinking of me at a time like this.

"Where is Jeff?"

"I don't know."

"Julien…"

"He's sleeping over at Laurent's. He told me he thought it was a better idea for tonight. And besides that, Laurent is beside himself with excitement that someone's finally going to test out his bloody guestroom."

I laughed a little. Julien leaned on the counter, setting down a huge frothy glass of banana daiquiri where I could see disappointing bits of banana floating.

"What happened?"

"Hmmph."

"Hmmph, what? He didn't tell me, Marine. He just said that knowing you, you were probably going to be in quite a state and that he thought it was better that he slept over there, just for tonight."

"He's pretty smart…"

Julien gave an exaggerated sigh before he took a big gulp of his drink. "Okay. Marine? I'm happy to believe he's pretty smart, and I'm happy for him and even happier for you, but in the meantime, could you please tell me what happened? Because I'm starting to disintegrate from the curiosity that's eating me alive, so if you don't tell me everything before I finish my fucking banana daiquiri, I'm going to make you drink one. Got it?"

"Okay! Okay!" As if my furious need for confession wasn't enough, the threat of the daiquiri did me in.

I tried to get everything in the right order in my mind. I have to admit, it was pretty mixed up, what with all the alcohol I'd consumed at my parents' so I wouldn't hear my mother repeating that it made no sense for me not to have someone in my life and that it was certainly because I was being too fussy (a theory she bitterly defended and that I found particularly insulting since it implied that my own mother thought my standards were too high, and that if she were in my shoes, she'd set them lower on something that was more in my range, in other words, more mediocre).

On top of this, my father seemed to be encouraging me, continuously pouring me more wine, because he undoubtedly knew, from his own experience, that nobody and nothing could raise your awareness like my mother, and that sometimes, between getting drunk and listening to her reproaches, a choice had to be made. So I'd come home pretty drunk, thank you very much, and in a sluggish state of helplessness that Laurent called "drunken self-pity." And I was wallowing right in it, miserable for myself because it was my own fault I was alone, because I couldn't stop feeling this way, accept being single and enjoy the other deep, fascinating elements concealed within the human soul. My thinking was all screwed up and I was thinking too much, sad and humiliated about being a bad person who cheated on her nice, young boyfriends (actually, I thought I was just an ordinary person and that depressed me even more. At least, I thought to myself as I staggered towards the living room, bad people are faced with possibilities of redemption and seeing the light. What was I doing to see the light? As I walked around the sofa trying not to step on the cat, I had the distinct impression that I was much too ordinary for any revelation worthy of being called an epiphany, which had to be reserved for people who were larger than life and whom I admired, but would never be).

In short, I was bitter, drunk and sad, not a good state for the young thirty-something filled with self-doubt. If I had even one iota of wisdom left, I would have gone straight to my room, but I didn't have the strength. And in the state I was in, that's exactly what I was emotionally dreaming of: someone's strength. Jeff, at six-foot-two and two hundred pounds and with his unbeatable assurance, seemed like just what the doctor ordered. No one could say I thought about it too hard.

I still clearly remembered going into his room, lying down against him, and crying like a baby when I asked him if he thought my life was over, and then kind of falling asleep. Where my memory gets blurry is just after that, when I turned towards him and looked at his face in the shadows for a few minutes. He had exceptionally long, thick eyelashes, like in a mascara commercial, and they were imperceptibly fluttering on his closed eyes. I might have kept up my observations (patiently reconstituting the features of someone you know so well you've stopped noticing them is a fascinating activity when you've had too much to drink) and then gone back to sleep, but, Jeff opened his eyes.

I had no idea how long we were like that, just barely a few centimeters apart, looking at each other like we'd never seen each other before. It did Julien no good to insist, I couldn't remember if it had been one minute or twenty. Really, I was waiting for Jeff to say something. Jeff always said something, he was the antidote for uncomfortable situations, the remedy for silences that became a little too heavy, the one who always knew the right thing to say. But this time, silence. Silence and a blue gaze – I'm saying blue because I know what colour Jeff's eyes are. With the night surrounding us, everything was blue anyways, and I felt like blaming the blue that covered everything, even the inside of my head, for what I did next.

"You slept together," said Julien draining his daiquiri. I wondered how he'd held out so long without asking, and I almost felt sorry for him because I knew how disappointed he was going to be when I answered, "No. No, we didn't sleep together."

I had, however, kissed Jeff. I hadn't really thought about it – first of all, I was very drunk, and, second, I don't think anyone anywhere has ever really thought too much before doing something absurd and impulsive. I still remembered his arm resting on my hip: more than his eyes or his mouth, that was what filled me with the absolutely irresistible desire to abandon myself to him. (Once again, it may be interesting to point out that desires are rarely resistible when you're drunk, and that this is a lesson no one will ever learn, or at least that no one will ever be able to apply, and that's just the way it is.)

I'd drawn in closer, slowly at first. I'd had a brief flash

of lucidity, which I still remembered and which had illuminated the frankly abysmal absurdity of the situation for
me, the astronomical quantity of completely avoidable
problems that it would probably create, and the fact that
there were probably very few more rotten things to do
when you were feeling alone and guilty about having two
lovers at the same time, than getting ready to do the same
thing with the first guy to come along, even if (and this is
the worst part) he was your best friend. I knew myself well
enough to know that it was just like me to do this, that
when I was feeling down, I went for a man's arms like others go for a bottle of wine (okay. To be completely honest,
that night I'd gone for both and found them).

The flash had only lasted a couple of seconds, but it
had been enough for me to get a glimpse of all this, and
worse, to make a conscious decision not to give a shit
about it. Beyond all reason and good sense, Jeff's arm was
on my hip and a brief eternity later, my lips were on his.

He hadn't seemed surprised. His lips had opened, gently, tenderly even, and I'd felt his hand squeeze my hip,
which got me awfully excited, and in one movement, I
pressed up against him, and his big, manly body whose
weight I wanted to feel on my own.

Julien looked at me, with his mouth wide open, in exaggerated surprise. In two seconds, I thought, he's going to
say "Oh. My. God."

"Oh. My. God." I started laughing, but he looked like he
didn't even see me. "I cannot BELIEVE he didn't tell me
any of this."

"Nothing at all?" To be honest, I was having a hard
time believing it, too.

"No! He wouldn't tell us anything. Just that something
had happened, not too serious, but that you were all
turned around. If you want my opinion, he looked a lot
more turned around than you."

"You think so?" It was stupid, but the idea of it made me happy.

"Oh my God," said Julien. "I'm *sure* he's going to tell Laurent everything." He raised a fist in the air and grumbled, "Bloody hetero secrets!"

"Julien. No. There's no such thing as hetero secrets. In any case, not for hetero guys, anyway. Guys confide in their girlfriends, occasionally their gay friends, and mostly in their German shepherd or their car."

"You're generalizing."

"Not by much."

He was making a rather unsuccessful attemp to peel another overripe banana so he could make another drink. "Anyway. It's better if Laurent doesn't know any more than me." He seemed lost in thought, then abruptly set down his fork and put one hand on his hip. "Besides that, would you mind telling me why he didn't tell us anything, the big dope? What kind of guy doesn't brag about that kind of thing? What's the matter, couldn't he get it up?"

"No." I got up to get another glass of wine. What a shitty week, really. "He didn't tell you anything because he's polite. Out of friendship."

"Oooohhh…" He nodded for a minute, then seemed to understand.

"Oh!"

"Oh," is right. I was plastered up against Jeff, still wearing all my clothes, and we were kissing in a way which, even in retrospect, seemed to me to be the very picture of passion. I'd put my mind aside and I was finally nothing but a body (sweet oblivion!). I only wanted one thing, and even if it still surprised me a bit, it persisted and continued to grow: I wanted to feel Jeff inside of me. That's when he woke up.

I say "woke up" because that is exactly what it seemed like and, for a few seconds, I was wondering if he hadn't been asleep the whole time we were kissing – after all, he might be a sleepwalker, and if there was one thing Jeff would do while he was sleepwalking, it was kiss women.

"Marine," he'd said, and I was immediately worried, because it wasn't the languid "Marine" of a man about to give in to pleasure, but rather the tense, frightened "Marine" of a man getting ahold of himself. I'd already heard this particular "Marine" in the mouth of another man, who'd followed my name with the statement "I'm married." In short, it was not a good omen, and I quickly stopped being a body and became a mind again that was all too aware of its body, which happened to be in the arms of its roommate, and of the undeniable drunkenness that had gotten it into that situation.

Jeff had pulled back a little, just barely a few centimeters, but I already knew he wouldn't be coming close again: with my arms still around him, I could feel a tension in his back, which was in sad contrast with the abandon of the previous minute. Slowly, very slowly, he'd removed the arm that was around me, and finally, I was the one who spoke up.

"Sorry," I said, rolling over onto my back and covering my face with my hand. I was wishing with all my might that I'd wake up in my own bed and realize that all this had been nothing but a dream, an exciting and humiliating dream that above all wasn't real.

"No," Jeff had said. "I'm sorry."

"Sorry for what? I'm the one who… I'm really sorry."

"Stop." He'd rolled over and put an arm out towards me, but this time I was the one who pulled back from his hand as if it would burn me.

"Let's not start that," I'd said, though I could still feel the embers of my desire in my stomach. "You're right. It doesn't make any sense."

"No, that's not it… Marine, it's not that I don't want to…"

When he said that, I got up – I didn't really know why, but it insulted me, it cut me to the quick. I just straightened out my sweater in a gesture of remarkable futility and I wanted to say something, but when I turned towards the bed, where Jeff was leaning on one elbow and running a hand over his face, half naked in the blue light, I felt myself give in completely and all I could say was, "I'm drunk, okay? I'm sorry," though we'd been drunk together hundreds of times before without anything of the sort ever happening, and "I'm going to bed."

Behind me, I heard him say, "Your life is so not over," and then, as I shut the door, "Fuck."

"Ooooohh," said Julien.

"Can you please stop saying 'Ooooohh'? It's not exactly constructive."

"Pffff…"

"Okay." If I was going to spend the evening listening to onomatopoeias and monosyllables, it would be better with a glass in front of me. I got up to pour myself some more wine, cutting a path around Julien who was still going "psss" and "tchk" into his daiquiri. Claude François was following me with his eyes and I leaned over to kiss his warm fur.

"Are you mad at him?" Julien asked.

"At Jeff? No. No, I even think he's fucking classy not to have told you anything." I took a swallow of wine. Julien looked at me, undoubtedly trying to see if I was really being honest. "And for not… you know… for not letting me… for not letting us… Anyways… For not giving in or wanting to… Christ, don't try to help, whatever you do!"

"But there's nothing I can do to help, Marine! Do you really think I know what was going on in Jeff's head? I think he was just being reasonable, that he figured it didn't make any sense, that it likely would ruin other things… and no offense, sweetheart, but it doesn't take a clairvoyant to see that you're in a bad way these days and that it wasn't exactly common sense that led you to do what you did."

"I know all that, Julien. That's why I think he did the right thing. Even if... Christ. At the time I wanted to kill him."

"I understand."

I wasn't even sure if I hadn't reacted badly because I was mad, or if it was in fact, because I saw, despite my frustrated desire and drunken state, that Jeff understood better than I did, and before I did, what had brought me to his arms.

"You can't be mad at yourself," said Julien.

"Hmmpf."

"No! You can't be mad at yourself. I don't know what gets into all of you, you and Laurent especially, to get mad at yourself for being human. What you did wasn't exactly smart, in fact, it was far from being a good idea, but, Christ, it's only human. Weakness is human. You're not going to start blaming yourself for being human, are you?"

I felt like telling him that with thinking like that, we'd be in a good position to start forgiving everybody for everything on the pretext that we're all human, from the best to the worst of us, and that the idea of embracing one's weakness, with a teary eye and a full heart, and the blissful smile of someone who's found a long-lost sister, seemed to me like it was opening the door to a dangerous flood of stupidity and idiotic acts, not to mention potential catastrophes (following Julien's logic, you could blame anything on the human condition: its shoulders were immeasurably broad. I imagined Hitler in his bunker, shrugging his shoulders and looking a little contrite: "What can I say, *mein Herren*, I screwed up, I know, but I'm only human").

"I know what you're thinking," Julien continued. "Maybe

it's because I'm gay, and figuring out you like men in 1980 in Percé isn't the easiest thing in the world and it forces you to think outside the box a little bit, just to be able to survive and put up with yourself, but, pretty early on, I decided there's nothing, absolutely nothing, we can do that is inhuman. There's no such thing as inhuman. It's just a word we made up to make us feel better when things scare us. Saying "It's inhuman" when a mother kills her child is just closing your eyes. Shit, it can't be inhuman since somebody did it. It's horrible, but it's human. At worst, it's a refusal of what's human, but trying to deny it isn't going to help anyone. And, on a much smaller scale, cheating on your wife, sleeping around, stealing petty cash from the restaurant where you work, being a bitch to your best friend, forgetting to call your mother for her birthday, trying to sleep with your roommate 'cause you're drunk and feeling down – all these are nothing but rather disappointing reminders of our humanity. I'm not saying you should celebrate, but you don't have to beat yourself up either. Because spending your time blaming yourself is just a way not to take responsibility for what you've done wrong."

He finished his tirade with the kind of tired, satisfied sigh that usually comes with the accomplishment of some difficult, daunting task, then he raised the bottle of banana cream liqueur up to his eyes to see if it was empty. There was about a half-inch left, and he immediately poured it into his glass and drank it down in one swallow. What had ever happened in his life, I wondered, to make him say things like that and finish bottles of banana liqueur in a single gulp?

I understood what he was trying to say, and, although I didn't agree with him completely, I didn't think he was wrong either, but I was dumbfounded to hear him, Julien, say it with something of a tremor in his voice. We always knew something sad and gray was hiding in Julien's past – Laurent and Jeff thought it was simply that he had to accept his homosexuality when he came from a family that considered it a mortal sin, but I'd always thought it was something else, something that was more serious but that he'd managed to get over and that had made him choose to be so violently cheerful, so constantly positive, and even decide to banish gray socks from his room and transform his wardrobe into a rainbow.

He wasn't looking at me, he was busy moving bottles around in the cabinet, looking for who-knows-what – after the crème de banane, I wouldn't have been surprised if he got out the Drambuie.

"Sorry," he said, with his nose still in the cabinet. "Sometimes I get carried away. It's just that…" His head was completely engulfed in the cabinet. If he could, I think he would have crawled all the way inside, shutting the door behind himself. "It's just that when you've been hurt yourself, sometimes it makes you mad to see people you care about hurting over things that shouldn't even be painful."

"What happened to you, Julien?"

He turned around, with a filthy bottle in one hand. "Peach schnapps! Just what I was looking for. I make excellent Fuzzy Navels." He was smiling, radiant, his beautiful eyes were dancing gaily as if they'd never seen any sorrow and I knew there would be no answer for my question, not tonight for sure, and maybe not ever.

"Listen," he said, taking the orange juice carton out of the fridge to make some of his damned Fuzzy Navels, which I would have to taste. "What I mean is that there's nothing wrong with wanting a man's body when you're not feeling great. It's my drug, too."

"Okay, but you've got a boyfriend, Ju."

He opened his mouth to say something, blinking his eyes.

"Okay, what?" I asked.

"Orange juice," he shouted as if he'd just woken up. "There's no more orange juice." I must have looked pretty

intrigued because, in an overly cheerful way that was supposed to sound like an answer to my question, he
immediately added, "Grapefruit juice. That'll do the job."
And he started pushing juice cartons around in the fridge,
and then he added, in the same perky way, "What do you
want, Marine, we're full of life – it has its good points and
its bad points."

"Yeah, but in the meantime, I'm stuck with a roommate who can't sleep at home, an awful guilt trip and a
fucking Fuzzy Navel."

"Taste it! I'm telling you it's not bad."

Strictly speaking it really wasn't bad, but the taste of
peach schnapps awakened the immortal memory of the first
time I got drunk and immediately made me want to throw
up, listen to some old Depeche Mode and write ridiculous
anarchist slogans on a backpack in an effort to relive the
glory of my sixteenth year. What had I done to deserve
friends who still insisted on drinking absurd cocktails at
nearly forty years old? Why couldn't we just get drunk on
wine or beer, like everybody else?

"Yes, yes. If you're good, I'll make you a Blue Lagoon
next. You have Curaçao, don't you?"

In a panic, I looked towards the liquor cabinet and
mentally calculated the number of meters separating it
from me and tried to figure out, just in case, if I could leap
over the counter to get to it before Julien and smash the
bottle of Curaçao on the first available hard surface.

"But," said Julien, as if the threat of the Blue Lagoon
were not still hanging in the air between us, "Jeff really did
treat you right."

"He treated me fucking great. Did he really look turned
around?"

Julien must have noticed my smile since he gave me
back one that was full of insinuation. "He looked unsettled. Maybe he's just afraid things will change between
you."

"Maybe." What if things did change. The idea of it made me sad beyond words. I didn't want anything between me and the boys to ever change even if I knew that things always end up changing and that some day we'd all really have to grow up.

"Did you ever think he might be in love with you?"

"Excuse me?"

"I don't know, it's just an idea."

"NO! No! God, no, no, no, no, no... Julien, NO!" The very idea shattered me. I loved Jeff with all my heart, and well, yes, I'd desperately wanted to make love with him, but it seemed obvious that if someone was going to mix love – real love – into all this, then nothing would ever be the same, nothing could ever be simple between him and me because once love comes into the picture, you can kiss simplicity good-bye.

"Okay! Okay! I was just wondering, that's all, I didn't mean to imply anything... Lord, would it be as bad as all that?"

"It would be completely absurd, Julien. It would imply that for three years I've been living with a guy who's in love with me... Oh my God, did he say something to you?"

"No! Cut it out..." He laughed a little. I really must have seemed pretty laughable, getting upset for no reason right there in front of my Fuzzy Navel. "He didn't say anything to us, I've told you forty times. And, knowing him like I do, I'm sure that right now he's watching hockey with Laurent – who's pretending to like it – and debriefing a little and hoping you're all right. Don't forget, Marine, Jeff is by far the least fucked up of all of us."

"That's funny," I said in a tone that was wavering between paranoia and bitterness and definitely didn't foreshadow anything pleasant. "The ones who seem the least fucked up are always the most fucked up."

"Okay, you need another drink." His voice was patient and a little weary sounding, and I could feel that he was perfectly conscious of the stupidity of what I'd just said. It was true, though, that Jeff was the least complicated of the four of us. He was transparent because he had no complexes, he was sincere and solid in his affection, and, with my shifting sands and awkward movements, I must have thrown him off just a little, but he never lost his way, and remained like a rock in the middle of our anchorless lives although, despite his big heart and good will, our frantic drifting left him confused.

"Sor-ry. You're right. I know Jeff isn't fucked up. "It's the Fuzzy Navel talking." As I was talking I did actually realize I was getting a little tipsy. "Watch out, Julien. If I happen to get drunk, I might make a pass at you."

He started to laugh and then he added some corny remark like, "Well, you know, Marine, that's all I'm waiting for to switch teams," then the doorbell rang. Curious, I got up to open the door and in came Flavie like a Technicolor hurricane, in her mustard yellow coat, her mauve Doc Martens, and to top it all off, a Phrygian cap she insisted on calling "revolutionary," although everyone else around here called it patriotic.

"Hello, darling!" she called as she took off her coat to reveal a long blue dress made of something that looked like felt. With her and Julien in the same room, it was like being in a Prismacolor box. "I've left Guillaume."

"Guillaume! I... Oh yeah?" It was the most uncertain "oh yeah?" I'd ever uttered in my life: I didn't exactly remember who Guillaume was, I wasn't sure if it was good news or not, and, to be honest, I had absolutely no opinion about the whole thing.

"That's right, oh yeah! Shit, oh yeah, oh yeah, oh yeah. Oh! Julien!" It took her two strides to get over to him, and send Claude François flying, because he was always terrified by this larger-than-life woman, and then settle on a bench, heaving a sigh the neighbors must have heard. "So, what are you making, handsome?" she asked Julien.

"Blue Lagoons."

"I have no idea what that is. Is there any alcohol in it?"

"Just about nothing but."

"Will you make three, then?"

She heaved another sigh before taking off her cap and then finally turning back to me. "What the hell are you doing in boxers? You okay?"

Julien made a gesture that said, "Not so hot."

"What's wrong?" Flavie asked, suddenly transformed into a red river of compassion. "What's going on?"

So the whole story had to be told all over again for her. I wanted to leave a ton of it out, because I remembered that Jeff had a little crush on Flavie, and I really would have been mad at myself if I ruined everything with my blunder, but Julien wanted to tell the whole story, while Flavie listened, shot me truly distressed looks and kept repeating "You poor dear."

"You poor dear!" she said when Julien's interminable story was finally over. "What were you thinking?"

"What do you mean what was I thinking? What do you think I was thinking, Flavie?"

"I'm asking what you were thinking when you left the bedroom?"

"What did you expect me to do?"

"Sleep with him, silly girl! I expected you to use all your dirty tricks, do whatever you had to do, but at least spend the night with that fine specimen between your legs."

"You think he's a fine specimen?" Shaker still in hand, Julien was leaning so far over the counter I thought he was going to come tumbling over the top of it.

"Of course!" said Flavie, as if it were the most obvious thing ever. "That boy is fantastic!"

"He thinks YOU'RE fantastic," I said.

"I know, I know. I'm not that stupid, you know. I can see how he looks at me."

I was suddenly very jealous of her, not for the way Jeff

looked at her, but for having the clearheadedness and confidence it took to recognize and accept such things. At thirty-two years old, I still felt like apologizing profusely when a man liked me.

"Why don't you come to supper?" I asked Flavie. "It'll be fun."

"Well... okay, maybe. Maybe we should wait until you two work things out, no?" Behind her red mane, Julien was furiously nodding his head "yes."

"Yes," I said. "I suppose, but it won't take too long. It's not that serious, after all."

"It's not that serious," said Flavie, stroking my thigh. "It's never as serious as you think."

"It's never that simple, either."

"No," said Julien, setting an electric blue cocktail in front of each of us. "It's never that simple."

"Thank God," I said with a smile. Flavie raised her drink and we all clinked glasses without saying anything, to life's beautiful complexity, I suppose, although deep down, I was hoping that it would be that simple, that beautifully simple, forever.

The next morning, the telephone woke me up at seven. First, I was startled and, for a short fifteen seconds, I wondered where I was and who I was, then I remembered the Blue Lagoons and, then as if my headache was simply waiting for this memory to surface, I felt a sharp pain squeezing my temples. I answered the phone – anything to put a stop to that horrible noise – and I heard the soft, fluty voice of Julien's boyfriend, Mathias, on the other end of the line.

"Mathias?" I looked next to me: there was Julien, lying on his stomach, still fully dressed, snoring softly, and images of the night before began to come back slowly, like bubbles resurfacing in churning waters. I could see the two of us, lying on my bed, finishing cocktails which, at that point, couldn't have had real names, laughing like fifteen-year-old girls, then I fell asleep, but not before muttering to Julien about him staying over if he wanted to – a useless measure on my part, since, if my shaky memory was accurate, he was already snoring.

"Sorry for waking you up," said Mathias… "I just wanted, um… Is Julien there?" In his voice, I could hear he was uncomfortable calling me, not to mention humiliated about having to inquire about Julien's nights this way and that he would have preferred not having to call his boyfriend's friends at seven o'clock in the morning, but that he couldn't wait any longer. He must not have slept a wink all night.

"Mathias, yes! My God, yes, Julien is here. Julien!" I shook Julien, who was a little hard to wake up, and I placed the phone next to him so Mathias could at least hear his characteristic grumbling.

"I'm sorry," I said. "We should have called you. We were acting like teenagers, we got drunk as skunks and Ju fell asleep here."

"No, Marine, I'm the one who's sorry."

"No, no, you can't be sorry. It's out of the question.

"Is he okay?"

"Well, he must have a hell of a hangover, but as for the rest, I suppose he's fine."

"Good."

"Mathias. You okay?" I was still breathing alcohol vapors from the night before and I was having a hard time carrying on a conversation. I wanted to be there for Mathias, to tell him everything was fine, that we'd drunk some banana daiquiris and some who-knows-what-else, but both words and ideas kept bumping into each other in my head.

"I'm okay," said Mathias. "Great, even. I'm really sorry, Marine."

"Stop it. You're not sorry, got it?" I wanted to add that

Julien was the one who should be sorry, but I thought that
Mathias might not want to share his conjugal worries with
me. I liked Mathias a lot, with his big black eyes, his gentleness and a sensitivity he cultivated although the boys
confused with being effeminate. We talked for a few more
seconds, with Mathias nicely asking how I was and offering me a secret-sharing session "over an herbal tea instead
of a barrel of booze." He hung up saying, "Thanks,
Marine. Thanks for looking after him."

I fell back heavily on my pillow, and I looked at Julien
who was fast asleep again, with his big secret hiding under
his colorful clothes. "Damn idiot," I said out loud,
untruthfully thinking that if *I* had a boyfriend like
Mathias, I would have showered him with attention.

I'd just fallen asleep when the bloody phone woke
me up again, but this time I let it ring since the nice call-
display told me it was my mother on the other end. I
tried to guess the number of minutes that would go by
before she called again – it took less then thirty seconds
before I heard my cell phone ringing in the living room,
then another fifteen seconds before she called back on
the home phone "just in case it didn't work the first
time" – since she always did. Ten minutes later, another
call, and this time I decided to listen to the message.

"Marine, it's your mother, Monique." "Oh," I'd always
wanted to answer, "that mother." "Listen, if you happen to
talk to your brother, can you please tell him to call us? We
haven't heard from him in a long time... Now, I don't want
him to pay long distance, so tell him to let it ring twice,
then I'll know it's him and I'll call back. Because calling
long distance from France, you know, Marine, is just a
short cut to bankruptcy. And he's already not super rich...
Okay. Anyway, you can call us back. 450-555-8321... Oh,
and Marine..." I was convinced that the idea of calling
Frédéric herself hadn't even crossed her mind. It couldn't
be explained, but my mother seemed to be incapable of

coming up with simple, practical solutions for life's little problems, rather, with fearsome energy, I must say, she sought out surprisingly ingenious ways of complicating things that, I thought, seemed impossible to complicate.

I was listening to the end of her message, an unending story of questionable interest about a woman who took out the wrong checkbook at the bank and consequently made her lose a HALF-HOUR of her time, and I waited from one second to the next for her to remind me of their other phone number, which hadn't changed in thirty-five years, as if it were humanly possible for me not to know it by heart, when I saw Jeff standing at my door. I hadn't heard him come in, busy as I was following my mother's intrepid adventures at the Caisse populaire de Duvernay.

He was looking at me with a particularly amused smile. I was lying on my back, still wearing boxers and a camisole, one hand on Julien's back, the other against my ear, and I realized I'd sighed out loud at least twice. "Jesus, *Maman*…" I threw the telephone on the floor and sat up, way too quickly of course, and sent my head pounding.

"Ouch… ouch." I raised my face towards him. "Hello? I… errr…" I didn't know what to say. I was almost mad at him for being there, for not leaving me enough time to make myself a little something or at least digest a couple of Tylenol. "You okay?"

"Yeah, I'm fine, but I saw a lot of dead bottles in the kitchen… You must be in bad shape… I didn't know we had liqueur de cacao."

"Liqueur de… ? Ugh…" Vague memories of absurd cocktails started resurfacing again. I got up slowly to go talk in the living room for a little while and get myself a glass of water. Jeff had already gone to his room.

"Listen," I said. I was lying on my stomach across the back of the sofa.

"Marine." He came and stood in the doorway. "It's all right. It's really, really all right."

"No. No, it's not all right, I..." I got up, with my face in my hands, and I felt a little like crying, mostly because I had an unbearable hangover, but also because for the hundredth time in two weeks I thought I was fantastically stupid and useless. I had become the kind of girl I hated.

"Marine!" He laughed, and I heard him coming towards me to put his arms around me. My face barely came as high as his pecs – I felt like I was about three inches tall and, if I could have, I would have climbed into his shirt pocket. I wanted to be tiny and invisible, a little bird in an incubator, a kitten on it's mother's tummy, even a bug, there must be happy bugs, snuggled up somewhere in their comfy cocoons, hidden from the eyes of the world behind wide, green leaves.

"Marine," Jeff repeated with a laugh. "It's really, truly all right. Jesus, we didn't commit a murder, did we? Nothing happened! Okay, a little necking. You think it's the first time in the history of roommates that a guy and a girl have necked a little?"

"Noooo. But why did you leave?"

"Because I knew you'd be all turned around. And besides, Laurent was so happy to have someone finally sleep in his bloody guestroom."

"Ah."

"Okay, look." He raised my chin with one finger. "Now, you're looking for reasons to be upset about things that aren't supposed to be upsetting. I know you've had a rough couple of weeks, and what happened with Christophe is really a pain, and your handsome doctor probably thinks you escaped from the psych ward, but what happened the other night really shouldn't upset you, okay?"

"Am I an idiot?"

"A little. But I have to run. I have to be in Québec City at noon."

"Why?"

"I have an interview with the premier."

"Oh." Sometimes I had a hard time following Jeff's career path – sometimes he did bios of pop stars, sometimes he did reports on the state of the schools around Ungava Bay, and today he was meeting the premier.

"Gotta go," he added, tweaking the tip of my nose, like I was nine years old, with braids and a lunchbox.

"Umm… You sure everything's okay?"

"Drop it already, okay? Everything's fine, Marine. I just don't want you to be all turned around, okay?"

"Okay…"

He gave me a beautiful, sincere smile and went out as quickly as he'd come in. In a daze, I was contemplating the bar, covered with glasses and empty bottles, and I heard Julien behind me. "Not a word," he said. He had one arm braced against my door frame and was leaning his head against it. "I don't believe a single word of what he just said."

"What?"

"Jeff. I don't believe him."

"Huh?"

He sighed, and then added, "But. What do I know…" and he ran a hand over his face. There were spots on his magenta shirt and they made him look strangely vulnerable, unlike his usual well-dressed self, the prince of the impeccable image. "Was that Mathias on the phone before?"

"Yesss… he was worried. You know."

"Yes, I know. I fucking know."

And I had the feeling my prince of the impeccable image was shattering before me. He made a strange noise that sounded something like a sob and something like a self-pitying, sad laugh, then, when he saw I was coming towards him, he put out a hand to stop me in my tracks. I stood there like a statue for a couple of seconds – his head was completely buried in his arm and he wasn't making a sound now, but the slight movement of his shoulders told me he was crying. My God, we're a mess, I thought when I saw us. It felt like seeing Julien break down was like seeing my own flaws, that his fragility worsened my own. Because if he was falling apart, I may as well just crumble.

"Julien," I said gently. "What… What's going on?" I had the vaguely panicked tone of children who see their mother crying.

"Mathias left," he said into the crook of his arm.

"WHAT?"

"He left. He's fed up." He raised his head. On his lips was a sad, pathetic smile. "And I know I've spent the last three years praising the single life and complaining and sleeping around. I know that, but…" His chin trembled. I tried again to come near to him.

"No," he said. "Not right away, okay?"

"Okay."

He nodded his head and as he went to sit on the sofa, he said, "I know I said all that. But… but now…" I went and sat down next to him, being careful not to touch him. "I just can't without him." He looked at me. I understood what he meant. Most of all, I understood that his pain was sincere and deep, and that he must have been carrying it around for a long time without knowing how to share it. He preferred to console me, listen to our little troubles, and pretend to try and pick up Andrew.

"Are there any cucumber slices left?" asked Julien, pointing to his swollen eyes. I laughed a little, compassionately, the only way I could.

We didn't say anything for a little while, then I laid a hand on his thigh. "Do you want to tell me about it, Julien?" He nodded yes, but he didn't say anything and we just sat there like that, bruised, me in my old boxers and him in his spotted shirt, and all I could see were our faults.

To: Fred
From: Marine Vandale
Subject: Self-flagellation

....

So, in the category of thanklessness and disastrous narcissism, I can tell you that I broke records this week. Can you believe that for days Julien has been walking around with his heart at half-mast and that the whole time, I was just filling his poor ear with my hopeless little worries?

To: Marine
From: Frédéric Vandale
Subject: Re: Self-flagellation

....

Yes, let me flagellate you a bit myself. Because the last time you wrote, you left me in suspense in the middle of a promising little story. Do you realize Jeff had to tell me everything himself?

To: Fred
From: Marine Vandale
Subject: Act of Contrition

....

Okay, okay, that's enough. My humblest apologies. But you should understand that I've been busy with Julien's problem. He doesn't talk very often, our Julien, but when he opens his mouth, it just doesn't stop.

To: Marine
From: Frédéric Vandale
Subject: Sad clown

....

What's wrong with our friend the rainbow?

To: Fred
From: Marine Vandale
Subject: Lonely clown

Mathias left him.

To: Martine
From: Frédéric Vandale
Subject: Re: Lonely clown

Really though, there's no reason to faint from surprise, is there?

To: Fred
From: Martine Vandale
Subject: "Really Though" Echo

Right, that's what everyone's been saying for two days. Including Julien. But it doesn't makes the boo-boos go away, you know. So, what he gets are back rubs, an attentive ear, and a bartender: I'm like Florence Nightingale for the lovelorn.

To: Marine
From: Frédéric Vandale
Subject: Paris wants to know

What happened, exactly? Did Mathias just get tired of it, or was there a straw that broke the camel's back?

To: Fred
From: Marine Vandale
Subject: One huge straw

I'll tell you on the phone because the straw wouldn't even fit into a single email. You shouldn't laugh when you have a friend in tears, but I'll warn you now, the word "hilarious" may cross your mind. Now, will *you* please tell me what Jeff told you? Because for days, he's been nothing but carefree and cheerful around here, and he's brought home Marie-Lune every night since. And just before it all let loose, Julien still managed to tell me that he didn't think Jeff was really as carefree and cheerful as all that.

To: Marine
From: Frédéric Vandale
Subject: Trust me, trust me

....

He told me, that's all. And maybe it's just kind of his style to go heavy on the cheerfulness, but don't you think you should look at the situation with a little distance and not be so suspicious? But I do agree that bringing Marie-Lune home every night may well be the sign that the man is in distress. Distance, Marinette. Distance. Maybe everything is not as complicated as you always want to think.

To: Fred
From: Marine Vandale
Subject: Sudden wisdom

....

You had to go to Paris to figure all this out? Tell me how you did it, 'cause from here, I can't see much. But you, on the other hand, seem to be nothing but distance and writing.

To: Marine
From: Frédéric Vandale
Subject: Parisian distance

....

Um, you're right about the distance, but as far as writing is concerned, it would be nice if you just avoided the subject, since my future book is currently only three paragraphs long. Of course, you can't say anything to *Maman* because she expects me to win the Prix Goncourt before the end of the week. So, mum's the word, and thanks.

To: Fred
From: Marine Vandale
Subject: *Maman*

....

Speaking of *Maman*, she's so fired up looking for you I'm surprised she hasn't sent the RCMP after you. She wants you to call her and use a code that I really don't understand, but that has something to do with two rings and a call back. It doesn't matter though, just call.

To: Marine
From: Frédéric Vandale
Subject: Re: *Maman*

....

Maman never wants me to call and she wants to call me even less because, in her mind, long distance means worry. She still sends snail mail, remember? So, what's going on?

To: Fred
From: Marine Vandale
Subject: RE: *Maman*

....

She wants to talk to you.

To: Marine
From: Frédéric Vandale
Subject: RE: Re: *Maman*

....

Wait a minute, you're not going to leave me hanging twice in a week? Marine what's going on?

To: Fred
From: Marine Vandale
Subject: *Papa*

....

Don't panic. You call, let it ring twice, hang up and don't panic. And above all, don't tell *Maman* that I told you anything at all.

:)

Chapter 5

"Okay, I know he's hurting and everything, but it's fucking weird," said Laurent, bringing a little blue tray over to the coffee table. On it was a bowl of marinated olives and another bowl of spicy nuts, a plate of thinly sliced *rosette de Lyon* sausage, and a slim vase, that was also blue, holding a daisy. I knew all of it came from the market on the corner – Laurent was incapable of making toast without burning himself and even less capable of slicing sausage without amputating an arm – but I appreciated the effort. The lighting was subdued and soft music filled the apartment.

The little world I'd lived in for five years hardly bore any trace of my presence anymore, the photos on the walls had changed, the furniture had been moved around and the contents of the pantry belonged to another woman. But, I thought, as I looked around the room where I'd been so happy and so sad, where I'd even had the luxury of being a little bored, I still bear the indelible mark of this place. I must really have been in bad shape, I was starting to make up bad poetry about the memory of places versus the memory of people, and I was saying to Laurent – who was patient, despite being slightly uncomfortable – that "we remember places long after they forget us," and I didn't even have the excuse of being drunk.

"Oh, I know," I said… "It's really…" I started to laugh through my nostalgia, then I got ahold of myself. "We shouldn't laugh… Poor Julien. The one time he tells us his problems instead of listening to ours, we laugh in his face."

"Not IN his face."

"No, no, Jeff literally laughed in his face. He almost fell over backwards."

"Yeah, but…" and Laurent burst out laughing. "It's a helluva comedy sketch."

Apparently, Julien had actually redefined the expression "to get caught with your pants down" and since we'd learned the whole story, I have to admit I feel a new respect for Mathias. Of course, he wasn't crazy and he'd always known that Julien had a roving eye – but they had a tacit arrangement and I think that deep down Mathias knew Julien loved him and he accepted his heart's fidelity even if he couldn't get his body's. The thing was, he didn't want to see other people; he often repeated he was the wife in the couple and, unfortunately for him, he was part of the small minority of men, gay or straight, who were ferociously monogamous.

The day after our banana daiquiri party, Julien told me they sometimes talked about it. He knew his one-night-stands hurt Mathias because he'd often make remarks that he meant to be playful, but his wounds were visible and growing, until the day he decided he couldn't take it anymore and told Julien so. Julien thought about it for a long time, he told me, and he weighed the pros and cons and realized that, despite his macho talk and his penchant for anonymous sex, he loved Mathias and the life they had too much to lose them. And he'd promised.

Then, a few months later, faced with a few suspicious absences and some lies that didn't add up, Mathias decided, despite his scruples, to search Julien's computer. On the dating site where they'd met years before, it didn't take him long to find Julien's new identity: "hotjules." Hotjules was exchanging messages with several different men (Julien said he was flirting, but knowing my friend the way I did, I was sure that the nature of said messages went well beyond the realm of flirting). Listening to no one but his broken heart, Mathias became "badboy69" and he and hotjules began to "flirt."

"He asked me what I liked," Julien told me. "He told me what excited him, he described himself – Mathias knows me by heart, so I don't have to tell you that he didn't have any trouble attracting my attention." He laughed sadly. "He asked if I had a boyfriend, if I loved him."

"What did you answer?"

"I couldn't say no. So I said I didn't want to talk about love." And I thought my relationships were complex.

Hotjules and badboy69 finally made a date in a part of the city where Julien was sure he didn't know anyone. He waited for badboy69 in his car, with his heart throbbing ("Um… I think you mean with your cock throbbing," Jeff corrected him, and even Julien laughed) and he was feeling a little guilty, but not guilty enough, when he looked up and, at the agreed upon time, the passenger door opened up and Mathias sat down next to him.

"It's not that it's funny," I said to Laurent. "It's just that… it's the kind of thing you don't even believe when it happens in a movie." Jeff had applauded when Julien got to the punchline.

"Well… Julien may be my best friend, but I'm not sure I wouldn't congratulate Mathias if I saw him on the street."

"*I'd* congratulate him. I love Julien from the bottom of my heart and he really needs to hear that now, but he really got what he deserves…"

"You think they'll get back together?"

"Um… don't you think it might be a little too early to ask that particular question? There's no doubt they love each other, but… anyway, if I were Mathias, I'd stay mad for a while. Poor guy, he called over to our place the other morning. He was worried." I nodded and took a drink of my wine. "I'm telling you, Loulou, I looked at us the other morning,

Julien and me, in the living room, with our hangovers and our cucumber slices on our eyes... And I thought we looked pretty fucking rough. Can you tell me how two people who are supposed to be somewhat intelligent manage to fuck up all their relationships so spectacularly?"

Raising his eyebrows, Laurent gave me a little smile. The two of us had crashed and burned, too.

"Marine... you don't know how lucky you are," he finally said, probably to get me to be quiet, I think. "You complain about not having anyone, about screwing everything up, but you don't know your own good luck." He said this more and more often. I remembered that Laurent was never deeply unhappy, but he really wasn't able to be perfectly happy either, and before he enjoyed anything good, he always looked for its downside.

"You shouldn't complain," he repeated. It's true I'd been complaining a lot the last little while. I grumbled stupidly about my situation, whined about being alone, and said extremely intelligent things like "nobody loves me and I'm alone in the world" which the boys enjoyed reminding me of the next day as they brought me a Bloody Caesar.

"You complain, too," I told him.

He shrugged his shoulders and swallowed a slice of *rosette*. "Hmpff. No more than usual." At least he was thinking straight. He'd been complaining about his relationship with Carole from the beginning, and my intuition told me he must have complained to other people about our relationship the whole five years we'd been together.

"You think it's displacement?" I asked him.

"Hmmm?"

"Displacement. It's a term Fred uses. Like, we complain about little things so we don't have to face our real problems."

"My real problem is that I'll never be completely happy in a relationship and I'm incapable of being alone."

He really was thinking straight today. "Tricky," was my only comment. Laurent took a drink of wine and went "Pfft," as if to say something like, "Who do you think you're telling?" For a minute I wondered why I'd come over – it was obvious neither one of us felt like talking, but I felt good in this living room that no longer looked anything like me. Some girls go to their mother's to forget themselves, I thought, I go to Laurent's.

"You're thinking pretty straight, anyway."

"Hmpff. I think we all see things more clearly than we think. You know what your real problem is?"

I thought for a second. I agreed with him: I'd always thought most people, including myself, were a lot more aware of what was going on inside them than they'd admit, undoubtedly because repressing things was easier and less painful, in the short term, of course, than facing things head on.

"I think…" I found the idea rather unpleasant, and even pretty humiliating, but it had a ring of truth about it that I could no longer ignore. "I think my problem is that I don't really have any problems."

"Um…"

"I don't know. Call it idleness if you want. I don't have any serious problems and I have a lot of time, so I make up troubles that take on ridiculous proportions in my mind."

"Hmpff."

"Okay, that's one 'hmpff' too many."

"All right, what do you want me to say: 'No, things aren't as bad as that.' Well, yeah, things are tough, but it's like that for everyone. Well, maybe not people who are just trying to survive in Darfur or somewhere, like Sudan…"

"Darfur is in Sudan."

"Really?"

Sometimes I wondered how Laurent's mind worked. He watched the news, but all he got out of it was the color of Bernard's tie, the weather in Saskatoon or the number of horses used in *Cavalia*. He'd already questioned me about west India to find out if it was really a region: "Is there such a place as west India?" and he looked all flabbergasted when I told him not only was there such a place, but that even his condo had a west side.

"Anyway," he went on, "I just mean you can't be the only person who does that. We all go a little crazy when we have too much time to think about ourselves. That's why we work too hard…"

"Um… you only work four months a year."

"Yeah, but the rest of the time, I'm at work in here." He tapped his left temple with his finger, and I started laughing. "That's why we work hard and that's why we want to fall in love so bad. So we don't go crazy."

He'd uttered the last sentence with his mouth full of spicy nuts. He swallowed another handful, and didn't add a word, until he said, "Wow." I took a drink of wine, as I tried to assimilate the idea that had come so unexpectedly from the mouth of a person I thought I knew by heart. "Do you really think that's it?" I finally asked.

"Well, yeah. What do you think we're all doing? What do you think Jeff is doing with Marie-Lune, of all people?"

"What do you mean, what's Jeff's doing with Marie-Lune? You still need me to draw you a picture?"

"You know what I mean." He paused and then said exactly what I expected: "Besides that, I can't believe you guys French kissed."

"Loulou…" He'd been repeating the same thing for two weeks, always insisting on the fact that he had no problem with the whole situation and that Jeff had done the right thing when he went to his house that night.

"What? It's all right, you can French kiss whoever you want, but it's something special." When he said "special," he meant "huge."

"Loulou, he's sleeping with Marie-Lune. And the whole

thing was a mistake. My mistake. Didn't he make that clear?" Laurent had never wanted to tell me exactly what Jeff had told him the night he'd slept over, and as much as I admired such beautiful masculine solidarity, I also wanted to skin Laurent alive and shake him till his secret fell out. I believed him when he told me it wasn't much, that Jeff has assured him he was "cool with everything," but I would have liked to get a tape of their conversation or, at the very least, a verbatim repoprt.

"I told you what he told me. It just proves my theory anyway. What you did, what he did himself, it's all the same, it's the same principle. Talk to him about it, I'm sure he agrees deep down."

"Yeah well, it's not like I have regular chances to talk to him these days. In two weeks, I don't think I've even seen him once without her being there…"

I knew I'd been paying too much attention to insignificant details. But ever since that stupid mistake I was still beating myself up over, I was just about counting every word Jeff and I exchanged, and despite his cheerful, carefree attitude, I was worried. I thought he was too cheerful and carefree, and I also thought I was crazy for thinking like that. And I was climbing the walls in the apartment, asking him twenty times a day if he was all right, and he invariably answered with an amused smile, "Of course, I'm fine!" And I realized that even though all I wanted was for nothing to change, it was the very absence of change in Jeff's behavior that worried me, because I'd been so disoriented myself lately that I had a hard time believing that anyone who wasn't as mixed up as I was must be hiding something.

And then there was Marie-Lune's presence, which seemed like an effort on Jeff's part to reclaim his territory, and though something like that would usually make me laugh, now it was depressing me – I'd have liked to reclaim a little territory, too, wash myself of the memory of Jeff by being in another man's arms, but I still had enough good sense to know, for the time being at least, that I was better off keeping away from men.

"You can think what you want," I said. "But I'm not biting. Your idea's too sad."

"It's not as depressing as it seems."

"Um... can you tell me how it's not totally depressing?"

"Oh, I don't know." He shrugged his shoulders. I couldn't ask him for much more, though: for someone who was as into introspection and romantic reflections as I was into astrology and the German bolt industry, Laurent had just opened up like he hardly ever did. I gave him a little pat on the shoulder.

"It's just that... I don't think it's sad," he said. "Isn't it okay if that gets our ass in gear, in the end?"

"Yeah, well, I don't want to disappoint you, but if for you getting your ass in gear means whining about your girlfriend or complaining because you don't have a girlfriend, or managing to lose a guy like Mathias, or sleeping with Marie-Lune, I'm not sure the results of your theory are exactly top notch."

"It's still funny."

"What's still funny?" I felt like asking him if he sincerely believed something constructive was going to come out of this sorry stew the four of us were simmering in. Did he really think we were going to emerge from it like a group of wiser, happier phoenixes? Then I remembered the German bolt industry and I thought it would be better to stop bothering him with my unanswerable questions.

"How's your father?" asked Laurent.

"Hmpff."

"I thought I'd used up the quota of 'hmpffs' for today."

I give him a little smile. "No, it's just that we still don't really know, and we may not know for months, and still, given that..."

"They're giving him tests?"

"Oh yeah... they send him from one to the other, he has appointments with shrinks, neurologists and ergotherapists... poor guy."

"But he's the one that chose to go, that's a good sign, right?"

"Yeah, but still... poor old *Papa*."

My father had decided, a month earlier, to go to the hospital to get some information on Alzheimer's disease. He kept repeating that it was his own decision, but I was sure that my mother had influenced him, since for years she'd been taking care to point out everything he forgot and everything he repeated, and they couldn't have anyone over without her saying, at some point, "Oh, you know, Raymond has become so forgetful..."

We probably never would have heard about what he did (my father, who'd been living for the last forty years with one of the most intrusive women in the history of humanity, had learned long ago to protect what he called his "secret garden," a term that still seemed to me to be out of place in a retired trucker's mouth) if, in an ironic twist of fate, he hadn't forgotten a piece of paper with a doctor's appointment on it in his pants pocket one day. My mother, who always emptied his pockets before doing the wash always took great care to inspect the contents, had called the doctor in question, asked some questions and went into a state of hysteria that lasted a good week. My father, who'd been almost superhumanly calm since the beginning of this whole thing, is the one who told me, laughing, about how she'd already imagined everything and called her sister in Québec City, crying that she didn't have enough time to think of prearrangements, and what was she going to do, a widow with four children?

"Maybe it's just old age," said Laurent.

"Of course it's just old age." That's what we'd been telling ourselves since the beginning and, personally, I was

almost convinced. Maybe it was simplistic optimism, but
I preferred it to my mother's innate defeatism: she'd never
been able to resist the idea of a juicy hardship, and had
always delighted in the worst even when nothing had happened ("Your sister's not home! They must have had an
accident. My God, can you imagine it, paraplegic at sixteen..."). Anticipating the worst from the beginning,
she'd also forbidden me from saying anything to my sisters because, "we have to spare the poor little ones." I
didn't see how they needed to be spared more than me
and Fred, but I figured if I could save them a few weeks of
interminable conversations with my mother, who had
gotten into the habit of calling me every day and would
have undoubtedly done the same with them, if they'd
known, so they at least benefited that way and it was a nice
gesture of solidarity between sisters. And, maybe because
of superstition, I thought it was useless to upset them,
since we would soon learn that my father, finally, was just
old and that everything was as good as it could be in what
nonetheless remained the best of all worlds, since there
was no other.

"But still," I said to Laurent. "It's not the best start to a
new year."

"Yup, we may have seen better."

"2005..."

"Oh! 2005!" The year 2005 was our golden age. All four
of us were single, my brother was still in town, and – was
it just a coincidence? or unadmitted certainty that it was
possible our last really carefree year? or, like Julien said,
was it a particularly mischievous alignment of the planets?
– in any case, we'd identified a kind of freedom that was
nearly absolute and a kind of euphoria that was even more
vivid because we knew deep down it would be short-lived.
We hardly left each other's sides, drifting from brunch to
lunch to cocktails, organizing trips to New York, Las Vegas
and even the festival in Saint-Tite, and I think that, in a

year, none of us had thought about the future for a second, not even once. Since then, we'd felt nostalgic about this time of excess and light, and the slightest mention of 2005 elicited a series of melancholy "Ahs."

"Not like 2005," sighed Laurent.

"Not like 2005…" I repeated. I was going to add something when Laurent's phone rang. He answered, went "Hmmm" four or five times in a row, then hung up saying, "You have to go out the back, Carole will be here in two minutes."

I almost burst out laughing. "Excuse me?"

"Carole's on her way. If she sees you here, she'll make a scene on me. Go out the back." He was already throwing the contents of the little tray into the garbage, being careful to put other garbage on top, as if two slices of *rosette de Lyon* and three spicy almonds constituted a real and serious risk of provoking a conjugal crisis.

"Laurent…" I knew Carole wasn't going to make a scene. I also knew I was going to go out the back, like the lover I wasn't, because Laurent, in that crazy head of his, needed to believe that Carole was a thousand times more jealous and possessive than she really was, because, if she wasn't, he'd lose one of his reasons to complain, worry and poison his own life. It was a particularly absurd form of masochism that Laurent practiced without really knowing it, but that consisted of stuffing his daily life full of potential dramas that never really risked being played out for the simple reason that they only existed in his head. Carole had a little trouble, and rightly so, with the fact that her boyfriend was still so close to his ex, but she'd never really made a big deal out of it. Nonetheless, Laurent insisted on telling us that yes, he came close to death every time she found out he'd seen me, and we'd stopped contradicting him long ago.

I put my boots back on while he was bringing me my coat and I said to myself that we were all in the same boat now and that, despite his lucidity, Laurent wasn't any more clever than me, and that, despite all the good sense I thought I possessed, I was still practicing a version of his ridiculous masochism where I got bogged down in dramas that really had no depth.

"Bye," he said, with a distracted kiss on my cheek. "Sorry."

"Of course." I couldn't bring myself to get mad, I thought it was too funny. "You know this is unbelievably ridiculous, right?"

"Yeah, yeah." He would have said yes to anything to get me out.

"Bye, Loulou." I stroked his earlobe and went out by the balcony, wondering how he was going to explain the big footprints in the snow, the sly old dog.

Evening was falling and, in the yards along the lane, Hassidic children were yelling and laughing as they played, creating a melody that had always irritated Laurent, but that I'd liked, and it reminded me of the years I'd spent there. I remembered one family, at the very end of the lane, whose yard was on the street corner, with seven or eight children, including three sets of identical twins, all as red-headed as foxes, who always waved at me when I went by. I could hear children shouting behind the off-level fence. From the side of the lane, you could see into the yard – two identical pairs of eyes were there; they were laughing and throwing snowballs and, something even stranger, plastic milk crates. One of them saw me, then shot a quick glance towards the inside of the house, then turned back with a little smile to wave a big hello, before he was called back to business by one of his brothers with a good knock on the head. I made a cartoonish sad face and headed towards the street. I was still waving mischievous hellos to the youngest twins when I turned the corner, a meter farther on, when I came face to face with my handsome doctor. I'd hardly thought of him the last few weeks and here he was in front of me, smiling with the ease and casualness of a man who spends his life bumping into young women in the snow, while all I could do, being leagues from feeling the least bit comfortable and miles from the tiniest speck of casualness, was open my mouth for an overly elated "Oh!" while my mitten was still raised towards the twins, though they couldn't see me anymore.

"Well now," he said still smiling. I gave a stupid little laugh and, remembering the last time we'd met, I thought to myself it was maybe about time to try to make a good impression on this man, who had a tremendous and inexplicable effect on me, even now, in the snow, with his ski coat and his red nose.

"You live around here?" I asked.

"Two streets over. *Et vous?*"

I was charmed and flustered by this use of *vous* that seemed to come from another era – I don't remember having ever said *vous* to a man I liked, except in my childish daydreams, when I was Madame de Chevreuse and I was reunited with Athos, my lover, after years of separation.

"I used to live around here," I said. "That's, um, a friend's place."

"It looks like you have a lot of friends in the area." He was pointing behind me, towards a little mitten waving behind the fence which, following a shout in Yiddish, quickly disappeared.

"Yesss," I answered. "The little Horowitzes and I used to have a street hockey league."

He laughed and I felt like I'd accomplished something marvelous and magical. He must speak, I thought, or else I'm going to say something completely idiotic in three seconds.

"Listen," he said. "We must have bumped into each other at least fifteen times now, so I'm thinking it's about time we get to know each other a little, so that at least when we see each other again, we'll have a good reason to say hello, right?"

Two or three times in my life before, I'd gotten the feeling that luck decided to be on my side, not just in my vicinity, but right there with me like it is for people who win million-dollar jackpots or survive huge car crashes. That night, for the few seconds that followed the doctor's questions, I felt luck had once again settled on my shoulder, offering me free of charge everything that had seemed unattainable.

"You want to go to the café over there?" I asked. "It's nice."

"And they make hot rum."

"And they make hot rum," I repeated with what must have been a clumsy smile. We started walking, and I was blessing both the little Horowitzes for slowing me down long enough to bump into Gabriel and Carole who had the wonderful idea of coming home early, and even Laurent's masochism, and I was so convinced that this providential luck would never leave my side again, that when my phone started ringing I answered out of habit, or perhaps because I was too sure of myself.

"Hello?"

"It's me," Laurent was whispering into the phone, and I knew right away I'd made a mistake when I'd answered. "You have to come back."

"What? No. Really. No."

"Shit, you can't be that far already, can you?"

"No, Laurent, I…" I looked towards the doctor who was walking on and politely looking like he wasn't listening. "I can't right now."

"Marine, Christ, you just left five minutes ago, you have to come back."

"Look, we'll talk later, okay?"

"NO! You forgot your toque here. Carole found it in the entryway, and she caught me by surprise so I told her you'd just gone out to get some white wine. You can't do this to me!"

Then I did something completely idiotic – I brought my hand to my head as if I could simply will a toque to appear, thereby releasing me from a completely ridiculous situation. It seemed that luck could have hung around a little longer than three minutes.

"Laurent, I'm sorry, but I really can't."

"No, no, no. It's too late now. I TOLD her you were coming back."

"Well, just tell her that I remembered an urgent appointment and that I had to go."

"Marine…"

"Laurent!"

"You're right here! I'll owe you one, a big one, anything you want, but get me out of this mess!"

I sighed. Carole may not have been as crazy as Laurent said, but it seemed to me he'd certainly managed to get himself into a big enough jam that I had to help him. "You're a fucking pain in the ass."

"Are you coming? She's changing."

"Yes. Shit. I'll go get the fucking white wine so it looks credible and I'll be right there."

I hung up, still cursing, and I looked up at Gabriel. We'd been standing still on the sidewalk for a couple of minutes and he'd stopped pretending not to listen and was following my conversation with a steady look of amusement, and, given the circumstances of our previous meeting, I couldn't actually blame him for looking like that.

"Listen," I said. I was already making up a stupid, pitiful excuse, something that ideally involved my family (less threatening) and a life in danger (that couldn be saved by a bottle of white wine). Then two facts occurred to me simultaneously: not only had I been letting my own inertia lead me around for weeks already, but also, this man I didn't really know who was standing before me must have had, for the same period of time, an opinion of me that justified the amused smile he always wore when he was around me. And, not only did he not ever look discouraged or bored, but he was also trying to get to know me better. And since he was still standing next to me, he undoubtedly deserved something better than a bad excuse.

"I…"

"You…" He was still smiling, with an encouraging look. I thought maybe I amused him more than anything, but again, I thought, why not?

"Do you want to come to the SAQ with me? My ex is in a mess and needs help."

He laughed again, and it seemed like I'd performed a little miracle and that the laugh was my reward. "I'll explain on the way, if you want."

"*Avec plaisir.*"

I smiled broadly: a man who accepted such an absurd proposition so readily had to be at least a little interesting.

"My name's Marine," I said as we were walking.

"I know. I'm Gabriel."

"I know."

When Carole came to open the door, she was wearing a pink-and-gray indoor tracksuit, that was very becoming, just like everything she wore. She was always well-put-together and even her casual outfits had a little something thought-out and deliberate about them. Her nail polish was impeccably applied and she possessed that one thing that still mystified me – a hairstyle. "Hi," I said. I always felt like a little girl around her – like I was twenty-two and just a little inadequate. She didn't answer right away, undoubtedly too surprised to see me come back with a man when I supposedly left alone.

"Carole, this is my friend Gabriel," I said. "I ran into him at the SAQ and invited him to come have a quick drink with us."

Laurent had said he'd owe me one, so it was better to play the game. Gabriel was on board from the get-go. He'd explained, as we looked at an aisle of New Zealand Sauvignons, that he'd been noticing my friends and me for a year already, and without really knowing why, he'd started imagining what our lives must be like. "You always look so happy together," he said. "Maybe I just live in a dead serious world, but I hardly ever see that. Hardly ever. Is your ex the tall guy who's starting to lose his hair?" We'd gone from *vous* to *tu* quickly, without getting hung up on it. I'd asked him what kind of doctor he was, which made him laugh ("Man, there are no secrets in that restaurant. Have you been drawing for a long time?"), and he made me guess, but finally, after I'd tried podiatrist, oral surgeon, PhD and Dr. Doolittle, he told me he was an ER doctor.

"Okay," I repeated as we climbed the stairs to Laurent's condo. "We've known each other for a long time, but we kind of lost track of each other, and we were so happy to see each other just now that I took it upon myself to invite you over."

"Where did we meet?"

"Wherever you want."

He thought about it, looking up at me, with a smile still floating across his lips. For a beautiful, brief second, I thought about leaning down to kiss him – I thought about it seriously since the situation seemed too unbelievable for someone not to take advantage of it, and since, evidently, this handsome man had a serious penchant for the unexpected. He was looking into the distance, as if he'd find help there, while his light eyes took on an indefinite color in the light of the street light. He must have a wife, I thought stupidly. Or a girlfriend, or a lover, or even fifty lovers. Men like this are not left to freely roam the streets, someone has already caught him and, unless that person is completely crazy, they'll never let go.

"In Maine," he suggested, pulling me back to reality.

"In Maine?"

"Yes." Then he started explaining it all very seriously to me, as if it had been a real event. "A couple of months ago, we met on a beach in Maine…"

"Carole goes to Maine a lot. What beach? It'll have to be near Biddeford Pool, that's the only place I know."

"Okay for Biddeford Pool. So, we meet, we hit it off, we have a couple of beers together with all our friends, but NOW, and here's the beauty of the thing, we've bumped into each other by chance, in Montréal, a couple of months later." For sure, my handsome doctor dreamed of the unpredictable and the unexpected.

"Are you sure that meeting at a mutual friend's isn't maybe a little more believable?"

"If you want. But, the advantage of my story is that people are more likely to believe a story if they think it's beautiful, not just if they think it's possible.

"You think so?" It was such a nice idea that I really wanted to believe it. He smiled, undoubtedly understanding my reasoning, and he gave me a little nod that said, "I'm sure of it."

"Okay then. Let's go with Maine." I returned his smile and was about to ring the bell when he said my name.

"Marine?"

"Yes?"

"Is your life always like this?"

"Hmmm?"

"Do things like this happen to you a lot?"

"Um… are you going to take off running if I say it's not a daily occurrence, but that it's not totally unheard of, either?"

"No, not at all." He looked happy, and I thought maybe he was bored, or at least he was looking for something he couldn't quite put his finger on, a little something extra, a little unknown something that was anything but ordinary. I'd always thought that was what we were all looking for, but this was the first time I'd ever seen someone doing it so obviously, without beating around the bush, without shame for the voracity of his hunger. I'd rung the doorbell and I heard him behind me murmuring "Biddeford Pool."

We'd followed Carole's gray-and-pink shape to the living room, where Laurent was setting down the same little blue tray, with the same nuts and the same *rosette*, on the coffee table. He saw how I was looking at the tray and shrugged his shoulders imperceptibly to say "What can I say..." and then he noticed Gabriel.

"Errr..."

"You remember Gabriel? Remember, we met in Maine, then we'd see each other from time to time for a while... I think you bumped into each other at the restaurant..." Carole was standing behind me, so I could make very deliberate gestures at Laurent who was standing there like a statue, with his blue tray in one hand. "Come on," I was thinking with all my might, while my lips were shaping other words. "Play along."

"We just ran into each other at the SAQ," I added.

"Gabriel!" Laurent finally exclaimed. "Yes! Oh my God, I'm soooo sorry." He put down his tray and came towards us, cordially extending a hand towards Gabriel, who accepted it equally cordially and added a very appropriate "Long time, no see."

"Ooof, it has been a long time," continued Laurent. "The last time we saw each other you were just finishing med school, weren't you? I thought he was enjoying this little game, too, maybe as much as Gabriel. They started exchanging remarks that would have been entirely ordinary if they hadn't been completely fictitious, until Gabriel noticed Laurent was getting carried away (he'd even asked if he still had his old Renault, a charming detail, though it carried the risk of tripping one of us up), and turned towards Carole to ask a few polite questions about her. I took advantage and followed Laurent into the kitchen, where he was opening the bottles I'd brought over. It was an open kitchen, only separated from the living room by a counter, but by bunching up in front of the fridge, which backed onto the living room, you could be out of sight of the guests.

"Okay, what the fuck?" Laurent whispered.

"You told me you owed me one."

"Yeah, but, no... You go bringing over guys you don't even know?"

"Well, we know who he is at least."

"He could be a serial killer."

I gave him a look that shut him up.

"Well, yeah, but..." He couldn't keep a straight face.

"I'll explain it to you later, Loulou. Can you believe it?"

"Um, no? Can it be any more surreal?"

"No, no, I don't think so." I was aware of my smile and my excitement.

"Okay, what's going on, you going to go out with him?" That slight, somewhat old-fashioned jealousy still made me smile.

"You're a jerk. And, anyway, serve the wine, there's company in the living room." He smiled and so did I, for a couple of seconds, within the bubble of our past intimacy.

In the living room, Carole's clear laughter welcomed Gabriel's remarks, and he seemed as comfortable as if he had known these people forever, and I thought that the situation, which under normal circumstances would have been unbearable, was somehow absolutely charming because of how he was enjoying this game. He was wearing old jeans and a maroon turtleneck, and he seemed perfectly comfortable in the old sweater that hung loosely from his wide shoulders. I was trying to imagine his body beneath the wool and when he looked up at me, I could see in his green eyes and in his smile that he knew exactly what I'd been doing. I almost wanted him to go, so I could get my bearings, close my eyes and relive each movement and each moment, call Julien and give him something else to think about and stop doing what Jeff called "over-analysis," which consisted of dementedly dissecting every detail, especially the insignificant ones, because, as Julien said, "You never know what's behind the bat of an eye or in a preference for pinot noir. Everything means something, Marine. EVERYTHING." If everything meant something, I thought as I sat down near Gabriel on the sofa, it's going to take us years to analyze this evening.

We kept talking like that for a good hour. Laurent seemed particularly comfortable, undoubtedly because, with a third party involved, he didn't have to worry about Carole's attitude towards me. He was even affectionate towards her, rubbing her back, in an awkward yet touching gesture that made me think he certainly loved her more than he wanted to admit to himself. With one hand on Laurent's thigh, Carole was talking almost exclusively to Gabriel; I again had the impression they were the only adults in the room, and that, if we could, Laurent and I would have slipped away to make a tent out of sheets or jump up and down on a bed.

The conversation was easy and pleasant and I was getting to know my "old" friend at the same time as Laurent and Carole were. He was born on the shore of Lac-Saint-Jean, and he knew he wanted to be a doctor when he was eight, when his cousin Harold fell down a little ravine and he saw his dislocated leg, and he had almost physically regretted that he couldn't do anything to put it back in place; he lived in Vieux Montréal; he'd been married. He was thirty-nine years old and loved the ocean.

When Carole got up to answer the phone, the three of us all waited for her to leave the room before we started slapping ourselves on the thigh in surprise and exchanging flabbergasted looks that asked thousands of questions.

"You so owe me one…" whispered Laurent.

"Excuse me? YOU owe me one."

"No, no, no. No way."

"Oh yes way."

And Gabriel laughed. "Listen," he finally said. "I'm going to go. I don't want this to go too far. I…" He hesitated for a moment, then turned towards me. "You want to get something to eat? Unless you're already busy, I don't know. Your life seems a little um… hectic." Laurent started laughing when he brought up our last meeting at Le Lulli and I thought they were going to high-five each other.

"I'd like that," I replied, trying not to look *too* happy. From the corner of my eye, I saw a scowl on Laurent's face and in Gabriel's eyes I saw a joyous sparkle that made me doubt my own good luck, and it seemed like such a good omen that I was afraid something would happen, that everything would stop and I'd wake up, because life was generous, but not that generous, and I'd stopped believing in miracles long ago.

Gabriel was already on his feet when Carole returned to the living room. "I hope you're not leaving."

"Yes," said Gabriel. "I um…"

"Well, just wait five more minutes, that was Jeff on the phone: he's coming over, and he was really happy when I told him you were here."

There it is, I thought. It's starting already. Laurent, from his chair, was looking at me with a silly smile. Gabriel turned towards me, looking unsure – he may have had a weak spot for the unexpected, but this handsome doctor from Lac-Saint-Jean was beginning to understand that we weren't going to be able to keep up much longer with this charade, that was really only intended for Carole, anyway.

"I don't know…" I said.

"Really," Carole insisted. "Jeff said it's been years since he's seen Gabriel and that he really wanted to see him again."

Son-of-a-bitch, I thought. Gabriel was still looking at me, waiting for me to answer, and I wanted to tell him that our charming, disorganized lives also had their downside, that there were layers it was hard to get through, levels that sometimes covered too much, knots we didn't remember how to undo.

"Let's go, okay?" I said, and he gave a little nod, "Yes."

We were in the entryway, putting on our coats, when Jeff rang the bell.

To: Marine
From: Frédéric Vandale
Subject: What's up, doc?

So? Did you call?

To: Fred
From: Marine Vandale
Subject: Lesson in tact

Didn't anyone ever teach you that there are some questions it's not polite to ask? If there had been any communication, and when I say communication I'm ready to include smoke signals and telepathy, I would have made such a fuss it would have been almost scarey! So, no fuss, no call and a well-advised brother who is welcome to act like nothing's going on.

To: Marine
From: Frédéric Vandale
Subject: Brother knows best

Your brother would like to advise you that in the category of "I-refuse-to-do-anything-at-all-to-put-luck-on-my-side," there are not many who could beat you. Would you mind telling me what's keeping you from calling him? Because, after the evening you spent together, I'd like to remind you, you had "man of my dreams" in your voice. Therefore, you can see how your silence seems rather thoughtless to me.

To: Fred
From: Marine Vandale
Subject: Brother's a pain in the ass

I sent a text message, okay? And it's been a week and my mailbox is so empty you wouldn't believe it. So, add it all up for yourself and be quiet.

To: Marine
From: Frédéric Vandale
Subject: Error in addition

....

You kidding me or what? I really don't want to play your personal life coach, but the man said "call me" and you sent a text
message and then you drape yourself in indignation 'cause he
still hasn't sent you flowers?

To: Fred
From: Marine Vandale
Subject: Male psychology

....

Anyway, what kind of guy says, "call me" to a girl who's
expressing a sincere and palpitating desire to see him again
rather than getting *her* number and calling her like a big boy?

To: Marine
From: Frédéric Vandale
Subject: Male logic

....

Maybe the man in question noticed that the above-mentioned
girl has an innate gift for getting herself into ridiculous situations, was a witness to an altercation between her boyfriend
and her lover and saw her for the last time at her ex's where a
bear showed up like a two-hundred-pound fly in the soup? I
don't want to act like a know-it-all, but, you know, I was just
wondering.

To: Fred
From: Marine Vandale
Subject: Bear in the soup

....

Ah, yes, I remember that. You should have seen it, it was the
National Innuendo Festival, with looks so full of words that
poor Gabriel didn't know what level of the game we were on

anymore. Those two idiots really screwed everything up. And plus, I have no idea what Julien could have told him on the phone when he called, but it couldn't have helped, because after that, Gabriel laughed every time he looked at me. So, you'll understand that I interpret the silence that met my text message as "Thank you. Good night!"

To: Marine
From: Frédéric Vandale
Subject: Diagnosis

....

Did it ever cross your mind that you analyze things too much? Just a thought.

To: Fred
From: Marine Vandale
Subject: Re: Diagnosis

....

I don't overanalyze, I deduce. And, I'll have you know, Jeff coined the word "overanalyze" a long time ago, so you haven't invented anything. And don't tell me it's overanalysis to logically deduce that if a man is interested in a woman and she sends him a text, he answers ASAP. I would have answered a minute later, at the most.

To: Marine
From: Frédéric Vandale
Subject: RE: Diagnosis

....

What do you want me to say? The big problem we all have is that everyone thinks that everyone else thinks exactly like they do, and that's what we all want, by the way, because as far as interpreting everybody goes, that would really simplify things. But it's not true, Marinette. So, don't base everything on what you would have done, drop your overanalysis and stop playing games, the doctor said "Call me," so call.

To: Fred
From: Marine
Subject: Amazed

Would it offend you if I told you that's the most intelligent thing I've ever heard you say?

To: Marine
From: Frédéric Vandale
Subject: Short term memory

No, but I'd like to remind you of the time when I told you to replace the vodka you were stealing from the freezer with water. In the long run it may not have been the best advice ever given, but it was pretty intelligent, though. Seriously, Marine, if you like the ER doc, don't play games. We're grown-ups now.

To: Fred
From: Marine Vandale
Subject: Hobbit complex

On this side of the Atlantic I don't feel particularly grown up.

To: Marine
From: Frédéric Vandale
Subject: The little Hobbit will grow up

Yes, but the doctor seems like a grown-up to me. Stop being afraid, Marine. Call him. Are you going to call him?

To: Fred
From: Marine Vandale
Subject: Need Gandalf

Don't you want to call him for me?

To: Marine
From: Frédéric Vandale
Subject: Gandalf has spoken

If I remember correctly, Gandalf said to Frodo, "All you have to decide is what to do with the time that's been given to you." So, decide, but I'm warning you: the only way you're going to see your Gabriel again is if you call him. It's no more complicated than that.

To: Fred
From: Marine Vandale
Subject: A matter of perspective

It sounds nice enough when you say it like that, but it's evident that you're not the one taking the chance of not getting called back, on top of having an empty in-box. Maybe I could send a gentle little text message, like "Is there, maybe, perhaps, a tiny chance that you didn't receive my first message?"

To: Fred
From: Marine Vandale
Subject: (none)

Fred?

To: Marine
From: Frédéric Vandale
Subject: Re: (none)

I don't want to hear from you until you've called.
    :)

Chapter 6

I opened the refrigerator door only to see, propped up against a pint of grapefruit juice, a big card with the word: "CALL!!!" and three aggressive exclamation marks pointing at me. Even Jeff was getting involved, it was bordering on the ridiculous. I got myself a glass of juice, gently replacing the sign, an absurd, inexplicable gesture that only dawned on me a minute later, when, for the fifteen thousandth time in a week, I was checking my cell to see if I'd gotten any text messages and to make sure Gabriel's number was still in the contact list.

"The number didn't evaporate?" Jeff asked as he came out of the bathroom. He had a towel tied around his waist and, when I saw the pearl drops of water still on his shoulder, the image of our embrace came back to me, alive and up close. Strangely enough, it wasn't unpleasant, but his tenderness made me uneasy and I abruptly shook my head no.

"No," I said, making a little face at him. "The number didn't evaporate."

"Marine." He was using the calm, patient tone people use with other people who refuse to understand something.

"Listen, okay? I know what you're going to say. I think I even know what you're going to say word for word. Fred has stopped answering my emails. Even Laurent says to call him, and if Laurent is encouraging me to call a guy, it has to be because he's bloody sick and tired of listening to me. So, I get it. I know I have to call him. Christ, Julien called me three times last night to say, 'Call him.' The message has gotten through. I really get it."

They were all getting on my nerves, even more than I was getting on my own nerves. I felt like a little girl, like the time when my mother told me to stop giving Frédéric the cold shoulder because he'd hurt my feelings. "Go talk to him," she'd said. "I know you don't really want to, but now you're ignoring him just for the sake of ignoring him and you're hurting yourself more than anyone," and I'd wanted to shout and call her names, first of all, because I knew she was perfectly right, but especially because I wanted her to share my bad attitude. She's my mother, I'd thought to myself. She should be on my side, stick with me even if I'd committed a murder, and even more so if I just wanted to ignore my brother unfairly. And now, twenty years later, rather than suddenly turning into the voice of reason and good sense, I thought my friends should embrace my ridiculous fear and misplaced pride.

"Jesus, you're really not with it these days," he said with a smile. He went towards the liquor cabinet, took out the vodka and poured a good shot into my glass, then he went and sat on one of the barstools. "If you'd waited three seconds before you jumped at me, you would have given me enough time to say that maybe, in the end – and I do mean *maybe* – it's better you don't call."

"Hmm?" My bad attitude, with a resilience that impressed even me, did a one-eighty and I had to bite my tongue so I didn't tell Jeff that he must really be a helluva lousy friend to discourage a girl from calling the man who, you never know, might be the man of her dreams.

"Okay." Again with the calm, patient tone. He probably had a straitjacket hidden somewhere just in case. I must have been even more annoying than I thought. "Now," he continued in an undeniably cautious tone, "I'm going to tell you something and I don't want you to get angry." A syringe and a sedative, I thought. He's talking like someone holding a sedative-filled syringe and would rather not to use it, but is ready for anything. "Are you going to listen to me?"

"Geez, I haven't turned into a moron, you know."

A nod of his head and a look indicated I wasn't far off.

"Okay," he said. "What I think is maybe – and again, I cannot overemphasize the importance here of the adverb *maybe* – you've imagined a relationship with this guy and if you're so hesitant to call him maybe it's not because you're afraid he'll hang up on you or not call back, but rather because he *might* answer. AND…" he raised one hand to keep me from answering. "… I specifically said *maybe*. M-A-Y-B-E. *Maybe*."

"That's enough '*maybes*' already. What's the matter, are you afraid of me?"

"Terrified. I'm terrified. Seriously."

I gave him a little smile and made an effort to think about his idea. The shot of vodka he had given me had indeed been quite substantial and efficient, and I was starting to relax a little.

"Okay, I see what you mean." Jeff gave an exaggerated sigh of relief and wiped one hand across his forehead like a man who'd just avoided a serious accident. "But I don't agree."

"That's okay. I'm not asking you to agree. It's just an idea. I just thought it was such a farfetched situation that maybe – and I do mean maybe…"

"ENOUGH!"

"Okay, okay. But still. Admit it, it was a fucking circus that night."

"Yes, and let's also say you didn't help."

When Jeff arrived at Laurent's, I'd turned quickly to Gabriel, as if he'd have a solution or could help me, and I sincerely wanted to go out the back way for a second time, without forgetting my toque this time. Gabriel had frowned slightly as if to say, "What's going on? Why?" and I suddenly realized for the first time since the beginning of this ridiculous evening ("It was about time," Julien would say later) that we didn't know each other at all.

"Hey, you're not going to leave now, are you?" Jeff had asked in a cheerful tone that was so overexaggerated that for a second I thought he'd top off his sentence with a "Ho! Ho! Ho!" and deposit a bag full of presents at our feet.

"Gabriel! It's been ages, eh?" He was walking towards him, his arms open, while Laurent and I exchanged a slightly panicked look. Jeff seemed out of control, and, possibly, a little drunk, adding a very volatile element to an evening that had been on the verge of disaster for quite a while. First he'd hugged Gabriel who, despite the fact that he was at least six feet tall, seemed tiny in my ogre-like roommate's arms, then Jeff took me in his arms and lifted me in the air like I only weighed a few grams.

"You must think she's even prettier than the last time you two saw each other, eh?" Gabriel nicely answered, "Still as pretty, no doubt," while I shot a mortified look at Jeff, whose reply was to give me a slap on the ass, which nearly made Laurent die laughing.

"A slap on the ass," I said. "I can't believe you slapped me on the ass."

"What? I wanted to look normal."

"Just when do you slap me on the ass in normal life, exactly?"

"Well…" He was laughing. "Okay, maybe I did push it a little."

"Jeff. If you could have peed in a circle all around me, I think you would have."

"Come on."

"No 'come on'! It was the first thing Gabriel said when

we left."

I'd finally managed to put an end to an evening that had
become perfectly unbearable by insistently reminding
Gabriel that we had reservations at a restaurant at eight-
thirty and that, really, it would be a shame to lose our
table, and, who knows when we'd be able to do this again?
He readily agreed, making me understand he himself was
disoriented in this ridiculous production which had
begun in an effort to alleviate Carole's suspicions, though
it had lost any connection to her a long time before.

"Wow!" he'd said when we were out on the street. He'd
looked at me, with the amused, incredulous look that was
becoming permanent, and he'd shook his head. "Your
roommate…"

"I know, I know. I think he was a little drunk. Don't
pay any attention."

"No, no, it's okay. It's that it kind of felt like he was
defending his territory…"

"His territory…"

He pointed in my direction.

"What?! No. No, no. Come on." I'd tried to laugh, but
images of the evening kept coming back to me, the way
Jeff kept talking to Gabriel about me, as if he wanted to
really show how well he knew me, how close we were. At
least three times he must have said, "If you knew Marine
like I know Marine…" Even Laurent, who was the one
who normally tended to play this game when other men
approached me, seemed a little confused by his attitude
and was shooting me perplexed glances over his glass of
wine.

"Listen," Gabriel had said. "Maybe I'm wrong, but… I
just don't want him to think… We don't even know each
other…"

"I know! I know!" I had to bite my tongue to keep

myself from shouting, "What do you mean you don't want him to think that?!" and betraying my disappointment and my sincere desire to think that. It also occurred to me that the fact that Gabriel had figured this from Jeff's antics meant he knew very well that my intentions were not exactly chaste and pure, and that I had shared this with my friends. Poor thing, I thought to myself, feeling stupid and ridiculous. He has the feeling he's been drawn into the most ridiculous trap in the history of male-female relations by a girl who needs the help of her ex and her possessive roommate to reach her goal.

"I…" I wanted to think of something particularly brilliant to say, but my head was full of Jeff's off-color jokes and the persistent impression that I'd just spent two hours with a man I'd been fantasizing about for months and not only had I not gotten to know him at all, but I'd certainly also managed to convince him that my friends and I were a happy band of simple-minded teenagers. But he, on the other hand, with his condo in Vieux Montréal, a marriage behind him, and a job that consisted of saving lives on a daily basis and not drawing big bad wolves, he had obviously left adolescence behind long ago, with its hysterical fits of laughter and useless plans, along with its emotional instability and lack of judgment.

"Gabriel…" I had so little to say that I pulled my toque down over my face. I heard him laugh beside me. "I'm sorry," I said through the cashmere. "Really, in the whole history of humanity, I don't think anyone's ever managed to show how foolish they are as quickly as we just did. I'm sorry."

I'd pulled my toque back up and turned towards him again.

"We'll make a deal, okay? We'll go eat somewhere and you'll explain a couple of things to me, all right? Because there's no way I'll be able to go to sleep tonight without understanding what all happened in the last couple of

hours. It'd be like reading a *roman à clef* without getting
the key. It takes all the fun out of it."

Jeff had been listening from his room. "And?" he shouted.
"Did you give him the key?"
   "Yes."
   He came out still buttoning a pair of jeans he had just
barely slipped on. "The whole key?"
   "The whole fucking key."

I'd followed the same reasoning I'd used a few hours earlier in the little lane. Maybe it was due to some underlying
Judeo-Christian ethic I couldn't get away from, but something was whispering to me that, in situations like this, it
was better to bet on the truth, no matter what it was. So I
placed my bet, awkwardly undoubtedly, but I did place it.
I told Gabriel about my relationship with Laurent, and his
worries about Carole, my relationship with Christophe
and the following fling with Patrick – which explained the
scene he'd witnessed at Le Lulli – and, when he asked if
I'd ever gone out with Jeff, I told him what had happened
in his room a few weeks earlier. I also told him that I had-
n't heard from Christophe since our messy break-up and
that sometimes I stayed awake at night thinking that my
relationship with Jeff really had changed, while Marie-
Lune moaned in the room next door.
   "Anyway, the least I can say is you're never bored,"
Gabriel had said, and I thought, no, I'm not bored, and as
pathetic as it might seem, in the end, there was at least
that positive side. Sometimes I still saw some old girlfriends who told me about the kind of boredom that
settled in slowly but surely between them and their
boyfriends, though they never saw it coming. They said it
just showed up one day, on the sofa, in front of Bernard
Derome's serious face or Chantal Fontaine's hair, this
boredom that was gentle yet solid and had made itself

comfortable like it really felt at home there.

"No," I said to Gabriel's green eyes. "I'm not bored. Are you bored?"

"I'm fucking bored to death."

I'd answered with a pretty flat "Oh" – it occurred to me that if Gabriel had agreed to come with me to Laurent's when he knew next to nothing about me, it wasn't because he was attracted to my blue eyes or my most beautiful smile, but because he thought, inexplicably, that I could help him. "You know, deep down, all people want is someone to save them," my father had told me. At the time, I'd thought it was just an SOS about my suffocating mother, but, that night with Gabriel, I thought that maybe my father had understood something a long time ago, and that this unpolished man who hardly ever spoke had felt the need to share this idea with one of his daughters.

Then Gabriel started talking, for a long time, about the life he was living and how it should have fulfilled him, although instead it left him with "a kind of emptiness." He described his condo, the hospital, the occasional rush he got when something really serious happened in Emerg and got him out of his usual routine, paperwork, bureaucracy, worried little old ladies who monopolized the staff over a cold, drug addicts pretending to have any sort of pain in order to get some narcotics, and distraught patients worrying about inevitable hangovers who came in a panic explaining they were nauseous, had a headache and felt dizzy while they were still reeking of booze and for whom he prescribed two Tylenol and some rest instead of giving them a couple of good smacks.

He also talked about his wife, a doctor like him, five years older, and whom he'd left when that same big bad boredom came and made a nest between them, after seven years of marriage and exhausted "Good nights" exchanged from opposite sides of the bed. Since, he said, women had sometimes slept between his sheets – which I suspected

were made of Egyptian cotton of a neutral color (beige or
gray without a doubt) – and they left him satisfied but not
fulfilled, because they didn't make him laugh and he was
well aware that he wanted to know their bodies intimately
but didn't care about their souls.

He was so handsome, in the restaurant's golden light,
he spoke so clearly and confidently about his feelings that
a couple of times I wanted to cut him off and ask him to
take me home and hold me in his arms all night, without
moving if necessary, simply so I could feel against me the
quiet strength that was coming, paradoxically, from his
admission of his weaknesses. I could see the two of us,
happy idiots spending our lives, going around in circles,
asking useless questions and not even thinking about
expecting an answer. I found Gabriel's lucidity, and the
perfectly clear self-image he seemed to have, extremely
sexy. Just as I was wandering aimlessly and turning away
from everything, he faced head-on situations that I still
refused to even imagine.

"You must think I'm as gloomy as death, right?" he'd
asked.

"No. You must think I'm fucking crazy, right?"

"I haven't made up my mind about that yet." He'd
looked at me with a wide smile that made me forget it was
winter.

Since then, the boys had given him the mean nickname
of "The Prince of Darkness," even though I kept telling
them he was funny, too, and that he'd surprised me a
number of times with a particular and charming sense of
humor. "He can't be as funny as we are," Laurent kept saying, thereby soliciting convinced nods from Jeff and
Julien, who then shrugged as if to say, "What can we say,
you'd better get used to it: the man who's going to make
you laugh more than we do still hasn't been born," then I'd
make faces at them, afraid as always that they were right

– these three clowns I loved so much, maybe too much.

"Anyway," said Jeff, "I'm not too sure a guy who spent an evening telling me how bored he was would get me excited."

"Unlike the girls you bring home who don't even have to talk to be boring."

"Hey!" he said smiling and poking me with his elbow. "Cheap shot!"

I poked him back. "I'm entitled to a couple of cheap shots. When you came over to Laurent's *that* was a cheap shot. I can blubber as much as I want when my mother warns me that spending my life with the three of you probably scares off other guys, but it didn't help for you to lay it on so thick the first time I met Gabriel."

"Oh, come on. If the guy was as scared as that he never would have come over to talk to you or invited you for a drink the first chance he got. You have to give that much to The Prince of Darkness, he's really not the type to be intimidated by three handsome specimens like us."

"Specimens is right! Why do you think he hasn't returned my message?"

"Oh no, not that again!"

"No, but did it occur to you that he might have been a little traumatized by you lot? And then there was Julien on top of it! Will you please tell me what Julien told him when he called?"

Jeff started to laugh.

"Okay, what? What, what, what? All this isn't very reassuring, Jeff."

"No, he was super cool!" And he laughed even harder.

"Jeff, shit…" I grabbed one of his ears – it was my only weapon against him: he was leaning on his side, towards me and if I stretched my arm out enough, he couldn't grab me for a good three seconds.

"Okay! Okay!" He was laughing and wriggling at the same time and finally managed to grab my hand and in less than two seconds he had me, got my back up against his chest, and held me firmly in place with one arm.

"Okay," he said from behind me. "If you want to bring out the big guns... He let Gabriel know that he was very disappointed that he wasn't there, because for months you and he had been fighting for his attention and that, if he had been there, he was sure that Gabriel would only have had eyes for him.

"Oh my God..." I buried my face in my free hand and slid towards the floor. Jeff held me against him, still laughing.

"This is so humiliating!"

"No way! It's funny!"

"Okay, it goes without saying I'll never call him again. Shit, he must think we live in Degrassi. Oh my God! I'm going to kill him. Shit, and he's supposed to be suffering from depression, innocent my ass! I'm really going to kill him. If you ever want to speak to Julien again, call him now because he doesn't have much longer to live."

Jeff laughed against my neck.

"Do you realize that you all have literally ruined my life?"

"Come on now," Jeff said, relaxing his hold. Honestly, we did you a favor. At least the guy has a very clear idea of who you are and what your life's like."

"Too clear. The word you're thinking of is TOO clear."

I could still see us, Gabriel and me, on the sidewalk still covered in snow. He'd insisted on paying at the restaurant, saying it made him happy, and I'd replied saying that it made me even happier, and therefore I insisted even more. We kidded like that another five minutes, debating how happy we each were until we finally decided on separate checks. He got up to go to the washroom, supposedly, but when he came back, he'd paid the whole bill and said, "You put up a good fight, but I'm happier than you," and once again his smile seemed like a beautiful fireplace lit up on a cold winter's night.

But in the street, fifteen minutes later, he'd kissed me chastely, once on each cheek. But still not knowing how to make the first move, I waited, catatonic, for the kiss I wanted so badly and the sweet words I'd been dreaming of – but nothing. He finally lifted one hand towards my face and caressed my temple with one hand, but I couldn't take it anymore and I said (in a terrible, painful concession to my habit of never making the first move!): "I'd like to see you again." He'd nodded his head, with the word "yes" dancing across his smile, and when I'd said, "I'll give you my number," he'd answered, "No, I'll give you MY number. And you can call me."

Claude François had settled back in to his favorite place – the fruit bowl, just under my nose. "I see what you mean," I said to Jeff, petting the cat's light-colored fur. "And maybe I'm deluding myself like no other woman before me, but I'm telling you that if I'm afraid to call him, it's because I'm afraid he won't answer. Shit, Jeff, I haven't had anyone constructive or promising in my life since Laurent. Let's not kid ourselves, we all knew Christophe was nice enough, but that it wouldn't last. As for him, I don't want to put the cart before any horses that don't even exist, but it seems to me..." It seems to me what? I wondered. I was lost, and part of me liked it. "It seems to me there's something real about him."

Jeff had nodded his head, not looking overly convinced, and had now started petting Claude François, too. "Okay," he said, without looking up from the cat. "If it's what you really want, Marine, we're with you."

"Jeff?"

"Hmmm?"

"Why did you come over to Laurent's?"

"And he never answered?" Julien asked.

"Nope. He shrugged his shoulders and laughed in a

way I can't interpret, then he left because he was late and he didn't come home the night before last."

"Interesting," said Laurent.

The server arrived with four wine glasses. She put one down in front of each of us, then looked to the spot where Jeff usually sat and asked hopefully, "Will there be three or four of you?"

"Four," said Julien. "Don't worry, he'll be here." The server looked a little uncomfortable, but couldn't hold back a smile, and she lightly set down an empty glass at Jeff's place.

"How's it going?" I asked Julien.

"Fine."

"Julien: *how's it going?*"

He'd cried for two days after he told me Mathias had left him and, uncharacteristically, he'd even accepted my offer to come stay at his place. Everything was in order, like always, and as I came into the spotless apartment, where there was no sign of a recent heartbreak, I realized that Julien was capable of keeping his sorrows at a distance, that as long as he didn't talk about them, they remained almost foreign to him. But he'd told me everything and his pain was literally exposed to broad daylight, and I'd almost cried myself, one morning, when I saw him come into the kitchen wearing black pants and a gray sweater.

He'd spent the whole day in those clothes, which seemed like a white flag to me, a surrender, and we'd talked about Mathias, who was still calling regularly to see how Julien was doing and to say touching little things, like "Don't forget there are still four steaks in the freezer," "You still have two shirts at the cleaner's," "The cleaning woman's phone number is on the little card I left on the desk," "Whatever you do, don't catch cold." Julien hoped to convince him to come back, but still didn't have the strength and really didn't know what magic words he could have used to regain his confidence.

He'd also told me about his first love, the one that had hurt him so deeply he thought he'd die, in ironically and pathetically similar circumstances to the way he'd hurt Mathias. An older man, whom Julien had surprised in their bed with a stranger, and who had tried to convince him it was normal and healthy. "Like Mathias," Julien had said, holding his fists against his eyes. "The same fucking pattern. He'd convinced me and I'd accepted it, until it hurt too much, then he made promises…" He laughed a sad, scornful laugh. "Then I found bills… he'd been saying he was working all day in Québec City, but he was really shacked up all day in a hotel in Vieux Montréal with a nineteen-year-old Thai boy. I felt so, so stupid, then… so humiliated by his lies, even more than by the fact he was screwing someone else. And now? I'm doing exactly the same thing to the only guy I've loved since." I was rubbing his back, unable to say anything at all. I didn't want to say something trite like "No, no," or "We don't always learn from our mistakes" so I preferred to keep quiet. "Christ!" he'd finally shouted. "I'm FORTY years old! Why am I still doing this stuff?" And, with a sob, he'd added, "Why do I do this to myself?"

But the next day, he was wearing a new shirt, such a bright violet that it almost made the spectacular emerald green shirt look pale, and I'd found the gray sweater in the bathroom wastebasket. Ever since, he'd refused to talk about it at all, except to say he was doing "better." I was on the verge of threatening to call Mathias, convinced that his overnight recovery was more cause for alarm than teardrops on a gray sweater.

"Seriously," I repeated. "Are you okay?"

"Yeah," said Laurent, always awkward in situations like this. "Are you… okay?"

"Yes, yes, I'm okay. Lord, it's not like I lost a kidney or something."

No, but it's your own fault you got your heart broken, I wanted to say, and it's at least just as painful. But I held my tongue.

"Shit!" he exclaimed in a spectacular effort to change the subject. "Is Jeff coming or what? I could eat a horse!"

"I think there was a girl in his room," I answered. "He still wasn't up when I left and that usually means he's not alone."

"Marie-Lune?"

"No, Marie-Lune went to New York with some friends. I know, because about two hundred times, she said 'Oh my God, we're going to drink Cosmos in New York, it's so *Sex and the City!*'"

"So who's he with?"

"I don't know, Julien. It's not like I was going to open his bedroom door to check."

"Does it bother you if he sees other girls?" Laurent asked.

"Why would it bother me?" Even I could hear the aggression in my voice.

"You'll have to discuss it another time, kids," said Julien. "The big guy's here."

Jeff slid in beside me, and with one movement, he managed to pour himself a glass of wine and give me a funny little poke and a satisfied smile, lean on the table and take a drink.

"How are you, Boy-who-looks-like-he-has-good-news?" asked Laurent.

"Excellent."

"Yeah, well, we'd all be excellent if we'd all spent the night screwing," I said.

Julien raised a finger, "Ummm...."

"What?"

"Well, *I* spent the night screwing."

"EXCUSE ME?"

"Hey, I've got a broken heart. Not a broken dick."

I felt like making an unkind remark, but I thought that the fact that he admitted that he had a broken heart was enough of a step in the right direction for me to keep quiet. I scowled. "Well then, you were both screwing, bravo."

"To tell the truth, I did too," said Laurent, and my scowl turned into a pitiful groan that made Jeff burst out laughing.

"Don't worry," he whispered, rubbing my back. "I wasn't screwing either."

"You're just saying that to make me feel better." I had a hard time imagining Jeff spending more than six hours screwing.

"No, it's true! I went to bed late, but I wasn't screwing." But he still looked so delighted, that Julien couldn't take it anymore and quite nearly shouted, "Come on, criminy, are you going to tell us what you did?"

"Criminy?"

"My mother spent last weekend in town. It rubs off."

"My God," sighed Laurent. "If I had to start saying 'Fudge' every time I see my mother…"

"My mother is more of a 'Gosh' girl," I said. "I can't tell you how much I hate that expression. It's like 'goodness' or 'lordy' – that's how old grannies swear."

"It's not really satisfying," Laurent agreed.

"I don't think my mother's ever sworn in her life," said Jeff. "My father's a big fan of 'drat.'"

"Drat?"

"Yeah, like in 'Aw, drat.'"

Laurent and I made sympathetic faces: there was something interesting indeed about "drat."

"But, still, there's nothing to beat a good fuc…"

"HEY! We don't give a friggin' shit about how your ancestors swear! The big guy's face is lit up like a teenage girl who's just discovered her clitoris, so, will you please tell us, for the love of God, what's going on? Because I may have been screwing all night, but I still have bags under my eyes and my complexion is borderline pallid. So drop the comparative swearing analysis and talk."

"Christ," said Laurent. "You sure you're okay?"

"Yeah, yeah, I'm okay. Sorry. I haven't been sleeping very well lately because of..." He made a vague gesture that meant "everything." "I have a hard time putting up with myself."

"Maybe if you spent less time fucking..."

Jeff and I burst out laughing. Julien smiled a forced, tired smile and I could see him lying on his sofa in his gray sweater, staring at the ceiling, and I wanted to take his hand in mine and hang on to it for a while, without saying anything.

"It's nothing," Jeff finally said. "I'm just in a good mood. I saw your friend Flavie at Le Lulli yesterday." I remembered how he looked at her when they saw each other and what she'd said herself, "That boy is fantastic." That's all I need, I thought. All my friends paired up, my roommate with my only girlfriend, on top of it – I was going to be like Joey at the end of *Friends*, the only single, innocent one left, and even if he seemed very pleased with his lot, I was going to sink into bitter and graceless sullenness.

"We chatted for a good hour," he continued. "Man, what a woman!"

Had anyone ever said, "What a woman!" about me? It seemed to me the chances of it were slim, very slim indeed. I could imagine "She's really cool," "She's so funny," and, in my wildest dreams an occasional "She's a really cute girl." In my opinion, "What a woman!" was reserved for tremendous, supernatural beings like Flavie, not for girls who were five-foot-four, over thirty, and unable to refrain from dancing to early Rick Astley hits.

"I don't know," said Laurent. "Flavie scares me a little." I smiled and stroked his earlobe. I wondered if, someday, another man would manage to make me melt the way he did. Maybe if I ever had a son. And even then, who knows?

"So, you chatted," Julien said. "Are you telling me all I have to do is chat with a girl who wears powder blue polyester…" He stopped, following Laurent's explicit gaze directed at his violet-and-green checked pants, then shouted indignantly, "… Hey, they're not polyester!" I fell onto Jeff's shoulder, laughing. I didn't think about Gabriel anymore when I was with them – or at least if I thought of him, it was without worry and bitterness, just a thought that was vague and soft, like everything that was outside our world. Maybe what I was really more afraid of than anything, deep down, wasn't Joey's tragic, humorless destiny, but rather losing the three men I was so dependent on, because they were so good for me. Did they worry about losing me? I could see Laurent asking me about Gabriel, "Okay, what's going on, you going to go out with him?" and Jeff's ridiculous scene, and I thought, smiling to myself, that I wasn't all alone in my makeshift boat.

Jeff was just telling me that his "fascinating" conversation with Flavie concluded with an open dinner invitation and that Flavie was just waiting for my call to confirm everything and I was just waiting for him to get up so I could ask Julien and Laurent what I could have done to deserve getting saddled with the role of Cupid, when Ariane showed up, in a cloud of patchouli, at our table.

Speechless, I looked at her for an instant. Ariane's presence in this restaurant, where you could find non-fair-trade items, possibly non-organic items, and, the greatest heresy of all, meat, was completely incongruous.

"You, there," she threatened me, pointing a finger emerging from a half-mitten. "You…" I knew her – she was incapable of staying mad longer than five seconds. I was counting in my head when her eyes went from me to Laurent.

"LAURENT!" she shouted. She turned back into the sweet, cheerful little sister I'd always known. She leaned over the table to give Laurent a kiss, and he seemed delighted to see her.

"We miss you SO much," she said. Her pretty, bright eyes were laughing under her Peruvian hat.

"I miss you all, too," said Laurent, and I knew it was true. Ariane was about to lean over the table to give him another kiss when she noticed his plate and another half-covered finger, full of lectures and criticism, arose. "Laurent... steak tartar. Really... you know what kind of message you give your body when you eat something like that?"

"Yum?" suggested Laurent.

"You're in enemy territory, here," Julien said. "When in Rome..."

"Okay, okay." She gave him a kiss, too, then, laughing, let herself be swallowed up in Jeff's arms.

"Okay," she said, emerging from his hug, "I may be laughing, but I'm VERY angry, Marine."

Ten minutes and one tea (whose box was studied in detail to be sure its contents were fair trade) later, she explained that the day before, when she was coming out of the hospital where she volunteered ("You only volunteer in one hospital?" asked Laurent. "That's not much") she'd run into our father who, taken by surprise, was unable to lie, and had told her everything.

"I CANNOT believe you didn't let me know. Marine, I'm your sister! And I'm his daughter, too!" She was in possession of a number of indignant looks that she displayed at all the different pacifist protests and demonstrations that governed her existence.

"Oooh," I answered. "You should be thanking me, Missy. Because for a month now, I'm been getting daily phone calls from *Maman* and..."

"Marine, she's your mother! She's the one who brought you into this world. You still owe her…"

"Do you really want *Maman* to call you every day?"

A shadow of panic passed over Ariane's eyes. She didn't insist. Across from her, Jeff and Laurent looked at each other and laughed.

"Do Élo and Fred know?"

"Fred does. *Maman* wanted to spare you."

"What do you mean, spare us? We're his daughters, too! We have…"

"Ariane, can you let up on the 'indignant' tone for two seconds? We don't even know what's wrong with *Papa*. Maybe it's nothing. You have to remember that if it was up to him nobody would know until he knew himself. It may not have been the best decision in the world, but it's justifiable, don't you think?"

She gave an annoyed little "Humpf" and looked like she was sixteen. Of the four of us, she was the only one who'd inherited our father's instinctive kindness. Frédéric, Élodie and I weren't bad people, but not one of us possessed that humanist fiber which, in its simplicity, sometimes approached naiveté and other times the sublime. My father pushed the experience even farther: while Ariane did feel some gratification from the idea of helping others, my father would have fallen off his chair if someone pointed out his kindness. Nonetheless, he had handed down to his daughter his disinterested concern for others that characterized everything he did, to the point that people often walked all over him, something that distressed me greatly, not only for my father, but also for humanity in general and all it said about it.

"We have to let Élo know," said Ariane.

"Oh boy," Julien and Laurent and I all spoke at once: I could already imagine exaggerated outbursts and Élodie wallowing voluptuously in this potential drama – she, on the other hand, had inherited a lot from my mother.

"We should be there for him," said Ariane. "Fred should come home."

"Fred thought of that. But we're going to wait to find out what we're talking about, okay?"

"Poor *Papa*..." she suddenly stopped, surprised by a ringing sound, then she started rooting through the enormous woven hemp bag she always carried and that generally held at least forty tracts and petitions, but never any money – Ariane didn't believe in "the power of money" and got by almost exclusively through a system of bartering, recycling and trading favors, which took up approximately seventy-five percent of her time. She took out a small cell phone and answered simply by saying, "I'll be there in ten minutes."

"Okay," I said. "Whoa. Whoa, whoa, whoa. My brain can't keep up. *You* have a cell phone? *You?*"

She looked down like someone being forced to discuss a painful subject. "I know," she admitted. "It's just that we're organizing a huge protest against smoking and I'm in charge of transportation..." She looked back up at us, suddenly proud and enthusiastic. "We're even bringing in people from Vancouver, and we're trying to keep track of all the travel, and all the CO_2 emissions we cause will be offset by planting trees."

"Oh, for the love of God..." Julien sighed, slumping down on the table.

"Of course, we encourage people to come by bicycle and to carpool, but, well, sometimes, we don't have a choice..." Jeff looked at her, shaking his head, a smile dancing across his lips, looking like a guy who can't get over what he's just heard.

"That's why I have to go. But you, Marine Vandale, are not going to get off that easy. I'm going to call Élo and we'll have a tea together, okay?"

"Okay..." Digging in your heels with Ariane required self-control and rhetorical skills I'd never possessed.

"What about you?" she said, wrapping her arms around Jeff again. "How are you? How's your love life?"

"Oh my God... forget about it, I..."

The boys didn't even let me finish my sentence and launched into a rather comic description of the fiasco my love life currently was – they complemented each other and passed the puck back and forth with such ease, that I wondered if they hadn't rehearsed their little number.

"But you have to call him!" Ariane finally shouted, in the same tone of voice she would have used to say, "You have to dress warm in winter!" and I felt like shouting back it was okay, it was obvious I had to call, that some-time ago, I'd figured it out for myself, even before the boys did. The boys looked at her, nodding their heads with exaggeration and lifting powerless hands towards me, undoubtedly in an effort to show me I was a hopeless case.

"Here," said Ariane, holding out her phone to me. "You have two minutes. The stupid thing ought to be used for something good."

"What? No! I'll call when I get home."

"Marine," said four threatening voices. I looked at my little sister's gloved hand and bright eyes and, as I remembered there was no way to fight kindness, I took the phone and stepped out of the restaurant.

To: Marine
From: Frédéric Vandale
Subject: Sagrada familia

....

Okay, I said I wasn't going to write, but, you see, I just spent an hour on the phone with Ariane, and the smell of patchouli was starting to make its way over here. I didn't understand a thing she said. She was saying something about *Papa*, and the fact that life had given you a sign in the form of a cell phone she had, and that it seems that you can now plant trees in order to be forgiven for having a car. Can you explain all this to me?

To: Fred
From: Marine Vandale
Subject: Holy Patchouli

....

Where do you want me start?

To: Marine
From: Frédéric Vandale
Subject: Nice try

....

Do you really want us to pretend not to know that the only thing you're interested in telling me is whether or not you've called your doctor?

To: Fred
From: Marine Vandale
Subject: R-E-S-P-E-C-T

....

Easy, there. I'm worried about *Papa*, too, I'll have you know, and even more worried about seeing our little sisters tomorrow and the fact that I'm going to have to make use of all the authority a calm, thoughtful big sister can muster to explain to them that no, they cannot come with me to his next appointment with him.

To: Marine
From: Frédéric Vandale
Subject: S-E-G-R-E-G-A-T-I-O-N

And why can't they come?

To: Fred
From: Marine Vandale
Subject: Family portrait

Fred, put yourself in the shoes of a man who's afraid he might
have Alzheimer's and who's even more terrified about looking
weak in front of his family and tell me: do you really want to
have your two youngest children with you, especially when one
of them is Élodie and there's a good chance the other one will
insist on burning sage around you and rubbing your wrists
with essential oils?

To: Marine
From: Frédéric Vandale
Subject: Half a good point

You see, I follow you, but I have a question, too: don't you
think you might be playing *Papa*'s keeper and that you're the
one who doesn't want to share the role of glorious savior?

To: Fred
From: Marine Vandale
Subject: Good shot

I'd actually like to share my role as savior if you weren't living
the good life on the banks of the Seine, too busy not writing a
book with the money *Papa* lent you, and I'd be delighted to
see you go with him instead of me. But, there you go, I'm the
country bumpkin and you're pretending to be a writer in the
big city. Maybe you think I should apologize, too?

To: Marine
From: Frédéric Vandale
Subject: The heart of the matter

....

He didn't answer, did he?

To: Fred
From: Marine Vandale
Subjet: Re: Heart of the problem

....

No, he didn't answer.

To: Marine
From: Frédéric Vandale
Subject: Reason to smile

....

At least you called.

To: Marine
From: Frédéric Vandale
Subject: (none)

....

Right, Marine? You really called, didn't you?

To: Fred
From: Marine Vandale
Subject: Re: (none)

....

Yes, I really called. Voice mail. Now, I'm the girl who leaves text
and voice messages here and there and gets nothing but silence
in return. And while Ariane's busy saving the world by planting trees, I can't even manage to put the situation my father's
going through before my own friggin' bad mood. So, you see,
I'm not feeling all that cheerful.

To: Marine
From: Frédéric Vandale
Subject: Merry-go-round

You're going around in circles, Marinette.

To: Fred
From: Marine Vandale
Subject: Duh

Tell me about it!

To: Marine
From: Frédéric Vandale
Subject: Beautiful Parisian merry-go-rounds

Why don't you come see me?

To: Marine
From: Frédéric Vandale
Subject: (none)

Marine? Why don't you?

To: Fred
From: Marine Vandale
Subject: Re: (none)

It's him. He's calling on my cell.

To: Marine
From: Frédéric Vandale
Subject: Dive in

Answer it, Marine. Screw regret. Answer.

Chapter 7

"Dive in…" I said out loud to Claude François. "Like it's so easy to do…" But it *is* easy to do, mostly because diving in implies a brief, impulsive movement that leaves little room for thinking, which, in my case, had started taking up way too much space lately. Two weeks of my analyzing everything, every single movement and every single feeling, everything Jeff said, everything Gabriel didn't say.

So, in one smooth move involving just my body and that good old reptilian part of my brain – a move that had the same urgency as eating or getting shelter from bad weather – I answered. My heart was pounding and, in the delicious half-second preceding my "Hello," I had the time to imagine myself perched atop a cliff, choosing to jump in, with a shiver.

"Marine Vandale?" said Gabriel's polite and perpetually amused voice.

"Speaking. Doctor Champagne, I presume."

He started laughing, and I started breathing again. I wondered if there were any cigarettes in the apartment, I was so nervous. I hadn't smoked in seven years.

"Your sister is charming," Gabriel said.

"My sister?"

"Yes, your sister. Ariane. Unless she's another one of your characters, but the number you called me from yesterday seemed to be her phone."

"Oh…" I put my head in my hand, then I looked up, absurdly, towards some god I'd never believed in, to ask why he'd made me such an oaf and exactly what I'd done in a previous life to attract so much of his wrath.

"No, it's okay, she really is charming. Now I know all about the burning of greenhouse gases and the amount of CO_2 an average-sized leaf can absorb in a year. You didn't tell me your father was sick…"

I tried to think of a way to slit Ariane's throat from a distance. Had she really let Gabriel in on our family secrets? I knew she must have done it out of kindness, on top of everything, and that kindness which had always remained beyond my reach exasperated me.

"Err… your father IS sick, right?" repeated Gabriel, who must have decided a few days ago to be skeptical about any statements coming from my friends or family.

"Yes. Yes, he's sick. Well, no. We don't know." I looked around frantically, wondering if the stuffing in the La-Z-Boy could be smoked, or if Jeff didn't keep a joint or two in his room.

"What does he have?" asked Gabriel. His tone was sincere, professional and, above all, reassuring. It was at that exact moment that I did something that would be inseparable from that memory for me: I held the phone receiver away from my mouth so Gabriel wouldn't hear me sigh. It was a nervous puff leaving me to finally be replaced by calm, serene breathing: it was the sound of me stopping.

"He's been forgetting things for quite a while," I said. I sat down on the sofa. We talked for two hours that night, as I held the phone receiver right up against my mouth. I'd stopped looking for cigarettes or joints – I preferred getting lost in the music of our budding interest, in the intoxication brought on by discovering someone new and the first timid steps we dare to take into their territory.

"Hey!" shouted Jeff as he came in a few hours later. I was comfortably settled on the sofa, snuggled up in one of his sweaters, and, for the hundredth time, I was watching an episode of an HBO series we'd bought the box set of, and that we both loved.

"Hey!" I answered joyfully. I'd been waiting for him for a while and I'd gotten my joke all ready. I raised the cardboard where he'd written "CALL!!!" then I turned it over – on the back, I'd written "HE CALLED BACK!!!" myself.

Jeff came closer, squinting – pointlessly miming that he was having trouble reading from so far away, though I knew his eyesight was perfect. "Oh," he finally said, before he made a face that was probably supposed to be positive, but instead it made me think he found the whole thing highly unimportant.

"Come on. You could at least pretend to be happy, for the last two weeks you've been on me to call him and talk to him!"

"Yes, yes, I'm really happy. If it's what you want." He went and got himself a beer out of the fridge and sat down hard on the La-Z-Boy. "You're sure it's what you want, right?"

I sat up on the sofa. "Yes, I'm sure it's what I want! You're getting on my nerves with that! Why would I be in such a state since we met if it wasn't what I want?"

"True enough." Once again, he pulled that little, less than convincing face.

"Jeff? Is there something about it that bothers you?"

"No. Not at all." Something seemed to dawn on him. "No! Are you insinuating that… No!"

"No, I'm not insinuating anything," I lied. "It's just that…"

I looked away and when I looked back at him, he was doing the same thing. For the first time in our fifteen-year friendship, I had the feeling we were uncomfortable with each other.

"It's just that you're usually happy for me. Or, at least, you laugh at me. But now it seems like you don't approve, and I don't exactly understand why, it's the first time since Laurent that I've felt like this."

He smiled, sincerely this time. "I know. Sorry. That may be exactly it, I can see where you're going and I'm afraid you'll get hurt."

"Do you really have to put the cart that far in front of the horse?"

"No. But I always worry about you. You know that. But you're right. We'll cross that bridge when we get to the river."

"Right, we won't try to catch a tiger by the tail."

"We'll try to catch a doctor by the tail."

"Hey, Gabriel's tail's not going to get caught anywhere."

"Except..." He pointed towards my crotch and I laughed and threw a pillow at him. "Well, then, I'm going to go to Le Lulli for a while. You want to come?"

"What? It's after midnight!"

"May I remind you the bars close at three a.m.?"

"Yeah, but, no. I'm too comfy, I don't go out when it's minus forty, no way, José."

"As you wish. If I see Flavie, shall I invite her to dinner?"

I didn't know what to answer. The idea that he could be alone with Flavie again bothered me so much I almost changed my mind and went to Le Lulli with him. I thought my reaction was as irrational as his and that now he must be the one, seeing me incapable of answering such a simple question, wondering what bothered me so much about it.

"Err, yes!" I finally exclaimed. "Err... tell her I'll give her a call."

"I'll do that." He gave me a smile and little wink, then he left. He'd barely closed the door when I realized he hadn't even asked if Gabriel and I were going to see each other again.

"It was the most *bizarre* situation," I said to Julien. "I

mean: we were uncomfortable. Both of us were."

"Can you walk any faster?"

" Julien…" I looked up at the sky, but I still picked up my pace: he had been taking the idea of power walking on the mountain very seriously the last few weeks. Just a few minutes earlier he'd left me to admire the view from the top of the stairs while he went up and down five times in a row. "I'm going to be forty years old," he'd explained after his fourth time up, out of breath, but ready to do it all again. I was keeping up as best as I could. His clothes were perfectly suited to this kind of exercise, the cold weather and his penchant for electric blue. I was wearing jeans, an old down jacket, a toque with a pompom and a scarf that was about ten feet long. I must have looked like my sister Ariane.

"He didn't even ask how our conversation turned out!"

"That *is* weird," said Julien.

"That *is* weird, but isn't it weird that Jeff and I are uncomfortable around each other? The endorphins are going to your head, buddy."

"Nay." For the last little while, he'd gotten into the habit of saying "Nay" and "Yea." Laurent suspected he was having an affair with a peasant who was still living in the sixteenth century. "It's normal if you're a little uneasy, Lord, you almost slept together and now both of you, and I do mean *both of you*, are wondering if maybe you should have."

"Whatever!"

"Marine. Do we really need to have this conversation?"

"Yes! You're saying insane things!" I stopped walking, thinking it would force him to slow down, but he kept on going, simply shouting: "If it was so insane, you wouldn't be getting so upset! Now, anyway, you're not going to get the thighs of a twenty year old by standing in the middle of the path!" I sighed and started running to catch up with him, shouting: "My thighs are quite firm, thank you!"

Almost in another jogger's face, so he couldn't help but laugh and take a look at my thigh muscles.

"I am not wondering if I should have slept with Jeff," I said when I caught up to him. It was ridiculous – I'd barely run thirty feet and I was out of breath. "Christ, what's wrong with all of you? He thinks maybe it took me so long to call Gabriel because I didn't really want him to answer, you think I want to sleep with him, and Laurent called me last night, drunk, to tell me his mother and sister had convinced him I was really still in love with him."

"He did that?" Julien squeaked. For I second I thought the shock was so much he was going to stop.

"He does that a lot," I said. "When he's had a bit to drink, he starts thinking deep down I still love him."

"Maybe you do still love him."

"Okay, now you're going to have to make up your mind, I can't still love Laurent, want to sleep with Jeff, and have a crush on Gabriel. Maybe I have the hots for you too, while we're at it."

"You know perfectly well that if I was going to sleep with a girl, it would be you."

"Ah. I know, sweetie. You know that if I was going to sleep with a gay guy, it would be you. Except maybe for the tall, blond guy who waits tables at Le Lulli on Tuesday nights."

"Oh my God, Gareth? He is SO hot!" Apparently, Gareth's hotness was enough to stop Julien. He planted himself in front of me, made an extremely rude gesture, smiled ecstatically, then started walking again.

"Anyway," he said. "What I'm trying to get you to understand and what I KNOW you understand anyway is that once you open the door to sexuality with someone, let me tell you, it's not so easy to close it."

"Yeah, but…"

"Tut, tut!" He raised an authoritarian hand covered in a blue-and-black glove. "Don't waste my time, Marine.

You know I'm right."

I did know he was right. I'd known for a long time about half-open doors leading to possible yet unexplored worlds that never closed again, even when you turned your back on them. But I also knew that the door that had opened when Gabriel and I bumped into each other in the snow was far more interesting. I'd left so many doors ajar in the past – behind me there was a multitude of places I hadn't explored and avenues I hadn't dared to follow, and it had never upset me. But I knew that if I didn't take the risk on this adventure, I was going to regret it.

"Christ, would you mind supporting me for once?!" Before I even finished my sentence, I knew I was talking too loud, but I couldn't stop. For the first time in twenty years, I was thinking that maybe my mother had been right all along and that spending most of my time with three guys wasn't a good idea. "The ONLY times you ever encouraged me was when you knew things wouldn't work out." I'd stopped and I was shouting, in the middle of the snowy path, in the direction of Julien, who'd finally turned around.

"Are you going to cry?" he asked, worried. I heard myself offer a little unconvincing "no" – in fact I wasn't really sad, but I was angry. And ever since I was little, when I got mad, I wanted to cry (a serious handicap for a woman whose aspiration is to be taken seriously in both professional and personal negotiations).

Julien hesitated a couple of seconds, his cheeks like two pink pucks under the toque that was as blue as his eyes, then he gave an exasperated "Aaahhhhh" before he finally came over and took me by the shoulder.

"Marine… what Jeff is trying to tell you so clumsily, and what I'm going to tell you with all my characteristic ease, is that if we're asking so many questions, it's just because we've never seen you so enthusiastic, and that your…" He made a motion that looked like he wanted to look like a pregnant woman or a very fat person. "All your… enthusiasm, well, it's just that it's coming so soon after you broke up with Christophe and everything that happened after… and before… and during, in fact…"

He was even making himself laugh, and I jabbed him in the ribs with my elbow.

"Okay, I get it. Sorry." He was still laughing, but we were finally walking at a normal speed, arm in arm. Other couples passed us and I wondered if they saw us as a couple, too, if they didn't say, after they got by us: "Did you see the guy in blue? What beautiful eyes… can you please tell me what he's doing with a little blond who can't even match her toque and her scarf?" and I really didn't give a shit, the idea of being part of a couple made me so happy, even if it was imaginary and involved a single girl and a gay man. Obviously, this was a problem, and I finally understood what the boys meant.

"You're worried I'm building a house of cards?"

"I'm worried you're forgetting that love isn't built from one day to the next."

"I know that, Julien. I also know I'm getting carried away, logically, way too early, and maybe Gabriel just wants to be my friend and maybe even one day I'll find out he's unbearable. But have we gotten so old that we're going to start making things up, for fear of getting hurt?"

Julien turned towards me – he was smiling. "When did we start wearing bicycle helmets?" I continued. "And listening to Health Canada's recommendations? When did we start hoping for a net every time we're about to jump?"

"Yeah, but I know you're afraid this time."

"Of course I'm afraid. I'm fucking scared shitless! And I'll be even more scared in a year, and ten times more when I'm forty, I know that! I have less and less time to lose and my heart is more and more fragile. But shit…"

Julien hugged me against him, still smiling. "Anyway,

champ. Shall we meet up at the lookout point?"

"Meet up? I'll be there five minutes before you!"

We both started running. Five minutes later, I'd lost sight of him and was panting in the middle of the path, grumbling about all the happy athletes jogging gaily around me as if there had never been anything simpler and less exhausting.

Julien was taking his pulse when I finally caught up with him at the lookout point. Frowning, with the fingers of his right hand applied against his left wrist, he almost looked like one of those healthy people I was always cautious of, the kind who walk the dog at seven in the morning and drink a lot of green tea – the kind of person Gabriel could be.

"You're too intense," I said to Julien, leaning against the railing.

"YOU'RE too intense."

"What do you mean, too intense? It took me forty-five minutes to get up here!"

"I mean in sentimental matters. You're too intense. And, boy, am I fucking jealous."

He turned around and faced the building. I was still looking at the city, but I still poked him in the thigh with my elbow.

"I know you're all jealous of me," I said, without turning around.

"Yeah, and we know you know, too. But we also know that we'd be scared if we were in your place AND that if you were in our place, you'd be worried about you, too."

"Okay, that really doesn't make a lot of sense, but I understand."

We didn't say anything for a minute; he, I'm certain was watching the breathless young men finishing their runs, and I was trying to see the difference, off in the distance, between the river and the sky, where they blended together in the March light.

"Speaking of Jeff…" said Julien.

"Stop! I don't want to hear any more about it, it's too ludicrous."

"If you say so … but I *still* think the only thing that's really bizarre, and certainly revealing, is that he didn't ask you if you were going to see him again."

"YOU haven't asked me if I was going to see him again," I pointed out, turning around myself.

"I was waiting for the right time." He gave me a little wink. "Well? So?"

"Well, *so*?" I was laughing.

"Yes, well, *so*! Are you going to see him again, for Chrissake?"

"No matter what I say, you're not going to judge me, right?"

"Nay. Promise. Nay. So? Do you have a date?"

"Yea, Julien. 'Yea merrily verily.'"

"Did you really say 'Yea merrily verily'?" asked Élodie.

"Yes, I said 'Yea merrily verily.'"

"What are you, a thousand years old? What about 'm'lord' while you're at it?"

"Élo, it was hard enough to get together, could we at least try to take it easy on each other?"

"Yes, I'll give you that. It's better to save it for a good reason. I'm going to go have a cigarette, okay? I'll be back." Ariane was a good half-hour late, and I still hadn't had the courage to tell Élodie that even if the reason was good, it was far from being pleasant.

Ariane had asked us to meet in a little café in Mile End – Ariane *only* went to little cafés in Mile End. I looked at the crowd around me, as Élodie made her way amongst the girls wearing see-through shirts they'd bought at Value Village, flat red lipstick and glasses with wide black frames, and the tall, scrawny boys, who, whether they were wearing ponchos, or thin, showy jackets, also demonstrated a preference for glasses with wide frames. They look like movie extras, I thought. They were perfect – as if the owner had called a casting agency to say, "I'm opening a little café in Mile End, I'm going to need the usual crowd."

Perhaps all these people who looked nothing like me were engineers or primary school teachers or bus drivers, but they all looked like eternal students, up and coming artists, people who wanted a lot, in any case, and who, in many cases, were probably laboring over a movie script or a first collection of poetry. They all seemed as morally certain as Ariane – doubt was not hovering over the café, these people, for the most part, seemed quite solidly convinced that they where on the right track and had understood a number of things that seemed to be beyond my grasp since, as was often the case when I was talking to Ariane, I was clearly feeling pretty impure and individualistic, and I would have bet my life that what culture I did have would have provoked more laughter than anything else, in this sunny and pleasantly disorganized place.

But what was most ridiculous about the whole thing was that I was intimidated by the young women with scarves in their hair and the boys who most likely wore sarongs in the summer. I suspected they each had a blog and asked questions about the future of the planet, while I had a hard time not getting bored if I kept a simple journal and the questions that tortured me usually had more to do with my love life and the quantity of vodka left in the freezer.

I was about to stand up and shout: "Yes, I buy jeans at the Gap, and I've even darkened the door of Walmart, I eat beef and I like it, the last concert I saw was U2, and I stopped reading *Adbusters* and *Vice* magazine a long time ago because I only did it to ease my conscience, I hate Facebook with a passion, but no matter how hard I try, in the end, I'm more personally affected by my cat's temporary disappearance than by the bombs falling on Baghdad and despite all my best efforts, I cannot manage to intrinsically, viscerally believe that I can 'make a difference.'" I was already planning to finish on a pathetic note, screaming, "I AM ORDINARY!!!" when Ariane showed up.

"Élodie's outside having a cigarette!" she said without even saying hello, in the same tone she would to inform me that Élodie was picking up clients and showing her tits outside the café.

"Yes, Ariane. Élodie smokes. She's smoked for ten years." The place had sucked the sense of humor right out of me.

"I know," Ariane shouted. "I've known for ten years, too, and do you know what smoking can do to someone who…"

"Shit, Ariane."

She fell silent with a little smile that showed she could laugh at herself, and I wondered, as I often did, how such a pure and charming person could be part of my immediate family.

"Sorry," I said, with a smile of my own.

"It's okay. Did you tell her about *Papa*?"

"No, I wanted to wait for you."

"Thanks, big sister."

I sighed the same sigh as every time she or Élodie reminded me I was somebody's big sister, while she ordered a tea with an interminable, convoluted name. Élodie came and sat back down, smelling a little like smoke and a lot like synthetic perfume.

"So," she said. "What?"

Ariane turned towards me and, for the first time in my life, I felt a sense of responsibility towards these two young girls, whom I knew less than perfectly.

"Girls," I said, truly feeling like I was a hundred years old. "You must have noticed that for the last while, *Papa* has been a bit…" A bit what? I had the feeling that if I used my mother's word, "forgetful," I'd be betraying him a little. "In a fog" was too vague, and "out of it" was frankly too disrespectful.

"A little what?" asked Élodie, as her left leg started to fidget, something that happened whenever she was nervous.

"Sometimes he forgets things," I answered.

Ariane made a sad little face – I could only see her out of the corner of my eye because I was too busy watching Élodie, who wasn't saying a word. Obviously, they were both waiting for me to go on, be specific, give answers. It was a strange feeling for me, as someone who always had a thousand questions and no answers, to be the one expected to offer a solution.

"We don't know if…"

"*Papa's* got Alzheimer's," said Élodie. "Oh my God, *Papa* has Alzheimer's?" There was a tiny question mark at the end of her last sentence, but it was so faint that I wondered if I'd imagined it, or if she'd added it on in a little leap of hope.

"No! No. *Papa* doesn't have Alzheimer's. We don't know what he has. He decided on his own to see if it's normal or if it's something else. It's going to take a little…"

"Is he going to forget us? Is he going to forget our names?" Her question was so naive, but also so sincere I almost cried. A few years earlier I'd seen a movie, *Se souvenir des belles choses*, and I'd been so touched by the idea, that I'd spent weeks making absurd lists of things I couldn't forget, just in case. Names, faces and looks, moments I couldn't describe because, though apparently insignificant, they held immeasurable happiness for me – a Saturday afternoon hanging pictures on the wall with Laurent; interminable brunches with the boys that ended at six at night with a copy of *The Godfather* in the DVD player; the time when *Papa* and I didn't jump into the lake at my uncle's cottage – we ran with all our clothes on to the end

of the dock just to stop at the last second and *Papa* still
said, "Would we remember it so well if we'd jumped?"; and,
since then, meeting Gabriel in the snow, and his smile
when he agreed to come with me to Laurent's.

"Élo," said Ariane, when she noticed I wasn't saying
anything. "*Papa's* okay, okay? We have to wait till he fin-
ishes his tests."

"You knew?" Élodie asked. She didn't look angry anymore, only hurt. "You really think I'm the baby of the
family, don't you?"

"No, sweetheart…" Ariane took her by the shoulders.
"I just found out by accident. The rest of the family thinks
the two of us have to be protected."

Élodie gave a quick, pale smile and Ariane kissed her
on the cheek – and, for an instant, I could feel the love I
used to have for them, unconditional and savage as it was,
though it had faded with the passing years and rare
moments together.

"Listen," I said, sounding as much like a believable big
sister as I could. I told them more of the details about
what *Papa* was doing and how our mother wanted it to
stay a secret. I also strongly encouraged them not to tell
Maman they knew what was going on, if they didn't want
to spend most of their time on the phone listening to her
wonder what she was going to do when she became a
widow. Ariane didn't let go of Élodie's shoulders, even
when people came over to say hi to her, which was about
every ten minutes.

"I'd like to be involved," Élodie finally said.

"What?"

"You said you were going to his doctor's appointments
with him, sometimes. I'd like to come, too."

"You sure?"

"Yes, I'm sure. Shit, what do you take me for exactly?"

This time, even Ariane didn't know what to answer.

GIN & TONIC AND CUCUMBER

Had we underestimated her, or had she misrepresented herself that much? Either way, I knew that Ariane, like Fred and I, thought that Élodie was the last person you could count on, in a time of personal crisis.

"Right," said Élodie. "No need to answer. Anyways, I know you're all just jealous because I'm the cutest one in the family." She smiled coquettishly.

"Um… in fact, I always thought Marine was the most beautiful of the three of us," said Ariane.

"Oh, you're too kind," I answered. "But I've known for a long time that you were the prettiest. I mean, dressing the way you do and still turning out dazzling takes a hell of a solid foundation…"

Sitting between the two of us, Élodie laughed. It had been years since we'd played that game, which consisted in pretending that no one noticed Élodie, even though, out of the three of us, she was the one, by far, who spent the most time making herself beautiful. The thought crossed my mind that there was something sadly ironic in the fact that what drew us closest to our childhood and our memories was our father's failing memory.

"Seriously," said Élodie. "The next time you go with him…" She hadn't even finished her sentence when a very surprised voice shouted my name. Completely surprised myself (the idea that I could know anyone besides Ariane in this café seemed quite unlikely to me), I turned around to see Carole, in a business suit, coming towards our table.

"Hey!" I said. "What are you doing here?"

"It's the best café around here. What are YOU doing here?"

"My sister Ariane," I said, pointing at her with my chin.

"Ah," said Carole, nodding her head as a slight smile stretched across her lips. I was thinking that for the first time since we'd met, we finally felt like we had something in common, in this place where being a family law attorney must be looked down on just like the non-fair-trade wool sweater I was wearing.

"My two little sisters, in fact," I added. I was unusually proud of them and I thought these two young women, whose diapers I'd changed and whom I'd fed Pablum, were quite pretty and unique. "This is Carole," I told the girls. "Laurent's girlfriend."

Élodie, true to form, swept Carole with a merciless look implying that she certainly wasn't as good for Laurent as a member of our own family, while Ariane shook her hand and stated that she "REALLY missed Laurent" – all to put Carole at ease.

"Hey," she said, to change the subject. "Are you going to see Gabriel again? He's a REALLY great guy."

For a second, I considered saying something horribly mean and unjustified: that she could again take a number since, apparently, she seemed to have a considerable penchant for men I'd loved before her. Then I thought maybe she was just being nice, that maybe she wanted to share what Élodie called "girl time," and I thought I was so horrible, that I almost invited her over for a glass of wine sometime, without Laurent. We really should get to know each other better, after all.

"Yes," I said. "I'm supposed to see him again this week. Tomorrow or the day after. We have to call each other."

"Wow," Carole repeated. "Anyway, good luck with him. Really." She smiled broadly, then put on her coat to leave.

"Carole," I called to her before she left. "Why don't we get together for a drink sometime? Without Laurent? Just us girls – we can talk about him behind his back."

For a second, she looked so happy, I thought maybe I'd missed something spending my life with guys, that maybe, for me, girls could be an unexplored reserve of tenderness and generosity that I'd underestimated all these years.

"We'll call?" she asked.

"Anytime…"

Carole hadn't even taken a single step towards the door when Élodie, who'd inherited my mother's penchant to believe that as long as someone wasn't looking right at her, they couldn't hear her, asked, "Hey, you're not going to collude with the enemy, are you?"

"She's not the enemy!"

"She's Laurent's girlfriend!" I had a quick thought for Gabriel. If, by some impossible chance he wasn't convinced I was completely crazy and that most of my friends were recent escapees from a psych hospital, and if, by some miracle, something developed between us, he would still have to face my family, who, I knew, would base their judgment on a single criterion: "He's not Laurent."

"She looks sad," Ariane remarked.

"Hmm?"

"Lo's girlfriend. She looks sad."

I was going to protest when I realized she was right. Carole was always cheerful, but I couldn't remember a single time when her face had been lit up by a sincere smile. I could hear Mathias' voice on the phone the other morning when he was looking for Julien, and I thought of the countless times I'd told Marie-Lune Jeff was out when he was looking at me from the La-Z-Boy with a beer in his hand. What were we doing then to these people that we supposedly loved at least as much as we loved ourselves? Did the four of us love ourselves too much, so much that we'd become shut off from the rest of the world? It was such a depressing thought that as I looked towards the gray, snowy street I felt a physical need for summer and sun.

"Gotta go," I finally said to the girls. "I'm meeting Jeff and Laurent for drinks. Plus, there are too many artistic and ideological convictions in here, I'm starting to get a headache."

"You're just jealous, Little Miss Conviction-less."

"Touché," I said with a smile.

"Can I come?" Élodie asked. "I'm always a little afraid of alpaca wool." A young woman passing our table, in an alpaca sweater and wearing a Che Guevara beret, gave Élodie an angry look. "Plus," she said, ignoring Miss Guevara, "I do love that handsome Jeff…"

"Okay," I answered. "Ariane, you hold her down a minute and I'll make a quick getaway."

Ariane pretended to hold her firmly by the shoulders, while I went to pay.

"You'll call to tell us about your date?" she said, and beside her, in a strange reversal of roles, Élodie was asking, in a far more serious tone, "You'll call me when you're going to the hospital with *Papa*?"

I smiled at them and as I got up, I answered, "Yes and yes."

As I was going through the door, I heard Élodie give a frightened little shriek: a very handsome young man, with dreadlocks at least four feet long and, at the end of a leash, something that could be nothing other than a Vietnamese pot-bellied pig, came up to their table to say hello to Ariane.

I was still laughing at Élodie's reaction when the pig sat on one of her little pink, faux crocodile boots as I stepped into Le Lulli. I noticed Jeff at the bar right away, and he and Andrew the bartender were gesturing at me incomprehensibly. I walked towards them, shrugging my shoulders to show I didn't understand when Laurent came out of nowhere to grab me by one arm and say, "Can you please tell me why you're not answering your cell?"

"What?" I took my phone out of my pocket: I had eleven missed calls – seven from Jeff, three from Laurent, and one other, which had just come in a minute ago, from Le Lulli. "What is it? What's going on?"

Laurent abruptly placed me in front of him as if he

wanted to hide something from me, then pushed me towards Jeff.

"We wanted to let you know," he said, looking behind us. "Maybe you would have preferred not to come, we don't know. Plus, since you didn't tell us where you were…"

"What's going on?" Gabriel must be right behind me, I thought, passionately kissing a girl who logically isn't me.

"He seemed surprised to see us, but he insisted on staying till you got here."

"Okay, if you don't utter a name in the next nanosecond, I'm going to scream."

"Just…" Jeff took my hand and looked at me very seriously. "Stay cool, okay? And be nice. He looks a little turned around. We'll stay."

I was getting ready to scream when I heard a voice that I had obviously not forgotten say my name, just behind me. "If those two other guys show up again," I heard Andrew say to Laurent, "I'm gonna die laughing." And, just barely an hour after I'd been wondering if we all didn't have a sad gift for making others unhappy, I found myself face to face with Christophe, whom I hadn't seen for more or less two months and who was now looking at me with wounded eyes full of questions.

To: Fred
From: Marine Vandale
Subject: No doubt

....

You know how there are people who like to say their lives are like a book? Well, in my case, it's time to face facts: my life is a summer stock play. Laurent was nice yesterday, he said it was more like vaudeville or maybe a Feydeau play, but I figure there's no use pretending since the triple meeting at Le Lulli and Laurent's ridiculous act: it's a summer stock play. I'm expecting a cameo by Gilles LaTulippe from one moment to the next.

To: Marine
From: Frédéric Vandale
Subject: Author at a standstill

....

Well, be a good sister and tell me about it, because at this point I've started about thirty novels and thrown them all away because frankly, inspiration has been playing hide and seek and if I'm going to write, I guess, what's wrong with a summer stock play?

To: Fred
From: Marine Vandale
Subject: One person's sorrow...

....

Do you believe that? That one person's sorrow is another's joy?

To: Marine
From: Frédéric Vandale
Subject: ... is an author's joy

....

If you're insinuating that your problems are going to catapult me to success at Rougemont or Terrebonne, then my answer is yes.

To: Fred
From: Marine Vandale
Subject: Order! Order!

....

Can you be a little serious, please? Just because Marcel
Leboeuf's on channel 2, doesn't mean it's funny.

To: Marine
From: Frédéric Vandale
Subject: Remembering Marcel

....

You know the only time in my life I ever went to a summer
stock play, Marcel was in it?

To: Fred
From: Marine Vandale
Subject: Re: Remembering Marcel

....

No shit, Sherlock, I was with you and *Papa* and Aunt Emma,
who were laughing their heads off, and we couldn't get over it.
That's why I mentioned him. Now, will you answer my question?

To: Marine
From: Frédéric Vandale
Subject: Cloudy judgment

....

Could you give me a little help, please? Because the way you
asked your question is a little vague for a man who has no idea
why it suddenly surfaced in his little sister's brain.

To: Fred
From: Marine Vandale
Subject: Clarification

....

To give you the (relatively) short version, I saw Christophe
again, and he was under the surprising impression that we
were adults and that we owed it to each other to discuss what
he called "the real stuff." And he wasn't lying: he said a bunch
of things that were all true and, as is often the case with real
stuff, they weren't easy to hear, because, coward that I am, I
would have truly preferred to believe I hadn't hurt him so
badly.

To: Marine
From: Frédéric Vandale
Subject: Growth spurt

....

Yes, well, maybe you don't remember, Marinette, but it always
hurts a little to grow. This being said, as far as I remember, it
was also incredibly exciting. But, if you don't mind, now, would
you please enlighten me about the link you see between one
person's sorrows and another's joys?

To: Fred
From: Marine Vandale
Subject: Explanation

....

The relationship is that I'm filled with the idea that next week
I'm going to see Gabriel, while my ex just told me he should-
n't have been hurt the way he was. Maybe I'm not saying it
right, you're the writer, stalled or not. What I mean is this, "Do
you think there's a universal balance in the world that means
that for every joy there has to be a sorrow?"

To: Marine
From: Frédéric Vandale
Subject: Incomplete growth

Okay, I'm going to try to say this as gently as I possibly can, but maybe you should stop thinking you're so important, little sister. You know I'm paralyzed with love for you, but I still don't think you have that much influence on the cosmos. There's nothing new about it, but I've always thought we were each responsible for our own happiness.

To: Fred
From: Marine Vandale
Subject: Cold, hard truth

Okay, okay. I get it. It may indeed be time to grow up a little. Complex process. What if I start right away?

To: Marine
From: Frédéric Vandale
Subject: Re: Cold, hard truth

Where?

To: Fred
From: Marine Vandale
Subject: RE: Cold, hard truth

I'm going to talk to Jeff.

Chapter 8

Obviously, talking to Jeff would have turned out to be easier if he'd been there and, another important detail, if I knew exactly what I wanted to talk to him about. I had a few vague ideas, I wanted to tell him I didn't recognize us anymore since what I was still calling "my screw-up," that sometimes I felt like there was a messy layer of things not said that was multiplying on its own, as if every single thing we left unsaid led to another, creating levels and strata of possibly insignificant but unrecognized things, and, because of this their importance was exaggerated. We had always told each other everything – I'd always been pointlessly proud of the fact that I could read Jeff like a book. Now, I had the feeling I was facing a being who was partly unfathomable, and whose story was no longer unfolding before me like a tale I knew by heart.

I didn't really see how I was going to bring all this up. Alone in the apartment, I rehearsed out loud – a rather ridiculous habit I'd developed when I was a teenager when I took advantage of every precious moment of solitude to soliloquize instead of savoring the silence, rare as it was in our house. Impassively the cat was watching me, and I was regularly asking him "What do you think?" but he didn't look like he thought much.

"Look," I said to a potted plant, "you might think I'm being ridiculous, but it feels like something's not the same between us anymore. And don't just say 'no' right away." I pointed an imposing finger at the silent plant. "If you say 'no,' I want you to really think it."

I wanted him to say no, but above all I wanted him to

think it. I wanted him to convince me, I wanted him to do what he always did, with reassuring words and his very solid presence, I wanted him to pull me out of my river of doubt for just a moment.

Suddenly, seeing the cat slowly blink as he watched me, I had the idea that if my true goal was to grow up and finally start acting like the adult I was, I was certainly not going to reach it by speaking so forcefully to the innocent vegetation. Christophe had talked to me. Directly. Well, maybe he'd practiced with a poinsettia or a cactus, but he had nonetheless made the leap to an animated being, and *that* was undeniable progress.

That night at Le Lulli, Christophe and I had gone and sat at a little table next to the big windows which, in the summer, opened up onto the street. I think he saw the look I was shooting towards the boys, which must have been wavering between supplication and despair, and I was relieved to see him almost laugh.

"I'm not here to yell at you," he said in an extremely gentle tone. I forced a weak little smile, and I had to hold back from running a hand along his face. I hadn't seen him for a few weeks and I thought he looked even younger, despite the little beard he'd let grow, and that looked pretty good on him. He was even cuter than I remembered, too. I remembered the beginning of our relationship; I was unable to mention his name without adding, "he's so fucking cute," insisting on the word *cute* as if it were something I'd like to bite into. I thought about Gabriel, too, and how handsome he was, and how these two adjectives that people often associated with each other were impossible to invert, just like the two men were as well.

"Christophe," I'd begun, though I had no idea where I was headed. A dozen trivial things were bumping around in my head, statements like, "If I'd only known" and "I'm so sorry," which were not only empty, but also partly false.

I *had* known, and I was perfectly conscious of the fact that I wasn't as sorry as I should have been (and that was what really made me sorry).

He laughed ambigusouly, as if he heard my hollow thoughts, and I said to myself that he undoubtedly knew, he knew me well enough, after all, and I wanted to hide somewhere, under the table, between Jeff and Laurent, inside myself.

"I didn't come here on purpose," Christophe finally said. "I mean, I didn't know you'd be here. I don't want you to think I'm following you around all the bars in town or something like that." He laughed again, gently, sadly. "In fact, I haven't been back here since…" He only waved his hand vaguely to allude to our break-up, and to what I'd done. "But now, I don't know, I told myself it was time to move on… I can't be mad at you forever, can I?"

"Were you really mad at me?" I hadn't even finished my statement when I realized how stupid it was. Christophe had raised his eyebrows, as if to say, "What do you think?"

"I'm so sorry, Christophe."

"I know." He took a drink of beer, then concentrated on examining the coaster where *My Goodness My Guinness* was inscribed in red letters. How could I have hurt someone who was so gentle and so tender? I extended one hand towards him, in an uncertain gesture – what I really wanted to do was take him in my arms, but I knew this wasn't possible, and that it would never be possible again.

"You know what hurt me the most?"

"What?" I didn't want to know. I was thinking that what I really wanted was for HIM to take me in his arms, and not the other way around. I'd always thought of him as a little boy, with his tussled hair, his trendy tee-shirts and his sensual nonchalance. But, now, sitting across from him in this bar where we'd kissed so often, I finally understood that he'd grown up, that he'd always acted like a

thirty-one-year-old man, while I'd remained stuck somewhere around twenty.

"It's when I realized that deep down you were never
really in love with me."

"Christophe…" But I stopped. There was nothing I
could say. We hadn't been together for a year – and we
hadn't even gotten to the "I love you" stage and, in my
teenage selfishness, I'd never even thought he could be in
love. I was blind, I told myself we were having fun, that
life was beautiful and simple because it's what I wanted to
believe, and what I refused to see then, was that even if
life was beautiful, it was also complex.

I protested a little, but he stopped me – he was right,
and I fell silent when I had to face how obvious it was.

"I know we weren't together anymore," he added. "I
know that. It's not even the fact that it happened with one
of my buddies, besides, it's just… It's just that… I understood that a girl who does something like that isn't a girl
who's in love. Maybe I'm the one who was naive."

I wasn't saying anything. I was looking at my glass of
wine, wishing I could melt into it. For a brief instant, I
thought I was going to start crying, but that would have
been adding insult to injury: Christophe would have easily seen that I was crying for myself and not for him.

I'd taken the slap without flinching. He was so right
that any kind of protest would have been pathetic as well
as useless.

"I'm a horrible person," I said. "Really…"

"No. No, you're not a horrible person. You just weren't
in love."

"Christophe, there's no use kidding ourselves, it's horrible that I did that."

"Okay, maybe it wasn't a stellar thing to do, but it was-
n't horrible."

"How can you say that?"

"Because I fell in love with you, Marine. With the girl

you are, and I know that girl isn't a horrible person. She may be fucking selfish and afraid of commitment and of growing up, but she's not a horrible person."

"I'm not afraid of commitment!"

He moved his hand vaguely and I didn't argue: we weren't there for a therapy session for me, that would really have been the biggest possible cherry on a sundae that was already enormous as it was.

"You're an incredible guy, Christophe."

"Pardon?"

"You're an incredible guy. Anyone else would have told me to fuck off."

"Oh, I thought about it. I spent a month telling you to fuck off in my head. I was telling you to fuck off when I was taking a shower, making breakfast, having a beer, writing my papers, having dinner with friends – I even told you to fuck off when I was sleeping with another girl. That's when I said to myself that maybe it was time to give it a rest." He half smiled – he was trying to joke, to be friendly and generous. I answered with a smile of my own.

"I understand," I'd answered. "I... You're probably going to chuck your beer in my face if I say I'm sorry again, aren't you?"

"I'm toying with the idea."

"Can I at least say thanks? For being so... I don't know... mature?" I was ashamed of myself. I couldn't get my thoughts out, all I could get out were the usual niceties, and not only had this young man loved me, but apparently I hadn't really even seen who he was. So I repeated the only thing that seemed absolutely sincere to me, the only thought I had: "You're really incredible. I mean it."

"Well, not incredible enough, it seems." He got up and placed a hand on my shoulder. "Ciao, Marine."

"I... Ciao?" It seemed like we'd only just started talking – and at the same time, I could see very well that we'd said all there was to say, and that I was very lucky to have met such a clear-headed guy who was willing to talk. Really, there wasn't anything else left to say.

"Ciao," he repeated. And he left with a wave at Jeff and Laurent who were staring at us from the bar.

Ever since, his words had haunted me. Not heavily, not horribly – in fact, they had the immeasurable, changing weight of the truth, they moved about within me, traveling around my mind, sometimes almost disappearing, and at others impossible to ignore, like the proof I would have preferred to ignore, but this was exactly what I couldn't do anymore.

I walked around the apartment one more time, as if this could make Jeff suddenly appear. I'd gotten worked up, like I often did, talking to the plants or the cat, and it seemed not only like I had a thousand things to say to Jeff, but that each one of them was of the utmost importance. Part of me, stubbornly lucid and able to fight off the ongoing attacks from my irrationality, knew very well that the answer wasn't in Jeff or in the unending emails I was exchanging with my brother, but rather within me. It was simplistic, but for years, I'd been asking other people and what I called "life in general" for answers about everything. I expected answers from Laurent, Jeff and Julien, and I was hoping to get answers from Gabriel.

When I thought of him, I couldn't help but smile. It was beyond my power to stop believing, to stop saddling other people with countless nice but crazy hopes, I couldn't help it. Laurent often teased me about it – he'd ask the same question about every man that came into my life after him: "Another savior?" but I knew he'd be as devastated as me if I stopped doing it, if I simply capitulated to the reality which, despite all the years and experiences, I outright refused to accept.

I knew it was one of the things that linked us, all four of us: our ferocious and almost violent belief in a fabu-

lous future, one worthy of our dreams, which we refused
to abandon. We lived in a state of expectation, I knew that
– that everything around us had a sheen that said "while
we're waiting." People, actions, relationships whose only
importance was that they preceded that final happiness
that we had declared was inevitable. Sometimes I wonder
if this wasn't what was going to do us in, too, if this
despotic optimism meant that all four of us were going to
end up eighty years old, in rocking chairs on a retirement-
home porch, grumpy, bitter and above all completely
alone because we'd refused to compromise in the least,
and had willingly remained children, out of fear of betraying what we had been.

"You don't make any compromises, either, do you,
boy?" I gave Claude François a little kiss on top of his fra-
grant head. The rather abstract idea that in reality he had
made THE compromise we all hated the most when he
agreed, without even knowing it, to become a domesti-
cated animal.

I texted Laurent: "Do you think we're free?" Two minutes later: "What's with the intense questions at 4 in the
afternoon?" I replied: "Seriously, do you think we're free
people?" And when he came right back with "You're asking a guy who's been a slave to worry and hare-brained
ideas since forever. What do you think?" Then, I said to
the cat, "That's exactly what I thought."

"How are you?" Élodie asked me as she pretended to
straighten out the pencils on my desk. I suspected that she
did absolutely, positively no work while I was out, but I
couldn't get mad at her. An overdeveloped penchant for
laziness had weighed on our family for generations (our
great-grandfather on our father's side, whom we had
known, bragged about spending more time asleep than
awake every day, and our mother's mother had brought her
children up on TV dinners, the most important discovery

since the wheel, according to her, and it was a close race). Personally, my laziness could be frightening and I knew that if I had a job like Frédéric's where no client was waiting for me to deliver my work at a set date that couldn't be changed, I'd have done exactly what he'd been doing for the two years he'd been living in Paris writing a novel, in other words, absolutely nothing.

"Fine, fine," I muttered half-heartedly, as I put down my things. She was moving the pencils from one spot to another, without any particular goal or order. I watched her for a minute, mentally challenging myself to figure out the logic behind her movements, but it was impossible. Markers, charcoals, pastels, without any thought for the brands or even the colors, were moved and re-moved by her hands. I would have almost smiled if I hadn't been in such a bad mood.

"Okay, okay, okay," Élodie said in a tone that was totally out of place in her – the one mothers sometimes use with their children when they realize their troubles come from their own whims. "*What's* wrong?"

I leaned against the drawing table and crossed my arms. "You want to know what's wrong?"

"Of course," sounded more like "Absolutely not, to tell you the truth."

"I'm thirty-two years old and I just discovered that the great liberty I thought characterized me is actually the exact opposite. In other words not only am I not free, on top of that, I've been wrong about myself for years. Any questions?"

Élodie looked up at me and gave a little, only slightly exaggerated sigh. She looked discouraged, like someone who's just found out there's not just one hour left in the car ride, but four. This time, I couldn't help but smile.

"Are you kidding me?" she said, and this time the sub-text read, "Are you really going to put me through this?"

"Hey... you're the one who asked," I said, still smiling.

She shrugged her shoulders to show that obviously I was too stupid to understand that her question was completely insincere, and that I was just about beyond hope. I was putting a fresh sheet on my drawing table when she said, "I could have told you that *years* ago. You and your fucking ideals. At least, with Laurent, you seemed to understand that it was all right if everything wasn't perfect all the time and maybe even that's what makes things interesting, but now… pshhhht!" At the top of her forehead, she made a gesture to simulate an open skull with its reason leaking out. "Off in the clouds again. Man, sometimes it's like you're fifteen years old or something."

"Oh, because I suppose your mental age is like forty?" I retorted, feeling exactly like I was fifteen years old.

"No," said Élodie with another shrug of her shoulders. "But at least I'm not fooling myself." Then, undoubtedly sorry about how harsh her tone was and how bitter her words were, she added, "*You'll* try to fool yourself with three pounds of lip gloss and a half-ton of hair spray."

"But I thought that was the point of lip gloss and hair spray – cultivating illusion!"

"In other people, sure. But not in yourself. I'll tell you, you're unusually clear-headed when you realize it takes you an hour to put on your make-up and do your hair in the morning. There's no chance of cultivating illusion when you can feel that your hair is literally solid."

"Élo…" I had a ton of jokes to make, but even I had illusions I didn't know how to cultivate anymore. I missed the comfortable attitude I had when I was twenty. Nowadays I had to work hard on it, I had to keep going over it, digging out the weeds that represented my most realistic thoughts. No, it's not going to go like you want it to – what you don't know yet is whether it's going to be just not completely or not at all. Yes, there will be personal disappointments and capitulations. You know that one day you'll feel like you've betrayed yourself and you know that the worst part is that this betrayal won't seem all that awful. No, love is not all powerful. No, your life will not be a luminous slideshow of images snapped in moments of pure happiness you still imagine. And no, nothing will be easy.

I pulled and pulled these thistles from around the glorious flowers of the life I dreamed, but sometimes, and more and more often, I wondered if the thistle deserved to be considered as well, and a part of me could see that it would eventually take over the whole garden, because it was inevitable, wasn't it? Weeds always end up covering over everything. And sometimes it was magnificent. But I wasn't ready to throw in the towel yet. I kept on hoeing and weeding, and cultivated impossible pictures of Gabriel and me, laughing in the sun, our arms around each other by a lake and surrounded by friends who were laughing too, because our happiness was so contagious.

"Okay," I said. "I cannot *believe* I'm going to ask you this, but do you really think I'm fooling myself?"

Élodie gave a surprised little laugh. "Wow, call the media, send out a press release, do something, my big sister just asked my opinion about a serious subject. The world has turned upside down!"

"Okay, sarcasm is nice and all that, but seriously, Élo."

"Marine," she laughed again – this time it was a spontaneous laugh of disbelief, "are you kidding me?"

"Hmmm… that bad, eh?" I'd started sketching – inexplicably, the conversation had made me uncomfortable, part of me was very ill at ease with letting Élodie see my weaknesses. On the white sheet, a horse was taking shape.

"Marine," said Élodie, "I've never seen such a thing. When I was little, I thought it was normal, but, no offense, after a couple of spins around the real world, uh-uh." She used her finger and head to make the caricature "no" gesture made on sitcoms by Black women with names like LaTeesha, or by white women when they want to imitate them. "No waayaaay," she added with the accent.

"Really…" My horse had an enormous tail that was starting to stretch across the top of the sheet, and dripping curls around him. "It's not THAT bad," I said.

"Hey now, I'm not saying it's terrible, or a real flaw or whatever, but if you're going to ask me the question, I'm going to tell you what I think, that's all. You've *always* dreamed of impossible things…"

I could still see myself, in my pajamas in the girls' bedroom – I must have been fourteen, they were eight and five – telling them crazy stories that I spent hours making up and polishing. I'd make up stories about myself, and tell them about the electrifying love affair that would happen to me when I was almost eighteen, when, in a lovely seaside restaurant, in Mexico, a handsome twenty-three-year-old American would ask me to dance, lightly pressing my lower back, just above my coccyx, to the rhythm of "Samba Pa Ti." The men would change – movie stars, characters from novels (how many affairs did I have with the Count of Monte Cristo!), boys who were older than me that I'd pass in the school hallways but never dared speak to – everything (and everyone) was a good reason to dream.

"Everyone does that!" I said, like an offended little girl.

"Not when they're thirty, Marine. And don't look at me like that – I know you still do it."

The horse's tail had turned into a torrent, cascading down the sheet, getting larger with every line.

"That's nice," said Élodie.

"Well."

"No, seriously. Can I have it when you're done?"

"Élo, really. It's nothing."

"I don't care, I like it. Can I have it?"

"Yeah… I guess so."

She came closer and stood right next to me. We were both looking at the pencil. She smelled like strawberries and candy, and I wondered if men really liked this sweet smell that in no way resembled the human beings we were. "You know," she said, "sometimes I wonder if I'm the one who's wrong, if maybe we should all hope for crazy things. What you have in your head is great."

I turned towards her and looked at her. Looking each other in the eyes, we smiled awkwardly and finally came back to the horse. "But I just don't know," Elodie continued. "Part of me thinks... you know."

"What?" I knew. Jeff had told me, Julien had told me, I even told myself rather regularly.

"That thinking like that you might just be setting yourself up for disappointment. It's rare for illusions to materialize."

And, as if her final words were a magic spell, the doorbell rang. It was a delivery from a florist, with a compact bouquet of orangish roses with a note: "You told me there was nothing healthier than giving in to your head. Well, here's my head. See you Monday, Gabriel. P.S. Would the pun be too bad if I said I was really giving in to my heart?"

Sincerely astounded, Élodie and I looked at each other.

"Okay," she finally said. "You set this up, didn't you? Is the guy from your stories hanging around somewhere?"

I didn't say a word, I was too busy standing there with my mouth open. After a few seconds, I started hopping around, stupidly, squeezing the poor bouquet against me. And I saw that Élodie wasn't as cynical or clear-headed as she wanted to believe when she started hopping around, too, applauding the wonderful intervention of chance that allowed us to continue to dream.

Laurent was furiously agitating an empty salt shaker over his steak tartar. "COME ON, can you possibly be any MORE retro? Sending FLOWERS?"

"Can you be any MORE bitter?"

"I am not bitter, but what's the next step in retro? Sleeping with your personal trainer, maybe?"

"Hey! My trainer is incredibly adorable, he has the most beautiful blue eyes in the world and an ass that would send a saint to hell…"

"Meow!" said Julien.

"He pees sitting down," I said to clear things up.

"I don't give a shit if he pees standing on his head, darling. I've seen his body and M-E-O-W, meow."

"B-A-R-F, barf?" Laurent suggested.

Julien and I burst out laughing and I thought it was the happiest moment of my week. "You know you're ridiculous, right?" he added. Julien and I nodded our heads with exaggerated seriousness. "FLOWERS. Who still sends flowers? FLOWERS."

"Maybe you could cut down a little on the emphasis?" I asked.

"Maybe?" Julien added.

"No, but, ffff… flowers." This time he didn't shout the word, he simply spit it out sluggishly, as if the entire floral kingdom was a known source of scorn all over the Western world. "Flowers…"

"You sent me flowers!"

"Yeah, for your birthday!" Laurent gave his usual sigh, but I could see he was really angry, that his absurd fit about a bouquet of roses had deeper roots.

"Come on, now, really!" he finally grumbled. "Who is he, anyway? He sends us flowers and we don't even know who he is!" And with the mention of "we," the childish slip from "he sends you" to "he sends us" my heart melted so noticeably that Julien felt the need to rub his hand down my back. At that moment, I thought that if I were a little more drunk or a little more courageous, I would have told them that "me" and "us" were inevitably going to have to go our separate ways, even if it was just for a little while. But I was still unable to, physically unable, because such an admission would have catapulted me into a life that, like my metaphorical thistles, I was still unable to accept.

"It's super sweet," said Julien. Then, turning to me, "Okay, exactly how many hours do you want us to spend on this? 'Cause it's a big topic. Thinking with the head, thinking with the heart. We have to debrief."

"Not in front of me," Laurent protested, in a very decisive tone. I objected with a futile, "Come on, now," but he was already on his feet, his tartar hardly touched.

"Loulou!" I had the feeling that if he got up, if he didn't approve of the gesture, that the roses would automatically wilt. I didn't want him to spoil my roses. "Loulou," I repeated – and I felt the sad begging in my voice. I wasn't ready yet to let them go, "I saw Carole last Tuesday."

"What?!" If I'd said I'd spent the day before screwing Donald Duck, he would have seemed less surprised.

"I saw Carole. At that ridiculous café not far from your place. I was glad to see her."

Julien's intelligent look moved back and forth between us.

"I figure," said Laurent, "I fucking figure you were glad to see her." He looked surprised, suddenly, as if he couldn't believe his own vehemence, and he looked around, looking for something, an idea that suddenly seemed to dawn on him. He started talking with more energy, with a sincerity I was unfamiliar with, and that hurt me. "I'm sorry, okay? I'm tired, okay? I'm really fucking tired. I'm EXHAUSTED." And he left without adding another word, leaving us with a half a tartar and a whole lot of frites that normally would have attracted my undivided attention. And since he was the only person who could still hurt me, I started to cry. Julien rubbed a tender, welcome hand down my back.

"I'm tired, too, okay?" My voice was weak and not very believable – but I was tired. I was exhausted in fact, and I was ashamed of it. When he saw my tears, one of the servers discreetly brought me over a glass of wine – a kind, disinterested gesture that made me cry even more.

"I have no right to be exhausted."

"Oh, fuck. Fuck what everybody thinks. Yes, Ti-Joe the Ethiopian is undoubtedly a lot more tired than you. But what are you going to do about that, Marine? Stop feeling anything until there's peace on earth? Because, I don't want to disappoint you, but that may take quite a while."

"Yeah, but…"

"Tut, tut, tut." He raised the glass of wine to my lips. "I don't know about you, but if I was a starving child or a miner in Sierra Leone stuck in a bad movie with Leonardo DiCaprio, normal Westerners who pretend to worry about my fate would get on my fucking nerves even more than the ones who have the decency to admit they can't do anything about it."

"Ju!!!"

"Stop!" he said. "Stop!" He had me by the shoulders. "Stop feeling guilty, okay? IT DOESN'T DO ANY GOOD."

He'd become as vehement as Laurent and I was aware that not only was I crying, but in addition to that we were talking very loud.

"Come on," said Julien.

"No, but the check… We haven't paid for everything…"

"Come on."

He was domineering, and I understood what his young boyfriends saw in him. He kept his arm around my shoulders till we got home – two short blocks in the March slush.

"Talk to him," Julien said, leaving me in front of our place. "Be a woman." He was smiling. Under normal circumstances I would have replied, "You're the one who dreams of being a woman!" but I couldn't do it.

"Hellllooooo?" I asked as I stepped into the condo. For a minute, I stood ridiculously on what my mother insisted on calling "the stoop," my head barely inside the door.

"Uh… hello?" answered Jeff's voice. "What are you doing, selling chocolate?"

"No…"

"Well, then, maybe you want to come in?"

Which I did. I felt tiny, with all my late-winter trappings, in addition to all the trappings of a little girl who doesn't know how to become a woman.

"What is it?" Jeff asked me when I finally stood there in front of him. He was sitting in his La-Z-Boy, with a beer in his hand. On TV, guys in red were fighting over a puck with guys in blue and white. "What is it?" repeated Jeff.

"Jeff…" I was avoiding my own question.

"What?" He had the encouraging look of people who really want to hear what you have to say. And, out of deference for this enthusiasm, but mostly out of cowardice, I answered, "Do you really think we're grown-ups?"

He started laughing. His laugh was a triumph over all the faults we possessed, it made our human condition acceptable. "Grown-ups?! No, Marine. No."

"No?"

"No."

I don't know if he saw me go to pieces right there, but he stood up to take me in his arms, as I weakly melted, under the skimpy weight of my own sadness, onto the sofa. He laughed and stroked my hair, repeating it wasn't that bad, that I had nothing to be mad at myself for.

"Do you want a drink?" he finally asked.

"Do I ever! Nothing weird like Julien, okay?"

"Nothing weird. I'll make your day, sweetie," he said with a bad English accent (he persisted in believing – and wanted to believe – that Brooklyn was pronounced Brookelinde). And as he got up to "mec maï daey," I was so afraid that he'd really make my day that I jumped right up.

"I'm seeing Gabriel on Monday." The words were barely out of my mouth when I realized I'd nearly shouted them.

"Wow," said Jeff, pouring what looked to me like too much vodka into the shaker. "Cool." He pivoted around to get the ice cubes from the freezer. "Flavie's coming to dinner next Tuesday."

"Oh."

"Oh?"

He turned around. "What? That's not good for you?" I heard myself answer, "Why wouldn't it be good?" and we found ourselves, housemates for three years, friends for fifteen years, face to face, without a single word between us, where there was nothing but silence and stares

To: Fred
From: Marine Vandale
Subject: Collapse

....

Be honest with your little sister: is there a universal law that
says as soon as the tiniest thing starts to go right in your life,
everything alse falls to pieces and everyone except you knew it
would?

To: Marine
From: Frédéric Vandale
Subject: Chaos theory

....

I would be of the opinion that it's better not to make any
sweeping statements, but that is indeed a rumor that's going
around. In any case, that's what my housemate says. You may
reply that it's arguable, but he claims that in order to keep us
from imploding as individuals, there has to be unhappiness to
balance out happiness, because too much happiness would be
too heavy.

To: Fred
From: Marine Vandale
Subject: Oh, you optimist

....

Your housemate sounds like a real blast. Did it ever occur to
him that too much unhappiness can be a trifle heavy? I have
half of Bangladesh on the other line to confirm it for you, you
know.

To: Marine
From: Frédéric Vandale
Subject: Lame theory

....

Yeah, honestly, that theory really hasn't been proven. I think it comes from a kind of Judeo-Christian background that wants us all to think you can be unhappy without bothering anybody else, but that too much happiness isn't appropriate. It's the idea that you have to pay some how.

To: Fred
From: Marine Vandale
Subject: Huge Debt

....

Are you telling me that I have to pay because somewhere up ahead of me the end of some vague tunnel is about to appear?

To: Marine
From: Frédéric Vandale
Subject: Blame the housemate

....

Hey, don't get carried away, okay? My housemate also firmly believes that happy people should be sent to concentration camps and that *Big Brother* is quality TV. So there's no reason to get worked up over what he says.

To: Fred
From: Marine Vandale
Subject: Influential housemate

....

Far be it from me to confirm the quality of *Big Brother*, but I have to admit that the way things are going, I really want to believe he's not wrong about paying for happiness.

To: Marine
From: Frédéric Vandale
Subject: The price of happiness

....

Did you talk to Jeff?

To: Fred
From: Marine Vandale
Subject: Re: The price of happiness

....

Yes, and I don't even feel like telling you what we talked about.
And then Laurent got all upset, too, and I feel like I'm not capable of communicating with them anymore. And, this will make
you laugh, but the happiness I'm finding in other places does-
n't really tempt me if I can't share it with those two clowns.

To: Marine
From: Frédéric Vandale
Subject: Complicated clowns

....

Yeah, but those two clowns of yours have never been simple.
That's why you like them though, isn't it? What would you do
with friends who literally lived with everything right out there
in the open? Depth is what makes us beautiful, Marine.

To: Fred
From: Marine Vandale
Subject: You been drinking?

....

Okay, do me a huge favor and keep that kind of statement to
yourself, okay? Especially since, as far back as I remember, as
far as depth is concerned, in your case, we'll let it go. I'm going
to write a pamphlet in defense of what's simple. I'm sick and
tired of everything being complicated. Complication is not my
friend anymore.

To: Marine
From: Frédéric Vandale
Subject: Let's get into the depths

....

Well, now, I will be nice and magnanimous and ignore your
unkind comment about depth, which you say I don't possess,

when everyone knows I'm a veritable human bathyscaph. Tell me what Jeff possibly could have told you to turn you into the poster child for simplicity.

To: Fred
From: Marine Vandale
Subject: Angry poster child

....

It's too absurd, Fred, the very idea of it makes me feel incredibly drained. If my two clowns were at least complicated the way other people are, I could take it. But we're complicated like spoiled children and I'm starting not to think it's funny anymore.

To: Marine
From: Frédéric Vandale
Subject: Back and forth

....

Will you be mad at me if I say that, from here, your stories are giving me the faint impression you're going around in circles?

To: Fred
From: Marine Vandale
Subject: I'm pouting

....

I'm never telling you anything again.

To: Marine
From: Frédéric Vandale
Subject: Re: I'm pouting

....

You know that when you were little, you only used to pout when you knew you were wrong or, in other words, when I was right? What did you say to each other, Marine?

To: Fred

From: Marine Vandale
Subject: RE: I'm pouting

....

Nothing.

To: Marine
From: Fred Vandale
Subject: Reaching out

....

Help me to help you, you little pouter.

To: Fred
From: Marine
Subject: Re: Reaching out

....

Fred. I'm all confused.
    :)

Chapter 9

I shut the computer abruptly – my own sentence scared me and I was mad at myself for writing it to Fred, and, thereby, admitting it to myself. The house was quiet. No noise came from outside, it was a lazy, snowy Saturday morning. Inside, nothing was moving. I was sitting at my desk, giving the computer an evil stare as if it were responsible for my secret, Claude François was sleeping in his fruit bowl, and Jeff's bedroom door was still closed. He'd come in late the night before, after he suddenly went out following our conversation. I'd heard him, at around three in the morning, walking across the condo as quietly as possible, using a low voice to guide a girl, it had to be Marie-Lune – he always turned to her when he was annoyed.

We'd said nothing for a minute, I was standing in front of the sofa, next to the refrigerator, he was holding the ice cube tray. I was waiting for him to answer my ridiculous question, and he was obviously waiting for me to go on. When it's pronounced in an aggressive, paranoid tone, "Why wouldn't it be good?" sounds more like a cry from the heart than a constructive question.

"Um… you want… um … you want a vodka-tonic?" He couldn't stand silence. This was often practical, but even if I was grateful to him for breaking the ice, this time, I would have preferred something a little less about drinking and a little more about us.

"Jeff…"

"Gin and tonic?"

"Jeff…"

"With cucumber? Well, you said nothing too strong...
A Ricard maybe?

"Jeff!"

"Christ! What? Christ! Do you really want to have this
conversation?"

"What conversation, Jeff? I don't even know what conversation we're talking about. In fact, I feel like we're not
having any conversations. So I don't even know which
conversation 'this conversation' is. Enlighten me."

"Oh, no, you're not going to get away with it like that
again."

"What do you mean, 'like that'?"

He had finished making what evidently was a mixture
of pure vodka with a drizzle of lime juice, with an energy
I'd never seen in him before. He was always the calm one,
and was such a master of the art of nonchalance that he
used it as a charming tool, but now his jerky, rapid movements were hurting me, and making me want to say forget
it, drop it, come sit next to me with your straight vodka
and pretend everything was like it was before. But of
course, everything wasn't like it was before, everything
couldn't be like it was before and I had to stop feeling like
it was something horrible like premature aging, the possibility I'd never be loved, and the idea that my father
could forget everything.

"What do you mean, 'like that'?" I repeated.

"Like that," he said putting a glass down in front of me
with an abrupt movement that was almost aggressive.
"You always manage to get other people to say everything
for you. It doesn't matter if it's me, or Julien or even your
brother, who's fucking six thousand kilometers away, who
answer your questions." He started imitating me with a
caricatured little voice which, I have to admit, was pretty
accurate. "'What am I going to do, Jeff?' 'What should I
think, Fred?' 'Juuuuuuu, what would you do if you were
me?' 'Guys, why is everything always so complicated?'

Geez," he shouted in his own voice. "We don't have any more answers than you do, okay? And we certainly don't have YOUR answers. So if you have something to say to me, say it. But don't ask me to say it for you."

I'd felt like chucking my glass in his face, or running to my room, where I could already see myself slamming the door, with fiery panache. My brother was right: when I was wrong, I pouted.

"Okay," I said, "okay." I'd mentally counted to five like someone about to jump into a pool that's too cold, then I started talking really quickly. "I feel like I can't talk to you anymore. I feel like something's changed between us because of what I did. I feel like you're anything but happy for me about Gabriel and…"

"And what?"

"Well, it bugs the shit out of me that you're cruising my only fucking girlfriend, and I feel like…"

"You feel like a lot of things, Marine."

"SHUT UP! You wanted me to talk, so I'm talking. So don't piss me off."

He looked a little surprised – how had we become these two vehement, unpleasant people? We'd never spoken to each other like this before – personally I'd never spoken to anybody like this before. "Shut up?!" I thought. Since when did I say "Shut up" and really mean it?

"So," I continued, "I feel like if you've suddenly set your heart on Flavie, it's partly to get back at me."

"I've always liked Flavie."

"Yeah, but…" Yeah, but what, Sainte Marine? He was completely right. "Well," I said as I took a drink that made me scowl. "Okay, then." We didn't say anything for quite a while, each keeping busy examining the pattern in the carpet.

"Sorry," I'd finally said. "I can't believe I said, 'Shut up.'"

He smiled a little. "It's okay. I might have gone a little too far myself."

"See? That's what I mean. How did we ever end up talking to each other like that?"

He'd sighed and sat forward on his chair. "Look, I don't think I invited Flavie over just to piss you off. Maybe on some kind of subconscious level..."

"YOU have a subconscious?" Somebody had to make a joke. He'd laughed, gratefully.

"It's teeny tiny, but it's there. So, maybe subconsciously that was a little part of it. Because it bugs me that you're hung up on some guy who's so ..." He rubbed his finger and thumb together as he searched for the right word. "So *real*. Something like that, and I'm not kidding around... We all knew it wouldn't last with Christophe. But Gabriel, I don't know. He's believable. So, it has an effect on me."

I'd opened my mouth to say something, but Jeff quickly raised a hand to interrupt me.

"Maybe it's because we're afraid of losing you," he went on. "Plus, if you really want me to be honest... do you want me to be honest?"

"Yes, I really do."

"There's no doubt that what happened in my room upset me. Because, once you open the door to sexuality with someone..."

"Hey! That's Julien's theory!"

"Hmmm?"

"Ah-ha! Jean-François Murphy, you've been talking to Julien!"

"You did, too?"

"What do you think?" We both started laughing. Laughter's sweet release. "So, you thought it might be special, too."

"Maybe," he said with a little grin.

"No chance you'd talk about it to me, Saint Jeff!"

"You weren't talking to me, either!"

"I tried!"

"Sure, by asking your fucking questions, again. 'Jeeeefff,

you okay?' 'Claude François, do you think *Papa*'s mad at
Maman?' 'Inanimate plant, has something changed?'"

"You know I talk to the plants?" He raised his eyebrows
like he always did when he wanted to say, "You can't hide
anything from me."

"So?" I'd asked.

"So, don't worry. I think we've clearly established we
don't want to lose each other, right?"

Suddenly, I had a gentle desire to cry. He'd smiled at
me again and got up, setting his empty glass on the coffee
table. "I'm going to go for a walk."

"You sure you're okay?"

"Marine…" I nearly reminded him that when he *went
for a walk*, it was usually because something was bothering him, but I thought that maybe it wasn't a good idea to
talk too much, either, and if things weren't going to
change between us, we were each going to have to let each
live their life, like we always had. Jeff gave me a kiss on the
head. "You know I love you, right?"

"Yes, I know." His hand had lingered on my shoulder,
then he'd gone out. I'd sat in the silence for a long time,
replaying our conversation in my head. But the more I'd
thought about it, the more I'd realized we hadn't said anything, really, and the door to sexuality that we'd both
mentioned was still open, maybe even wider than before.

"I can't believe he didn't say anything more than that,"
I said to the plant. "Shit, that's the second time he did that
to me!"

I made a face at Jeff's closed bedroom door. I was anxious
to see him, and, also to face him with Marie-Lune, and
find a little bit of our routine in a more or less quiet morning with him. Maybe having Marie-Lune present at
breakfast would also make it possible for me to dream a
little of Gabriel, whose bouquet of roses still brightened
the dining-room table, without constantly tripping over

Jeff.

Mechanically, I removed one of the roses that was starting to fade from the vase, but its petals were only the softer for it, like the cheeks of very old women. I took my coffee and my rose and settled in quietly at the big table.

I was doing a Sudoku (a vile, repulsive little game that only requires one thing: not having any qualms about wasting your time or, like in my case, a serious desire to waste it), when the girl came out of Jeff's room. I looked up at her – it wasn't Marie-Lune, but a girl who looked a lot like her and who must have been about Élodie's age and who also could have been her best friend: she was pretty like her, with deliberately more of a girl's beauty than a woman's, and she had the same joyful, carefree and impulsive air that reminded me of a canary or a parakeet or some other hopping, little bird. Stupidly, I felt a wave of relief when I noticed it wasn't Flavie. I knew this kind of girl was only passing through. The Marie-Lunes never stayed long. I thought again about what Jeff had said, that Gabriel was "real."

"Hi!" she said, much too cheerfully for my taste, reaching a hand towards me. "Marie-Soleil." That's a hell of a joke, I thought to myself.

"Marie-Soleil?" I asked, taking her hand. "Really?"

"Umm… yes… really…" I looked behind her to see if I could spot Jeff, because I had to share how funny the situation was with someone. But his bedroom door was shut, and Marie-Soleil was standing there in front of me, perhaps waiting for me to entertain or feed her. She was wearing one of Jeff's shirts – Why do they all do that, I wondered. All the girls Jeff brought home came out of his room wearing one of his shirts. What made Jeff's lovers want to put on his clothes? I was perfectly aware of the custom of putting on the guy's shirt after a night of love. But in his case, they did it systematically. I'm going to have to talk to Julien about this, I thought. He must have a theory.

"I think Jeff's in rough shape this morning," said Marie-Soleil. "He's going to stay in bed a while." Jeff could have drunk all the grappa in the world and he still wouldn't be in rough shape. I knew him; I'd seem him knock back whole cases of wine and get up the next morning with hardly a wrinkle. I made a mental note to make him pay for his fake hangover which left me face to face with a girl who was in an unnaturally good mood for nine a.m. on a Saturday morning. I imagined the rest of my existence, a series of coffees drunk with Marie-Noëlles, Marie-Avrils, Marie-Québecs and Marie-Sourires, while Jeff pretended to recuperate in his room.

"You want some coffee?" I finally asked.

"That'd be super sweet of you!"

I pointed at the coffee maker. "The coffee's in the jar next to it, and the grinder's on the right." I was not "super sweet," no, ma'am. Not today. But it would have taken a thousand times more to diminish Marie-Soleil's good mood (was Jeff that good in bed? or maybe Marie-Soleil was just perpetually cheerful. What a terrifying idea), and she went and made herself some coffee while she sang to herself. I observed her for a minute – she really was very pretty, and she used an espresso machine like she was born with one in her hands. She must be a server or a barmaid, I thought. Jeff had an almost supernatural knack with those girls. He'd go into a bar, choose the prettiest one, and leave with her, no exceptions. Laurent had made him promise to teach him.

"You work in a restaurant?" I asked her.

"In a bar. At Le Lulli. I've seen you lots. Marine, right?" I looked at her more closely. Her face didn't look at all familiar, and I felt a little bad about it. But she went right on smiling, apparently without noticing that my gaze had gone completely hollow.

"You're always in *such* good company," Marie-Soleil

went on. "You know we even have kind of the same taste?"

"The same taste?"

"Yeah!" Her reply suggested it was the most mar-velously delicious bit of news since the invention of chocolate. "Well… I was with Christophe for a while."

I didn't say anything. I did *not* want to know she'd been with Christophe for a while, and I was incapable of figur-ing out how she could think this bit of information would interest me.

"You know, Christophe? Cute little Christophe? The one with the beauty mark and… you know, your ex?"

"Yeah, okay, I know."

"So there's Christophe, and now Jeff."

"I'm not going out with Jeff. I've never gone out with Jeff." I'd spoken too fast, my tone was abrupt and rushed, and, according to Claude François' ears, much too high-pitched.

"You two *never* went out?" Marie-Soleil seemed aston-ished. "Oh, girl, you're really missing out." Had she been brought up by some powerful sect to say exactly what I didn't want to hear? I expected her to finish off by telling me she was Gabriel's girlfriend. "Really. Seriously. Jeff…" She sat down and lowered her voice like girls do when they want to emphasize that what they're about to say is part of the magical, marvelous world of girl talk. "He's so dirty… Yesterday, he…"

I was saved by Claude François – sweet, sweet kitty – who jumped up on the table, blond and cute as he was, causing Marie-Miss-Sunshine to release a stream of laughter and "Helloo, baaabyyyy" that I could have found delightful at some other hour of the day. Once the cat left, undoubtedly frightened off by so much cheerfulness, Marie-Soleil came and sat behind me. Fortunately, she seemed to have lost her train of thought and magically forgotten how dirty Jeff was, just as he was coming out of his room, in boxers, with his hair a mess.

"How's it going?" asked Jeff in his best hangover voice.

"Fine."

"You met…"

"Marie-Soleil. Yep." My smile must have been at least ten inches wide and I had to hold myself back not to start teasing him right away, in front of Marie-Soleil. You're one to talk about your attraction to strong, flamboyant women, I felt like saying. You always come back to Marie-Morning-or-Evening-Stars. Besides, I didn't know why he couldn't simply admit that he preferred being with kind, young girls instead of exuberant women. He must have been trying to live up to some idea of himself. We all did that, I knew, but Jeff? I always thought he was the most at ease with himself of anyone I knew. Just goes to show, I thought. There was something touching in the discovery of his little weakness.

Three-quarters of an hour later, he was sitting in front of me, with Marie-Soleil on his lap, trying to focus his attention on a crossword puzzle, when, in the entryway, I heard Julien's voice.

"Anybody home?" Jeff shot me a panicked look, but I was already on my feet, literally hopping up to go head off Julien.

"Hello, hello," he said, as he took off his coat and boots. He was wearing red jeans, a violet cashmere sweater and green socks. It was like information overload. I was about to make a remark when his eyes popped open wide – he'd just spotted Jeff, who suddenly decided to pour all his concentration into a sports article. Marie-Soleil had stood up, and was standing next to him, radiant.

"What the hell's he doing here?" said Jeff, to no one in particular, or, perhaps, to Réjean Tremblay's picture.

"I'm all out of coffee."

"Isn't there a coffee shop downstairs from you?" I

asked. It was a very bad excuse. Julien lived pretty far from us, but since he couldn't stand to be alone, he usually showed up at our place every Saturday morning, blaming a lack of milk, oranges, newspapers or oxygen. Jeff sighed as he unfolded his paper, then, folding over another page and without looking up, he added, "We really have to stop giving our keys to just anybody."

"Julien," I said triumphantly, "let me introduce…" I paused to savor the moment, but Julien had already extended a hand to her.

"We've already met, haven't we?" he asked. "Don't you work at Le Lulli?"

"On weekends, I do. Marie-Soleil," she added, with a radiant smile on her lips, taking Julien's hand, though he nearly didn't notice, busy as he was giving me a doubtful look.

"Really?"

Marie-Soleil seemed a little surprised by this repeated reaction, but she smiled cheerfully, and I wondered if there was anything she didn't do cheerfully. She probably even screwed cheerfully. Laughing even.

"But, errr…" Julien stammered after saying hello to Marie-Soleil, and giving a hand first to Jeff, then to me. "What about you two… everything okay? Did you talk?" He was pathologically unable to be discreet. Neither one of us answered, and obviously, Julien insisted. "Seriously, did you…?"

"Tut-tut-tut," interrupted Jeff, raising a finger at Julien that demanded he be quiet.

"Tut-tut-tut?" asked Julien.

"Yep, tut-tut-tut," I confirmed.

"Tut-tut-fucking-tut," Jeff clarified.

"Tut-tut," Marie-Chickadee hummed to herself, as she went to make herself another cup of coffee. Julien gave a sigh that was disappointed and also revealed his slight anger, then reached towards the newspapers.

"Can you pass me the first section, Jeff? OOH! Mario Dumont. Did I ever tell you I fantasized about Mario Dumont?"

"Christ," sighed Jeff.

"Hey, I didn't say I agreed with his politics. Lord, far from it, but… I don't know… I don't hate that carnivorous smile of his."

"Personally, I like Marc-André Grondin," chirped Marie-Soleil.

"Any coffee left?" asked Laurent as he came in. He was wearing black linen pants, huge boots and a heavy coat that revealed the top of his long johns and had a furry hood that was still snug to his face.

"Hey, Bernard Voyer, how's it going?"

"What?" he asked me. "Mountain biking in the snow is a sport."

"You live three blocks away."

"And there's *a lot* of snow!" he shouted in an indignant little voice. "Oh… hi, Ju. Hello, Claude François." He came forward and noticed Marie-Soleil. "Hello."

Laurent also seemed to recognize her and was evidently searching for a name to put with the face, but Julien, beside himself, leapt in front of him and, with one arm stretched towards her, he shouted, or rather he sang as if it were the finale of an opera, "Marie-Soleiiiiiiiiilll!"

Laurent pointed at Marie-Soleil, a smile already dancing across his lips. He looked at me, then looked at Julien, then Jeff, who settled for looking stupid and bringing the newspaper up closer to his face. If he could have, he probably would have wrapped it around his head.

"Ummm…" Laurent looked like someone who walks into a surprise party on a day that wasn't his birthday and then wonders if he's supposed to look happy or if people are making fun of him. "Really?" he finally asked.

"Yes," replied a delighted Julien.

Marie-Soleil, despite her supernatural pep, was starting to think we were seriously lacking in the class department and put her hands on hips to ask, still smiling, "Okay, what's going on?" She must have thought our house was open to every crank in long johns or red jeans there was and that, inexplicably, each of these cranks fell over laughing at the simple mention of her name. The four of us were pretty unbearable, and I wondered how Gabriel could have been attracted to the incestuously exclusive dynamics of our little group. If I hadn't been part of it, it would have been *exactly* the kind of group that seemed too self-satisfied and sarcastic to be nice.

"Don't take it personally," I explained to Marie-Soleil. "It's just that for a while, Jeff was going out with a girl named Marie-Lune, and she looked a little like you, so it's pretty funny. That's all. It doesn't take much to get us going on a Saturday morning."

"Ah! Okay!" Marie-Soleil said in a sing-song voice, before she went over and lightly sat down on Jeff, smashing the paper into his face. "Um… how do you all know each other?" Marie-Soleil asked. Nobody had bothered to explain the sudden presence of two other people in our apartment, acting like we'd always lived together. I was explaining – since Jeff was making no effort, absolutely none, with his nose buried in his paper, undoubtedly hoping Marie-Soleil would leave, which didn't seem at all likely – when the phone rang. Jeff jumped on it and, looking at the call display, he joyfully shouted, "It's your mother!"

He answered, and his first words were, "Madame Vandale. Hello. Fine, fine, thank you. My recipe for osso bucco? Anytime. No, no Marine isn't here." I rolled my eyes, the guys didn't move a muscle, and Marie-Soleil looked even more confused. He spent a good ten minutes talking to my mother, about me (he was actually discreet, or at least he didn't make up anything that would make

my mother even crazier than she was), about himself
("I've been working tons lately"), about his osso bucco
("No, no tomatoes. I know, but that's how it is"), and a lot
about the weather ("Yeah, I know. Minus twenty-three.
Cripes!"). Then he finally hung up.

"Your sisters are on their way over," he said. "And you
can get down on your knees and thank me, because she
was calling to try to talk you into going to your aunt's sev-
entieth birthday in Québec City."

"Oh my God. Thank God. I got her to think I had a
meeting with a superimportant French author who was
only going to be in town for the weekend."

"She believed you?" asked Laurent. He knew my
mother and he knew she was skeptical of everything – if
I'd told her I couldn't come because of an accident, I'd
have to go over and show her the ax stuck in my skull in
order to get her to believe what I'd said. It was the first
time he'd spoken to me since the scene he pulled on me
the night before at the restaurant. I turned towards him
and he gave me that little smile, the one that made him
look like he was ten and a half years old, and was his way
of saying sorry. I puckered my lips, which was my way of
accepting his apology, in a routine we knew by heart. I was
sure that was the only reason he'd come over, unable as
he was to stand having anyone be mad at him.

"No. Of course not. She didn't believe me. But I think
she was being compassionate. Even she'd rather get all her
teeth pulled out than go over there on a Saturday afternoon. It's kind of like she said, 'Save yourself.' Christ, you
know my father's family..." Two nuns, a priest, a golf
fanatic and my seventy-year-old aunt who would have
preached to the Dalai Lama if he showed up at her house.
At least one of the nuns was funny and charming, but she
was currently on a mission in Pondicherry.

"Yeah, well, your sisters didn't get out of it," said Jeff.

Anyway, they're on their way to your mother's but they're going to stop by over here to get you to sign the card."

An hour later, Ariane was in the kitchen, wearing a pair of pants made out of parachute cloth, something like eight sweaters layered one over the other, and, of course, a Peruvian hat.

"Where'd you come from?" she'd asked Laurent when she saw his outfit. "The North Pole?"

"What about you? You come from Machu Picchu?" They both laughed and gave each other a hug.

"You could have forced yourself," Ariane was now saying to me. "It's not like we have to visit *papa*'s family every weekend. And Aunty Livia isn't so young anymore, you know?"

"I have an important meeting this afternoon..." Ariane didn't even pretend to believe me and crossed her arms disapprovingly – sometimes I had the feeling she was the only adult in the family. Poor thing. She turned around to say hello to Marie-Soleil, who seemed completely disconcerted by so much virgin wool, then did what seemed to come naturally to her: she offered coffee.

"Yes, it's fair trade," said Jeff before Ariane could even ask her predictable question. In return, she made the appropriate face and refused.

"Élodie's waiting for me, she's parking the car." Jeff, Julien and Laurent exchanged a panicked look. I had a vision of a car parked vertically on a snowbank.

"In the meantime," said Ariane, "would you mind telling me why your own sister doesn't have a key to your place, but these three boys all do?"

"That is an excellent question," Jeff said.

"Because if I give you one, I'll have to give one to Élodie, and she'll come sleep here every time she's in the neighborhood."

"Julien already does," Jeff pointed out.

"Whatever you say, champ. But you know Élodie, she's

going to sleep in your bed." Marie-Soleil frowned while Julien explained that that was where he'd slept, too. Jeff looked up at me, with a gaze that was filled with words I replied to by turning my head.

"Here," said Ariane, handing me a card, like the kind you find at Jean Coutu's, something with embossed roses and gold lettering evoking the birthday girl's long, wonderful life. I leaned over to write in it.

"Happy Birthday, Beautiful Livia, from your great-niece who loves you and thinks of you often. See you soon, Marine XXX." How many lies where in that little message? "Beautiful Livia?" No, it had been easy to mix Livia up with Martin Scorsese since she'd gotten new glasses and a new set of dentures that were too big, but I did think of her often – as for the "See you soon," I wasn't too straight with that either. I could have easily written "See you in two or three years." There was something unfortunate about these uselessly hypocritical family relationships (on MY birthday cards, with the same embossed roses and the same pompous lettering, Livia always wrote, "To my favorite niece," though the only one of her seven nieces and nephews she could stand was Ariane). Finally, in a futile effort to personalize things, I made a little drawing next to my signature (a winking dog – Livia loved dogs so much that she had them on her doormat, pillows, coasters, a tea service, and who knows how many frames with beagles, terriers and poodles).

"I'll give Aunt Livia a kiss for you," Ariane said to me as she left, and I knew she really would. She always did little things like that, and, like all the causes she took on, it was her way of fighting against the indifference of the world. I found it touching, and even admirable.

She'd barely closed the door behind her when Marie-Soleil said, "Does anyone feel like going out for brunch?"

Jeff, Laurent and I all looked at Julien. The fake hangover hadn't worked, neither had the unpleasant roommate, or the long john–wearing snowman, or the cashmere-wearing clown, not even the sister with a parachute where her pants were supposed to be. It was a case for Julien. He sighed, clasped his hands together enthusiastically and decidedly, then said, "Marie-Soleil, Marie-Soleil, Marie-Soleil..."

"Well, I don't want to bring up something disagreeable," said Laurent when Jeff came back from seeing Marie-Soleil to the door, "but weren't you the one who warned me that unless you already know you want to spend the rest of your LIFE with the girl, you must never, NEVER bring her home – you have to go to her place?"

"I know, I know," answered Jeff as he sat down next to me. I threw a crumpled-up wad of newspaper at him and it bounced off his head.

"And on top of that, I'm the one who had to do the dirty work," said Julien.

"You did a good job."

"Thanks, beautiful."

Julien really did do a good job. He had a way of making people understand what they didn't want to understand without making them feel like they'd had to compromise or abandon some idea they were attached to. It was very useful in his work ("No, no, you're not giving up $25,000 by buying this RRSP. You're *making* $2,800. That's what you want, isn't it?"), and even more helpful when it was time to convince Jeff's lovers that, first of all, they wanted nothing more than to leave the house with their heads held high, and, second, not to call Jeff again for a few months.

I threw another paper wad at Jeff. "You'd better pay attention. Someday some Marie-Happy-Go-Lucky is going to give you a taste of your own medicine. Be honest, Mr. I've-got-it-bad-for-Flavie.

"You're one to talk."

"What does that mean, I'm one to talk?"

"It's not like you're the queen of *honest-being*." He raised one eyebrow, intending it to be full of insinuation, while, out of the corner of my eye, I could see Laurent doubtfully mouthing "*Honest-being?*" at Julien.

"Excuse me?" I asked.

"You know. Gabriel, whatever…" He pointed a finger at him knowingly.

"Arrrgggh… That's fucking arrogant!"

"Okay, whoa, whoa, whoa," said Julien. "Everybody just cool their jets."

"Why aren't you sleeping with him?" Laurent offered.

"Jesus Christ!" I leapt to my feet, with the firm intention of yelling something, but my momentum was broken by the phone.

"Hello?" I answered aggressively.

"Marine? It's your father." I immediately felt a wave of affection wash over me. I'd spent several silent afternoons with him since his tests had begun. He'd never talked much, but when I was with him, I was in the same comfortable, serene state as when I was little, when I could let myself be rocked in his solid love, a love that didn't need words, but settled for a rub on the back, a kiss on the forehead, a cone of soft-serve from the ice cream parlor on the corner.

"Hi, *Papa*! How are you? Did the girls get there yet? Sorry I can't come." It was hard for me to lie to him.

"I'm calling to tell you that the girls are going to come by your place," he said as if he hadn't heard me. "For Aunt Livia's birthday. Are you going to get a ride with them?"

"No, no, *Papa*, I can't come, I…" I'd already told him twice that I couldn't come. I felt my heart tighten up. All I wanted was for him not to be sick, it was visceral – and painful when I had trouble believing it. For a few seconds, I thought of telling him I'd be there and then jumping in a cab, then I heard my mother telling him as nicely as possible that she'd already talked to me and that I couldn't come. It confirmed for me that she was really worried about my father's condition: she'd stopped telling him he was always forgetting everything. Then my sisters got there, and I heard my father say hello to them, give them a kiss, and tell me he loved me before he hung up.

"Is he okay?" Laurent asked me.

"Yeah, he's all right."

We were all quiet for a little while, each of us was pretending to be completely absorbed by an item in the paper that we would be incapable of summarizing, even if our life depended on it.

"Sorry," Jeff finally said.

"No, it's okay." I didn't feel like being mad anymore, and I thought he was at least partly right, and that was enough for me not to get into a fight that would be pointless and unnecessarily painful. I started reading again – for real this time – the movie section. Jeff still had his nose in the sports section, Laurent was drawing little stickmen on a circular and Julien had dived into the indecipherable columns in the business section.

After about fifteen minutes, Laurent looked at his watch. "Man, it's eleven-fifteen. Anybody want a Bloody Caesar?" Jeff and I raised our hands without looking up from our papers, and then Laurent did the same. Nobody even pretended to get up to mix the drinks.

"Okay, okay, okay," said Julien after a minute or two. "I'll do it…" He got up, walked around the kitchen bar muttering, "Geez, I do have to do everything around here…"

"Make mine a double," shouted Jeff, who insisted on believing there was nothing better than a solid dose of vodka to get you back on your feet the morning after.

"You know, I really want to see Flavie," said Jeff as he finished his drink and automatically held it out to Julien, who got up with a sigh to go make him another. "I know I'm always with these charming young girls, but I also know I'm with them because they're harmless."

"You!?! You're afraid of something?" Laurent asked as he petted the cat.

Jeff gave him the expected face. "Maybe I'm afraid of trouble."

"And Flavie *really* looks like trouble…" shouted Julien from the kitchen.

"I know," answered Jeff. "That's just it. You know that theory that says it's exactly when something scares you that you have to jump right in?"

He ran into three blank stares apparently stating that they'd never heard of any such theory.

"Come on, now. It's not Kierkegaard or anything, everybody's heard about it!"

"So, if I'm afraid of getting killed on a seedy little side street, I should jump right in and go for it?"

"Laurent…"

"I'm just saying…"

"What I mean is," Jeff went on, "that I want to be with a woman like Flavie – not necessarily with Flavie herself, I don't know her. And I know that all the Marie-Lunes and Marie-Soleils are just distractions, even if they are great. Like you and Christophe, Marine."

I didn't say anything. Laurent and Julien were listening to him, too, as if he were making some very wise proclamations.

"Okay, I know it might seem ridiculous, and maybe it's because I'm almost forty, but I'm just saying, shit, I'm going to check it out, at least. See if I can do it; try to understand what I really want."

I nodded. "I understand. That's why I'd like you to understand when I say that Gabriel… of course he scares me, Christ, it's like being a grown-up…"

"We *are* grown-ups!" said Laurent.

"...like being responsible and mature." Laurent nodded approvingly. "I just want... I'd never forgive myself if I didn't go through with it. Even if a big part of me is convinced he'll wind up realizing I'm just a joke..."

My statement was greeted by the usual chorus of "No, no" and "Come on, now."

"So, Gabriel and Flavie this week," said Julien. "You're going for it?"

"We're going for it!" I confirmed. I thought of my father and said to myself we had no right not to go for it, that we owed it to him, and to so many others, to go for things while we still could.

"I want to be honest," said Julien. "I want to be honest with Mathias, so he can make a decision that's not based on another one of my lies. I want him to come back to me with his eyes wide open." Jeff and I looked at him with wide eyes. "What? It's true."

"I want to explain to Carole that I don't want to have kids," said Laurent. "And make her see that if she wants us to stay together, she's going to have to accept that. Not that I want to lose her, but..."

The four of us all looked at each other for a minute – we were not accustomed to such group-sharing sessions, and we all smiled, looking uncomfortable but amused. So, here we are, I thought. At the crossroads, together, after so many years. And for the first time since we'd known each other, we accepted it, we admitted it. And knowing that these three men who I loved like family were in the same boat as me made me feel almost confident, with just the right amount of fear and butterflies in my stomach to go meet Gabriel the next day.

To: Marine
From: Frédéric Vandale
Subject: Release

....

I started writing. I started writing and it's not complete crap, like I reread what I wrote and I'm not ashamed and don't want to pluck out my eyes with suction cups. I feel like I've been drunk for two days.

To: Fred
From: Marine Vandale
Subject: Drunk from what?

....

Just to be clear, does this feeling of drunkenness come from creation instead of a half a bottle of Ricard, like the last time?

To: Marine
From: Frédéric Vandale
Subject: Ricardicide

....

Creation, Marine, nothing but creation. I chucked the Ricard in the garbage. I can't get over it. And so, of course, I'm so not used to feeling like I'm finally on the right track that I think maybe I'm just blinded by myself, or maybe by too much lucidity in the absence of the Ricard... do you think there's any such thing as too much lucidity?

To: Fred
From: Marine Vandale
Subject: Lucidity Overdose

....

It would make a good name for a band, don't you think?

To: Marine
From: Frédéric Vandale
Subject: Re: Lucidity Overdose

...

To: Fred
From: Marine Vandale
Subject: RE: Lucidity Overdose

Okay, okay, I get it, sorry. Yes, I do think it's possible to be too lucid. Not that it's a bad thing, but it can make you dizzy in a way Ricard can't. It's scary to see everything clearly, don't you think? Otherwise, why do you think we spend so much of our lives trying to muddle everything up?

To: Marine
From: Frédéric Vandale
Subject: Scrambled waves

I didn't think we muddle things up on purpose. I know that's not your case, but personally, I never felt like sitting down at my desk and saying, "Okay, now, let's muddle everything up."

To: Fred
From: Marine Vandale
Subject: Freudian Scramble

You want to hear my theory? I get about one every decade, and so far none of them will make it into the history books, but, what I think is that we muddle things up unconsciously, because it's a lot easier than seeing things clearly, and because it takes a colossal effort by our consciousness to actually open our eyes.

To: Marine
From: Frédéric Vandale
Subject: Eyes wide shut

....

You know what? That's not such a bad theory. But now I'm thinking that maybe I BELIEVE I'm seeing things clearly, but my eyelids are really shut as tight as can be, and that I'm getting as excited as a little girl about a book that'll turn out to be about as interesting as the instructions for putting together a Börg bookshelf or an Inglund coffee table. And don't make the joke about IKEA instruction books actually being interesting. I can see that one coming a mile away.

To: Fred
From: Marine Vandale
Subject: Censure

....

If you keep it up, I'm going to start a file on the mediocre jokes you censure. And besides, what kind of grown-up gets mad in advance about a joke they end up making themselves?

To: Marine
From: Frédéric Vandale
Subject: Little boy

....

One who has the distinct impression that he just started Grade One in short pants and suspenders, carrying a book bag and an apple, picture it, with marbles, and everything. I was just getting ready to enjoy my first few pages like a prince, and now I'm almost afraid of my computer. Shit, Marine. Thirty-five years old and still afraid of what I really want.

To: Fred
From: Marine Vandale
Subject: Welcome to the club

....

Well, Freddy, my boy, if it makes you feel any better, you're not
the only one who's afraid. You should have seen the boys and
I yesterday, four clowns with Bloody Caesars saying exactly the
same thing, that we've all get a knot of fear in the pit of our
stomachs when the time comes to face what we want. You
know, I don't want to turn the knife in the wound, but there's
not only the chance that we don't know what we want, but it's
also possible – and this is worse – that we may not even attain
the obscure objects of our desires.

To: Marine
From: Frédéric Vandale
Subject: Imbedded knife

....

Boy, have you ever got a knack for making people feel better.
That's quite a gift you've got there.

To: Fred
From: Marine Vandale
Subject: Same boat

....

I only mentioned it because, while you may be afraid of your
computer, I've been going into tachycardia for an hour because
I've got a date with Gabriel in an hour, and Jeff is about to
make me start breathing into a brown paper bag.

To: Marine
From: Frédéric Vandale
Subject: Epidemic

....

Do you think everyone's caught it, or is it just that we're making a huge effort to share our big scary virus with each other?

\

To: Fred
From: Marine Vandale
Subject: Pandemic

....

We've all got it, *mon frère.* And, if you don't mind, I'm going to
go now, because I still have to get control of these shakes, AND
my date's in less than an hour.

To: Marine
From: Frédéric Vandale
Subject: 28 days later

....

We'll get through it, Marinette. Good luck tonight. Keep your
eyes wide open.

To: Fred
From: Marine Vandale
Subject: (none)

....

Do you think he'll notice if I have a brown paper bag OVER
my head?

Chapter 10

"Come on," said Jeff. "You're going to be late."

"Oh, shit… don't you want to go in my place?"

He crossed his arms and smiled the way he always did when he thought I was really acting like a little girl. "Go," he mouthed, pointing with determination at the door, which, I was now convinced, was going to open onto a chasm, cliff or canyon, or any other thing that would be very deep and very, very lacking in bridges.

"And could you please tell me what this date thing is all about? Why can't we just do what we've always done, meet by chance, get drunk, go to bed together, then see where that takes us? That's what we've always done, isn't it? That's what YOU still do."

"Let me remind you that the idea was to move to another level. You're the one who wants to be a grown-up."

"Aaarrrgggghhh!" I made a gesture that really didn't mean anything, and spun around to lean, face first, against the wall. "Too much anticipation…" I moaned into the wall. "Not enough spontaneity…"

"Have you not *ever* had a date before in your life?"

"Well, no! That's what I'm trying to tell you! It's always been, 'Oh, hi, what a surprise seeing you here, yatta, yatta, yatta, it'd be fun to see each other again, hey, will you look at that, we're going out together.' Then, if we were really lucky, we eventually realized we were also falling love. But all this dating stuff… There's something hypocritical about it, something fake… aarrgghh… Like when you get to the restaurant, and he sees you, but you're still looking

for him, then, you have to walk all the way over to him,
then…"

"Marine… it's already seven-thirty. Far be it from me
to attempt to be your dating guru, but if you don't want
him to be pissed off 'cause he's been waiting for you for
half an hour, it might be a good idea for you to get going."

He handed me my coat. I felt like throwing myself into
his arms and asking him to hold me tight, but something
told me that would be going a little too far. He'd already
wanted to leave an hour earlier, but I'd held him back with
an annoying, begging voice because I knew that, left to my
own devices, I'd probably empty the liquor cabinet, drive
the cat crazy and have an absolute fit somewhere between
the house and the restaurant. Jeff's presence made me feel
better – it had occurred to me that my request was terribly selfish, but I also remembered that Flavie was coming
to dinner two days later and, unlike him, I was going to
have to stomach the flirting that was likely to take place.

"Okay," I said, slipping on my coat. "Okay, okay, okay,
ooooookay, okay, okay, okay, oooooo…"

"Marine!" Jeff took me by the shoulders. He looked
amused, but also sincerely confused by this worrying that
seemed completely unjustified to him.

"Okay," I repeated one last time. "Jeff?"

"What?"

"I really need you to wish me good luck. I know it's a
silly thing to ask, but I really need it."

He smiled at me. "Good luck, baby."

"Really?"

"Of course, really, silly." He gave me a kiss on the forehead. "Remember what we said yesterday: eyes wide
open."

"… and don't lose track of yourself."

The four of us had finished the bottle of vodka, talked
about our fears and desires, and came to the conclusion
that I had proudly shared with my brother a few minutes

earlier. Even once the effects of the vodka had worn off, I still believed that it was one of the most constructive things we'd decided to do in a long time. I kissed Jeff where I always kissed him – where I hadn't dared to in a little while – on the top of his chest, where his unbuttoned shirt let a bit of skin peek through, exactly where I could reach without having to stand on my tiptoes. "Bye."

I raised my head towards him one last time and the look he settled on me was full of the comfort and confidence I was expecting. "Thanks," I whispered to him. Then I opened the door, my eyes wide open, and saw there was no chasm or cliff outside, just a snowy path like the one that led me to Gabriel the first time, when we met by chance, in the middle of winter.

I saw him before he noticed me. He was crossing the street in the snow, tall and dark-haired, and I stopped for a moment to watch his long legs and the way he walked – to watch this man I didn't know, who was still unfamiliar to me, but who, possibly, would be soon. Would I still notice his figure? The way he walked? With joy and nostalgia, I remembered other first meetings, the discovery of other unknown bodies, all the beautiful and rare moments that happen as you get to know each other, when everything is still possible and nothing is taken for granted. Were there things, people, loves that you could get used to without having them lose their sparkle? I almost closed my eyes, so all I'd see would be fog as I convinced myself everything really was possible, but I kept them wide open and focused on Gabriel, walking towards me through the snowy night.

"Hey!" he said as he came closer. He slipped a bit on a little patch of ice, but he caught himself and laughed. I laughed, too, until his smile was right up close to my face and his eyes were settled on mine. Then something I never thought would happen in my life happened – something in fact that I suspected was almost a lingering adolescent myth, from the time when we felt everything so strongly and wanted so badly to believe things could happen: I reacted physically, I got what we used to call butterflies in the stomach and felt like I was melting from the inside. My heart or my stomach, I really don't know which, seemed to gently, sensuously explode, and I could have sworn I felt light radiating everywhere, even on my face, which I had no idea what to do with at that moment. I would have begged anyone, right then, I would have done anything so Gabriel would be with me always, so he'd take me in his arms.

"I'm late," I finally stammered.

"Well…" He pointed at himself, then at the ground, looking amused. Actually, he was just as late as I was. I realized I was looking into his eyes with an intensity that was even bothering me, and I turned away.

"Shall we go in, *mademoiselle*?" he asked, offering me his arm. He smiled, relaxed, and his easy manner was starting to wear off on me – he looked so sure of who he was, he had his eyes so wide open, to use our weekend expression, that you couldn't help but go along with him.

He'd picked the restaurant himself, a warm, kind of noisy place that I didn't know too well. I was happy – a stuffy place where all the patrons spoke in low tones around paraffin candles probably would have done me in.

"Would you like a drink?" he asked as we sat down, and I thought for the first time that maybe he was a little nervous too, normally this would have flattered me, but now I found it a little upsetting: at least ONE of us had to be at the helm. Otherwise, I could be washed away with the current and float aimlessly to the ends of the Earth.

"Would I ever," I finally answered. "Would I eeeeeeverrrr." Honesty was the best policy.

"You know what's a really good drink before dinner?" I felt like answering, "Anything at all." I would have drunk turpentine if I thought it would calm me down. "A gin and tonic with some cucumber," said Gabriel. I must have looked so astonished that he thought he needed to justify himself. "Okay, maybe it is a little summery, but… you just slice up some cucumber and…"

"I know. I… I have a friend who's a big fan of gin and tonic with cucumber."

"You'll have to introduce us, we have the same taste."

"It's Jeff."

His smile was so knowing and charming that I had to hold myself back to keep from stamping my feet in joy, or squealing something, or shouting out to the other tables.

"Okay," he said. "I have a better idea. Did I already go too far with the flowers, 'cause, now, if I order champagne, will I not only look like a guy who's making a stupid joke about his last name, but also like the guy who might be capable of bringing over the mariachis or reciting poetry?"

I started laughing, but my laugh was a little too flirty for my own taste. But I couldn't fight it, I was crazy about him. "No," I answered. "And anyway, I really like champagne. If I have to listen to poetry or even singing telegrams in order to have some, then I'll manage."

"Okay." He was laughing, too. And I started thinking of the title of a book I'd never read, *Everything Is Illuminated*. Golden light was dancing in the mirrors, on the light wood bar, on the copper beams surrounding it, and most of all in Gabriel's eyes, as he kept on looking at me, the way we should always look at people. Everything was illuminated, including me.

Two hours later I'd calmed down, for the very simple reason that Gabriel would have managed to calm down even a chronic anxiety sufferer. He gave off something solid and anchored, which, ironically, made me reel, and was very unlike the strength Jeff had. Although he'd always made me think of a boulder, something unmovable and eternally stable, Gabriel made me think he was like a tall tree. I could make out his deep, solid roots, and his leafy branches were stretching upwards towards something unknown, towards lighter air.

I listened to him talk and wondered if the gift he had for reassuring and calming people was a corollary of his profession or if, rather, he'd chosen this profession because he'd always known, more or less unconsciously, that he had this talent that could neither be acquired nor learned. I asked him and he gave the charming, modest laugh of people who are used to receiving compliments, but don't know how to react.

"I don't know," he said. "I… I really have *no* idea, in fact. I never thought of myself as reassuring." He laughed again and repeated, more for himself than for me, "Reassuring… Reassuring?"

"Yes. Calming. Soothing."

"Okay, we're two attributes from 'soporific.' I'd rather you stop now."

"No! No! Not soporific at all. No! God, why does every-one think that 'soothing' has become a negative word? It's like you always have to be *up* and *peppy* and *stimulating*…" I exaggerated the accent on each adjective as if I were in a Broadway theatre.

"And exciting, too," Gabriel added in the same tone.

"Exactly!" I was afraid my cheeks would split I was grinning so happily. Élodie would have thought Gabriel was exciting. To be honest, *I* thought Gabriel was excit-ing. Exciting and soothing. I imagined myself as a B-list celebrity that someone would ask, "Mademoiselle Vandale, what kind of man are you looking for?" and my idiotic reply, "A man who is exciting and soothing."

"I don't know," I continued. "I don't know if it's because I'm in my thirties, or tired, or something else, but it seems like after spending my life looking for something that was

going to send me over the moon, I finally want…" I could-
n't find the words, so I mimed setting down a weight. "…
something that's going to ground me. It's as if…" I stopped
for a second. I didn't talk like this to people who were nearly
strangers. I especially didn't talk like this to men I hoped to
seduce, like always, with my sense of humor and my light-
heartedness. Then, in Gabriel's eyes, I could see true and
sincere interest, so I kept going. "It's as if everything that
was attractive just five years ago has become totally and
utterly senseless. I don't know if you see what I mean…"

"Yes. I really do."

He didn't go on, so I did: "Then, like I was saying, I
don't know if it's because something specific has happened or if it's some sort of unavoidable law, but it seems
like now, all I really want to do, you know, is fly like a
kite…" I started laughing, a little uneasily, for having used
such a stupid expression as "fly like a kite," but Gabriel
didn't say a word: he was listening to me. "Fly like a kite
with both feet firmly on the ground," I finally said.
"Because being high as a kite a thousand feet up in the air
doesn't amount to much. Or, in any case, I don't think it
can amount to much anymore."

I could still hear the conversation that I'd had with the
boys the day before, the questions we'd asked each other
with adolescent urgency: "But is that what we really
want?" "But are we just kidding ourselves 'cause we're
scared?" "Isn't having both feet on the ground the most
boring thing you've ever heard of?" and I wondered if we
hadn't said all those things out of bitterness, because, after
all these years of missed flights and painful crashes, we
still didn't want to believe that high-flying joys were now
behind us and that terra firma was better than seventh
heaven.

"Have you ever been in love?" Gabriel asked me.

"Pardon?"

"Have you ever been in love?"

"Uhhh… yeah!" I had an absurd and unjustified feeling that I'd just insulted Laurent. "I was with Laurent for five years and I…"

"Ohhh," he said. "I believe you. It's okay. But I don't think it's a matter of years. I was with Suzie for eleven years…"

"Suzie…"

"My wife."

Oh. His wife. I knew he'd been married, and there was something huge about a union that had been made official by the famous bonds of holy matrimony. Even though I'd never wanted to get married, I suddenly thought that it added extra weight to a relationship which, in my head, was already bending beneath eleven years of history and love.

"We were together for eleven years, and I don't think I can say we were ever really in love."

I didn't say anything. I wasn't sure if what he'd just said was completely stupid or if he, Gabriel, was seriously a moron. I couldn't imagine it was possible to spend eleven years with someone without loving them.

"Don't look at me like that," he said with a smile that was already forgiving me. "You can be really happy with someone without being in love with them. You can get along impeccably, you can even have great sex, and not be in love. I'm sure of that."

I finally gave in. Maybe he was right. Since Laurent and I had broken up, I often wondered if we'd really loved each other, or if our relationship wasn't more of a manifestation of a profoundly deep friendship, with such unique closeness and such rare understanding that we, and all our friends and family, had passionately wanted to believe it was love.

"I want to answer 'yes,' anyway," I said. "What about you?"

"Yes. Once. Lana. I was twenty-five. I could see myself

with her at sixty-five, at eighty… I wanted to be with her always. I wasn't afraid, you know?"

Yes, I could understand that. I thought quickly and pleasantly of Jeff. I wasn't afraid with him. The only thing I was afraid of was losing him. The thought of it knocked me off balance for an instant, but Gabriel was already continuing.

"It was… it was her smell, you know? The smell of her drove me wild. I was literally addicted to her presence."

"What happened?"

He smiled a sad little smile. "She had a lot of problems. She was always anxious and, who the hell knows why, maybe because I loved her like crazy, but she didn't trust me. She even started parking outside my place to make sure I wasn't cheating on her. But I'd come home late, I was in med school, I was studying my fucking brains out, and at one point, I choked. It was too much. It was just too much."

"You're the one who left?"

"Yes. And I *never* saw her again. I heard some news about her a year later, she'd gone back to live with her family in Texas."

"Oooh-ohhh, a Texan…"

"Howdy, cowgirl!"

I started laughing. "Did you just say 'howdy'?"

"Yes, ma'am, I just did. I always try to slip in a 'howdy' or two the first time I meet someone. I know it adds some depth to the experience."

"Yeah, personally, I use 'hunky dory.' I've been trying to fit it in for half an hour."

We both laughed, more from enjoyment than anything else, as we looked into each other's eyes. I remember thinking, "I'm not alone. People don't look at people they don't care about like that." And because it was so easy to talk to him, I asked him the question I normally would have tried to avoid: "Do you think you're over her? The

Texan?"

"Ahhh…" he took a drink of champagne. "I don't want to make empty declarations, but do we ever get over love?"

I nodded. He always seemed to have the right answer or, in this case, the right question. In any case, his declaration didn't seem empty – not with the intonation he'd given it and the look that went along with it. I thought of Laurent and I understood that neither one of us was completely over the other, and that such unbreakable bonds, though they are heavy and infinitely precious, that sometimes outlive love are sad, beautiful things.

"At the time," said Gabriel, "I didn't think I'd ever get over her, that's for sure. Then I met Suzie, and the pieces started coming back together – you know how it is."

"There's nothing that can't be put back together."

"No."

"I still haven't decided if that idea is sad or marvelous. Sometimes, I think it's both."

"*I* think it's both."

"Do you ever regret it?"

"Leaving her, you mean? No. Not anymore. Not at all. I wonder what it would be like, sure. Often. But no regrets. They're pointless."

"That's easy to say."

"What about you? Do you have regrets?"

I made a quick review of all the little failures I'd collected, the more or less big disappointments punctuating my life, the countless times I'd said to myself, "if I could do it over again…"

"No," I answered Gabriel. "No regrets." It was true, and I realized I was smiling as I said it: my errors and erring ways were part of what I'd become, side by side with my love affairs and my victories, and I was recognizing for the first time that I loved them all the same and that, in a certain way, they'd even become precious. I'd always thought it was people's faults and shortcomings that made them beautiful – sometimes I'd look at the people I loved as they fought more or less heroically with their little demons and bad decisions, with what they'd never had the strength to change about themselves and the memory of what they'd lost, with certain painful decisions they'd made and certain things they wished they'd never done, with their hearts that had been broken and mended a hundred times, and I couldn't help loving them even more, because they moved me, because we were all in the same boat and the simple fact of living was as painful as it was dazzling. I would never have admitted this to anyone, at least, not sober. It was the kind of belief people prefer to keep hidden, like 'life is great' because it sounds too naive and sentimental, but then they end up telling their psychologists, or a stranger in a bar, or their best friends after they've knocked back two bottles of wine and a banana daiquiri.

"No," I repeated. "I'm… I'm not really capable of regret. I don't have that gene, or that stubborn streak. There are things… times in my life that I'd really like rework, or even change… but I can't regret them. What's done is done."

Gabriel looked at me, with one eyebrow raised as if he doubted what I was saying.

"It's true!" I said. "It's not that I don't WANT to regret or that I've made it a policy to have a regret-free-only-look-to-the-future kind of life, that's just the way it is. It's not in my genetic make-up." I stopped – the image of my father had popped up between Gabriel and me. Did he have any regrets? The two of us had never really talked – in fact, he'd never really talked at all. And if, by some awful chance, he had to be struck with this horrible disease, what memories were going to flee from him without our ever even knowing about them? Regrets, sorrows, private joys. I felt rich to still have all my memories, and I got upset with myself for it – I felt like a rich person who is even more grateful for the wad of cash in his wallet after he's bumped into a destitute friend.

"You thinking of your father?" Gabriel asked.

"Okay. What's going on? Are you really perfect? Handsome, brilliant, gallant and you can read minds, too?" I felt myself blush: it was ridiculous, but I was more uncomfortable about telling someone I thought they were handsome than about telling them they were brilliant. Opposite me, Gabriel laughed, his green eyes reflected the restaurant's thousand lights, and a few others as well.

"I think it's a sense that gets developed after years of working in Emerg. Plus, you said 'genetic,' so I figured you must have made the connection." Suddenly, he looked professional and almost detached. "Is he being properly looked after?"

"I guess so… Honestly, I don't really know, I don't know anything about all this. I'm going with him tomorrow for an appointment with another psychologist… I don't even understand why he has to see them, it seems to me…"

"No, he has to see the psychologists. Who's he seeing?"

"Umm…" I found the psychologist's card and handed it to him. He looked at for a second, then he seemed to hesitate.

"Listen," he finally said. "I don't want to impose where I don't belong, but my… the woman I'm seeing right now specializes in handling this kind of case. If you want, I can mention your case to her."

"More rum!" shouted Julien. "MORE RUM!"

"She's already drunk," said Jeff who was making another round of mojitos.

"I said: more rum."

"MORE RUM!" I yelled.

"Okay, okay, more rum. You sure you don't want me to go over and beat him up?" Jeff asked again for the hundredth time since I'd come home. I was still holding the card that belonged to "the woman I'm seeing right now."

When Gabriel left me in front of our house, he said, "You have the longest eyelashes I've ever seen in my life." I didn't add anything. In fact, I'd hardly spoken at all since "if you want, I can mention your case to her." I was so astonished, so disconcerted – and possibly this was really an advantage – that I was unable to rebel, to get angry, or even to ask the questions that had to be asked. Was I too resilient or too stupid? The fact was, I finished off the evening drinking a little more than usual, though I kept up a pleasant conversation with Gabriel. My heart seemed to have gone to sleep, but my brain was running at a hundred miles an hour, generating questions to which there were no answers – Why did he send roses? Why was I so unlucky? Did I give off the wrong signals? Was I too blind to see he was only looking for friendship? Who, exactly, in the history of humanity had managed to convince us that women were more complicated and harder to read than men? And, above all, did I really want to believe that I'd started falling for men who weren't interested in me?

As he was leaving, Gabriel had turned back around and, in the falling snow that seemed to have become a characteristic of our encounters, he said, "You are one of the most astonishing women I've ever met in my life, Marine Vandale."

"Astonishing, my ass, shit! What the hell does that mean, I'm 'astonishing'? That I'm the only girl who's stupid enough to think that I've got a chance with a guy who sends me flowers... FLOWERS for Chrissake! Stupid, bloody, fucking FLOWERS!" I pointed towards the dining-room table.

"It's all right," answered Julien. "You already chucked the flowers out the window."

"With the vase," Jeff clarified.

"Sorry about the vase…" I wasn't crying. I was beside myself, literally. Not even humiliated, just beside myself. Jeff was bringing over our mojitos when we heard the door open.

"Okay, I'm really on Carole's shit list right now, she doesn't exactly understand how I can have an emergency at eleven o'clock at night, so this had better be serious," said Laurent as he came in. I turned around – this time, he was wearing a big sweater and a toque and he was standing in the entryway holding a bottle of champagne. "I brought champagne. I know it cheers you up when you're down. What happened?"

I didn't have time to figure out if it was his kindness, the champagne or the fact that one of the other boys had thought to call him, but when I saw him, in his snowy boots, standing on our little yellow straw welcome mat with the red letters that said "At your own risk," I leapt over the back of the sofa and ran towards him shouting "Loulou!," which turned to sobs at the second "Lou," and I fell into his arms.

I cried as he held me for a good half-hour. Laurent was not used to this kind of outpouring – and, unlike Jeff, he didn't have the gift of comforting embedded in him. He slowly led me back to the sofa, whispering platitudes that made me feel better, while Jeff and Julien gave him the short version of what had happened.

"Do you want me to go beat him up?" Laurent finally asked, and I managed to chuckle through my tears – the idea of Laurent beating someone up was so incongruous and impossible that it simply touched me and made me laugh.

I spent the rest of the night crying and shouting in the arms of one of my three boys who were taking turns consoling me separately and together, until I didn't know what hurt me more: the illusions I'd built up around

Gabriel or the love I received from these three men who were not my lovers but who gave me more than any love affair ever had.

I woke up the next morning, in Jeff's bed, next to Julien. Feels like déjà vu, I thought as I looked around, one eye open, the other closed, where could Jeff be? A question that was quickly cleared up the next second by the sound of a solid weight hitting the floor, followed by an echoing "Fuck!" and a shrill "Meow!" Then I heard the cat run across the apartment, before he jumped on the bed, looking insulted.

"Is everything all right?" I shouted. "Did you just fall on the cat?"

"What the fuck am I doing in the living room?"

I was so surprised by the state he was in that I started laughing. "I don't know, but can you tell me what I'm doing in YOUR bed with this queer?"

"Shut the fuck up…" groaned Julien next to me.

I gave him a little kiss on the shoulder and set about getting up – slowly, gently – before I realized I was wearing Julien's bubblegum pink polo shirt and that he had on the violet satin blouse I'd worn the day before. How many times had we already done this? Dozens of fabulous nights and less glorious mornings passed through my head: me wearing blackwatch pants and a yellow vest, and Julien in a dress with a plunging neckline or a tailored cashmere sweater and leggings.

I laughed even harder when I saw myself from the front, then the details of the previous night slowly came back to me, drop by drop, like they usually did on such mornings. What I mostly saw was Gabriel handing me the card of the woman I didn't know and who had instantly become ridiculously and disproportionately important in my life. The night before, I'd staggered over to my computer to Google her, and the boys and I spent a good

half-hour examining the three photos I'd found of her
and trying to decide if she was pretty or not. I had to
admit, despite the boys' polite protests, that she was magnificent. And she worked in the same field as Gabriel, and
she looked disconcertingly grown-up, in a way I'd given
up hoping to ever attain. I groaned something at Jeff, who
was working on getting up, from between the sofa and the
coffee table.

"Oh boy," he said, still on all fours. "Laurent is going
to be in deep shit."

"Come on, now. It was barely two a.m. when he left,
wasn't it?

"*Four* a.m.," said a dying voice next to me. "I know
because I wasn't wearing your clothes yet."

"Laurent always leaves when the clothes swap starts. I
think he's afraid he'll think you're too cute in ladies' wear."

"Va-va-voom," said Julien, just before he hid his face
behind his satin-draped arm.

I could hear Jeff, in the kitchen, putting the glasses we'd
used the day before in the dishwasher. "Argh," he said, "we
even finished the crème de menthe."

"That was Laurent!" Julien and I shouted in unison,
which made us both laugh. Laurent spent part of the night
repeating that, deep down, he was jealous of me, since I
was still free and there was nothing better or more comfortable in the world than being single, while Julien and I
kept on rambling, "Love is the answer and you know that
for sure" – until Laurent declared, "Okay, seriously, isn't
John Lennon just a little over the top?" following which
Jeff rushed over to the stereo and flooded us with all of
Lennon's best for the next hour. Around two in the morning, Laurent was crying like a little girl, too, crushed, he
said, under the weight of a relationship, the responsibility
that came with love and the ordinary ugliness that accom-
panies everyday compromises. Incoherent, Julien tried to
get in touch with a couple of his former one-night stands

in the hopes of losing himself in sex: alcohol wasn't enough. For people who had, just the day before, made beautiful, constructive resolutions, it was impossible to say that we'd been very successful.

"Jeff," I called, from his room.

"Mmmm?"

"Why are we in your bed?"

There was a moment of silence. "You said you wanted to sleep in my smell," Jeff finally answered. I turned towards Julien, who'd raised his arm and turned towards me, then nodded to confirm that I had indeed said such a thing.

Two hours later, the three of us were sitting around our table at the restaurant. Laurent had refused to come, saying he had a monstrous headache, which we interpreted as "a lot of explaining to do with Carole."

"I don't understand," I said. "I mean, I can see why Carole thinks it's weird that Lo and I are still so close, but Jesus... if she still hasn't figured out that after all this time, it's really over between us..."

"Did it ever occur to you that maybe Laurent encourages it?" Julien asked me.

"Come on, now," said Jeff. "Why would he do that?"

"That's Laurent."

"Christ the world is complicated."

Julien and I hardly had a chance to inhale before the customary, "You're one to talk," before Jeff raised a hand to us, letting us know it really wasn't necessary.

One of the pretty servers I'd often seen in Jeff's shirts came over to our table with our three Bloody Caesars — and, in Jeff's case, an extra vodka shooter: things were serious for him, with a second hangover in two days. Desperate times call for desperate measures.

"Shit," I said, pushing back my glass. "Would you please tell me what the hell we're doing? I feel like I'm stagnating so bad it's not even funny."

"Come on…"

"No! That's exactly it! We rush around, live at a hundred miles an hour, have a drink, but ABSOLUTELY nothing ever happens. We don't do anything! And on top of it, in my case, nothing *happens*."

"Okay, cut it out," Jeff said, pushing my glass back towards me. "You had a shock yesterday because of a guy who honestly laid it on a little thick for someone who wasn't interested. But let him eat shit, okay? Tomorrow's another day."

"Oh, yeah, I've got *hours* of pleasure ahead of me tomorrow… I'm meeting my father at the hospital in the afternoon, and Élodie insists on coming. I don't know about you, but personally, I think hospitals are awful enough without having to put up with my sister blubbering the whole time, that's for sure." The boys nodded their heads compassionately.

"Are you going to have time to come to the Jean-Talon market with me tomorrow morning?" Jeff asked me. "Try not to forget Flavie's coming to dinner."

"No, I haven't forgotten…" In fact, I *had* forgotten and I really would have preferred not to remember. I was ashamed, too, because this dinner bothered me infinitely more than going to the hospital with my father. The idea that Flavie and Jeff might have everything I didn't have with Gabriel, that maybe they were going to kiss, fall into each other's arms and make love languorously made me want to dump my Bloody Caesar on my head. I tried to chase away such selfish thoughts: It would be my first test, I said to myself. Dig deep down inside and find enough confidence and generosity to be happy for my friends. Then, I immediately thought: Stupid fucking test.

And since problems never come alone, and "when it rains it pours" my cell phone started ringing. I didn't even have time to turn towards my bag before Julien had already opened it, found the phone, and checked the caller id screen before he sat on it.

"Julien…"

"No."

"Julien…"

"No. Jeff, hold on to her. No."

"Julien, is it Gabriel?"

"Hmm? What? No. No, it isn't Gabriel."

"Since when are you such a terrible liar? Give me the phone, Julien."

"No," answered Jeff, holding me by the wrists. "I think we've established pretty clearly that it isn't good for you, right?"

I looked into his eyes, and all I saw was sincerity, and such a disinterested concern for my happiness that I almost started to cry. "Okay," I said.

"Okay," repeated Julien, as he placed the phone on the table between us. *I'm* going to listen to the message and then we'll see. I didn't say much to you yesterday, because we were in 'crisis mode,' but I don't necessarily think he's a monster. Maybe it's true that he needs to understand that he acted a little ambiguously, but I don't think it's as terrible an offense as you think."

"A LITTLE AMBIGUOUSLY?"

Julien gave me the little look I always got when he thought I was getting upset over trifles. "Yes, Marine, a little. And maybe you got carried away a little too quickly, too. Jesus, you haven't even slept with the guy yet and already you're making plans for the future." I could almost hear Jeff, opposite me, doing everything he could not to shout, "I told you so!"

"Maybe you're right," I said. "Actually, you're definitely right. We promised each other, eyes wide open, grown-ups, no more living in an imaginary world. I. Am. Not. Getting. Carried. Away. And beside that, I'm still fucking mad at him."

But as I looked at the little phone on the table, with its blinking, message-announcing light, I felt nothing, absolutely nothing, except irrational joy and the blind conviction that everything was still possible.

To: Fred
From: Marine Vandale
Subject: Let's talk literature

....

You have to tell me what your book is about. And even if you've only written three paragraphs, you have to describe them to me, read them to me, and paraphrase them for me like no other paragraphs have ever been paraphrased before.

To: Marine
From: Frédéric Vandale
Subject: Literally

....

You know, I could be unusually sneaky and grant your wish? I can already see you sleeping at your computer, never to wake again. Do you REALLY think it was a spinning wheel that put Sleeping Beauty to sleep? Tsk-tsk-tsk. That is one of my paraphrased paragraphs.

To: Fred
From: Marine Vandale
Subject: A whiff of doubt

....

Tell me if I'm wrong, but do I detect a whiff of uncertainty? Aren't you happy anymore?

To: Marine
From: Frédéric Vandale
Subject: More like a torrent of anxiety

....

My doubts are solid, Marine. To clarify, I'm nothing but doubt, one hundred and forty-five pounds of doubt walking through Père Lachaise Cemetery every evening – can you smell the sad caricature? An aspiring author wandering indulgently around Père Lachaise?

To: Fred
From: Marine Vandale
Subject: Re: More like a torrent of anxiety

Hold it, you weigh one hundred and forty-five pounds? I'm calling *Maman*.

To: Marine
From: Frédéric Vandale
Subject: Weighing the pros and cons

Marine, if you tell *Maman* that I'm down to one hundred and forty-five pounds, in addition to the twenty pounds I've already lost, I'll also lose what little mental health I have left, and she'll literally start FedExing me Tupperwares full of *creton*. So, hush. Hush. Don't worry, I'll start eating ham and butter sandwiches tomorrow. So, how about being nice and wonderful and encouraging your brother's healthy weight gain by reading what I've already written? Even if you detest it, your opinion will help.

To: Fred
From: Marine Vandale
Subject: An honor

With pleasure, my dear beanpole. But I want to see the receipts for the ham and butter sandwiches.

To: Marine
From: Frédéric Vandale
Subject: Returning the favor

The receipts will be sent in due course. Now, will you please tell me what's going so wrong in your life that you're demanding paraphrasing?

To: Fred
From: Marine Vandale
Subject: Not paraphrasing

....

In short, Gabriel, who will, from this point forward, be referred
to as Dr. Jekyll, because of his double personality, has a girlfriend, news he shared over a glass of champagne. Flavie is
coming for dinner tonight and I have to spend the afternoon
at the hospital with *Papa* and Élodie. Dr. Jekyll called again,
which explains the urgent need for paraphrasing to combat
the desire to jump up, grab the phone and dial his number in
heretofore unseen record time, and finally, I feel like I have the
moral fiber of a piece of shit because the thing that's having
the greatest impact on me in all this is Dr. Jekyll's call.

To: Marine
From: Frédéric Vandale
Subject: Diplomatic effort

....

Tell me, between Julien and Jeff, has either one already told you
you might be overreacting a little, or am I the first to risk my
life with such an idea?

To: Fred
From: Marine Vandale
Subject: Diplomatic blunder

....

It's okay, really. Julien already said it. But I'd like to remind you
that just because you know something rationally and for a fact,
that still doesn't mean you really know it. And don't even try
to make me believe that you don't see what I mean. I know you
follow me 100%. My pride is hurt, Fred. I feel like such an ass
for believing in the whole thing.

To: Marine
From: Frédéric Vandale
Subject: 110%

....

Okay, I get it. Still, did it not occur to you that he might be just
as scared of you as you are of him?

To: Fred
From: Marine Vandale
Subject: Psych 101

....

Too easy, Fred.

To: Marine
From: Frédéric Vandale
Subject: Still funny

....

Think about it.

To: Fred
From: Marine Vandale
Subject: Re: Still funny

....

I'll call right now.

To: Marine
From: Frédéric Vandale
Subject: THINK ABOUT IT

....

I didn't say "Get stupid," I said, "Think about it." If you think
it's going to be painful, don't do it, concentrate on *Papa* and
Élodie and Flavie, and ask me to paraphrase something.

To: Fred
From: Marine Vandale
Subject: Pale imitations

Not sure that the perspective of my day is what's going to restore my joie-de-vivre. But, if you send me what you wrote, that might do it. ☺

To: Marine
From: Frédéric Vandale
Subject: Don't underestimate the pale imitation

I've attached the document here. Don't keep reading if you get bored. And if you can't resist trying to get in touch with Dr. Jekyll and you think it will be painful, just call me. Anytime, little sister.

:)

Chapter 11

Two hours later, I'd called my brother five times and was getting ready for the sixth when Jeff came into my room to say we had to get to the market right then if we wanted to have time to have lunch and get dinner ready.

"I can't help you with dinner, Jeff, I'm going to be at the hospital."

"Oh, shit. That's right."

"Anyway, you're the one who's good in the kitchen."

"Yeah, but who's going to finely cut up the vegetables? Who's going to grate the chocolate and chop the garlic?"

"You just need someone to help you with the little stuff. You just need a little helping hand."

"Yeah, but…" He stepped closer and took my right hand in his. "Have you ever seen a prettier little helping hand?"

I rolled my eyes while he kissed my fingers. "Flattery will get you nowhere, Jeff Murphy. It doesn't work with me. And I don't think it's too hot with Flavie either, for your information."

He dropped my hand with an exaggerated sigh. "Psshhht. What hard hearts! And you're even proud of it!"

"You're starting to realize you're going to have to change your ancestral cruising techniques, aren't you?"

"What?"

"Don't even try, Casanova. Girls like Flavie are not caught with winks and handsome smiles. You're going to have to work for it, champ."

"It's just dinner."

"Mmm-hhmm." I couldn't help but smile. Maybe Fred was right. Thinking about something else, even this dinner

I'd been dreading for days, was changing my perspective. I'd spent the two previous hours talking to him instead of reading his manuscript, claiming there was no ink in my printer and that I couldn't read anything longer than a page on a computer screen. He'd listened to me politely, laughing at me just enough, until he finally got bored and, just at the end of our conversation, as I was calculating exactly when I could call Gabriel back and not look desperate, but just a little interested, he said to me, "Stop playing games, okay? Just stop playing games. No one's ever found happiness by playing games."

"I listened to Gabriel's message," I said to Jeff, who was lying down on my bed while I got dressed. He had his arms crossed behind his head, and his feet went well past the end of the bed. There really must be different beds for big boys and little girls, I thought as I slipped on a wool sweater that covered my whole butt, but only one shoulder.

"What did he say," Jeff asked.

"He let me know that he'd had a great evening and wondered if we could do it again... But at the end, he added, 'Maybe... no, nothing...' and... Okay, can you listen to it, please? I've already played it twenty times."

Jeff looked at me with a smile that clearly said he was expecting me to ask and he stretched out his hand to take the phone. I quickly dialed my voicemail number and handed the phone to him. He listened, frowning, then he pushed the button that played it again.

"He's wondering if maybe he shouldn't have told you he was screwing a psychologist."

"That's not what he's saying!"

"No, Miss Innocent. But that's what's implied between the 'maybe' and the 'if' you ever want to do it again." He emphasized the *ever*. He must know it wasn't very clever to tell you that."

"OKAY, SO." I sat down on the bed. "If he thought he wasn't being smart, it might be because he wants to be more than friends. If he just wanted to be buddy-buddy, he wouldn't give a shit about mentioning his fucking slutty psychologist."

"Marine, stop playing games, okay? If you want to call him back, call him."

"Hey, now, what's gotten into all of you today? Fred said the same thing."

"Maybe it's because it's *the* right thing to say, don't you think? Anyway," he added, giving me a little slap on the thigh. "Put on your jeans so we can get the hell out of here."

"You know what?" Jeff asked as I was trying to get into a pair of jeans he'd left in the dryer too long and would now only fit a pygmy. "If what he wants deep down is to be with you, then I'd be ready to say he was very clever, in fact."

"How do you figure, exactly?"

"There's nothing that excites you more about a guy than when you think he's unattainable."

"No WAY!"

"Yes way. If you'd slept together before yesterday, if he'd never mentioned another woman to you, and right away wanted to see you again, you'd already be cooling off."

"That's crap!" I said and threw the pygmy jeans in his face.

"It's absolutely right," he said through the pants. "Think about it. *All* the guys you've had the hots for had something about them that made them unattainable." He pulled the jeans off his head. "Either they weren't inter-ested, or they already had a girlfriend, or they were beyond complicated, or they lived in Los Angeles."

"San Francisco."

"Whatever."

I finished getting dressed in silence, while Jeff's look said he was completely satisfied with himself. I really did-n't have much to add. I thought he was right for the broad strokes, in so far as, yes, I'd strewn the path behind me with a series of rather impossible relationships and affairs. But I'd long ago persuaded myself that this was due to nothing other than chance, a little bad luck mixed with a slight penchant for things that weren't necessarily simple.

Then, as I was pulling back my hair, it occurred to me that Jeff hadn't mentioned his own name or even made a direct allusion to himself, but that was what he was thinking as he drew up his list of unattainable men. Would I have been as upset if we had slept together? I turned away from him. No, I thought. I never would have been this upset. Then I realized it was the first time I used the word *upset* when I was thinking of him and I wanted to throw something else at him – another pair of jeans, a boot, my chair.

"You're one to talk," I finally said as I left the room.

"GOOD," shouted Jeff behind me. "I was wondering what you were waiting for. I've been waiting ten minutes for my 'You're one to talk.'"

I was distractedly squeezing tomatoes while Jeff was carefully picking out mushrooms one by one like a maniac, when, across from the fruit and vegetable store we were in, I saw Laurent and Carole, walking hand in hand. I punched Jeff in the arm and he looked up and happily shouted "Hey!" before he went towards the door to call them.

"No, wait," I said, holding him back. "Wait." It was the first time I'd seen the two of them when they didn't see me, when they didn't know I was there. Jeff seemed to understand and we watched them for a little while. Carole was leaning on Laurent's shoulder and he was smiling. Then, he said something and she started to laugh, cutely tossing back her head.

"God," I said to Jeff. "They look… so happy."

"They ARE happy," said Jeff. "It's just that Laurent

doesn't know it."

I turned towards him. His statement struck me, mostly because I was realizing for the first time how true it was, how deep down in Laurent's heart there was some true happiness that he did his absolute best to ignore. And I finally understood, after all this time, that he loved Carole.

"Wow," I whispered. Watching them walk with their arms around each other, Carole's pink down jacket against Laurent's long gray coat. "Wow." I was absolutely moved and felt like a mom who finally understands her kids are grown up. Again, I looked up at Jeff, and he hadn't taken his eyes off me.

"Yeah, eh?"

He smiled and I knew he'd understood. "We'll call them," he said. "In ten minutes. You want to?"

"Yes, I do. Really." I looked at my watch. I'd told Élodie to meet me at 2 p.m. on the corner of Jean-Talon and Saint-Denis. "If they have time, we'll have lunch together," I said. "But in the meantime, finish your mushroom auditions."

Jeff started laughing and he took me by the waist and kissed me on the forehead. "Thanks, baby. In the meantime, you want to go get the herbs?"

"Right away, baby!" I gave him a wink and turned around and ended up face to face with the owner's wife, who we ran into almost every Saturday.

"Oh, my darlings!" she shouted, tapping my cheeks. "It always makes me happy to see you. So much love… I'm a grandmother five times over, and I'm always glad to see young people like you who really love each other. Good job, little ones."

She walked away, tiny and chubby, in her apron. Jeff and I looked at each other laughing, between a mountain of button mushrooms and a container of green bananas, and I couldn't have said which of us was happier.

"Little?" Laurent asked Jeff. "Sorry, but I'd say you're anything but little."

"It's an expression, idiot," I answered. "Don't you think it's cute she thinks we're together?"

"No." Laurent shrugged his shoulders. It was naive of me to think that anything would change simply because, from a distance, Laurent had looked happy with Carole. Beneath my gaze, which must have reminded him of too many things and seemed like a pitiless camera, he was again filled with the reserve and ill ease I'd always seen in Carole.

We were sitting in a little trattoria, looking out onto the market, and I was already regretting having called Laurent, who was looking outside glumly, and, I figured, already mad at me for having disturbed an otherwise pleasant day. He was uncomfortable when he felt like he was stuck between what he called his "two lives," simply because he was unable to reconcile them, which, from the outside, didn't look that hard to do.

Carole and I did our best – which wasn't much – to maintain an easy, light, conversation, but it was really an homage to dullness. I finally gave up after a long exchange about the appalling price of Jerusalem artichokes and I fell silent, settling for being like Laurent, who emptied the contents of a salt shaker onto the table and was keeping busy drawing abstract designs in the little pile of white grains. Jeff, who'd lost interest after a few praiseworthy efforts, was rereading his shopping list for the twentieth time. I looked up at Carole, to give her an apologetic look I hoped she'd know how to interpret about how helpless I was around this Laurent who, when we were both around, became a conversation vacuum, canon of awkwardness, and a silence factory. She answered with a little smile and raised eyebrows, then she got up, apologizing to no one in particular. Laurent was still absorbed by his pile of salt and Jeff by his grocery list.

"Um, you okay, Sad Sack?" I asked after Carole left.

"Yeah, but what were you thinking of, calling me? What did you want to prove?"

"What do you mean, what did I want to prove? When I see my best friend and his girlfriend at the market calling them seems like the least I could do, doesn't it?"

"No, it wasn't the best thing. Jesus, Marine. You know these situations aren't easy for Carole."

"Oh, bullshit!" I was more angry than I'd thought. I thought of Julien, who was going through some really hard times, of my father, even of all these strangers around us who probably fought day after day with demons and regrets that were much heavier than Laurent's. "Bullshit," I repeated. "You could at least have the decency not to blame Carole for this."

Laurent looked up, and I saw Jeff do the same thing, looking like someone who's just smelled danger.

"What are you going to do?" I asked Laurent. "Are you going to spend your whole life like this? Becoming completely moronic and disagreeable every time your girlfriend and your friends are in the same room as you?"

"Not my friends. Just you."

"Ooohh. Just me, eh? Wow." I gave an offended laugh and turned my head towards the window. A short bald man was walking along and shouting stupid things to no one in particular. You're right, I shouted to him in my head.

"Christ," said Laurent, "it's obvious isn't it? For Carole, you'll never be my 'friend.' You'll only ever be my 'ex.'"

"What about for you?"

He looked me in the eyes, and didn't say anything. Carole was back from the bathroom and was already putting her coat on – she obviously had no desire to be there and, given the atmosphere reigning at the table, it was hard to blame her.

"Okay, well… See you around," said Laurent in a voice that was so natural that Jeff stifled a little laugh and I settled for waving good-bye. I watched them leave in silence, tense and sullen, and I ended up getting angry with myself for having ruined their nice day. I could still see what they'd looked like an hour before and, despite how angry I was with Laurent, I would have loved to give them back the carefree happiness that had been surrounding them then. I sighed.

"That was fucking unpleasant."

"It was very unpleasant, baby," answered Jeff, his nose still buried in his grocery list. I threw a little packet of sugar in his face and he laughed, without looking up. Outside, the little, bald man went by again, in the opposite direction, still shouting insults at some invisible person or perhaps at the world in general.

"Christ, sometimes I think we're all going to end up like that," said Jeff.

"Stop it. I know. We can't."

"We really can't."

"That's where the hope of love comes in."

He gave me a very soft smile. "Yes," he said. "Yes, I suppose."

Two hours later, Élodie was parking her car in front of our parents' house. "I am so driving the rest of the afternoon," I told her, "you have no idea. Would you please tell me who gave you a driver's license?"

"The Driver's License Bureau."

"More like the Liquor Control Board. Anyway."

She looked at me and laughed and we got out of the car. The walkway to the door had again been perfectly shoveled by my father. "How many times do you think he shovels every day?" Élodie asked me as we were waiting at the door.

"When it's snowing? At least ten times," I answered. "Easy."

My mother came and opened the door, with a perfectly

distressed look it must have taken her hours to get right.

"He's not doing well," she said, even before she kissed us hello. Behind me, I could feel Élodie tense up.

"What do you mean, he's not doing well?" I turned back towards her to give her a look that said "don't worry" – even if she loved him with every fiber of her being, my mother wanted him not to do too well, because she fed on drama. Frédéric had already pointed out to me that she never looked as radiant as she did at a funeral. She'd cry, bathed in tears and looking compassionate, shaking hands with infinite empathy, and her eyes would sparkle because she was just so delighted to be sad.

"He reminded me FOUR times this morning that his appointment was this afternoon."

"Oh, *Maman*… that's normal."

"What do you mean, four times," asked Élodie.

"FOUR times," my mother repeated. "Four times."

"Okay, *Maman*, okay. We get it." I gave her a kiss. "And, by the way," I pointed out, giving her a little tap on the bottom, "that makes THREE times that you've repeated to us that he told you FOUR times he had his appointment today."

She couldn't help but smile. "Anyway, come in for a couple of minutes, he's not ready yet. I'll go help him get dressed."

"Monique…" said my father as he came towards us. "I'm still capable of dressing myself."

My mother gave a disappointed little sigh, as Élodie rushed towards our father and wrapped her arms around him like she hadn't done in years. My God, they love drama, I thought. Over Élodie's shoulder, my father shot me a little wink.

"Okay, we've been waiting FIFTEEN minutes," said Élodie.

"Élo, the day when people don't wait at least fifteen minutes for a doctor's appointment, you can assume the apocalypse is at hand."

Exactly seven minutes later, the doctor called my father. He got up and gave us a smile. "You know," he said, "it's just a blood test. I could have come by myself."

"No! No," Élodie nearly shouted. Then doing something that was really out of character, she took one of our father's big hands in her own and kissed it.

"Oh, my God," she groaned as she watched him leave with the doctor. "I really hope he's going to be okay."

I looked at her for a minute. She almost had tears in her eyes. "Élo... come on..."

"Yeah, but... it's *Papa*!"

"I know, I know..." I took her by the shoulders. In the end, I thought, she's the one I had to keep company. I almost told her she didn't have to wait for the first signs of a possibly incurable disease to show her *papa* how much she loved him, but I bit my tongue.

I still had one arm around her, when I heard someone, just next to me, say my name. I turned around, and there was Gabriel, looking even more handsome than I remembered (Did he really get more and more handsome every day? I had the chance to wonder) and absolutely delighted to see me.

"How are you?" he asked, putting a hand on my shoulder that gave me an electric shock.

"Uhh... good! Good... considered." I made a vague gesture towards our surroundings – except in obstetrics, what good things could happen in a hospital? "What are you doing here?" I added, in a tone that I immediately thought was aggressive, but made Gabriel laugh.

"My best friend is an endocrinologist here."

"Oh. I see." I didn't know what to say to him. He was smiling at me and I was thinking that I had missed that smile, with its mix of amusement and deep affection – he always looked unbelievably *surprised* by me, by what I said, by who I was. But, stupid me, all I could think of was

"But you have a girlfriend!" and "You are so, so hand-some." I could see myself, lying next to him, spending hours looking at his face, caressing his cheeks, getting lost in his eyes. Getting lost in his eyes, I thought. I'd always found that expression incredibly stupid, but with him, I didn't. And it made me mad at myself.

"Hi," Gabriel finally said as he put out a hand to Élodie. "I'm…"

"Gabriel, I know," said Élodie, before she nearly knocked me out of the way to take his hand. "Nice to meet you. Really." Suddenly I was fifteen years old again, and I had to hold myself back to keep from kicking Élodie and looking like a panic-stricken teenager.

"The pleasure is all mine," said Gabriel, his hand still in hers. "Well…" He looked at me and a voice in my head screamed that I had to say something, but I felt like I looked like a deer caught in headlights, and was unable to do anything but look. "Well… call me?" he finally said, and I liked the question mark at the end of his sentence. "Call me," he added, and I adored the period at the end of his sentence.

"Oh, my God, that was pathetic, eh?" I asked as I collapsed on Élodie's knees.

"Honestly?"

"Yes, honestly."

"That was pathetic."

We started to laugh. "You see," I said as I straightened up. "The guy is certainly going to prefer a girlfriend who's a grown-up with a real job, and probably even a real hair-style."

"It's still funny."

"Mmmm."

"Marine?"

"Élodie?"

"What are we going to do if *Papa* really is sick?"

I looked at her for an instant. Her question was perfectly sincere – she didn't want to wallow willingly in unhappiness like our mother. "We'll stick together," I answered. And even as I was thinking to myself that that was the stupidest answer in the world, I saw in Élodie's eyes that it was true and it was exactly that: it's what we did, in the end, it was what was in Jeff's eyes when I said "That's where the hope of love comes in," that's what I could see lately in Julien's grateful attitude: we were sticking together.

The snow had turned to rain during the course of the afternoon and I was completely soaked when I got to the apartment. Élodie had insisted on driving back from my parents' and she'd let me off at the corner because, she claimed, she was "in a huge hurry." And easygoing and calm as I was, I pretended to believe her though I knew the only urgent thing she had to do was get home and spend an unending amount of time getting ready for another one of the dates she collected.

"Oh, my God," I said as I came in. "It smells so good in here!" I felt like I'd walked into a warm, welcoming cocoon – I felt keenly and deeply happy, the kind of happiness that comes from security, familiar surroundings, a fire in the fireplace, and the marble of scarlet that settles in the bottom of a glass of red wine, and the presence of someone you know perfectly and really love.

"Chicken with candied lemon," said Jeff as he lifted the cover off a big pot that let off a puff of sweet-smelling steam. He'd set the table, and only when I noticed the third placemat and the third wineglass did I stop smiling. Why had I agreed to attend this dinner? We all knew it was ridiculous. I was sure of it. I took off my coat with a sigh and went towards Jeff who was holding out a glass of red wine. The light is so pretty here, I thought. That was why I liked the house more in winter than in summer. When it was dark out at four-thirty, the large room changed into a showcase of golden light nestling pleasantly against the brick wall, the big bookshelves and the table where the glasses sparkled.

Jeff, leaning over the counter, was concentrating on grating an enormous chunk of dark chocolate which, I knew would be transformed into delicious chocolate fondants, a classic that never failed and that was, according to Jeff, a powerful aphrodisiac. (I always felt like pointing out that, according to him, *everything* was an aphrodisiac, except maybe leeks, and even that wasn't sure.) "How did it go?" he asked.

"I ran into Gabriel at the hospital."

He laid down his knife and rested his two fists on the counter. "Marine. Shit."

"What?"

"You could at least pretend to be more interested in what's happening to your father." He was smiling affectionately – he wasn't horrified, or even shocked, but it was obvious that he found my attitude unbelievable and I could only agree with him.

"Christ…" I said as I sat at the counter. "Christ, I'm awful."

"No, no," he said laughing. "Well, yeah, you are awful. But it doesn't matter. We're all the same, Marine. So?"

"So, what? My father or Gabriel?"

"Your father, Miss Innocent. We both know very well that's what we're interested in and that if your father wasn't doing well, you would have told me as soon as you came in."

I gave him a grateful smile. "He was there to see a friend of his. We didn't even talk for five minutes."

"And?…" He was talking without looking at me, he was too busy trying to separate out the yolks from half a dozen eggs.

"And even Élodie agreed it was pathetic."

"Pathetic?" When he was distracted, he had a tic that consisted of repeating the last word he'd just heard, and adding a question mark.

"Pathetic, pathetic. I acted like I was twelve years old, and when he said, 'Call me,' I nearly peed my pants. Christ, I don't know what's wrong with me, but it's like when he's around I'm a complete idiot."

"Idiot?..."

"Could you please stop repeating the ends of all my sentences?"

"Sentences?..."

"Jesus, you're getting on my nerves."

I started to laugh, and so did he. He finally raised his eyes, looked at me and smiled for an instant.

"What?" I asked.

"Christ, you're beautiful."

I sat in stunned silence for an instant – complete, absolute, dumbfounded silence – then I stammered, "Are you drunk, or what?" It was easier to be just a little unpleasant and aggressive. He laughed, then, with his eyes back down on his chocolate, he answered, "No, not even." I looked at him, begging my heart and my mind to come up with something intelligent, or at least something nice, to say, but no luck. So a kind of silence we weren't used to settled over us, it was heavy and full of unspoken words, and I was wishing that Flavie would show up an hour early to save us from the weight neither one of us wanted to carry, because it was so unlike us, princes of light-heartedness and regents of easygoingness that we were.

"So, Gabriel?" Jeff finally asked. "And your father?"

But I didn't feel like talking about my father with him. He'd come out of the examining room with the funny little courageous smile that he'd been wearing for weeks and that broke my heart because it was first and foremost a sign of worry, and he told us that he wouldn't hear anything for two or three weeks, and maybe, always maybe. Since he'd started having tests, we'd been swimming in a lake of maybes, kilometers away from any solid information we could hold onto. I had to start getting used to uncertainty – I'd been surrounded by it for months already, and I was wondering if I'd ever even touched anything else, if at any point in my life I'd ever had firm footing. Maybe before, I hadn't minded the wandering, I thought as I mechanically grabbed a sliver of chocolate. Maybe I'd just simply run out of breath.

"Gabriel…" I started, but I didn't feel like talking about Gabriel either. I didn't know what to say – what was there to say, anyway? He's handsome, lalala, I looked like an idiot in front of him, lalala? I wasn't fifteen anymore. Above all, I didn't *want* to be fifteen. I suddenly felt very tired and I wanted to go far, far away, to the beach, maybe, or some huge city where no one knew me and I could finally rest, invisible and anonymous. I went and stretched out on the sofa, next to Claude François, who stretched out to his full length and replied to my petting him with a grateful meow. Jeff had his back to me, he was stirring, mixing, sniffing, blending, and I knew most of what he was doing was pointless, it was just to fill up the silence between us. I was a little upset with him – my vanity wished he'd say more about the beauty he seemed to have discovered in me, and above all I would have preferred that he not try to forget that sentence amid the noise of clanking pans. I put my glass down on the table, and I closed my eyes.

When I woke up, Jeff was sitting in his chair, opposite me, reading. I observed him for an instant, happy to look at him when he didn't know what I was doing. The golden light shone on one side of his face and his fingers were against his temple, and I thought he was handsome and human. How ridiculous is it to find someone "human," I thought. Obviously, he was human. Finding the cat human would be surprising. But with Jeff, it went without saying. Still, that's the word that came to mind, and there was something touching and almost disturbing in the idea. I didn't like thinking of Jeff as fragile, and I understood that my definition of "human" was dangerously similar to my definition of "fragile."

Jeff turned a page. "Did I sleep long?" I asked him. He raised his eyes, but didn't move – his blue eyes looked almost black in the semi-darkness – and he made the same face he always did when he didn't know the answer to a question or hesitated. "A half-hour?" he answered. "I don't know. I had time to get everything finished. I'm the most ready guy in town."

"Sorry… I wasn't really much help, was I?"

"No problem. Technically, I'm the one who invited her."

"Yeah, I know." I rolled over onto my back and stared at the ceiling. Thirty seconds later, Flavie rang the bell. I sat up, settled for pointing at the door with my thumb so Jeff would get it.

"You sure?" he asked. "She's YOUR friend." I gave him my famous "Are you kidding me?" look and he got up. I was getting ready to do the same when I heard the door open and someone said, very loudly, "No, no, no. Out. Out. What…? HEY!" and Julien burst in, ignoring Jeff, like a green and yellow arrow (were those pink Ugg boots I saw on his feet?) and came to a stop right in front of me.

"He agreed to see me! He *agreed* to SEE me!!!" He looked so happy and ridiculous, with his arms flung open, that I started to laugh.

"Julien…" Jeff said in a voice that was almost pitiful, "we're having company tonight. And… shit, are your boots pink?"

"I AAAAMMM YOUR… singing telegram," Julien started singing, and even Jeff laughed. Still, he came closer after a couple of seconds, just as Julien was nearly lifting me off the ground, and said, "Really, Ju. Please."

"Please? No, no, no. This is me saying please. I can't stay by myself, I'll explode."

"Pretty please," I added. I thought that if Julien stayed, I'd have at least one ally in case of a heavy necking session or too many sweet nothings between Jeff and Flavie.

"No!" said Jeff. "And besides, there's not enough food." This time, Julien joined me for the famous "Are you kidding me?" look – Jeff always cooked enough for at least twelve people, even if he was eating alone.

"Oh, Christ!" and with that "Christ," in came Flavie through the still open door, looking superb in a long hound's-tooth coat, with her red mane tied up in a spectacular bun.

"So, you're having company?" she said, looking happy, and she hugged Julien, who was standing closest to the door – and I felt a little bad for Jeff, and extremely happy for myself.

An hour later, there were already three empty bottles on the table and we'd barely started the first course of the meal. We'd stuffed ourselves on a cold cut platter Flavie had brought for hors d'oeuvres and we were saturated on fat – and on speculations about the future of Julien's love life. Flavie seemed particularly interested, and she advised him, cautioned him and encouraged him, and I'd gotten to the point where I said to myself that I was going to scream if I heard "You can never take ANYTHING for granted. Julien. Never. Take. Anything. For. Granted" one more time, from a girl who's making it sound like she knows all there is to know on the subject and has lived just a little more than others.

"Seriously," I said, "you can't forget that, whatever happens, Mathias may have some trust issues."

"But I love him!"

"Of course you love him, you big jerk!" said Jeff. "But if a guy who cheated on his girlfriend or boyfriend only had to bleat 'I loooove you' in order to be forgiven, people would know about it."

"That's really not that stupid," said Flavie. "But don't get carried away, sweetie. One step at a time."

"Baby steps," I added.

"NO!" Julien banged his hand on the table, making the cat, who had been peacefully asleep on an empty chair, jump up. "NO!" he repeated, and Claude François took off, giving him an angry look. "I'm almost forty years old, and I'm sick of counting my steps, being careful, and hoping – but not too much, because it might hurt if I hope too much. I want giant steps, get it? I want to dive right in, I want to take the plunge, I want to believe anything is possible."

He stopped – he was halfway to his feet when he seemed to suddenly notice our stunned faces and the fact that he was flirting dangerously with the absurd, with one arm in the air, a napkin clenched in his other fist, and spitting out his sentences with uncharacteristic vehemence, which, given the situation, had nearly pathetic connotations. I looked towards Jeff who, I was sure, was just waiting for a few seconds to pass before he came out with something like, "You okay, Mr. Midlife Crisis?" He was looking at Julien, with a slight smile on his face. Here comes the bad joke, I thought. But Jeff raised his glass and, sincere as could be, he said, "Bravo, Ju. That's probably the worst idea in the world, but I like it. Here's to giant steps."

Out of the corner of my eye, I could see Flavie looking at Jeff with a smile. She raised her glass, too, while Julien sat down, looking surprised by his own remarks, and even more surprised by the reaction of the other two. What else could I do? I raised my glass, too, thinking that we were on the verge of believing literally anything, we wanted so badly to believe in something, period.

I spent the rest of the evening feeling like I was watching a play, where, for some inexplicable reason, I was sitting right on the stage. Flavie getting closer to Jeff, while he started rubbing her back more or less subtly. I was there, present, right next to them, but I didn't feel like I was *with* them. I was lost in a maze of disconnected thoughts, and the phrase "giant steps" was echoing in my head, and the image of the Giant's Causeway, which I'd seen in Northern Ireland years before was floating before my eyes, like a stupidly easy analogy that I was too tired to push away.

I was thinking of Gabriel, about the idea that maybe it was wiser to jump right in, than try to patiently calculate my chances of finding the safe, direct road that would lead me to straight happiness.

Around two in the morning, Julien, who was completely drunk and literally jumping for joy to come and optimism, finally proclaimed maybe it was time for him to go home, that he was going to see Mathias the next day, so maybe it would be a good idea not to be in too bad a shape, and reek of alcohol to the high heavens. "It's a little late for that, old man," said Jeff, making every laugh the happy, tender laugh of drunkenness.

"Do you think you could give me a lift?" Julien asked Flavie, who only lived a block away from him. She smiled, pulled up her hair with a magnificent, Amazon-like movement, and looked at Jeff. I motioned for Julien to come with me into the kitchen, to leave them alone for a minute, but Jeff, in a frankly encouraging voice, was already saying, "That might be a good idea, Flavie. I'm sure Mr. Pink Boots here isn't in any shape to drive, or even walk home."

"I can take a cab," stammered Julien.

"No, I'll drive you," Flavie said. And I caught her as she shot Jeff a wink that meant "We'll make up for this next time." They gave each other a smile and I thought, okay, giant steps.

"Everything okay?" I asked Jeff as we finished off the end of a bottle of white wine while we cleaned up the kitchen.

"I'm okay. But what about you? You looked kind of… off."

"Yeah, maybe. Sorry. That thing of Julien's about giant steps. Gabriel, my father, I don't know. Maybe I'm just drunk." I finished drying a pot. "Did I spoil your evening? Is it because I was here that things didn't gel with Flavie?"

"No! Not at all… Mr. Pink Boots may be all excited about diving right in, but there's no need to be hasty, is there? You know me, I'm not in a hurry."

"It's still weird."

"You're one to talk."

I laughed, half-heartedly, and turned back towards him. He was looking at me, making that little doubtful, hesitating face. I still had the cast-iron pot in my hand when he kissed me. I dropped it on the stove with a big clang and put my arm around his neck as he lifted me up onto the counter. This is it, I thought to myself through a fog of alcohol and desire. We're jumping in.

To: Fred
From: Marine Vandale
Subject: SOS

....

You asleep?

To: Fred
From: Marine Vandale
Subject: SOS!!!

....

YOU ASLEEP?

To: Marine
From: Frédéric Vandale
Subject: Regarding the nature of sleep

....

First, of all, if I was asleep, I don't see why my computer would be on, nor how I ever would have heard the nice little "ping!" sound it makes when I get email, since the computer is in the office and, strangely enough, I usually sleep in the bedroom. And besides, why would I be sleeping at eleven in the morning? And now, the corollary to this question – what are you doing up at five in the morning?

To: Fred
From: Marine Vandale
Subject: Amazing lack of insight

....

Just in case the SOS didn't put a bug in your ear, I'm in deep, the absolutely deepest possible shit. And, by the way, the last time you got up before noon, you were still in high school.

To: Marine
From: Frédéric Vandale
Subject: A new man

You wouldn't recognize me anymore, little sister. For the last
three weeks, nine a.m. has found me typing away at my computer to achieve creation, cerebral activity and health through
work. It's a sweatshop over here.

To: Fred
From: Marine Vandale
Subject: A deaf man

Is there something you don't get about the letters S.O.S.?

To: Marine
From: Frédéric Vandale
Subject: I'm listening

Okay, I get it. What's going on?

To: Fred
From: Marine Vandale
Subject: Deep, deep caca

You remember when I told you I'd made a little boo-boo with
Jeff? Well, the boo-boo has taken on astronomical proportions,
it's not a boo-boo anymore, it's a catastrophe.

To: Marine
From: Frédéric Vandale
Subject: Astronomy 101

Can you give me a few more details, please? Because, right now
I'm thinking of one thing, and if the catastrophe in question is

indeed what I'm thinking, I may be left speechless and need an emergency glass of pastis.

To: Fred
From: Marine Vandale
Subject: Re: Astronomy 101

Go get the pastis.

To: Marine
From: Frédéric Vandale
Subject: RE: Astronomy 101

Oh no. Are you KIDDING me? You didn't, did you?

To: Fred
From: Marine Vandale
Subject: Correction

Did it even occur to you that HE might be the one who did it? Has it never struck you there has to be two people to do it?

To: Marine
From: Frédéric Vandale
Subject: Apologies and questions

Okay, sorry. Now, if you don't mind, I'd like to ask, as politely and deferentially as I possibly can, what, exactly, were you thinking?

To: Fred
From: Marine Vandale
Subject: Your stupidity astounds me

What do you think I was thinking, you jerk? Has France really made you that stupid?

To: Marine
From: Frédéric Vandale
Subject: Soft-headed

....

If you don't mind, I'd like to chalk it up to creativity. But, okay,
I can guess what you were thinking. But... Marine? As we say
in Québec... *Câlisse?*

To: Fred
From: Marine Vandale
Subject: Câlisse, period.

....

Câlisse is right. And I'm figuring if it got you to give me a good
old Québecois *câlisse* when you've been wallowing in that
French *putain* and *bordel* for months, then it must really be as
bad as I think.

To: Marine
From: Frédéric Vandale
Subject: Let's stay calm

....

Listen. I don't know. Maybe not, no? Maybe love and all the
trimmings have been discovered and there's sudden joy at the
idea that my beloved sister is going to go out with my best
friend.

To: Fred
From: Marine Vandale
Subject: No, let's panic

....

I'm not going to go out with your best friend, Fred. And there's
even less of a chance that I'm going to go out with MY best
friend. I don't know what got into us, but I do know what got
into ME. Yes, indeed, I know exactly WHO got into me, and on
the counter, on top of everything, and... Oh, my God, Fred,

he's still asleep but panic has replaced my own skin, my whole body is covered in panic and the strong desire to wake up in a few seconds.

To: Marine
From: Frédéric Vandale
Subject: No, let's stay calm

Marine, it's eleven a.m. and I have a pastis as big as a swimming pool in my left hand, so, stop getting all worked up and give me some details. How did it happen?

To: Fred
From: Marine Vandale
Subject: (none)

Fred. I've spent the last two hours feverishly trying to get the details out of my own head. So, give me a minute, or even three or four years before I share them with you.

To: Marine
From: Frédéric Vandale
Subject: Final effort

Whatever you say. But tell me, was it good?

To: Fred
From: Marine Vandale
Subject: Resisting the effort

Don't you think that at five in the morning that's exactly the kind of question I'm trying to avoid? Do you really think that if I'm avoiding sleep to this point, it's exactly to avoid dreaming about it? Fred, I've thought of blowing this Popsicle stand.

To: Marine
From: Frédéric Vandale
Subject: Perseverance

....

So if I try my, "Was it good?" again, I've got no chance, eh?

To: Fred
From: Marine Vandale
Subject: Re: Perseverance

....

Okay, that's it. Suck on your pastis as long as you like, I'm out of here.

Chapter 12

So, I ran away. In the darkness of my room, where I refused to turn on any lights for fear of waking up Jeff, I mechanically slipped on an old sweater and a pair of quilted cotton pants I'd had since high school. A useless image suddenly popped into my head, a bubble from the past that I hadn't called to, but that had risen up nonetheless, gently, to the surface of my conscious: I could still see myself, sixteen years old, in the huge high school gym, miserable and wearing the same pair of pants, with a badminton racket in one hand and my eyes fixed on the handsome Mathieu Saint-Laurent who was kissing the beautiful Clara Toussaint, next to the net. "Oh the dejection and despair of adolescence, oh those carefree days," I murmured, mocking myself. And still, as I put on my boots with Claude François rubbing on my legs and meowing, I was upset with myself for not having appreciated the simple joys of those times.

I looked around the apartment one last time before I left, and I held back a vague desire to cry and gently pushed the cat away, though he kept trying to follow me. Where was this ridiculous nostalgia coming from, as if I were leaving forever? That's not it, I said to myself, as I closed the door. It's that I know this place will never ever be the same, it will always be stained now – absolutely, indelibly – with the memory of what had just happened. "Can you please tell me what got into us?" I said out loud, as I stood on the landing outside and wondered, exactly, where I was going with my handbag, my quilted pants and my confused conscience. What had gotten into us?

Jeff had picked me up as if I weighed no more than a feather. I felt myself being lifted off the floor, then lightly set on the counter, where we'd had so many drinks together, free from desire and its terrible, beautiful consequences. And once again, I felt the dizziness of my empty mind and of my body, which I'd finally settled completely into. I could feel my skin and my stomach, and Jeff's tongue talking a long walk across my epidermis. And? That was it. Abandonment, which apparently is what I'd wanted for a long time already, maybe forever. Bad idea, I thought. Terrible, terrible idea. And I'd smiled on the inside, because the fact that the idea was terrible made it all the more irresistible to me.

"Shut up," said Élodie as I walked into her place. "Shut up and just tell me what happened because you'd better have a fucking good reason for waking me up at this hour." I'd finally made my way to her house, for lack of a better idea – Laurent was living with Carole and wasn't talking to me anymore, Julien was probably dead drunk, Flavie obviously had an eye on Jeff. Élodie opened the door, with a stuffy nose and smeared make-up, and on her face one of the most spectacularly stupid looks that I'd ever seen in my life.

"I slept with Jeff," I finally blurted out. With her raccoon eyes almost bulging out of her head, she let me in and only let me take my coat off when she'd heard every last detail (especially the indecent ones).

"We did it on the counter," I added, with my stupid toque still on my head. "Then we did a lot of other things on the kitchen floor, and when I thought my epidermis was going to fall off, I was so excited and stimulated, we went to my bedroom."

"And then?"

"What do you think, silly?"

Images were coming back to me, like in a bad movie, damp bodies, passionate hands, exploring tongues and hips bumping feverishly in the darkness with intoxicating, delicious and almost painful urgency.

"Oh!" said Élodie. "Oh boy."

"Oh boy is right," I confirmed.

"What are you going to do?"

"Élo…" I tried not to get mad, but if I'd listened to myself, I would have yelled at her, I would have called her stupid and inexperienced. I would have criticized her for her stupid, sterile questions. "Do you really think that I would have knocked on your door at five-thirty in the morning if I had the slightest idea of what I was going to do? I ran away, Élodie. I'm thirty-two years old and I ran away from our home like a thief in the night because I'm frightened by what I did with my housemate, who, incidentally, is my best friend. So, I don't know. I don't know, I don't know, I don't know." I started slapping myself on the head.

"Okay, okay," said Élodie, as she removed my toque. "Ooooo. Kay. It's not that bad, is it?" I quickly turned my head and gave her such an explicit look she didn't add a word.

"Do you want something?" she finally asked. "A coffee?"

"No…"

"A glass of something?"

"No! No, it's five-thirty in the morning. Just a glass of water. I'm going to try to get some sleep."

"Now that's a good idea. That's a seeeeeeriously good idea. Come sleep in my bed with me. There's room."

Wonderful, I thought as I followed her into her white-and-blue bedroom. I'm going to sleep in my little sister's bed with her, after I slept with my best friend, got into a fight with my ex and looked ridiculous in front of the only real man to cross my path in years. Won.der.ful.

"I'm just going to brush my teeth," I said. But my phone

was already ringing, sharp and incongruous at this hour, and I knew before I looked at it that it was Jeff. Élodie did, too, obviously, and we stood there facing each other, both stamping our feet, talking at once and making a series of gestures that were both incomprehensible and useless.

"Answer it!" Élodie was shouting.

"No!"

"Answer, then it will be over with!"

"No! No! Oh my God, Élodie, what am I doing?"

"Jesus Christ, answer it, or I'll do it for you!"

"Okay! Okay! No. No, no."

I held the phone towards her and she pretended to take it then raised her hands in the air, desperately mouthing, "Answer it!" We were in ridiculous poses when, suddenly, the phone stopped ringing, leaving us motionless, Élodie with her arms in the air and me, inexplicably on one leg and holding the phone as far away from my body as possible. "Fuck," we said together, staring at my cell phone. Then we looked at each other and burst out laughing.

"Okay," I said, getting into a more normal position. "This is ridiculous." Élodie nodded yes, still laughing. "I should call back, shouldn't I?"

"Mmm hmm!" We laughed even harder, and I sat down on the sofa. "I'll go get you a drink," said Élodie. "Exceptional circumstances."

"Yeah, I think so, too."

She went towards the kitchen in her little blue pajamas, and I could still hear her laugh as she shouted, "Man, what was that thing you were doing when you were waving your hands on each side of your head like you were swatting flies?"

"Hey... I'm not the one who had both my arms stretched up in the air, okay?" I laughed a little more and looked at the phone. Of course I had to call him. Jeff must have woken up a little while after I left, he must be looking for me and if I didn't check in in a few minutes, he'd call Julien, then Laurent, then my mother, then Flavie. Very bad. I pinched my nose high up between my eyebrows – a useless gesture people make when they want to think hard – but in my case, it only elicited one thought: Can you please tell me why people pinch their nose when they want to concentrate? I was terribly tired and completely incapable of reasoning.

"Okay," I said out loud, in order to give a little depth to my thoughts. "Have to call. And the truth is, it's not THAT bad." I opened my eyes. "Oh God. It was THAT bad... ÉLODIE!"

"What?" she yelled from the kitchen

"On a scale of one to ten, where ten is the worst worst and one is the least worst, where would you put me right now?"

She came back into the living room with two cups. "I'm sure you feel like you're at about eleven or twelve, but objectively, I guess I'd say, you're at about a... I don't know. Three? Four? Obviously, there's an annoying part to all this, 'cause it might change things between you two, but look at it this way, you didn't cheat on anyone, and it's not THAT true that sex ruins friendship."

"No. No, that is true." I made a little mental list of the men I'd slept with, who were still friends, some close, some not so close, but friends nonetheless, and I gave her a grateful little look.

"Yes," I said, "BUT. Jeff wasn't just a friend. He's my housemate. I live with him. And he's my best friend."

"I know. Five, maybe? But I'm not going any higher than that."

I pensively nodded my head as I took a drink from my cup, and immediately began to choke. "Jesus, what is that?"

"A grog."

"A grog? You know you're supposed to put water in, too."

"Really? I just warmed up the rum."

"Jesus, what are you doing, taking night classes with Julien?"

"How is he?"

"Over the moon. Mathias agreed to see him tomorrow... well, today, actually, he's so far up in the clouds, I'm afraid he's going to fall down hard."

"But maybe not."

"No, maybe not. But maybe he will."

"Did you ever notice that you tend to expect the worst so you don't get disappointed?"

"It's not to avoid disappointment, it's superstition. Like, if you hope for the best, it won't happen."

"That's completely stupid."

"Yeah, I know."

We didn't say anything for a minute; just the fumes from the rum were going to my head.

"Marine?"

"Yes?"

"Phone."

"Hmmm?"

"Phone, Marine! Call him! Stop being so naive. The longer you wait, the weirder it'll be."

"Okay, okay! I hate it when you're cleverer than I am. All right, all right, I'll call."

I was reaching for the phone when it started ringing again. I turned to Élodie, who was looking at me so seriously that I almost laughed, then she shouted, "If you don't answer in two rings, I will."

"Okay, okay..."

It's like ripping off a Band-Aid, I said to myself. Do it quick and it'll be over. "Hello?"

"Hello..." his relief was almost exaggerated.

"Hello," I repeated. Too much to say. Too much to say, and no idea where to begin. I pushed Élodie away, after she'd just about glued herself to me in order to hear the conversation.

"You left," said Jeff. It wasn't a question, but a statement, and our habit of always making fun of each other almost led me to say, "No shit, Sherlock."

"Yeah. Sorry. I freaked out. I'm still freaking out, by the way."

"Where are you?"

"At Élodie's."

"You okay?"

"Well, I don't know. I don't know." And that was the truth: I didn't know.

"Look, Marine. It's not that serious. It's nothing."

"Hey!"

"No, no, no! I don't mean nothing like that! It's just nothing."

"It's nothing." I stupidly insisted. Did I really want him to throw himself at my feet and announce that screwing with me had changed his life? Was I that arrogant? Probably, yeah.

"Not a bad nothing! A good nothing!"

"Jeff, that doesn't make any sense."

"What, what happened?"

"No, what you just said."

"What?"

There was a period of silence and we both started laughing, a nervous, happy laugh, because anything was better than tension and not saying anything.

"Christ, Jeff, what got into us?"

"I don't know… I've been trying to figure it out for an hour."

"An hour?"

"Yep, an hour. I was awake when you left. Too stupid and chicken to hold you back."

"Look, don't blame yourself. I'm the one who was too stupid and chicken to stay."

"Good point."

Images of his body over mine on the super cold kitchen floor, then of my own straddling his in the tangled sheets came back to me, and I uselessly covered my eyes with my hand. "Jeff… shit…"

"I know, I know."

"Yeah, but what…"

"Stop asking what got into us. We don't know, okay. You're all mixed up with everything going on, as for me…"

"What about you?" Sudden and intense panic: was he going to admit he'd always secretly been in love with me?

"I've been jumping around for years from one thing to the next, from Marie-Lune to Flavie, thinking I'll find what I'm looking for, but no matter how tough you act, it still leaves you empty. Watch out."

"Oh. Okay." Sudden and intense humiliation and relief: the man wasn't in love, and I was seriously presumptuous. "Are we going to tell the guys?"

"Eh? No. No, no, no. No, eh?"

"Jeff, we always tell each other everything. It's bound to come out."

"We'll let it come out at the right place and time, okay?"

"Okay…" I looked at Élodie who was listening to my side of the conversation, looking so greedy for it, it was almost funny, and, when she saw me look at her, she felt the need to give me two thumbs up to encourage me.

"Was it my fault?" I asked. "Because of what I did last month?"

"Don't ask yourself questions like that, Marine. It's a miracle it didn't happen a long time ago."

"Sorry?"

"Jesus, Marine! You're pretty, I'm a pig. You do the math."

I laughed. "Are we going to be okay, Jeff?"

"We have no choice. I don't want to lose you."

"Neither do I."

"You want to come home?"

"No. I'm just too tired. I'm going to go to bed."

"Okay. Love you tons."

"Me, too."

I hung up and the "tons" floated in front of me toning down the verb, and I understood perfectly. And I also thought we weren't going to be as "okay" as we were letting ourselves think, that for a long time, between us, there'd be the memory of what we shouldn't have done, what we had done for the wrong reasons, and that we regretted for even worse ones. Pride, desire, fear of losing the other, and of losing face, it all added up to a pretty disgusting mixture.

"You okay?" asked Élodie. I shrugged my shoulders, thinking that if things kept going the way they were I'd save quite a bit of time and a good number of tantrums if I just had a tee-shirt that said *I don't know if I'm okay* made for myself.

"Pretty okay, if you know what I mean."

"But you're not okay, either."

"Here's a clue: it's six in the morning and I'm drinking a cup of hot rum at my little sister's."

"Personally, I'm glad you came over."

It was such a cute, sincere statement that I couldn't keep from stroking her hair maternally. "What about you? What about your love life?"

"Well, I think David's seeing other girls."

"David…"

"Yeah! David! You know! We've been going out for three weeks."

Did I know? I wondered. There was no trace of a David in my brain – but, I had to admit that for years that, in the interest of my own survival and not getting overloaded, I had decided to aggressively filter all information about Élodie's love life. Too complicated. Algebraic theorems were simpler and took up infinitely less room.

"David…" I said evasively. "Yessss…"

"Well the other day, I found a condom wrapper on his bedside table. And he hadn't opened it with me. Do you think that's a clue?"

"Ummm…"

"You think it is? Oh no, you think it is?!"

"If you prefer, I can say that maybe he suddenly felt like using his rubbers to make water balloons to throw at people passing by."

"What am I going to do?"

"If he's throwing water balloons?"

"Marine!" She put on her offended look. How could she be so lucid about other people's love lives and so stupid about her own? Then, I thought, I do exactly the same thing, and I put my arm around her.

"Did you talk about being exclusive?"

"*Now* you have to talk about it?"

"Sometimes, I think. We've become modern and open, what can I say."

"Can't you just take it for granted?"

"Élodie, my dear, let me take this opportunity to share an important truth: you can never take ANYTHING for granted. Remember that and you'll save yourself a lot of trouble.

"You're one to talk, Mrs. I-was-insulted-when-Gabriel-told-me-he-was-seeing-someone-because-I'd-taken-for-granted-that-he-was-single."

"I didn't say I didn't take anything for granted. I just said it's a bad idea. Because, in case you haven't noticed, I'm in a heap of trouble myself, thank you very much."

"It's not THAT bad."

I hope they have a two-for-one deal at the tee-shirt maker's, I thought. The one saying, "I know it's not THAT bad" had a good chance of wearing out before the first one did.

"Can you live with that?" I asked.

"With the fact that he see's other girls? NO!"

"Well, then, you know what you have to do."

"What?"

"Tell him!"

"Then what, he dumps me because he's not ready to be 'exclusive'?" She made air quotes with her fingers, and a little face, too.

"I was thinking more that YOU would dump him if he isn't ready for that."

"Yeah, but I looovvve him!"

"Okay. No. No, no, no. Enough of that. You don't love him. Besides, you're going to have to stand up for yourself, Élodie. It's a sure thing that if this guy can have you and other girls, he will. He's not that stupid, is he?"

"Bastard."

"No. He didn't make you any promises, as far as I know," and I thought of Christophe again. I hadn't promised him anything either, but there was an implied commitment, and I knew it.

"I'm not going to say anything to him," Élodie stammered in a weak voice.

"As you wish. But you have to be honest with yourself."

"You're not being very nice!"

"Okay. Okay." And I took her in my arms. "It's just that I'm beyond tired. But, admit it, I do sound a little bit like the voice of reason."

"Reason is not nice!"

"No. No, that's for sure." I kept my arms around her for a minute. Through the window, above my fingers, I could see a strip of blue sky. "Come on," I said to her. Let's try to get a little sleep. It's been a fucking long day."

In Élodie's single bed, I dreamed of Jeff. He was standing

in the snow, wearing nothing but a tee-shirt. He wanted to
tell me something, but every time he opened his mouth,
colours were all that would come out. Red curlicues, blue
curlicues, green curlicues, and he tried to catch them.

"Sorry," I sighed, sitting down at my spot. "Oh, sorry,
sorry, sorry." Julien looked at me, his arms were crossed
and his look was angry, then suddenly confused.

"What did you do to your face?"

"Hmmm?" I raised one hand to my face. I'd been
woken up, after five hours of absolutely unrestorative
sleep, by a call from Julien, who was waiting for me at the
restaurant, where we were supposed to have brunch
together to prepare for Mathias' visit. Not only had I completely forgotten our date, but I had a hard time believing
he'd managed to get out of bed himself. "I've been on
Gatorade since ten a.m.," he'd told me. "It's a red-letter
day, you know. We've gotta get going. No excuses. I
ordered us some mimosas."

A brief inspection in one of Élodie's countless mirrors
had confirmed what I was afraid of: I really did look like
shit. AND I was wearing quilted pants. So I'd given Élodie
some frantic shakes to wake her up so she'd give me a pair
of jeans and a decent sweater, and to presort for me the
fifty million beauty products she possessed. But all her
blushes were sugary pink, and she'd insisted on putting
some concealer on me herself, and some "tanning powder"
which was supposed to give me the look of "vitality." The
results being that I now looked like Barbie, and that I was
wearing a tiny sweater that I had to keep pulling down so
it didn't ride up over my breasts, and a pair of jeans with a
waist that came six inches below my navel. I should have
kept on my cotton pants, I thought, when I saw Julien lean
over the table to have a good look.

"So, where should we start exactly?" he asked. One of
the servers I saw there almost every day walked by our

table and gave me a look that was a little worried.

"It's a long story. I spent the night at Élodie's."

"I was thinking you reminded me of someone... But... why?"

I took a drink of my mimosa. "We'll let it come out at the right place and time," Jeff had said, but I couldn't believe the time and place was already here and now. And without missing a trick, his eyes suddenly popped wide open and he slapped a hand against one cheek, in a gesture that made me want to laugh.

"Nooooooooooooooooooooo." It was the longest "No" in history.

"Yep." And the shortest "Yep."

"No."

"How long are we going to keep doing this?"

"As long as it takes for me to digest the information." He emptied his glass. "Nooooo."

"Oh, yes."

"No."

"What, no?" I looked up. Laurent was standing beside the table, with a silly little smile on his face. "What?" he said. "Just because I acted stupid yesterday, doesn't mean I'm going to start missing Sunday brunch, you know?"

"Loulou!" I said. He was all things good and reassuring. I put my arms around his neck as he asked Julien, "Is she already drunk?" He finally sat down. He looked like he was in a particularly good mood. "I talked to Carole."

"Talked about what?"

"I told her... um... what's with your face? What kind of make-up is that?"

"It's a long story. What did you tell Carole?" Across from me, I could see Julien, stamping his feet, completely devoured by his desire to shout out the news.

"Well, after the market yesterday, we got in a fight, because yes, as you can imagine, I made a scene." I said "sorry" with a smile. "But instead of just shouting incoherently…"

"Do you regularly shout incoherently?"

"Oh, yes. I'd show you an example, but it'd scare the other customers. Anyway. I told her if she wanted things to continue, she'd have to accept that you were still part of my life and that Sunday was my morning with my friends. Some guys have poker nights, I have Sunday brunch."

"Manly."

"You do what you can," bringing a delicate glass of mimosa up to his lips, with his little finger waving in the air.

"How'd she take it?"

"Not well."

"So?"

"Well, we talked about it, and talked and talked and talked some more until my ears were ringing."

"Why didn't you just tell her you love her? That would have helped the medicine go down."

"Okay. Wow. I told her she was very important to me."

Julien and I exchanged a semi-appreciative look: it wasn't fantastic, but it was a start. And, in Laurent's language, that was practically a declaration of deep, undying love.

"Jesus Christ!" said Laurent. "I know it's not easy for her, but you have to make compromises, don't you?"

"Do you ever make any compromises?"

"I do. I live with her."

I put a hand on his thigh. I knew that, if given the choice, Laurent would have preferred, by a long shot, to live alone. I also knew he'd probably be a better lover if that's how things were. But he was never able to sell that idea to any of his girlfriends and they all ended up moving in with him, and then he'd start to complain. He'd give in, faced with love's demands, without even trying to negotiate. "That's a very, very bad strategic move," we'd tell him over and over, knowing full well that we all gave in, too – faced with different fortresses or minefields, but it was all the same in the end.

"Anyway," Laurent went on. "I'm happy. Christ, I feel like I've lost twenty pounds. I just wanted her to understand that, you know? I can't change that much. A little is okay, but not that much. That's not the way to keep people close to you."

"I'll drink to that," approved Julien, raising his glass.

Laurent turned to me again. "Now, can we get back to your face? You look like Murielle Millard."

"Come on, now. Take it easy, it's not that bad, is it?"

Julien looked at me, looking sorry for me and shaking his head, while Laurent now leaned under the table.

"What's going on? Are you disguised as Élodie?"

"Yess! Yesss!" said Julien, pointing two overexcited fingers at him.

"Why? Didn't you have a dinner at your place last night?"

"Yes…"

"And then what, Jeff and Flavie started screwing on the counter? So you left?"

"Okay," I said to Julien. "Wouldn't you like to believe that, too?"

"I left with Flavie, she drove me home."

"Oh yeah."

"So," asked Laurent. Julien was practically lying on the table, his arms stretched out towards Laurent, begging. Laurent seemed to hesitate for a moment. He scrutinized my face, and, as I counted the seconds before the revelation, I saw it arrive, with great big eyes and a wide open mouth.

"Nooooooo."

"Yes."

"No way."

"Yes. Way."

"Nooooooooooooo."

He turned back towards Julien, looking stunned, and they started nodding their heads like two idiots, their hands spread apart, in a gesture of powerlessness, and I put my hand beneath Laurent's jaw because it was about to come unhinged from one second to the next. Then, Julien cooed something, one finger pointed towards the entryway, and I didn't need to turn around to know Jeff was there.

"Well, that really did take an awful long time before it came out," said Jeff as he sat down. "I figured that... Shit, what did you put on your face?"

"Élodie's make-up," answered Julien as quickly as he could, so no time would be lost before we got down to the juicy stuff. "Jeff. Really. Nooooooo."

"It looks like."

"No," said Laurent. "I can't get over it."

"Yep."

"Noooooo…"

"Don't worry, they've been blithering like that for half an hour."

He smiled at me and looked me in the eye for the first time since... since, in fact, we'd found ourselves stuck to each other, damp and out of breath twelve hours earlier. "You okay?" he said to me, and I answered with a smile and a nonchalant shrug of my shoulders. "I wasn't sure about coming…"

"That's what I thought, too," said Laurent. "But, boy am I glad I came," he said, imitating André Dussolier in *Les Enfants du marais*.

"He's in a good mood," I explained to Jeff. "He had a talk with Carole."

"Oh yeah? Well?"

"What do you mean, 'well'?" screamed Julien. "I. Don't. Think. So. I love you, Laurent, but your case is not our priority right now. Okay, we'll debrief for Shrek and Barbie here, but later on, because right now, I want all your brains working together to help me with seeing Mathias tonight."

"Julien," I said, "think about it for a second. Do you really want *our* brains, the three of us here, now, at the point we are all at in our lives, to be the ones to help you? I don't mind, but…"

"But yes, of course! I've noticed that the more idiotic you are in your own love lives, the better advice you give about other people's."

"Hey!" I said happily. "Me, too. Élodie had great advice this morning, and I had good advice for her."

"You should have fucking good advice," Laurent muttered into his glass. I gave him a shot with my elbow, laughing, and buried my face in my hands.

"Christ, I'm so tired it's not even funny."

"Hi, Marine," said a voice nearby. It was Gabriel. I still had my face in my hands and when I remembered the coat of paint Élodie had applied, I settled for just moving two fingers to be sure it was him. And there he was, the same black curls tumbling onto his forehead, the same green eyes with the halo of super sexy wrinkles when he laughed, even the same smile exuding charm and self-confidence.

"Hello?" I said through my hands. "Come on, now, I'm going to seriously start thinking you had some sort of gizmo installed in me, like in science fiction movies, so you'll always know where I am."

"Hey, now. I've been coming here for years, Mademoiselle Vandale. I have rights to this place."

"What about Le Lulli?"

"You can keep Le Lulli." He was laughing.

"What about the hospital?"

"Well, there," said Julien, "you have to play fair, sweetheart. He's a doctor."

"It wasn't *his* hospital."

"I think he wins all the hospitals," said Laurent.

"Even the psychiatric ones?" asked Julien, sounding

much more interested, and they got into one of the interminable, pointless debates that amused them way too
much for my taste. Gabriel was still smiling, with his eyebrows raised, then he turned towards Laurent, and made
a sign with his hands to ask him just what I was doing
with mine.

"Oh, dude. You DON'T want to know what's underneath."

"Okay, okay, that's enough!" I took away my hands and
rolled my eyes like a teenager.

"Ho-ly-sh-it!" shouted Gabriel. "Why? Seriously, why?"

"Do you really want to hear the whole story?" The
three guys turned towards me, their eyes as wide open as
possible, their expressions motionless and overly serious.

"I've got all the time in the world," said Gabriel. "I'm
sitting alone at the bar, so…" The boys were still staring at
me with their bug eyes, so I took it upon myself to invite
Gabriel to join us. He'd hardly turned his back to go get
his coat, before six bulging eyes turned back to the table
to say, what boiled down to, "Are-you-crazy-come-on-if-
you-hope-to-have-the-slightest-chance-with-this-guy-*shut*-
your-mouth-what's-wrong-with-you-did-you-fall-on-
your-head-and-besides-it's-none-of-his-business!!!"

"I'm not going to tell him everything, you idiots."

"Are you going to lie?" asked Julien, saucy and
delighted.

"No, I'm just going to do a little editing." I winked at
Julien, as he rubbed his face in discouragement, and
Laurent, true to form, muttered into his glass, "This, I've
gotta see."

"So," said Gabriel, sitting down at the end of the table
between Jeff and Laurent. "What's this long story?"

"We've never met," said Julien, practically lying down
across the table to take Gabriel's hand. "Julien McKay.
We've spoken on the phone."

"Nice to meet you," said Gabriel. "I've heard a lot about

you."

"So have I," Julien answered, then, a second later, he was wincing from the kick he got in the shin. I shot a look at Jeff, who seemed like he was wondering what he was doing there and finally turned to the server to ask for his famous double Bloody Caesar. Laurent, across from him, was running his handsome almond eyes from him to me, gently trying to figure out our thoughts, what we weren't saying, especially what we weren't saying to *each other*.

An hour later, I'd finished my famous "long" story, which, after my attentive editing, was nothing but a short, everyday story, and we'd been talking about Julien for a long time.

"If I had one piece of advice to give you," said Gabriel, "it would be to really not try to be forgiven right away. Admit your mistakes, my man. Out of respect for him. And, don't ask him to trust you again right away. I don't mean to be unpleasant, but it'll be great if he does trust you again some day. And he has to understand that you understand that."

Julien was listening to him attentively, frowning, nodding from time to time, like someone who's listening to the explanation of a complex theory.

"Don't jump on him," Gabriel said, as he got up to go to the washroom. "Let *him* talk. Because, seriously…" He was obviously thinking of the whole story and was laughing as he left us.

"Okay," said Julien, leaning over towards me. "If my theory is right, that guy must be in a really bad place in his love life, because his advice is REALLY good."

"Yeah, eh?"

"Oh yes. You think it would look bad if I asked him to hide behind the sofa to whisper what I should say when I'm talking to Mathias?"

"You know," I said, "it's almost a miracle we haven't

done that yet. It's exactly the kind of stupid plan we'd come up with."

"Gabriel!" shouted Julien when he saw him coming back. "You want to be my Cyrano?"

"Hmmm?"

"It'd be the first time Cyrano was cuter than Christian," said Jeff.

Julien elbowed him, while I leaned on Laurent's shoulder, laughing.

"Is he serious?" Gabriel asked me.

"Unfortunately, he may be."

Once again, Jeff ran one hand over his face. He looked tired and vaguely bored with what we were saying, and by the situation in general. We're going to have to talk, I thought. We can't pretend nothing happened and put everything behind us, hoping that, if we ignore the whole thing, we'll wind up forgetting it. We deserved better.

The main courses had just arrived when Jeff's phone rang. He took it out of his pocket and looked at it curiously. "It's your mother," he said. Then, in a slightly panicky voice, he said, "My God, it's your mother." No, I thought, she can't... Would Frédéric or Élodie have? No... Laurent and Julien obviously had the same idea and they looked at Jeff, who finally decided to answer.

"Hello? Yes? What a surpr... What? Yes, yes, she's right here, why? Her cell? I don't know, maybe... Marine, don't you have your cell?" We were all listening to him in reverent silence, except Gabriel, who was happily eating. "WHAT?" Jeff finally exclaimed. "Yes. Yes. Yes. What hospital?" He looked up at me. "Your father is in the hospital."

"WHAT?"

I was still looking at Jeff, but out of the corner of my eye, I saw Gabriel immediately set down his fork. "Where?" he asked Jeff. It was his hospital. He got up and was already putting on his coat. "What happened?" And while Jeff was relaying information between my mother and Gabriel, I was catching phrases like "stroke," "burst vessel" and "brain."

"Shit," I finally said. "What did he say?"

"Hang on," said Gabriel. He gestured to Jeff to give him the phone and quickly introduced himself. "Madame Vandale, I'm a friend of Marine's. I'm an ER doctor where your husband was admitted. What have you been told?"

"Oh, he's really hot now," said Julien, earning himself three irritated "Shut ups" and a smack on the back of the head from Jeff.

"Okay," said Gabriel, "Come on. We'll go see what's going on."

"Is he going to be okay?"

"We'll see. Get your coat. I'm calling a cab."

"I'm parked just out in front," said Laurent.

"Okay, go then." He was on his feet, had his coat on and the four of us were still looking at him with unblinking eyes. I had the nearly physical feeling that I was still trying to absorb an oversized piece of information into my exhausted brain. He didn't say he was going to be all right, I kept thinking to myself. He'd said, "We'll see."

"GO!" shouted Gabriel. "Let's go, what are you doing?"

"Yeah, yeah, *go*," Laurent repeated, getting up and putting on his scarf. "Marine! Go!"

"Christ," said Julien, getting up, too. "I'll come with you. Come on, Marine, let's go."

He held out a hand to me and, as I was still thinking, "He said, 'We'll see,'" without moving, he gave a little irritated sigh and literally lifted me up under my armpits. "Marine," he said, drawing his face close to mine. "Hospital. Now."

"Yes. Yes, okay." I stood up, feeling distinctly like I was made of stone or dreaming, and I started putting my things on. Opposite me, Jeff was still sitting there, and I finally woke up. "Are you coming?" I asked.

"Hmmm? No. No, there's enough of you as it is."

"Jeff…" I wanted to tell him I wanted him to come, that I needed him, but the words got stuck in my throat, because they'd become too heavy – they were now loaded down.

"Go on," he said. "I'll be at home."

I opened my mouth, but I couldn't find anything to say and I could only look back at him, as Julien pulled me by the arm. When I turned around, I saw that Gabriel was looking at us and that he had, apparently, understood something.

"Come on," he said, grabbing my other arm. "We're going to take care of your father."

To: Fred
From: Marine Vandale
Subject: Crisis Action Team

I'm here. Did you talk to *Maman*?

To: Marine
From: Frédéric Vandale
Subject: Ruptured eardrum

No. *Maman* talked to me for about an hour. And seeing as you were with her, you don't need me to comment on her level of hysteria. She was shouting all kinds of words at the same time, and went on for a long time about how being a widow at her age was just too unfair. So, I don't have any idea what's wrong with *Papa*. What's going on?

To: Fred
From: Marine Vandale
Subject: Boo-boo on his head

He had a blood vessel burst in his brain. You'll understand if I don't go any further, because I don't understand a thing they say in all that medical jargon. It wasn't a stroke, if that's any help, and they still don't know what caused it. But it could explain the memory troubles.

To: Marine
From: Frédéric Vandale
Subject: Re: Boo-boo on his head

Is your medical jargon so bad that you can't even tell me if he's going to be all right, or are you just having fun making me wait?

To: Fred
From: Marine Vandale
Subject: Can you figure it out?

....

Don't you think that if I knew if he was going to be all right or
not, I would have told you? The last time I heard a story about
a sister who teased her brother about a life and death situation
involving their father, I don't remember falling down laughing.

To: Marine
From: Frédéric Vandale
Subject: Re: Can you figure it out?

....

You're right. Sorry. I'm slightly panicky. Do you think I should
come home?

To: Fred
From: Marine Vandale
Subject: Superstition

....

Don't come home right away, Fredou. Because if you make the
trip home, I'll have the hopeless feeling that it's to see *Papa* one
last time.

To: Marine
From: Frédéric Vandale
Subject: Bitter lucidity

....

Okay, I get it. But what if that's the case? These are not words
I enjoy saying, Marine, but it's possible that my father will pass
away and that my last memory of spending time with him will
be a Tim Hortons coffee I had with him at the airport.

To: Fred
From: Marine Vandale
Subject: Grace period

....

Fuck, Fred. Of course, I understand. Nobody wants Tim to be mixed up in that kind of memory. But listen, I'm going back to the hospital later. I just came home to change, and mostly to take off my make-up, while they're doing tests, because I don't have to tell you, it's been a pretty long day.

To: Marine
From: Frédéric Vandale
Subject: Subtle change of topic

....

I suppose so, yeah… What's going on in the matter of your housemate? And what kind of girl leaves her father's bedside to take off her make-up?

To: Fred
From: Marine Vandale
Subject: Murielle Millard

....

As far as the make-up's concerned, I'll spare you, but Laurent managed to sneak a photo, so I'm sure he'll send it to you. All I can say is that Élo is the one who painted me, and in Emerg, patients were running away screaming. And there was nothing I could do, except stand there like an idiot. It's enough already that some of the nurses were seriously contemplating tying *Maman* down to a stretcher so she'd leave them the hell alone. And besides, he's in good hands, Gabriel is there.

To: Marine
From: Frédéric Vandale
Subject: Superhero

In that case, there must have been a lot of coming and going between the stretchers. Have you managed not to succumb to the savior doctor's charms?

To: Fred
From: Marine Vandale
Subject: Bar humor

You're a jerk. He's been marvelous, and, though it may surprise you, I'm not exactly in "succumbing" mode, if you see what I mean. My father's in a coma and I spent the night with my best friend. So, you see, a bit of self-control. On the other hand, Julien was flitting around like a little girl, and it wasn't because he was going to see Mathias, it wouldn't have surprised me if he'd tried to corner Gabriel.

To: Marine
From: Frédéric Vandale
Subject: The real questions

Forgive me, little sister. I'm a little shook up myself, and you know how I am when I'm shook up, I make awful jokes. But tell me, how are *you*?

To: Fred
From: Marine Vandale
Subject: You'll never guess

I really don't know, to tell the truth. I don't know. Jeff isn't here. And I have no right to hold it against him, but he's all I want now. And I wish you were here, too.

To: Marine
From: Frédéric Vandale
Subject: There in thought

....

You know you can get in touch whenever you want. And when you want me to come home, you just have to say so. You're all alone, there? Didn't you let the little sisters know?

To: Fred
From: Marine Vandale
Subject: Having a good friend

....

No, Laurent is with me. I'm going back to the hospital in a little while, but I was waiting to have something concrete to say before I let the girls know… Shit, Fred. The doorbell's ringing. I've gotta go. I'll let you know what happens.

To: Marine
From: Frédéric Vandale
Subject: Feeling of déjà-vu

....

Do you know the one about the guy whose sister kept dumping him in the middle of an email conversation?

   :)

Chapter 13

"It's okay," shouted Laurent from the living room. "I'll get it." He'd spent the afternoon with us at the hospital, then he'd taken me home as night was falling when Gabriel had explained to us that if we wanted to get a little rest ("or, just an idea, maybe take off some of your make-up") it was a good time to go, because it would take at least a couple of hours before they could offer any kind of diagnosis.

"Come on," said Laurent, taking me gently by the shoulders. "I'll give you a ride home."

"No, I'm going to stay... and don't you think you're living a little dangerously? I mean, I know you talked to Carole and everything, but come on... The idea that you spent the day at your ex's father's bedside may not exactly thrill her."

"I'm not going anywhere," he'd answered, and I almost started crying, something I hadn't yet done (luckily, by the way. With the amount of make-up I had on my face, the consequences of even a single tear would be cataclysmic).

I had firmly decided to stay, but my mother, who had not yet stopped talking or shouting at the entire hospital staff, including the people who worked in the cafeteria and the secretaries, demanding a precise diagnosis on her husband's condition because she had "the right to know if she had to prepare psychologically to become a widow before the end of the day," came back over to me, bombarding me with questions, too, though she was breaking them up with comments about the make-up, which, "frankly, made me look easy" and about Gabriel whom she was probably going to knock out as soon as my father's survival was assured so she could drag him, unbeknownst to him, to Las Vegas and force him to marry me. "Marine. A doctor! A doctor in the family!"

I jumped up. "I'll take you up on that offer, Lo. It'll do me some good."

"Take your time," said Gabriel. "As soon as I have any news, I'll let you know." He gave me a hug. My head barely came up to his shoulder and I felt him place a light kiss on my hair, and it made me shiver deliciously. It was a gesture that seemed terribly intimate to me, despite its apparent insignificance, and that intimacy finally warmed me back up again.

I'd spent the longest afternoon of my life in this busy hospital, where we'd blown in like a whirlwind, a disorderly, rainbow-colored group, with Gabriel in the lead, followed by Julien, who had me by the hand, and Laurent shouting he was going to go park the car. He'd joined us in the family waiting room, where everyone was talking at once, my mother louder than anyone. The three of us were sitting together, me between Julien and Laurent, for hours while Gabriel came and went, and my mother attempted to bribe innocent employees in order to get access to her husband (the poor man, I thought. It's a sure thing that if there was anything in the universe that could cause an aneurysm rupture, it was my mother).

In the car, on the way back to the apartment I'd left twelve hours earlier, very upset, Laurent hardly said a word. But he'd reached out a finger to stroke my left cheek, a small, but tender thing that he used to do when we were together and which, knowing as I did how reserved he was, had always held a great deal of sweetness for me.

"You should go home, Loulou."

"No, no."

"Loulou, I'm not saying that to be a martyr." I'd thought about the previous afternoon, which seemed now like it had been months earlier. "I'm sorry about yesterday at the market."

"Did you *really* sleep with Jeff?"

"I said, 'I'm sorry about yesterday at the market.'"

"No, no. I'm the one who was a jerk." He'd opened the window to half-heartedly insult another driver whose car was already three blocks ahead. "I know I'm the one who was a jerk about all this. You know I know, right?"

My usual "No, no, you weren't" was about to come out, but the last twenty-four hours had removed all desire for lies or even hypocrisy. "Yeah, I know, Loulou."

"I know you know I know."

I laughed tiredly and stroked his earlobe. "You know I'm not mad, right? And that I don't judge you and I love you?"

"Hey, take it easy with those four-letter words." He treated me to his little grin, then to a sigh, then, again, "Yes, but *Jeff*... What got into you?"

"Okay, if I hear that question one more time, I'll swallow my own tongue. Nothing got into me. It just happened, that's all."

"You okay?"

"Come on. Nobody died, right?" I was biting my bottom lip. Laurent, almost unconsciously, stroked my thigh, paternally.

"It'll be okay," he said. "Everything'll be okay." Coming from him, the most worried and pessimistic person I know, that was the most comforting statement I could imagine.

"Wait! Wait!" I said in the strange tone people use when they want to whisper and shout at the same time.

"What? Are you afraid it's Jeff?"

"No, no, no, Jeff has a key, you know. But what if it's one of my sisters?"

"Marine, you're going to have to deal with them."

"No, not right away, I…"

"Okay, I can hear you," said Gabriel's voice through the door. So Laurent flung it open and the two of us stood there smiling stupidly, while Gabriel leaned against the railing with his arms crossed. "Your door isn't very sound-proof," he said with a smile.

"Is my father okay?" It seemed to me that if he'd come all this way, if he'd gone to the trouble of coming over, it must be because the news was really bad.

"Your father is stable." Stable? It was a meaningless, worry-filled word that I usually heard on the news or read in tabloids that usually implied that the person was hanging between life and death, BUT – what joy, what relief – without being wracked with spasms.

"He's okay," Gabriel added, when he saw how shattered I looked. "Stable means good. They're going to operate on his brain tomorrow…"

"What?!" I wasn't aware of the slight inner collapse that either preceded or followed that question, but I remember that Laurent caught me as I tried to sit down on the sofa… three feet away from the sofa in question.

"Hey! Hey…" murmured Gabriel as he came near. He almost looked like a parent who was sorry and distressed about the pain their child was going through. "I know… I know." Of course he knew. It was his job to know. He followed us as Laurent gently guided me towards the sofa, as he explained to me in a surprisingly stable voice what had happened in my father's brain.

"Gabriel," I finally said. "Can you just tell me that, right now, he's okay?" Silence obviously. "I know it must be written somewhere in the Hippocratic oath…"

"Hypocritical?" asked Laurent, but no one was listening to him.

"… that you can't lie or give false hope, but, please, can you ignore the rules for a minute and give me some?"

"Some what?"

"False hope."

"You want me to give you false hope?"

"Yes."

"Even if you know it might be false?"

"Ohhh... What are you having a hard time understanding exactly?" A completely ridiculous thought went
through my head and I nearly said that was what he was
doing anyway, sending flowers to women he had no intention of pursuing, and I buried my head in my hands, more
out of disgust at myself than out of love for my father.
With my eyes still shut, I heard Laurent go towards the
kitchen and start rummaging around in the liquor cabinet, and I felt Gabriel come over and sit next to me.

"Listen," he said in a gentle voice, pressing a warm
hand upon my shoulder. "He's going to be all right."

"Really?"

He gave me a little smile, meaning, "Don't push it."

Laurent, in the kitchen, was pouring the contents of a
variety of bottles into the mixer. "Stop it, Marine," he said.
"You wanted false hope? There you go. And if you're lucky,
it may turn into real hope. You never know. Right,
Doctor?"

"Um... yes. Yes, that's right. That's right," he repeated,
giving me a kind smile. "Those aren't the exact medical
terms, but yes, that's true."

Laurent came and brought us two glasses. "What is it?"
asked Gabriel. "I'm not working tonight, but I'd like to
remain relatively clear-headed to follow Monsieur
Vandale's case."

"Long Island Iced Tea," said Laurent.

"You don't know how to make Long Island Iced Tea!"

"Taste and see..."

I tasted it. It was absolutely disgusting. "Perfect," I said
to Laurent. Beside me, Gabriel made a spectacular face as
he took his first drink.

"Shit, what did you put in here, man?"

"I'm really not sure. They've got a really well-stocked liquor cabinet here. With Drambuie, and everything... You ever had Drambuie?"

Gabriel looked at his glass, distressed.

"I'm sorry," I said to him. The "Laurent Iced Tea" was already having an effect, undoubtedly due to my emotional state and the fact that I had hardly eaten a bite since that morning, but what did it matter. For the first time since I'd heard the news, I wasn't feeling aggressive. I'd spent the day being mad at the world in general, and at my mother for driving me crazy, and at Gabriel for being unable to come up with a miracle cure, and at my father for needing a miracle cure, and at Élodie for slathering three inches of foundation on my face, and at Jeff for keeping me from having a good night, and at Julien for possibly being back on track for true love – which made me jealous, and even at Laurent, just because his father wasn't in a coma – the very good reason for which was that he was dead, which was certainly sad, but still let his son avoid the throes of worry that had invaded me.

"Well," said Gabriel. "I don't want to take anything away from you, Marine, but I've seen people react a lot worse than you. Nobody accepts these situations. Nobody expects you to accept them. Nobody's asking you to, either."

I didn't say anything. A little "meow?" was heard from my room and Claude François slowly came out, his eyes half closed, and his tail standing up in the shape of a question mark. He came and sat down in front of us, and looked at us calmly before giving an unnecessarily huge yawn and then lying down in the exact spot where he was standing.

"I don't exactly remember when my father died," Laurent suddenly said. But my mother told me I didn't react. I just didn't react. I didn't cry, I didn't get mad, I went and sat in the corner with a comic book, and at the funeral, I put on a little comedy sketch with my cousin Raymond. Over and over, my mother kept saying, 'Let yourself go, sweetie, let yourself go,' and I really had no idea what she meant."

"How old were you?" asked Gabriel.

"Eleven."

He didn't add anything, but I knew that he did let himself go at the age of thirty-six, and one night between Christmas and New Year's, though nothing had prepared us for it, the thirty-year-old repressed holiday memories poured out without warning. He'd spent hours prostrate on the sofa, crying like a baby, then he'd left, after midnight, to go see his mother in Alma to tell her he'd finally let himself go and that she'd no longer be mourning for her husband alone. It had been, as Jeff said, "unbearably intense," but that was Laurent.

"Yep," I said, taking another drink of my indescribable cocktail. "Maybe I am getting too carried away. He's not dead yet, after all."

"Far from it," said Gabriel.

"Does anybody ever recover from this?"

"Lots of people."

"Really?"

"Really."

In the glass of the picture hanging opposite us, I saw Laurent's reflection leaning behind me and mouthing to Gabriel, "False hope?" as he replied "No," with a laugh.

"I can see you both in the picture frame, you bunch of dopes."

They both laughed. On my left, Gabriel rubbed my back. "Taking off that make-up was a good idea," he said. "Now you've got your own face back. All the better for me."

"False hope?" I felt like asking in a sly voice, which I would have done in other circumstances. "What do we do now?" I asked instead.

"We wait a little. I have my pager, and my cell, your family has all your numbers, and if I could give you ONE piece of advice, it would be to wait at home instead of in a waiting room, if you have to ever wait for news about a loved one."

"Yeah, but what if he wakes up and he's stuck alone with my mother? Couldn't that send him back into another coma?"

"If he's smart," said Laurent, "he'll send himself into another coma." I giggled into my glass. Really, Laurent Iced Teas should be patented and sold in hospitals next to the coffee machine. They were excellent for relaxation.

"Even if he wakes up right away, he's going to be pretty groggy, so that you'll have plenty of time to get there," Gabriel went on. He seemed to think for a minute and then added, "And anyway, even if you were there, I don't think you have the physical strength to stand between your mother and any damned thing she's got her sights set on."

"She's something else, eh?" remarked Laurent.

"Shit…"

"Um… That's enough collusion now between you two boys. No one is allowed to say anything bad about my mother except me. Got it?"

"What? We just said she was something else!"

"Yeah, but…" I was about to go on, but my phone on the table rang out a message alert and I jumped on it. It was Julien. "M gone to washroom. Letting me have it. Good sign?"

I sighed and held the phone out to the guys. "Is it really worth it to answer, in your opinion?" Laurent made a gesture that meant, "Is it really worth it for you to ask that question?" but Gabriel was already typing away on his phone.

"What are you telling him?"

"I'm telling him that yes, it could be a good sign.

Especially if he continues to keep his mouth shut."

Laurent and I exchanged a glance. "Listen," I said, "are you speaking from personal experience?"

"Maybe a little." He was still hunched over his phone. "In the beginning, with my wife. Before she became my wife. I committed what they call an 'indiscretion.' And the more I tried to apologize or get her to forgive me, the more she pushed me away. Finally, one day, I called her up, and told her she was right, that there was no excuse for what I did and that I had no right to ask her for anything. So, it took a few months, but a year later, we were married."

"And eleven years later, you got divorced."

"Eight years," he clarified, still without looking up. "We were together eleven years, but married eight years."

In the glass of the picture frame, Laurent's reflection made an appreciative face. Sure, we may have laughed, but really, neither one of us had ever come close to an eleven-year relationship and *he* was one year older than Gabriel.

"Just because it ended in failure, doesn't mean it wasn't a success at some point."

That would be a great principle to apply in medicine, I thought. "Your husband is dead, ma'am, but he had some great moments during the operation, so we really can't look at this as a defeat." The idea instantly made me think of my father and then, I ricocheted onto my mother.

"Mmmm, doesn't it make you a little worried that my mother still hasn't called yet?"

"Are you *really* complaining about the fact that your mother isn't calling?"

"I don't know, shouldn't I?"

"Pager," said Gabriel pointing to his belt. "Cell phone. We're the easiest to reach people in town."

I looked at him for a second. He seemed strangely familiar, as if he'd already been in my life for almost as long as the three boys. Perhaps it was because he was so easygoing, because he was sitting next to me, on my old sofa, as if he'd been there thousands of times before. He was playing distractedly with the cat, peacefully drinking his drink, he was joking with Laurent as if they'd known each other forever. Perhaps it was my own tired gaze or my appreciation, I don't know. I wanted to reach out a hand towards him, touch his arm or his thigh like you do with a lover, kiss him on the neck, naturally, like people who have been in love for a long time.

"Wilaya?" said Laurent. "What the hell is *wilaya*? That's not a word!"

Impassive, Gabriel slowly counted his points. "With the triple letter score for the *w* and the double word score, that makes... 33, 43, 44... 88."

"Could we get back to the fact that it's not a word?"

"Algerian administrative division."

"Oh, *come on.*"

I grabbed the dictionary and checked. Then I looked up at Laurent, sorry. "Yup. Wilaya. It's right there in black and white."

"Who knows words like 'wilaya'?"

"Someone who plays way too much Scrabble," I said.

Gabriel gave a little laugh. "Hey, it's not my fault. With my wife, at the end, we didn't... let's say we didn't have much to say to each other."

"So you discovered wilayas, zymases and yttria."

"And koumys. I looooooooooove koumys."

"Okay, can you be any more nerdy?" asked Laurent.

Gabriel and I looked at each other, like we were thinking about this, and then, in unison, we answered, "Ummm... no," which made all three of us laugh.

"Besides," said Gabriel. "I'm being very fair, because I could play all kinds of medical terms that no one knows and everyone would think they were just invented to score big in Scrabble. When I was finishing up med school, my friends and I would have theme games. As many medical terms as possible and…" He stopped, glanced at Laurent, then at me, and added, "Okay, that's depressingly nerdy, isn't it?"

"Did you say 'depressingly'?" I started to laugh, as Laurent, his face so contorted with concentration that I was afraid it would split into two, carefully placed the word "amased" on the board.

"Okay," said Gabriel. "THAT isn't a word."

"Come on, really: they were very amased that… oh. It takes a *z* doesn't it. Oh boy. Sorry. It's a little embarrassing, eh?" he asked.

"No, no," answered Gabriel, as I nodded yes vigorously.

"Hey!" said Laurent, elbowing me. "At least I'm not a nerd."

"Excuse me? You spent all your teenage years making daily news recordings of what happened in your class. I KNOW where the tapes are, I'll have you know. AND your favorite superhero was Robin. Not Batman, Robin."

Gabriel giggled into his glass. "Oh man, Robin?! Nerdy AND gay. Even in med school we weren't that bad."

Laurent grumbled as he moved the letters around on his wooden tray. "You're one to talk, Madame I-had-the-map-of-Middle-Earth-on-my-wall-and-I-drew-out-the-different-characters'-paths-as-I-read-the-story."

"You did that?" asked Gabriel.

"She also wrote 'Marine + Edmond' in all her planners."

"Edmond?"

"The Count of Monte Cristo," I stammered.

"What? Oh my God! I've fallen into the biggest den of nerds in all Montréal!" He was laughing very, very hard now.

"I was eleven years old!" I shouted.

"FIFTEEN," Laurent corrected me, and I shot a pillow at him, but missed by two feet.

"Seriously," Gabriel asked me. "What were you like?"

"As a teenager?"

"Yes."

"Oof…" What was I really like then? I had a hard time remembering when I was a teenager. Or rather, through a fog, I could see a confused and troubled time – sometimes, though, the fog would lift and here and there I could see bright patches – first kiss, first feeling of being absolutely invincible and immortal. I'd been a good kid and, it's true, pretty nerdy. The few friends I had, mostly boys, and I would organize trips into the woods surrounding our suburban subdivision at the time; we thought we were explorers, or adventurers, discovering still virgin territory.

But the center of my world was still my brother. We had a book club that had ended the day he decided to become cool, and thereby broke my heart and left me alone with my books and my drawings. I used to draw what I read, musketeers and cheating countesses, elves and sorcerers, castles and unsettling prisons rising up out of the ocean. And I had few girl friends. I'd want to talk about Quasimodo or Excalibur, knights and the courtly poetry I was slowly discovering, but girls my age wanted to talk about love and boys, and love frightened me.

Then, one day – had I stopped being frightened? No. But there was a boy who flustered me so much, I couldn't go near him. It was like I was dizzy: he was so tall, my attraction and fear were so strong that I took that one step too many, the one I *had* to take. Then everything shifted and for years my books and sketch pads did nothing but collect dust in the basement, next to the sagging sofa where I'd spent hours in his arms, kissing him. All we did was kiss, but we were so serious about it, it was almost funny and my heart would beat a mile a minute from beginning to end, the whole time we were in each other's arms. I was sixteen, and even if I went back to my books and pencils after a while, I never stopped searching for that unfolding of sensations that love and desire meant. I had chased after that kind of dizziness. And I still did.

"Do you think love is always scary?" Gabriel asked me, and I thought to myself that maybe I'd gotten a little carried away. Laurent was looking at me, and he was surprised, too. I opened my mouth to answer, but I didn't say anything: had I been afraid with Laurent? In the beginning, yes. I was terrified. Then, time and the strange way he loved me reassured me. Was that why love had disappeared? If it was, I was off to a very bad start.

"I don't know," I finally answered. "I don't know if it HAS to be frightening, but I know it frightens me, all the time."

"Doesn't that get tiring after a while?"

"I think it's exquisite."

He smiled at me. "What about you?" I asked him.

"What about me, what?"

"Does it frighten you?"

"Love?" He seemed to think about it, then looked into my eyes. "Never." I thought he was going to add something else, but next to us, Laurent shouted out "HA! Noted! N-O-T-E-D. The things I noted in my notebook. And it's a triple word score on top of it! Twenty-one points, ladies and gentlemen!" He grabbed the score sheet and triumphantly wrote down his score before he said to Gabriel, as he fished out his new letters, "Anyway, man, if you're telling the truth, you're my idol."

My cell phone started ringing, and I nearly knocked the game over as I quickly reached for it.

"Damn! You could have told me you weren't at the hospital anymore. I'm in the washroom so I could get away from your mother – she doesn't want to let me leave and, frankly, I'm starting to get a little scared." It was Julien.

"How's my father?"

"They're prepping him for the operation. Your mother gave me a detailed description of every move the surgeon will make, I didn't understand a word of it, but it seems he has very handsome eyes and looks well groomed, which has reassured your mother a lot. Where are you, for Christ sake?"

"At home. I'd rather wait here than with my mother."

"Well, don't you think I'd rather do that, too? Right now, I'm going to try to get out of here, and if I have to, I'll knock out a male nurse, steal his pale green suit, and jump out a window. Marine, she's un-bear-a-ble. Like, worse than usual."

I gave a compassionate little laugh and looked up at Laurent and Gabriel. "Julien went back to the hospital. My mother got her hands on him."

"Who are you with?"

"Laurent and Gabriel."

"Gabriel, eh? Hmmm... The doctor's getting involved..."

"Okay, shut up. How did it go with Mathias?"

"I think I might have a chance..."

"Really?"

"Really!" He seemed so happy and his joy was so contagious that I let out an overexcited "Yeah!"

"Come tell us all about it," I said. "Knock out the nurse and get over here."

"I'll be right there. Oooh! Cute doctor..."

"Julien, get over here." I hung up and gave Laurent a knowing look. "It hasn't even been an hour since he saw Mathias and he's already cruising a doctor. What are we going to do with him?"

"What have we been doing with him all these years?" asked Laurent. "We take him like he is."

I nodded my head and I saw Gabriel smile.

I was in the kitchen with Gabriel, putting the seventeen thousand sushi rolls Julien had brought over onto plates. "When I'm feeling down, sushi always makes me feel better," he'd said as he sorted the bottles of sake and plastic containers filled with countless kinds of rolls.

"There's just four of us," I'd said.

"Um... Hello? Exceptional circumstances?"

"Are you talking about Monsieur Vandale or your love life?" Laurent had asked.

"You know," I said to Gabriel, "you don't have to stay if you don't want to." Though it was ridiculous and childish, it was my way of asking him why he was still there.

"Well," he said, placing a little mound of wasabi on each plate, "I want to stay." Then, as if he understood the question beneath my remark, he added, "You know it's true, Marine. We hadn't gotten to know each other very well, but there was something about your friends, the way you are when you're together, really tha... that fascinated me, you could say. Maybe because you're so different from me. Or maybe not. It doesn't matter. But I feel good when I'm with you. So you could even say it's selfish of me. I'm here because it makes me feel good."

I didn't know what to say. What kind of man said that kind of thing to a woman he hardly knew? What kind of man even talked like that, period? I was used to things being left unsaid, and now, I felt like I was in a zone where nothing was left unsaid, there was too much transparency.

"Oh my God," he said. "Is that your way of saying I'm imposing? Maybe you want to be alone with your friends."

"Finally! Finally, a little insecurity! Thank you, Gabriel, thank you."

He laughed and I added, "No, no, I don't want you to go. It's reassuring for me to have you here. Besides..." God, I was bad with words. They always seemed heavy and awkward, too close to the ground when my thoughts wanted to soar. "Besides, I feel good, too. When you're around. It's a little scary."

"Is it exquisite?"

"Okay, smart ass, that's enough. It would be fun if your head still fit through the door when it's time to leave to go back to the hospital."

He bumped me with his hip, laughing, and I thought, even if he does have a swollen head, all I wanted was for him to lean in to kiss me, to touch my throat and my breasts.

"Have you had a lot of girlfriends in your life?" An absurd question that popped into my head and that I immediately regretted.

"What do you mean by girlfriends?" Welcome to the twenty-first century, I thought. Between girlfriends, mistresses, boyfriends, lovers, and one-night stands, fuck friends and true love, it was starting to get hard to figure out.

"I don't know," I said. "Answer however you want."

"Okay…" He thought about it. "I was married, I had true love. I've also had several lovers and a couple of girlfriends. I never held back if that's what you mean." Then he seemed to realize his statement could be misinterpreted and he added, "Not that I've spent my life jumping on every woman I meet or cheating on my wife or my girlfriends, no, no. I cheated on my wife once, like I told you. Not good. It's a horrible, horrible feeling to cheat on someone."

"Yes, I know."

"You know?"

"Yes." I pointed towards Laurent with my chin.

"No…"

"Once. A horrible, horrible feeling, indeed. I don't know why people do things like that. And it so wasn't worth the bother, on top of everything. And when I say bother, I mean bother. I'm still upset with myself."

"Does he know about it?"

"No! No, my God. I never want him to find out. It would do absolutely no good. He's the person I love most in the world."

"Do you think he did, too?"

"I don't know. And I don't want to know. What good

would it do to know that now?"

"That's true." He took the last sashimi rolls out of their containers. "Nothing's ever easy, is it?"

"No. No, I don't think anything will ever be easy. But it's okay like this, too."

He seemed surprised by what I said and looked at me for a second, seeming undecided. "I think so, too."

"I figured that."

There was a silence between us. Too many things had just been said, too quickly. I was searching for something to say, a joke, something to lighten the situation, when Julien shouted, "Phoooooone!!!" as if we might possibly not have heard it ringing. Then, he literally jumped up, stepped over Laurent and went to answer it.

"Hel…" He didn't even finish his hello. I was staring at him, immobile and catatonic, my mind empty and my heart switched off. I could see he was trying to talk, going "but…" "we…" "it's just that…" Then he hung up.

"Um…"

"WHAT, FOR CHRISSAKE?" I was screaming. Gabriel put a hand on my waist and I sharply pushed it off. "WHAT?!?"

"It was Ariane. Your mother called her. She called Élodie, too. They're not happy. They're on their way over."

"Is that all? Is that ALL?" I started crying. Mostly from relief. "Julien, shit, why didn't you say so right away? I thought my father was dead! I thought my father was dead! They're… they're on their way over?"

"Yes, your mother told them we were here. So, you see, it's a good thing I bought a thousand pieces of sushi!"

I felt like laughing, just a little. But the tears were still flowing, tears of exhaustion, tears of being overloaded. Gabriel put his hand on my waist again and this time I fell into his arms, and they smelled so good. "Shhh…" he whispered. "Shhh…" Then the door opened and I turned my head, my right cheek was still against Gabriel's chest when I saw Jeff come in, followed by Flavie.

To: Fred
From: Marine Vandale
Subject: Calm after the storm

....

Ooof... can you believe it's the first time in a week I've had the
chance to sit down and write you? It's just not cool, Fred. When
I can't write to you, I really feel all alone.

To: Marine
From: Frédéric Vandale
Subject: Relative solitude

....

Were you really all alone?

To: Fred
From: Marine Vandale
Subject: Figure of speech, perhaps

....

For a writer, you're not exactly quick on the uptake, you know?
I don't have a single minute to myself. Well, okay, maybe I have
one or two, and, would you believe, I used them to soak in the
tub with a good book.

To: Marine
From: Frédéric Vandale
Subject: Book club

....

What are you reading?

To: Fred
From: Marine Vandale
Subject: Future Goncourt winner

....

The first chapters of the first novel by a guy named Frédéric
Vandale.

To: Marine
From: Frédéric Vandale
Subject: It's not nice to make fun

....

You are absolutely not allowed to make jokes about that, okay?
Because, now, if, naively, I ask you if you really liked what you
read, and you say "Yes" just to get rid of me or kidding around,
you're not my sister anymore. In that case, Élodie and Ariane
would be all I'd have left and, even though I love them to death,
it would leave me a little empty feeling.

To: Fred
From: Marine Vandale
Subject: Dead serious

....

Fred, I think it's brilliant. And I think it's even more brilliant
because, and this may surprise you, I know you pretty well and
I know what it must have taken for you to write all this. You've
never been the king of self-disclosure, if you see what I mean.

To: Marine
From: Frédéric Vandale
Subject: Man in the Iron Mask

....

And here I thought I disclosed everything to you. You should
appreciate the irony, anyway.

To: Fred
From: Marine Vandale
Subject: Cliché?

....

I don't want to slide into ridiculous platitudes, but, as you may
know, we're never as transparent as we think, and there's no
doubt we lie to ourselves as much as we lie to other people. But
in your book, I see transparency and truth, and I think it's

beautiful and sad. But if you don't mind, I'll wait till I read the whole thing before I give you all my thoughts. And maybe till my mind's a little more rested, too.

To: Marine
From: Frédéric Vandale
Subject: Rest for head and heart

Maman has kept me up to date on the hospital news, but what about you? First, how's my little sister's heart, and second, how's my father's brain? Because, from time to time, I get lost in *Maman's* explanations. The last time we talked on the phone, it was a circus at your place. Ariane and Élodie where there, and the roommate, the ex, his girlfriend, the Queen of Adultery, and the doctor, and let's just say that your level of coherence was a little off.

To: Fred
From: Marine Vandale
Subject: Circus maximus

Yeah, well, next time we see each other and we have two or three hours to kill, I'll tell you about the whole scene. I'm just barely getting over it myself. And besides, the week following it didn't exactly help either, I spent more time at *Papa's* bedside than at home. And you know what else was at *Papa's* bedside? *Maman.*

To: Marine
From: Frédéric Vandale
Subject: Compassion

It's okay, I can imagine. She hasn't calmed down at all now that we know he's going to come out of it okay?

To: Fred
From: Marine Vandale
Subject: Maternal filter

Listen, when *Maman* says he's "okay," it means, "We think he might come out of it okay." Things are okay now, he's awake, he recognizes us, but we can't say he's talking our ears off, or even that he's in A-1 shape. It's not easy.

To: Marine
From: Frédéric Vandale
Subject: Leavin' on a jet plane

Will you stop bugging me with your superstitions if I tell you I found a ticket for three hundred eighty euros and that I'll be home in ten days?

To: Fred
From: Marine Vandale
Subject: Get on that plane

Not only will I stop bugging you with my superstitions, but I'll welcome you with the widest open arms possible. Come home, brother. *Papa* is just going to keep getting better, and, spring is here.

To: Marine
From: Frédéric Vandale
Subject: What about your heart?

So, I'm coming. And, just so that I can be up to speed on the important files, tell me how it's going with your doctor and your housemate.

To: Fred
From: Marine Vandale
Subject: No man's land

....

The doctor's working and the housemate spent four days in
Québec City, and I'm on the verge of pitching a tent at the hospital. But, like I said, spring is here.

Chapter 14

What I said about springtime is true. It showed up like it always did, with no warning, or any advance notice at all – but one morning, I'd stepped out of my house, all bundled up in my coat and scarf, and there I was, standing with my two feet in the sun and in a river of melting snow, with my toque quivering in the warm, soft breeze. I'd felt my heart leap, or rather literally expand in my chest and I rushed back inside, tripping over the tiny step on our threshold and I shouted, "Jeff! It's fucking springtime!" His bedroom door opened and Marie-Lune came out, still half asleep and, of course, draped in one of Jeff's shirts, and she greeted me in a bit of a fog.

"Hi, Marine."

"Oh, Marie-Lune. Long time no see."

She went, "Hmmm…" waivering between a smile and a yawn. I was triumphantly removing my toque, mittens and scarf when Jeff's voice came to me from his room, "Don't fall for it, Marine, there's still more cold weather and snow left to come." I didn't say a word, but just went out into the warm air, wearing a light coat.

The ambiance at home had been strange since that huge day when everything seemed to happen to us – Jeff and me, my father, Julien making up with Mathias, Laurent having a talk with Carole, my sisters showing up in a rage, and, in the middle of all this, Gabriel coming into our lives, seemingly to pour a bit of order and sanity into our panic-stricken hearts.

Jeff really had worked a lot since then – in fact, I suspected him of making up excuses for going to Québec
City, of writing phony stories about subjects he wasn't too
interested in, because he was afraid of me. I talked to
Laurent about it for hours, while we were at my sleeping
father's bedside. Was he afraid of me, of us, or of the conversation we hadn't had yet? He was avoiding me, I could
feel it, and it hurt me too much to even bring it up, especially now that I was spending most of my days at the
hospital and getting home exhausted and emotionally
drained.

"Don't rush too much," Julien said to me. "We'll get
through this, you know. We're very good at getting through."

I'd always believed that, too. But after that first night,
when we were all together in the living room and everyone started shouting at once, I'd had some doubts about,
shall we say, our ability to get through. And since, I'd
thought maybe it was time for us to really stop trying to
get through, that we clean house and talk about what we
couldn't get through anymore.

I'd just gotten over the shock of seeing Jeff walk in with
Flavie (what's he doing with Flavie? wondered my brain,
through the fog of fatigue, alcohol and the circumstances,
until I realized that I was in Gabriel's arms, with my head
pressed against his chest). I stood up quickly and there
followed a series of absurd and slightly hypocritical greet-
ings.

"Hi!" "Hi?" "Jeff?" "Oh, Flavie!" "Hi, guys!" "Oh, Marine,
I thought you'd be at the hospital." "You thought?"
"Gabriel?!" "Aren't you in Québec City?" "Julien? I thought
you were with Mathias!" "How's it going?" Obviously, no
one was asking the questions that were actually running
through our heads. Then, Julien got up, as Laurent and I
exchanged panicky looks – he was completely capable of
shouting to Flavie or Gabriel that Jeff and I had slept

together, just to add a nicely wrapped little scandal to this unending day. I had the time to think that he'd been here, less than twenty-four hours earlier, along with Jeff and Flavie, light years away from where we all now were.

I was looking at Laurent, who was looking at Julien and obviously wondering if he should jump on him and pin him to the floor or muzzle him, but Julien simply yelled, "Mathias is going to give me a chance! A chance!" And he stood stock-still for a second, with his arms in the air, in his lime green turtleneck and turquoise pants, but nobody said anything. Jeff was making the little face that meant that he'd heard but really didn't care much about the news, Laurent sighed in relief, Gabriel and Flavie were laughing – it was pretty funny in fact. Julien was still smiling, and occasionally saying, "Eh? Eh?" demanding unbridled joy from Flavie and Gabriel, and receiving in return nothing but a pout and an affectionate laugh. His arms were still in the air when Élodie's voice could be heard behind Jeff.

"Come on, I'm telling you! If she's too stupid to lock her door, then we're just going to go right in. Because, I'd like to remind you, that, shit, her fucking faggy friends have keys, but we don't. So, go! I'll give you… oh!"

She stopped dead in the doorway, with Ariane following behind, but Ariane had been running and then bumped into Élo, which sent both of them flying into the room where we all were. Élodie got her balance back then looked at me, almost said something, then her gaze fell on Gabriel, which caused her eyes to pop open spectacularly, and then she looked at Julien, with his arms still in the air, but he gave up and dropped them as he let out a loud "Huh!" Then she noticed Jeff on her left and gave a silly, knowing smile.

"Hi, Jeff…"

"Yep, yep, hi."

"Hi."

"That's enough," Jeff said, rolling his eyes. "Hi." Élodie had turned her head and gave an "Oh! Ah!" that was completely devoid of subtlety, then she noticed Flavie. She seemed a little off balance in front of an audience she hadn't expected, and I knew she was wondering where to begin.

"I'm not a fag," Laurent finally said.

"Huh?" We all looked at him, trying to find the link and wondering if there was a reason for his sudden declaration which wasn't news to anybody.

"I'm not a fag," he repeated. "'Her fucking faggy friends have keys…' *I* have a key. And I'm not a fag. *Julien* is a fag."

"Hey!" Julien had said. "It's true, but it's a bit insulting, Élodie Vandale."

"Well… I didn't mean…" She put on her pitiful face – Élodie was so afraid of the idea of being disliked by anyone at all that she could cry if she thought she'd hurt someone she didn't know or offended a saleswoman in a boutique. "It's just that…"

"Okay, whoa!" Ariane had shouted, bumping into her and positioning herself in front of her. Mauve Doc Martens, ripped black tights under turquoise leggings, at least three gigantic wool sweaters, with little red squares pinned to her heart to show her support for the students. She looked so small under all that wool that I wanted to take her in my arms, despite how angry and indignant she looked – *because* of how angry and indignant she looked, in fact, which made me want to laugh, and made her all the more dear to me. "You'd better have a good excuse, Marine. A DAMN good excuse!"

"I wanted to wait till we had something specific to tell you. What good would it have done to panic you and …"

"My father was in the hospital in a coma and I didn't know it! How could that seem like a good idea to you?" Next to her, at the mention of the word *coma*, Élodie began to cry. "When are you going to stop treating us like little ten-year-old girls?"

It was a good question. "Never," I said. "I can try to stop treating you like that, but you'll always be my little sisters." Élodie was collapsing onto the sofa, next to Laurent, going "*Papaaaaaaaaa*" through her tears. I'd held an arm out towards her to show Ariane that, apparently, there still was a little girl in Élodie. And there's one in me, too, if you only knew, I thought.

"And besides that, what are you doing here? *Papa* is in the hospital." She was speaking slowly as if there was something about the idea that *Papa* was in the hospital that I hadn't yet digested.

"I'm the one who suggested she come home," Gabriel had answered.

"Who's he?"

"Ariane, I'd like you to meet Gabriel. Gabriel, my sister Ariane."

"Gab... oh!" I could have strangled her on the spot. She shot a look towards Élodie, undoubtedly looking for an accomplice, but Élodie now had her nose buried in Laurent's sweater, so he was looking helpless, cradling her awkwardly and mumbling "Of course not, of course not."

"Your father's going to be okay," said Gabriel. "But right now, they're getting him ready for an operation that's going to take a long time and you won't be able to see him. There's no point in staying there. People just go crazy. And we're only two minutes from the hospital here; she can go back whenever she wants."

"Well, let her go back when she wants, I'm going now."

"*Maman* is there," I said, and Ariane, who'd already turned around and was headed for the door, stopped dead.

"How is she? I just talked to her quickly on the phone."

"What part of 'people just go crazy' didn't you understand?"

She went "hmm" a couple of times and hesitated. Jeff,

still standing next to the door, finally spoke up. "Um… I think I'll go to Le Lulli, because…"

"That's it, leave again." I had no idea why I said that. It was completely unjustified.

He looked at me, and appeared hurt. "Um… I'd like to point out that if anyone's left around here lately…"

"What's he talking about?" Ariane had asked.

"Let it go," Laurent and Julien both answered together.

Flavie, who had remained silent from the beginning, finally let out a big sigh, and at the same time she took off her hound's-tooth coat and her black beret with the big white flower. Then, in two steps, she was over by the bar. "If we're going to stay, let's at least have a drink." She reached one arm towards a bottle of sake and the other towards Gabriel. "Hi, I'm Flavie. Very, *very* pleased to meet you." She gave me a look that showed her appreciation, although it was highly lacking in the discretion department, then she shouted, "Jeff! You want a drink?"

"No. No, no. I'm going out."

"Hang on, your housemate is having hard times and you're taking off? What's wrong with you? We're not going anywhere, Marine."

Go, I felt like saying. Please, go! Gabriel was watching the scene and I knew he was putting the pieces of the puzzle together in his head, patiently, just as he had done since we'd met.

"*Papaaaaaaaa!*" Élodie had moaned.

"Oh, shit, Élo, shut up. That's no way to get her to stop treating us like babies."

"You're not niiiiiice!"

"Of course not, of course not," Laurent was still droning half-heartedly.

"Can't someone be happy that Mathias is ready to give me another chance?"

"Christ, you idiot, will you please shut up?" Jeff interjected. "Her father is in the hospital."

"Hey! Just because you…"

"OKAY! OKAY! WHOA! Quiet." I nearly leapt over the bar and stuffed twelve sushi rolls into Julien's mouth to shut him up. As for Jeff, he stood stock-still in the middle of the room for a minute then he rushed towards the bar where he quickly sniffed what was left of Laurent's Iced Tea in the mixer, then tossed it back. He looked at me as he put it back down on the counter, without a word, then he extended a hand towards Gabriel. "Hey, man." He didn't look him in the eye.

"I'll *bet* you that Fred knows?" Ariane had asked.

I hesitated a second. At that point we were at "*Maman* called him this morning." So she started shouting again and repeating that "even *Maman* doesn't think much of us" and I suspected her of thinking about founding a union, a club, an NGO, anything at all, to defend the rights of little sisters – it was what she did best, her way of expressing herself, after all. Jeff, who seemed completely discouraged, went and put a hand on her shoulder to calm her down. She'd turned her anger against him while Julien angrily put his winter clothes on in protest of what Jeff had said. Behind the counter, Gabriel served the two of us a glass of sake and raised his in my direction, with a little smile.

"You were right," said Jeff as he came into my room. I jumped at least a meter. I'd been jumping a lot the last little while and I didn't know if it was fatigue, the state of permanent alert you're on when a loved one is in the hospital, or because, on some level, I was afraid of Jeff, too. I'd just finished writing to Frédéric – it was a little after midnight – and I wanted to go to bed and finally get some sleep, so I could get to the hospital early the next morning.

Ariane and Élodie had finally calmed down, and they'd slept at my place that night, one on the sofa, the other one curled up on Jeff's old La-Z-Boy. Everyone else left a little before midnight, when Gabriel got a call telling him that the surgery would happen during the night and that he'd come out of recovery around eight o'clock. He'd put his arms around me before he left, and I nearly clung to him, nearly asked him to stay near me, to sleep beside me – just sleep, because at least if he were there, it seemed like I'd be less afraid.

The next day, the three of us sisters arrived at the hospital to find our father still asleep, with an enormous bandage around his skull. A tired-looking surgeon explained to us that they'd had to open up his cranium in order to remove a blood clot and clean up something I didn't quite understand. The words were getting mixed up in my head; I'd stopped understanding after the word *cranium*. I was tired and kept thinking to myself I would ask Gabriel later; coming from his mouth, the words would scare me less.

Ariane started crying when she saw the bandage, and, strangely enough, Élodie was the one who kept calm. "Okay," she'd said with a decisive tone in her voice, placing a hand on one of our father's broad shoulders. "Okay. We're going to take care of him. I propose we each take a shift."

"Hmmm?"

"Well, there's no reason for the three of us to all be here all the time."

"The four of us," said my mother as she came into the room. She looked exhausted and seemed to have aged ten years. She's so small, I thought. I put my arms around her and for a couple of seconds, I wondered who I felt worse for: my father, who was resting in a hospital bed after having his skull opened up, or my mother, who'd spent the last twenty-four hours struggling with the idea of a life without him, which was obviously killing her. Ariane was gently stroking my father's face, as she silently cried. I'd thought of Fred, whom I'd told not to come the first time he offered, and whom I was missing bitterly.

"We won't leave him alone," Élodie had continued. And the three of us, tired and docile, listened to her as she set up a schedule. When I got home that night, I finally realized I'd been had and that Élodie's revenge had been to give me the shift that started every day at 8 a.m. – of the three of us, I am the farthest from being a morning person.

Since then, she'd been at the hospital non-stop. Shift or no shift, she was there. Arriving just after I did in the morning, not leaving our father till the evening. She'd turned into a responsible nurse – she read books to him and softly spoke to him when it seemed to her it didn't tire him out too much. Surprised and moved, Ariane and I looked at each other – our little sister, whom we had considered a perfectly selfish person, absolutely incapable of the tiniest thought that didn't directly concern her, was proving to be the most altruistic and devoted of the three of us. I'd never been so happy about being wrong about someone. In fact, I was almost ashamed, because I compared my involvement to hers and I could see a flash of joy in my father's tired eyes when he saw her come in. "Your sister Élodie is a good girl," he repeated and repeated, and I could feel he was as surprised as I was. "If I'd known," he said with a sad, tender smile, "I'd have gotten sick a lot sooner."

"What do you mean, I'm right?" I asked Jeff, hugging my chest.

He was smiling and his eyebrows were raised – he was amused by how much I'd jumped. "About the springtime," he said. "You were right."

I smiled back at him. I must have looked like Jennifer

Beals in *Flashdance*, wearing a low-cut sweater over a camisole, and leggings with thick socks that came up to my calves. All I needed was a headband and a perm.

Jeff seemed to hesitate, then he came and sat on my bed, with a big sigh. He's waiting for me to say something, I thought, so I sat down in front of him, on my office chair. He wasn't looking at me, his elbows were on his knees, and he was distractedly playing with an embroidered pillow that seemed to be taking up all of his attention.

"Look…"

"Listen…"

We both started to laugh; we'd both spoken at the same time.

"Go ahead," he said.

"No, no. You go."

He was still spinning the little pillow in his big hands, so I jumped in, "Listen, we're not going to pretend…"

He looked up at me, suddenly, "Do you feel like going down to Le Lulli?" I quickly thought, No, I was tired. No, I wanted to get up at seven the next morning. No, we could easily talk here. No, it was raining cats and dogs outside. No, it was the cowardly way to do things and we had to be able to talk at home, without making an effort not to be alone together by getting lost in a crowd. So I said, "Sure. Good idea."

We ran the two hundred meters between our place and the bar. It was raining, but the air was almost warm and the windows at Le Lulli were glowing with a warm, golden light that always made me think of Paris, though I really didn't know why. Maybe it was because Fred loved the place, and because now I associated everything connected to him with Paris and vice versa (the aroma of hot chestnuts reminded me of Fred). We went in, shouting a joyful "Hi!" at Andrew, who raised his arm high in the air to greet us. It was a good idea, I thought. A little cowardly, maybe, but there was something good about being on neutral ground, in a light atmosphere.

We went over to the bar to order – an unnecessary move, really, since in front of him Andrew had already set down a glass of white wine and a gin and tonic. Jeff picked up the glasses and indicated a table near the window.

"This okay with you?" he asked.

"Oh, come on, guys!" Andrew begged. "It's a slow night. I'm bored. Come sit with me."

Jeff didn't say anything, but I saw him give Andrew a knowing look. Andrew made a wide-eyed face back at him. "Oh! Oh… Tonight's the talk…"

I turned towards Jeff. "Come on, now. You told him?"

"Oh-oh," said Andrew. "Sorry, man."

Jeff was looking at him like he'd just had a lobotomy. "Dude! What the fuck?"

"You told him?"

"Hey! I didn't have the two queers to confide in."

"Laurent's not queer."

"Whatever."

"Listen," said Andrew. "I'm a bartender. It's my social role. Secrets. It's fine. It's not my role to judge at all. No judgment, Marine. Trust me on that one."

"Fuck…"

"Sorry…" Jeff said to me.

"No, no, it's all right. It's okay. Shall we sit down?"

"The drinks are on me," said Andrew.

"Yeah… they better be." Jeff still gave him a grumpy smile, and we went to sit down. There was a candle on the table, the wind was beating against the big window, and when Jeff settled in opposite me, I knew everything was going to be okay. I felt okay, and I was happy to be there with him. It was the first time since my father's accident I'd relaxed, thought about something else, and I knew that, somewhere, Jeff's presence had a lot to do with it.

He'd always reassured me a lot, this Shrek of mine, and I
was almost touched that nothing had changed on that
score.

"Hi," he said.

"Hi…"

We both smiled lovingly and he took my hands.
"How's your father?"

"My father?" I wasn't expecting this question, and it
left me speechless for a few seconds. "My father is…"

"We haven't talked all week, Marine."

"I know. Weird."

"I know, so talk."

About my father, I felt like asking. Weren't we here to
talk about something else beside my father, something a
lot less serious, but that weighed on me almost as much
because Jeff was at the center of my life, of my everyday
life, of what I was, even more than my father was? But I
started talking, and I quickly felt a weight leave me: I told
the same stories I'd been repeating for a week, but that's
what had been missing the last few days: telling them to
Jeff. Isn't that what I'd always done? I talked to my boys.
And since that night, one of them had been missing, and
since then, things had been off balance. I was missing part
of myself. So I told him about the operation, about the
atmosphere in the hospital, and the fact that Élodie was
proving she had a little Mother Teresa in her, about my
mother and the fact I'd gone over to see her twice at home
and make her eat a little something, and that I felt worse
for her than for my father.

"And Gabriel?" asked Jeff.

"Gabriel what?"

"You seeing him a lot?"

"Well… at the hospital, I do. He comes around sometimes when he knows I'm with *Papa*."

"What about outside the hospital?"

"What do you mean outside the hospital?"

"Well... do you see each other a lot?"

"You mean in real life?" Stupid question, I thought. Where did he think we'd see each other? In the after life? In hell? In our dreams?

"No, Marine, in a parallel universe."

"Okay, okay, it was a completely ridiculous question. But, no."

"No what?"

"No, no. We don't see each other in real life. Or in a parallel universe."

"No? Because I thought..."

"Eh?" How could he think that?

"But I don't know, when I got there the other day and you were in his arms. I just thought that maybe..."

"When you got there with Flavie. Are you seeing her?"

"No... I see her here, sometimes. Well... once."

And I felt like shouting at him, "Are you seeing her like you're seeing her, or are you seeing her like you're screwing her?" but not only was it a little vulgar, it was also completely inappropriate.

"Okay," said Jeff. "Is this what we're going to do? Are we going to spy on each other like little girls?"

"No. That's really a bad idea." And I thought of Marie-Lune, leaving his room the other day in his pale blue shirt and I pinched my lips. "No, but, surely..." I wanted to be honest. I didn't want any more of this weighty silence between us, the two people who had always been so close, the ones that people at university said were on the verge of communicating telepathically.

"Surely what?" I could see in his eyes that he was thinking the same thing I was, and was wondering the same thing, too: was it really a good idea to say it point blank? To ask each other if we just felt friendship, hoping that our answers would be the same and knowing for sure that, since we were prideful and human, an affirmative reply would hurt us as much as it relieved us?

"I'm glad you're not with Gabriel," Jeff said, looking into his glass.

"I'm glad you're not with Flavie," I answered, watching a drop run down the windowpane.

"It's a little silly," said Jeff.

"It's very silly."

"Oh, because you're in a position to…"

"Yes! Yes, I know. For you it's…"

"You think it'll pass?" Oh my God! We were getting dangerously close to a turn in the conversation I wasn't sure I was ready to take. I thought of Gabriel, how he always seemed like the sun when he came into my father's room, with his white coat, his handsome eyes lingering on mine, who hadn't once asked if I felt like getting a drink, or a coffee, or even a mineral water, and made me repeat over and over to Julien all week long that it was clear, obvious, undeniable that he wasn't interested. Julien had stopped listening and all he said, without looking up from the magazine article he was reading, was "Ask him yourself."

I looked up at Jeff. What was I going to tell him? That I don't know if it'll pass, and that I don't know if I want it to pass? It had taken years with Laurent, and even if we knew beyond the shadow of a doubt that we weren't in love anymore, every time one of us had a relationship, it really upset the other one. So what? Jeff's blue eyes were staring at me and I could see them again, but above me, burrowed into mine as we were both catching our breath. I sighed in an attempt to push aside this troubling image that kept me from fleshing out the slightest rational thought, and I almost fell off my chair when a light blue shape rushed up to the window and knocked on it joyously, just above and to the side of my head.

"Shit!" I shouted.

"Can you please tell me what he's doing here?"

Julien gave us a big wave, with an oversized smile, then

came into the bar. "Helloooo," he shouted, and Jeff and I exchanged a look that was falsely discouraged and sincerely relieved. "Saved by the queer," I said and we giggled into our glasses.

"Guess who has a date tomorrow?"

"Um… Not me. Is it you, Jeff?"

"Nope?"

"Well then, who has a date tomorrow?"

"Andrew?"

"No…"

"Your downstairs neighbor who always wears pants that are too short?"

"No…"

"The guy you work with? The heavy one who stutters a little?"

"No…"

"Your aunt who just lost her husband?"

"No…"

"The old guy who always eats alone at the restaurant while he looks at the servers' asses?"

"Okay, exactly how long are you going to keep this up?"

"Well, we have *all* night in front of us!" We started to laugh and Jeff and I clinked glasses.

"You're both a pain in the ass. *I* have a date tomorrow. With Mathias. A real date. I'm going to pick him up after work and we're going out to eat. Sushi. We're starting at zero."

"*From* zero."

"*From* zero?"

"Of course, *from* zero."

"Okay. Anyway, yeaahhhhhhhh! I have a date!"

"I'm happy for you, old man." Jeff gave Julien a pat on the back and signaled Andrew to bring him his scotch. "And, if I may, I think it's very wise of you to do it like that. Baby steps."

"I followed Gabriel's advice," Julien said, giving me a wink.

"Now Gabriel's giving relationship advice? Does he have a lonely hearts column?"

"He's the Louise Deschâtelets of the hospital circuit," said Julien. Then he froze, his gaze riveted on the door, looking like a guy who's just seen a ghost. I turned around – a handsome man of about sixty was standing there, in a big beige raincoat, closing up his umbrella. He then extended an arm behind him to encourage a young man of about thirty to follow him in. The younger man, who could have been his son, had a lock of blond hair that tumbled across his face and a soaking wet bomber jacket. He smiled at the older man and they went towards the bar, passing by us without seeming to see us.

"Is it still possible to get something to eat this late?" the man asked in impeccable French, with a slight accent. When Andrew replied in the affirmative, he was delighted and complained about how few restaurants were open late and encouraged "Kevin" to come sit down.

"It's him," said Julien. He was livid.

"Him who?" asked Jeff, as the answer dawned on me.

"He didn't even see me! He didn't even…" He was stammering. Andrew came over with a scotch, which Julien appeared not to notice at first, then he grabbed it, his eyes still on the door, and drank it down.

"May as well bring another," Jeff said to Andrew. "Julien, who is that?"

"Ex-lover," I explained. "Broke his heart. Twice."

"Oh." Jeff tried to turn around, but he got a hard elbow in the ribs.

"If I see you move…" He finally stopped staring at the door and ran his hands over his face. "Twenty years, for Chrissake. It's been twenty years."

Jeff and I looked at each other without saying anything. What was there to say? Some relationship scars never heal and we both knew it – even after love is gone, the marks remain. It was nothing new, but it was the first time I'd seen a wound open back up so spectacularly. Julien was practically doubled up over the table.

"Is this what I'm doing to Mathias?" he asked, still holding his hands over his face.

"Of course not... Come on now..."

He looked up at me and looked me square in the eyes. "Marine. Don't lie to me. This is exactly what I'm doing to Mathias. You know as well as I do that if we get back together, I'll start cheating on him again."

"No! You..." I didn't know what to say. I'd really thought there was a possibility of a new beginning, of being redeemed. Of real commitment. Was I really that naive?

"If I really loved him," said Julien, "I'd help him get rid of me."

"Stop."

"Do you two really believe that? If you love someone set them free?"

"I do," Jeff answered immediately. "But what I don't believe is that there's anyone on this planet strong enough to do it. We're only human. When we love, we hold on. There are no saints around here."

"Yes there are," I said.

"Okay, maybe, but we don't know any of them."

"And we're not sure we want to know them," I added in vain, trying to get a smile out of Julien.

"I'm going to go talk to him," said Julien.

"What? No!" I put a hand on his arm. "Julien, you're just going to mess yourself up."

"No, it's a good idea! You should go for it, Ju. Fuck, it's been twenty years; you're better off lancing what's left of that abscess."

"Okay... Okay..." He took a few deep breaths like an athlete preparing to accomplish some remarkable feat, then he emptied his glass, again, in one gulp. "Okay," he repeated, in a more decided tone. But even as he was getting ready to stand up, the two men passed by our table

again, with their coats on. "We'll just get room service,"
we heard Julien's ex-lover say. Apparently, Andrew
explained to us when he came over to refill our drinks, the
younger man had expressed the pressing but inexplicable
desire for pasta, which wasn't to be found on Le Lulli's
simple yet exquisite menu.

Julien had started staring at the door again. Jeff and I
didn't say a thing, settling for sign language or mouthing
a word or two. "Should we..." and "I don't know..." made
up the better part of our exchange.

"Julien," I finally said. "It's all right. It's just all right.
You knew that guy was still somewhere on the planet.
You're stronger than that now."

"Shit, that's exactly what I want him to see!"

"Ju, it's been twenty years."

"You can't understand. You've never had your heart
broken like that."

Jeff shrugged his shoulders, forced to give in to the evidence.

Julien continued, "I was very intense when I was
twenty years old. And don't go making any stupid 'What
a surprise!' jokes, because it has nothing to do with what
I am today. I was a kid, I was super naive and just wanted
to fall in love. And I fell square in love with Harold. He
was handsome, he was cultivated, he took me to shows,
he helped me discover the world, literally. I mean... I
thought I'd die, you know?"

Beside him, Jeff raised his eyebrows.

"I know it seems ridiculous now, but... I don't know...
it's the memory I have of what I was, I suppose, that gets
me all turned upside down like this. Then there's
Mathias..."

"Ju... do you love him?"

"Yes, I love him. But I think Harold loved me, too,
somehow."

"Yeah." We didn't say anything for a minute. There

wasn't much to say, really. I wasn't going to give Julien a hard time for thinking too clearly, after all. Ten years earlier I might have. But not anymore. The idea made me a little sad. We were getting older despite how things looked. We were growing up and, by that simple fact, we were abandoning some good things.

"Now, look," said Jeff. He was looking through the window at Laurent who was headed toward the door to the bar. He came in, saw us right away and took long strides straight to our table.

"Well now, this is quite a coincidence," he said, without taking off his coat. "I didn't dare call you at this hour. Carole kicked me out."

"Of your place?"

"Well, technically, it's become our place."

"What happened?" I gave him a peck on the cheek. Opposite me, Jeff and Julien were smiling a little, too – there was something joyous about these unexpected meetings, no one was going to complain.

"We got in a fight," Laurent explained. "For the same fucking reasons as always. I was very unpleasant. She told me she didn't want to see my face anymore and I answered, 'Good,' and I got the hell out. When I was out in the street, I realized I was being ridiculous, since… I thought I'd have a drink and calm down and then go back. But um… how are you all?"

"Okay," said Jeff half-heartedly.

"As you'd expect," I added.

"I just saw the man who broke my heart twenty years ago," said Julien.

There was another silence as Andrew set down a scotch in front of Laurent. Even he didn't dare talk anymore. The bar was almost empty and the four of us were there, glasses in hand, almost like we were on hold behind the big window that was still being struck by the rain.

"Fred's coming home in a week," I finally announced.

The three boys were delighted. "Maybe it's a sign," said Laurent.

"What kind of sign?"

"I don't know, a sign of renewal?"

We all looked at him like he'd just said the stupidest thing ever.

"What?" he asked.

"You're right," said Julien, raising his glass. "Really, things can only get better, right? It can just get better."

"You mean it can't get any worse," said Jeff.

"No, I mean it can just get better…"

So we raised our glasses and toasted in silence, the four of us together.

A week later, half hysterical, I called Julien to tell him he had no idea how right he had been, and that his statement had been downright prophetic.

To: Fred
From: Marine Vandale
Subject: (none)

....

Oh my God. Oh my God. oh my God oh my God. Omigod.
OH. MY. GOD. Omigod! Ohmygodohmygodohmygod.

To: Marine
From: Frédéric Vandale
Subject: Oh mon Dieu

....

Marine, I'm holding my passport between my teeth, I've got
my suitcase in my hand, my toque on my head and my computer on my lap: the portrait, as you can see, of a man about
to get on a plane and who, therefore, has very little time to offer
his sister when she's pretending to be autistic.

To: Fred
From: Marine Vandale
Subject: Political correctness

....

Eh, oh… no joking about autism, it's not funny. I've been trying for eight years to rehabilitate Laurent about his imitation
of Dustin Hoffman in *Rain Man*, so cut it out.

To: Marine
From: Frédéric Vandale
Subject: Behavioral problems

....

Would you mind being coherent? Because when I say I'm holding my passport between my teeth, I'm not kidding. I have a
flight in two hours and fifteen minutes, Marine, and my butt
is still on my sofa. So be nice, in other words, brief.

To: Fred
From: Marine Vandale
Subject: Time management

Why is your bum on the sofa if you're taking off in two hours?
Smells like self-sabotage to me. Don't you want to come? Is
that it? Because *Papa* is expecting you and he knows very well
you're coming, now that he is the very picture of lucidity
("Well," you could say, "we could have a long debate about the
exact nature of lucidity" to which I would reply, "Yes, Fred, but
let's come to an agreement all the same: he hears, he understands, he answers, he is coherent").

To: Marine
From: Frédéric Vandale
Subject: Exact nature of lucidity

Do you really want to debate about lucidity? Because, I don't
know, Marine, but if I look at the current conversation, I can't
say you're exactly a champ. Will you please tell me what's going
on?

To: Fred
From: Marine Vandale
Subject: (none)

Guess.

To: Marine
From: Frédéric Vandale
Subject: Re: (none)

Let's play a little game, okay? Go into one of the drawers of
your memory bank and find the memory of when you and I
were little and you would tell me, "guess." Now. Do you
remember how I used to react?

To: Fred
From: Marine Vandale
Subject: Denial

....

You're not going to get me like that today. For twenty years I've been trying to forget that you'd spit in my ears to punish me for the offense in question. Cruel. Too bad for you.

To: Marine
From: Frédéric Vandale
Subject: Wet ear

....

Did I really spit in your ears?

To: Fred
From: Marine Vandale
Subject: Wet pride

....

Oh, yeah. You also put me in a suitcase and promised me a piece of grape Hubba Bubba if I stayed in there five minutes. *Maman* is the one who found me an hour later.

To: Marine
From: Frédéric Vandale
Subject: Bad deal

....

For ONE piece of Hubba Bubba? Wow, Marine, you really were a bad negotiator.

To: Fred
From: Marine Vandale
Subject: Re: Bad deal

....

Like I would have come out ahead for TWO pieces of bubblegum. Here's a hug, I miss you, brother. Go catch your plane.

To: Marine
From: Frédéric Vandale
Subject: Scandal

....

Wait, WHAT? You flood me with Omigods and you leave me
with a "Go catch your plane"? You crazy or what?

To: Fred
From: Marine Vandale
Subject: A man's sleep

....

Okay. Since you insist. He's asleep. Just next to me. Well, two
meters from me, to be absolutely precise. But you can deduct
that if I'm two meters from his sleeping body, it's because I was
right on top of him a little while ago.

To: Marine
From: Frédéric Vandale
Subject: The ghost of the suitcase

....

You're playing with fire, Marinette. If you don't tell me who it
is in the next five seconds, I'll shut you up in a suitcase as soon
as I land and I'll put you on a plane headed for Cyprus. It's the
doctor. It has to be. Not Jeff again? Not Jeff again, right? No,
you wouldn't be so happy. I know you're happy because happiness has always made you incoherent, it's both idiotic and
very touching. Although... Marine! My plane leaves in two
hours!

To: Fred
From: Marine Vandale
Subject: Hubba Bub-BET

....

Okay, you've got me feeling sorry for you. For a piece of grape
bubblegum, I'll tell you. When you get here.

To: Marine
From: Frédéric Vandale
Subject: (none)

....

You're not my sister anymore.

Chapter 15

Gently, I closed the computer, trying not to make any noise, but to this day, I'm still certain I couldn't hold back a mischievous laugh. I was, indeed, incoherent. I'd gotten up right in the middle of the night after I realized sleep wasn't an option.

Gabriel had fallen asleep rather quickly, holding me close, one arm around my waist, one hand on my left breast, his legs intertwined with mine. I'd heard his breathing slowly become peaceful, then take on the tender, docile rhythm of sleep, and I'd felt his body become heavier and warmer, like little children's do when they fall asleep in your arms. But my eyes were wide open, staring at the white ceiling in his bedroom, perfectly conscious that I was going to wake up with at least twenty-four cramps, I was so tense. I didn't want to move, for fear of waking him up, for fear of disrupting the beautiful fragility of the moment. He'd said, "Stay." And I had, only too happy to obey.

But two hours later, it was obviously a failure, I was unable to fall asleep, and it had taken me a good twenty minutes to get out of his embrace as gently as possible so I wouldn't wake him up and so he wouldn't hear me heading for the living room, where I'd finally found the phone. It was three in the morning and I was completely naked, and I was sitting on the floor, leaning against the kitchen counter (which, according to my exceptional surveying estimates, was the farthest possible place from Gabriel's bed) and I called Julien. Who, of course, wasn't answering.

And who, therefore, I called again. After the fifth call, a hysterical, overexcited voice bellowed:

"What is it? Marine? What's going on? Where are you? Marine, my God, it's spring, you have to come dancing with us. Wooooooo-hooooooo! Springtime! … What? … No, you shut up, you old shit. I can shout on rue Sainte Anne if I want, it's springtime! What d'you mean it's three in the morning?… Um, nice watch… Yeah, but… IT'S THREE IN THE MORNING? Marine! Are you okay? Marine? Where are you? Who's number are you at?"

"My cell's out of juice, and…"

"But where are you? It's springtime!"

Since what we were calling his "non-meeting" with Harold, Julien had probably only slept about twenty-two minutes and spent ninety-seven percent of his time staying awake in the bars in the gay Village, where he'd dance until the wee small hours against the moist, perfect bodies of boys who were half his age. "I haven't touched a single one," he'd tell us so proudly it made me feel sad. Neither Jeff nor Laurent nor I had the courage to tell him that his absurd demonstration of faithfulness was not only pathetic, it was unnecessary – and above all it had nothing to do with love. But it had only been a week. Only one week, I kept telling the boys.

"Come dancinggggggggg!" he'd shouted.

"Ju, it's three in the morning. There's no more dancing left."

"We're going to an after-hours club!"

"Ju, I'm a thousand years old. I don't go to after-hours clubs anymore. I used to go to after-hours clubs when I was nineteen and even then, I hated it."

"Yeah, but it's so cooool! I'm thirty-four and I still like it…"

"Oh, my sweet baby, you're almost forty years old."

"Shhhhhhhhh. Shh, shh, shh. Rod will hear you."

"Rod?" Being named Rod and dancing in a gay bar seemed, in my opinion, to be either a miracle or a sham.

"Yes… Rod. Handsome boy. A very handsome boy. But nothing will happen. Did I tell you I'm not cheating? *Even* if technically I'm not with Mathias? I love him, Marine. I loooooooooove him!"

"Ju, what are you on exactly?"

"Love, Marine! Nothing but love!"

I rolled my eyes and laughed. It didn't really matter if Julien was drunk or sober or just high on love.

"Julien… You know when you said things could only get better?"

"Yes…"

"You were right. You were right! You were so right!"

"Does that mean you're coming dancing?"

"Juuu! No!"

"You happy?"

"I… I suppose."

He'd laughed, and then I'd laughed and then I hung up. I was all alone, sitting on the beautiful, orange, ceramic tile floor of a man I hardly knew. And I kept on laughing, almost physically missing the presence of a cat, who, that particular night would have been my silent, indifferent confident, who I could have taken in my arms, and simply laughed into his warm little neck, and felt his fur against my naked skin.

Four seconds later, Gabriel's phone was ringing. Panicked by the idea it would wake him up, I jumped on it.

"Okay," said Julien's voice, suddenly sober. "I didn't ask the right questions. What happened? What's making you happy?"

"Rod dumped you, eh?"

"Totally. Moving on. Shoot."

So I told him. About our first kiss.

I'd gone back to see my father, but I had the night shift that day. Ariane was busy cutting out squares of red fabric for the student movement. "Commendable work," I said as I wondered how bits of fabric could help anything. "You can replace me tomorrow."

"So! So! So! Solidarity!" she'd replied.

I spent some time by our father's side, as he slept, with the peaceful breathing of an active volcano. His snoring was a poem, a phenomenon, an event that even the nurses' aides we'd gotten to know a bit over the past two weeks thought was fantastic.

I'd fallen asleep, with one hand in his, and I'd been woken up by a warm palm against my back. It was Gabriel, who'd just stopped by to see how everything was.

"Everything okay?" I'd answered with the eternal question mark that had been following me around since I'd found out my father was sick.

"Everything's fantastic," Élodie had answered, whom I hadn't seen come in though she was standing right behind Gabriel. "I've brought some books that *Papa* likes."

They were bad detective novels and the sight of the worn, old-fashioned covers brought tears to my eyes.

"I'm going to read for *Papa*," Élodie had said. "You leave for a little while. Take a break."

"Élo…" I'd just woken up, I wasn't thinking. "Okay, what happened to the real Élodie? When did you turn into this girl?"

She laughed gently – obviously, she'd been caught by surprise too – "I don't know, silly. But, you can take at least an hour break, okay? I'll be here."

Delighted, I made my way towards the sinister room where we could obtain such delicacies as Joe Louies, muffins the consistency of a good brick, Doritos, the same old kinds of chips, Mars bars, disgusting bags of "traveler's mix," expired Yoplait yogurts and over- or underripe bananas. There was also a little microwave for heating, I imagined, dishes brought by people luckier than me, who thought in advance about bringing lunch. The light was green and sad, and I wondered what had inspired the architects, or designers, even in a hospital, to come up with such a place.

I was hesitating between an excellent package of dried apricots and a protein bar that was as dense as a stone when Gabriel walked in. He gave me a little smile and went straight for the coffee machine, and put it on. Then, he turned his head toward me and gave me a little smile. He was wearing his white coat and although the room's green light made the rest of us look like corpses, he still managed to look handsome. Locks of black hair tumbled loosely onto his forehead, and his smile, as always, seemed to be filled with words, as if the wrinkle digging along its left side, was saying to me, "Come," repeating that it knew more than I could imagine. I can't hide anything from him, I'd thought, as I looked at him without speaking. And I didn't know if it was true, or if he'd simply attained the status of master of smiles that seem to know everything, but it was totally intoxicating – and most of all, it was terribly sexy. I felt like I was completely naked when he looked at me like that. Not physically, but on some other, even more intimate level. Some people must have hated that. Personally, it made me crazy.

"You okay?" he'd asked me.

"I'm okay." I was still standing in front of the snack machine, and he was still in front of the coffee machine.

"You can go, you know. Your sister will stay the whole night. She stays every night."

"No… She already spent the morning here…" He'd shrugged his shoulders, seeming to say, "Whatever you want," then he came towards me. "The Mars bar," he'd said.

"What about the Mars bar?"

"It's probably the healthiest thing in there."

"I would have thought it was the tasty traveler's mix…"

"Trail mix. Traveler's mix has dried pineapple and papaya in it. Trail mix is just apples and bananas."

"Oh… Is there a couch potato mix?"

"No, but you can make it yourself. One Mars bar and one bag of Doritos. It's my favorite."

I'd looked up at him and laughed. It was more of a smile in fact, that remained there, floating between us. He was so close to me – I could feel his chest against my shoulder. He smiled ever so slightly, too, then he came closer. I thought he was going to say something, but he seemed to hesitate. Then he smiled more openly and that's when, in front of a pack of salt-and-vinegar chips, under the vibrating neon lights, a few meters from the bed where my father was sleeping, I kissed Gabriel Champagne.

"*You* kissed him?"

"Yup."

"You kissed each other."

"No, no. *I* kissed him. I literally grabbed him by the coat and I kissed him. I never do that."

"I know! I've been telling you to do it more often for almost ten years. Out there, girl. You gotta be out there!"

"Okay, that's enough now. He was going to kiss me any second there, it was obvious. It's just that it was too long."

"Two seconds?"

"An eternity."

I couldn't see anything but his eyes. Their jade irises, full, black lashes like a woman's, and they seemed to never want to let me go, to see nothing but me. He's going to do it, I thought. It's going to happen. I felt very light, almost ethereal, like I no longer had a body. Then, after moving towards his chest, all I had to do was pull him the few centimeters still separating us, for him to find my body, and for me to find his. It was the most impulsive and logical thing I'd ever done in my life. I hadn't thought, I'd acted, very simply, because that's all I could do. It was inevitable, like eating when you're hungry or jumping into a stream of running water when you're overheating. And besides, and besides, it was what I wanted. For those two eternal seconds I had a feeling of clear-headedness that was almost blinding.

"And…"

"And what?"

"Marine, it's three-thirty in the morning, I'm sitting on a crummy bench in the Village, I have a feeling you're hiding behind a chair or under a desk with a cordless phone, so don't give me a hard time."

"What do you want to know? How it was, if he's got a nice body?"

"Marine… Ma-rine… Sometimes you are hopelessly naive. I know what he looks like, Marine. And when I say I have X-ray vision when it comes to handsome guys, I'm not kidding. I *know* he's got a nice body. But… um… his…"

"No. I'm not answering that."

"You're dying to."

"No. No. Seriously, if there was an expression that meant the opposite of dying to, that's exactly what I'd be telling you right now."

"*Come on…* What about his ass? His chest? He isn't hairy, is he? Is he?"

"I'm going to hang up. But no, he's not really hairy. And everything is perfect. Voilà."

"Meow. I knew it! And? And? What does he do with it?"

I knew he was dreaming of getting the juicy details. Details that I refused to provide; instead I was making him wait by giving him details about how our bodies had come together – became truly molded together in that sad room in the hospital. I told Julien about his hands on my face, his mouth on mine, then on my neck, about my hands in his hair.

"I knew this was going to happen," I'd murmured to Gabriel, holding his handsome face in my hands.

"You knew?"

"Yes, I knew." And as I said it, I realized it was true. Though I didn't normally believe in anything, liked black cats and walking under ladders, made fun of Flavie and all the time she spent with clairvoyants, I had, without realizing it, cultivated a strange certainty that had no basis in reality and that, at that moment, reassured me as much as it frightened me.

"You could leave, you know," Gabriel had said. And once again, I was looking at his smile that was full of words and his eyes that seemed to just want to eat me all up.

"Yes, I said. I could leave."

And five hours later, there I was, sitting in Gabriel's kitchen, eyes wide open in the darkness, replaying each move we'd made, me hastily grabbing my coat as Élodie – tired, complicit and inexplicably indulgent – looked on, the rearview mirror reflecting the amused eyes of the taxi driver who couldn't ignore the fact that we were acting like love-struck teenagers, our awkward entrance into his apartment – bodies backed up against walls, clothes feverishly removed, my hands grabbing the door frame as he lifted me off the ground. Then, his body against mine, his mouth kissing my shoulder, my teeth against his skin and his eyes fixed on mine as he felt my orgasm.

I placed one hand over my eyes, knowing perfectly well that I was wearing a stupid smile and that I had no intention of chasing any of these images out of my head. Instead, I thought to myself, I'm going to cultivate them, watch them again and again, caress them till I'm satisfied.

I was mentally reviewing a particularly delicious moment of our night when I suddenly realized I was cold. I must have been feeling cold for a while already, but I was in that strange, rare state that keeps us miles away from unpleasant sensations and any thoughts we don't feel like thinking. "You mean like when you're completely drunk?"

Laurent would have asked and I would have answered, "Yes. Exactly like that." Because I was afraid, more than ever, of the morning after.

I got up to get my sweater, when I noticed, on a chair, a wool coat. I observed it for a moment, I hesitated – I almost spoke to it, in fact, to ask what it thought of its owner and if it might have a couple of good stories to share, or even two or three secrets to confide about the man whose shoulders it sometimes covered. It was an old coat, the kind most men keep hidden in their closets, a little worn on the elbows, with only two buttons left, dark green, warm and soft. I grabbed it and slipped it on easily, then continued to walk through the apartment, trying not to touch what I saw, not to pick up every book, every magazine in hopes of finding out something, any miniscule clue to Gabriel's true personality.

It was a nice apartment, that didn't look at all as I had imagined it. Certain walls were made of gray stone, and there were beams in the ceiling, and the floors were hardwood. Everywhere, there where old objects that spoke of a life I didn't know, an early-twentieth-century suitcase served as a storage unit for CDs, heavy Canadian armoires were full of books, there was a heavy, varnished wooden table, and there were pedestal lamps that had obviously known other generations than ours. I saw life, everywhere, layers of existence, and I felt stupid and naive for thinking that Gabriel lived in a space and time that only touched the present, and that his life had never had any consistency before I'd showed up.

Standing in front of one of the Canadian hutches, I contemplated Gabriel's books – our books say so much about us and I wanted to know so much about him. In this particular hutch, there were only books in English – the ones in French were elsewhere, a bit scattered throughout the apartment, on a mauve bookshelf in the dining room, in another hutch, in an old trunk that looked like it had been made to hold gold coins. Classics, first off, Forster, Waugh, Kipling, Faulkner, Fitzgerald, and Hemingway, Woolf, Joyce, Miller. Then a whole shelf of contemporary works (which I couldn't locate among the French titles, as if Gabriel had abandoned francophone literature after Sartre): Zadie Smith, Jonathan Franzen, Paul Auster, Mordecai Richler, Michael Ondaatje. Ah, I said to myself proudly, picking up *The English Patient.* I'd at least read those. A copy of *Barney's Version*, which apparently had also been well loved, was signed. I made an appreciative face, and as I looked up, I noticed my reflection in one of the big windows.

"Marie-Lune," I whispered. It was the wool vest: all the times she'd come out of Jeff's room in one of his shirts passed before my eyes. And so, I thought about Jeff. I thought about Jeff and his arms, about the night we'd spent together, about the Jeff who I knew so well and so intimately. What did I know about this man, who was such a voracious reader, who saved lives and loved the sea? Not very much. And I finally understood why Jeff's shirts were so important to Marie-Lune: it was because they were a way for her to be closer to him.

I suddenly felt very small in this apartment, in this wool coat that was too big for me, in the middle of this life I knew almost nothing about, beside the fact that it was inhabited by old trunks, books, and... He'd never again mentioned the woman he was seeing, that admission that had startled me so, weeks earlier. Was she still part of this dense, distant life? Gabriel had a way of talking about himself that gave the impression he was revealing intimate details, but I realized, at this time of the night when paranoia came so easily, that I knew almost nothing about how he spent his time, what he did in the evenings, at night, in the gray early morning. I didn't know anything about his day-to-day life, and this idea suddenly frightened me.

"You're *trying* to frighten yourself," Laurent would say

to me later (for lack of any better options, I just made a face in reply).

It was undoubtedly the fact that it was night, my accumulated fatigue from the preceding days catching up with me, but I almost felt like leaving, like running for home, where I'd be in my own little cocoon, far from sickness, desire and oversized dreams of love. I was putting the book by Richler back on the shelf when I heard Gabriel's voice.

"You okay?"

I jumped. He was on the other side of the room, leaning against the wall, with tousled hair and sleepy eyes, completely naked.

"I'm okay," I said. "Couldn't sleep. My father."

He smiled politely – we both knew very well that my father wasn't what was keeping me from sleeping.

"Okay. All right." He raised a finger to signal me to wait, went back to his room and came back wearing pajama bottoms. Clever man, I had the time to think. You know how handsome you are just wearing that. He settled down on the sofa, propped up against the armrest, his legs stretched out, and then extended one hand towards me. "Come on. Come here."

"Hmmm?"

He laughed a little, like you do when you're touched by someone's naivety. "Come here!"

So, I sat down between his legs. He put one arm around me, and with the other, he pointed the remote at the huge plasma screen opposite us. An image appeared, a grid that seemed sibylline and complex to me (Jeff and I had basic cable, an old eighteen-inch TV and about as much technical knowledge as a chimp of average intelligence). Gabriel pushed a couple of buttons, then put down the remote, looking satisfied. "There," he said. "Nothing like a good, old movie when you can't sleep." On the screen, a movie company's logo appeared, along with a light tune that sounded familiar. Gabriel put his two bare arms around me and, with his hands resting on my belly, he said, as if by way of an excuse, "It's because of my work schedule. At one point or another, your sleep patterns get kind of fucked up. So it's always practical to be able to watch a movie whenever you want."

I finally recognized the tune, and the movie's first scene confirmed my idea: *Four Weddings and a Funeral*?! I looked up at him, with an amused smile on my lips. Except for Laurent, I didn't know a single other man who admitted to liking this movie. I knew that some had liked it, but they all pretended to prefer *Gladiator*, *Slapshot*, or *Magnolia*, depending on whether they wanted to seem macho, funny or intellectual.

"What?" said Gabriel, with a little embarrassed smile. I turned back to Hugh Grant who was repeating "Fuck" for the sixth time, while Gabriel was giving me little kisses on the temple. You're the one who's perfect, I thought. And I shivered a little, with fear and with pleasure.

"I know, I know," I said as I walked into the apartment. "I know, I'm late. Give me ten minutes."

Jeff and Laurent, leaning on the kitchen bar, were both giving me the evil eye, their arms crossed, looking mockingly angry.

"I was…"

"It's okay, we know," said Jeff.

"You know?" At the same instant, I heard the far-off sound of flushing and Julien came into the great room zipping up his mauve jeans. "Ta-daaa! I couldn't hold it in!"

"Seeing that you're coming out of the washroom," said Laurent, "I think you'd better reconsiser the way you phrased that statement."

Beside him, Jeff laughed silently.

"What are you doing here?" I asked Julien.

"You really think I'm going to let you go to the airport without me? And miss out on all the fun?"

"You just wanted to chat, you big blabbermouth."

"Ohhh. You were very happy to have someone to chat with at three this morning."

"Okay, that's enough!" said Jeff. "Marine, we have to be on the road in fifteen minutes, max."

"I'll just take a quick shower."

I dropped my coat right on the floor and ran to the bathroom with light steps. When I went by the boys, Laurent said, "Maybe you want to sleep with Julien, too, while you're at it? Talk about promiscuity! Geeez..." He wasn't being mean. He was teasing me more than anything else.

"You're just jealous," I said.

"Of the doctor?"

"No, of me. You're jealous 'cause you wish you could sleep with whoever you want."

I went into the bathroom. Behind me, I heard Jeff's voice saying, "Touché" and Laurent answering with a contrite little "Eat shit."

"We have the same conversation *every* time," groaned Jeff.

"I knew we should have taken my car." Julien was leaning on the roof of Laurent's car. "There's more room in the back seat. Your fucking Audi is cute and all that, but except for maybe two Hobbits, I don't know who you could fit back there."

"That's exactly my point. The two dwarves in the back, Jeff and me in front."

"Hey!" I shouted as Julien wrapped his multicolor scarf around in his neck to express his outrage. "We aren't dwarves."

"Do your legs measure four feet? No. I don't think so. Are you six feet two inches tall? No. I don't think so. Jeff and yours truly, six-foot-two. So, front seat. And besides that, I'm driving."

"*Every* time," sighed Jeff, kicking a little pile of snow that was still resisting the arrival of spring.

"Okay, okay," I said. "It's all right. I get it. But, um, where are we going to put Fred? In the trunk?"

"Maybe on the roof," suggested Julien.

"Hey, if anyone goes on the roof, it's going to be you. I'd like to point out to you, Bozo the clown, that you're the one who insisted on tagging along, so you're going to have to live with it."

"No, but really?" I asked.

"We'll put him in the back!" Jeff finally shouted, obviously annoyed. "Shit, it's a good thing you're not ushers in a theater, you'd get yourselves lynched. It's not complicated. Christ, Marine in the middle, then Bozo and Fred on the sides."

"Okay, when did we decide my name was Bozo?"

I raised a finger.

"Yeah, but… Fred is six foot one, after all."

"Okay," Jeff said to Laurent. "Get in the car. I'm leaving these two idiots right where they are on the sidewalk."

"Grrrr!"

Ten minutes later we were all sitting in the car, in the same seats we were always in. "Anybody know a song we could sing?" asked Julien.

"Jesus Christ," said Jeff, as Laurent and I burst out laughing. I was completely exhausted, but on such a high that I could have run a marathon or tap-danced or even done a little cheerleading number. I felt like hopping and that's exactly what I was doing, on the backseat, just behind Jeff: I was stamping my feet. I noticed him looking at me in his outside mirror. "You okay?" he asked.

I wanted just to tell him that things were better than they usually were and that I was violently happy and that it scared me, that everything around me seemed to be a promise of happiness and fulfillment: my father could only get better, Élodie was turning out to be a generous soul, my three best boys were in the car with me, I'd be hugging my beloved brother in less than an hour, Gabriel had held me against him as I fell asleep right before the fourth marriage and just after the funeral and he'd looked into my eyes again, with his head leaning on the back of the sofa as we made love in the pale morning light. I felt invincible and naive – I felt as strong as I had when I was sixteen.

But, despite all my efforts, Jeff now seemed imperceptibly separate from me, by something blurry and indefinable that was linked both to unspoken desire and to the questions we didn't dare ask. So I answered, "I'm fine." And in the mirror, his reflection smiled and he nodded his head with a look that was approving and completely lacking in sincerity. There always has to be a catch, I thought. A little stain on our happiness, since it wouldn't be the same if it were spotless. Too bad. I knew that these moments of intense joy that we feel with almost supernatural lucidity don't last and I had no intention of letting mine slip through my fingers so quickly. Too bad about the catch, I said. I'll look after the stain later.

I was still fidgeting in front of the Arrivals door that Fred was due to pass through any minute now. I was so excited about seeing him, that I was almost afraid of the moment and I sporadically clapped my hands and shot hopeful, worried looks at Laurent, who finally started laughing.

"Will you please settle down?"

"Didn't get enough sleep."

"Okay, okay, we know." He turned his head so he didn't have to look me in the face, which is what he always did when the conversation intimidated him. "Everything go, umm, okay with the doctor?"

"Loulou…"

"What?"

"Do you really want to know?"

He seemed to think it over. "Hmm. No. Maybe not."

"What do you mean maybe not?" Julien almost pushed him over the metal barrier. "Yes, we want to know!"

"Do you want me to stuff his clowny scarf down his throat?" Jeff asked me.

"No... maybe just gag him with it... Or maybe... FRED!!!" I grabbed hold of the metal barrier so I could slip under it more elegantly (or rather, I should say, less ridiculously), I bumped into an old woman and two children, shouted "Sorry" without much feeling into their conversation, pushed the cart with Fred's luggage into the wall, and finally leapt into my big brother's arms. With my legs around his waist and my arms around his neck, I could hear him laugh and feel him squeeze me with all his might. We gave each other a kiss that was almost abrupt, one on each cheek, then we finally looked at each other, still laughing. In that position, in his arms, my face was higher than his and he had to look up to see me. "Your hair!" I said, running my hands through the blond waves. "Your hair is so long!" Then I put my feet back on the ground and I had to look up to see the top of his face.

"*Ça pogne au boutte*," he said to me with a little wink. Two minutes in Québec and he'd already gotten back our wonderful accent. He gave me a big, noisy kiss on the top of the head, then, noticing the boys up ahead, gave a big, "Hey!" and then it was one greeting after the other – a kiss for Julien, who managed to run a hand through his hair, a macho hug complete with some strong slaps on the back for Laurent, and an inevitable bear hug from Jeff who lifted Frédéric off the ground before giving him a smack on the back that almost sent him reeling into the lady I'd already bumped into a few minutes earlier.

"Okay," said Laurent. "Drinks."

"Well, maybe we could wait till we get home..."

"Did you fall on your head? Drinks all the way! To the airport bar." He slapped Fred on the back again. "Right, *l'frère?*"

I rolled my eyes. I'd forgotten Jeff, Laurent and Fred's unbearable habit of calling each other "*l'frère*," which they pronounced with such a thick accent they would have made my Uncle Marcel blush.

"Let's go, *l'frère*. Hey, it's eight at night for me!" And all three of them started laughing, slapping each other on the back, giving each other manly pokes in the ribs, and booming, "*Ostie, l'frère!*"

"He's even more handsome than I remembered," Julien whispered to me.

"Shut the hell up, *l'frère!*"

An hour later, Jeff was gesturing to the server who, despite being sixty years old, had fallen under his spell. "Another round, Adèle *ma belle.*"

"Adèle *ma belle?* Adèle has lost all her teeth, Jeff." Laughter on all sides. We were so happy to be all together again, after all the great years at Le Lulli and so many other bars and restaurants, after celebrating our love of life in at least a dozen apartments – some elegant, some dives, after singing 'Unchained Melody' and 'Le Feu sauvage de l'amour' at the top of our lungs in big rental cars, we were so delighted to share a drink in this soulless place, where people only ever passed through, and we thought everything was funny and charming – starting with us. I never wanted to leave this bar for travelers, never wanted to leave behind this precious moment where we all were happy. We were all thinking the same thing, I knew, because we hesitated to admit it to ourselves, as if the fact of mentioning our happiness would chase it away – like sometimes when you mention the long-awaited presence of the sun, and it goes back behind the clouds.

"So, you got your hands on your doctor," Fred repeated. "Good work, little sister."

"Well now, let's go easy there. I spent one night with

him. Let's not put the cart before it hatches."

"Cut it out… I know you well enough to know you're already imaging little scenes of falling in love, getting married, having babies, and walking hand in hand down the street."

"No…" I tried to hold back a smile, but without much luck. Then I shot a quick look at Jeff who was staring at me with an expression I'd never seen before and that didn't look bitter or annoyed – it was a silent question, a calm and attentive observation, as if he thought that by staring at me like that he'd get an answer or be able to read it in me. "Really?" his big blue eyes seemed to be asking me. "Can you really be sure?" My smile faded and as I turned around, I saw that Fred was looking at Jeff, too.

"Don't listen to her," said Julien, who hadn't seen any of this. "That girl is on fire. On FIRE, Fred."

"What about the rest of you?" asked my brother.

Julien and Laurent each muttered something.

"*L'frère*. Still with Carole?"

"Mmm. Yep."

Frédéric started laughing. "Still as communicative as ever, I see. Really, things are good with her?"

"Hmmpf."

"Loulou…"

"Yeah, yeah, things are okay. It's all right, okay?" He'd gone back home after Carole had "kicked him out" and he simply told her he was "tired." That he couldn't take the tension and their countless squabbles anymore. When she asked him if he wanted her to leave, he said no, looking her right in the eyes. I knew it was true because Carole had told me so: the day after he said it, she'd called me to suggest we go for a coffee so unexpectedly that I almost choked on my delicious handful of trail mix. And, stupidly, I'd hesitated, foreseeing an unending scene of condolences and an hour of being very ill at ease, but when I saw how nervous she was, and her sincere smiles,

I knew she was reaching out to me, and, if I really loved my friend, I would have to take her hand.

We talked for nearly two hours, mutually reassuring each other, carefully laughing over Laurent's shortcomings ("Did he ever make you his famous omelet? Poor guy, he's so proud of his famous omelet..." "Wait, he just discovered frittatas. Three Saturday mornings in a row, I've had to eat a frittata." "Ouch..."). The exact words were never spoken, but we understood each other: at the end of the day, we really had no reason to criticize each other, no reason to be jealous of each other, and everything to gain. I'd left the café feeling light and relieved, repeating to myself that we really were quite a bunch of idiots for waiting so long to offer this kind of simple, healthy gesture.

As for Laurent, he had decided a few days earlier that healthy optimism would pave the way to conjugal happiness. He was as suited for optimism as I was for, say, the trapeze, and ever since he'd been struggling with a resolution that didn't suit him, but that it would be hard to criticize him for. Sometimes he amazed me with his almost supernatural gift for complicating what could have been so simple. He was living with a woman who was intelligent, beautiful and lively, who undoubtedly had some faults (but who really wants a perfect partner? Who doesn't want to love someone for their faults as well as their strong points?), but who loved him and who, despite what he said, despite what he might even think, he loved.

"The more things change, the more they stay the same, eh?" said Frédéric. "What about you, Ju?" I gave him a little kick under the table, not for fear that the question would make Julien feel uncomfortable (nothing, but nothing in this universe made Julien uncomfortable), but to avoid the unending story of Julien's love life, which Jeff, Laurent and I couldn't stand to hear again and which, of course, he had just launched into again.

"I'll take his legs," Jeff murmured to Laurent, "and you

get him under the arms. Marine…"

"I know, I should have agreed before when you wanted to shove his fucking scarf down his throat."

"Okay, okay! I get it already!" Julien squeaked. "Too bad for you. Long story short, and believe me, Fred, you're missing a *fabulous* story, Mathias dumped me because…"

Laurent and I looked at each other then started to giggle. "Okay, it really was pretty fabulous," said Laurent. And the four of us started telling the story, with Jeff, Laurent and I adding details as if they were about us, while Frédéric laughed with pleasure.

"What about you?" Julien asked Fred. "Hop, hop, hop?"

"Hop, hop, hop?"

"Bing badabing?"

"What?"

Julien sighed in discouragement. "Are you getting any, for Chrissake?"

"Oh… THAT'S what you meant…"

"Come on, hop, hop, hop, bing badabing, shaky shake shake, everybody knows what that means, right?"

"You know what the worst part is?" Jeff asked me. "It's that *I* understand Julien perfectly."

"Yeah, I know…" We laughed together and I felt a gentle warmth inside, the kind that radiates within you when nothing, but absolutely nothing, is missing.

"It's okay," Fred said laughing. "I've been working a lot lately."

"Making progress?" I asked.

"I brought you the rest and…"

"Keep gooooiiing…" Laurent said to him between clenched teeth. "We want stories about the French girls, we *demand* stories about the French girls."

"Well… let's just say I haven't been bored. I don't know if it's the accent or what… But, I swear, for a while I was seeing four of them a week. And not necessarily the same ones from one week to the next."

"Okay. WHOA! Maybe I don't really want to hear about my brother's sex life?!"

"Coming from the girl who spends twelve hours a week on the computer sending me details about HER sex life, that statement seems a little out of place."

"Yeah. Maybe." I pouted pitifully and Fred pulled me in close to kiss my hair. Across from me, Jeff wasn't saying anything.

"So, l'frère," I said to Fred. "It's getting to be time to go see l'père."

"What about l'doc? Am I going to meet him?"

"Don't be a smart ass," I said as I got up, and as Julien was already struggling with Jeff about where we were going to sit in the car.

As we left the terminal, Frédéric looked up towards the perfectly blue sky. We could feel water all around us, dirty, joyful water on the shiny asphalt, on the yellow, soaked patches of grass, in the delicate sounds of droplets in the gutters. The Great Melt. "Springtime," he said. "Shit, I missed spring." I looked at him with a smile, almost with adoration. I'd missed him terribly since he'd left, but it was only now, in his presence, that I realized how much. I examined his profile, his incredibly long eyelashes, his eyes that were the same color as mine. With his hair tumbling in waves almost to his chin – golden hair, with loose waves that always fell perfectly, hair women were always jealous of, his gray scarf and his long coat, he looked like a portrait of a young poet.

"How's the 'I think I'm Rimbaud' style working for you?" I asked him. "You the king of Saint-Germain?"

He looked down towards me, laughing, then he put his arm around my shoulders. "Christ, I'm glad to see you."

And I laughed in the sun, as I snuggled up to my brother, because he was back, and I could finally hold him in my arms, because, in front of us, the three boys were walking shoulder to shoulder and I could hear them laughing and talking like they always had ("Why not get a Winnebago, then?" "I told you we'd all end up in a commune." "Oh boy, I don't know if Carole would like the idea of a commune." "As long as there are Egyptian cotton sheets and banana liqueur, I'm all for a commune." "What kind of liqueur? You big fucking degenerate." "Cut it out, you love me." "No, no, that's exactly where you're wrong. I don't love you at all. At all." "Come on… a kiss. Give me a kiss. I know you want a kiss, Jeff Murphy." And then Jeff grabbed Julien in a stranglehold to plant such a big, violent kiss on the top of his head that it left him with tousled hair, and Laurent in a state of hilarity).

I watched them go and held on to Frédéric's hand, I was thinking about Gabriel and I felt the sunshine where my heart should be because I was content. And I was stupidly trying to not really admit it, not even to myself, because, didn't we all know, there was only one direction to take from the top of the mountain? Later, I kept saying to myself. Later is the time for the big questions. Right now, just happiness and fulfilment. The unavoidable shipwreck was for later. And I was so happy I believed it.

To: Gabriel
From: Marine Vandale
Subject: From the Plateau to the Big Apple

....

How's New York?

To: Marine
From: Gabriel Champagne
Subject: From the Big Apple to the Clam

....

Actually, I'm in Boston. We planned to arrive tomorrow, but we managed to get free sooner, so we got here early.

To: Gabriel
From: Marine Vandale
Subject: Apple vs Clam

....

You mean when you managed to carve out a bit of free time, you deliberately tossed out the apple core to go wallow with the mollusks?

To: Marine
From: Gabriel Champagne
Subject: Nerd 101

....

I know we've only been seeing each other for two weeks, but if you still don't know what a nerd I am, you'll forgive me for having doubts about your powers of observation. I have some old friends here. And plus, Harvard and the exquisite atmosphere that precedes the unending conferences at the Med School are kind of like the Playboy Mansion for me.

To: Gabriel
From: Marine Vandale
Subject: (none)

....

Watch what you write, plans like that could give Hugh Hefner
a heart attack. Although he'd be in good hands, I suppose. But
tell me about New York. Or even about Boston, if you want. I
mean, if you must.

To: Marine
From: Gabriel Champagne
Subject: A monk's life

....

You know, as hard as I've tried, I really don't know how to
make the tale of the two days I spent with colleagues in a con-
vention center interesting, even if it was in New York. Your
brother could undoubtedly do a better job than me on that.
But, we're eating like kings, it's like the organizers wanted to
make up for how boring the days are by stuffing us in crazy
restaurants where every dish requires more work and knowledge than the first year of med school.

To: Gabriel
From: Marine Vandale
Subject: Darn

....

I told you I'd be jealous, so there's no reason to add insult to
injury, as far as I can see. I'm spending almost every day at
Laval with my father, and despite the daughterly love that char-
acterizes me, the job is a little less thrilling than your
gastronomic escapades. It's a good thing Fred is here, because
otherwise the combination of "*Maman* who's worried to
death" and "*Papa* who seems to prefer to stay sick because then
he doesn't have to talk too much to *Maman* who's worried to
death," I don't know how I'd manage.

To: Marine
From: Gabriel Champagne
Subject: *L'frère*

I adore your brother.

To: Gabriel
From: Marine Vandale
Subject: *LE frère*

Yeah, I thought I noticed something at about the fifth bottle of wine you two opened together the other night. That being said, can you please be a good boy and never, never use the expression *l'frère*? You may not have noticed, but it's just a little unbearable.

To: Marine
From: Gabriel Champagne
Subject: Yes sir

As you wish, Miss Vandale.

To: Gabriel
From: Marine Vandale
Subject: Miss Curious

What are you doing tonight?

To: Marine
From: Gabriel Champagne
Subject: Mr. Indecisive

I don't know yet. Maybe dinner with an old friend, or maybe go to a pub with two guys who were in my class in Montréal. I'm telling you, the Clam is overflowing with possibilities.

To: Gabriel
From: Marine Vandale
Subject: (none)

When you coming home?

To: Marine
From: Gabriel Champagne
Subject: I'll be back in Montréal

Tuesday or Wednesday, I'm not sure yet. But it'll be in a big, sea blue Boeing, I promise.

Chapter 16

"No, but seriously, Ju. Seriously. An old friend? Not exactly sure when he's coming back? Seriously."

Julien was slumped down in his old sofa, with a copy of my correspondence with Gabriel in one hand. "I can't believe you printed this. Marine, you've reached a level of pathetic that has never before been seen in our little group."

"Jeff once told a girl, 'Do you have twenty-five cents, because my mother asked me to call her when I met the girl of my dreams…'"

"It worked."

"Okay, Laurent spent three hours sitting on the floor behind the bar at Le Lulli so he wouldn't be seen by a girl he'd slept with."

Julien thought it over. "Yeah, it's certainly not worse than that… But, still, that probably gave him a great view of Andrew's *quite* extraordinary crotch. So… no… you're still number one on the pathetic scale."

"Okay. Whatever you say. You're forcing me to remind you that you once sent something like fifteen erotic letters to a twenty-year-old guy who didn't want to have anything to do with you."

"Those were VERY beautiful letters."

"It was cheap porn."

"You never read them."

"Oh, don't you believe it, young man. You'd printed a copy on Jeff's printer and…"

"You all read them?!"

"Oh, yeah. We even had public readings. Cocktails and *erotica*. Quite a success."

"They weren't pathetic."

"My curious tongue travels up your trembling dick and…"

"Okay! Okay! That's enough. We're even."

I crossed my arms and raised one eyebrow, staring at him the whole time.

"Okay, okay, I'm number one. But still, Marine, you have to give it a rest."

"*You're* giving *me* advice on giving it a rest?"

"Can you stop turning everything back on me for two seconds? You're starting to become the girl no one likes, Marine!"

"Oh my God. Oh my God. You're right."

I had one hand on my forehead and I was pacing back and forth in front of him. It was true. I'd become the girl with no confidence, who was too sensitive and incapable of any critical distance, and who falls in love with a man in less than forty-eight hours and plans house-kids-growing-old-together after seeing him for just two weeks. I flopped down on the sofa next to Julien, who spontaneously lifted one arm and put it around my shoulders.

"I don't know what's happening to me, Ju. I don't know if I'm acting like this because Gabriel has more of an effect on me than any guy has in years and I'm getting that mixed up with love, or if it's because I AM in love, or because I've just become another crazy desperate woman… I wasn't like this when I was twenty."

"Honestly?"

"What, honestly?"

"Honestly, you've always been a little intense around the edges." I sat up, looking offended, but only half exaggerating. "And that's why we love you, Marine. But admit that now…"

"I've gone a little crazy, eh?"

"It's only been two weeks, sweetie. And I know it's something special and…"

"And you know that, eh? You know! You know…" I had my hands folded under my chin like a little girl in love. Julien gently took one of my arms.

"Get out of your body, Marine. Look at yourself for two seconds."

I got out of my body. I must have looked like my friend Mélanie and I did, when we were twelve and watched *Dirty Dancing* in our pajamas, eating popcorn and rolling around on the floor whenever Patrick Swayze was onscreen. "Julien. You have to help me. We promised we'd grow up and I'm more of a teenager than ever."

"I'll help you, sweetie. If you want love to last forever, you can't scare it off by pouncing so hard on it."

"Or by making a date for sex online with a guy, without knowing it's your boyfriend behind the screen name."

"Yes. That's true." Things were going a little better between Julien and Mathias. They'd been seeing each other again for a little while, for coffee or a drink, or for dinner. But Mathias was playing hard to get, and even if part of me thought he was going a little overboard, or that he was only pretending to be calm and distant when he was dying to give in, I admired his pride and his willpower. All I did was get carried away, without thinking, and let my heart imagine beautiful, impossible stories, I let it stifle my reason, and I didn't know if it was because it was too full or too empty. "But we're talking about you," Julien continued. "And about the fact that our ears can't take it anymore. So, you're going to have to stop analyzing everything as if your life depended on it." I opened my mouth. "And don't tell me that your life DOES depend on it."

"Okay…"

"Marine. He's a great guy, you saw each other almost every day for two weeks, do you want to tell me what's got you so worried?"

What's got me so worried, I felt like asking. It was

absurd, and I knew deep down that Julien was right, but my worry and my perpetual questions seemed completely justified to me and if I stopped even the least little bit being reasonable, and if for just one second I followed the natural path I'd been heading down the last two weeks, I'd have a thousand pieces of evidence to offer.

In barely ten days, I'd opened up to Gabriel like I'd never done with anyone before. I knew, deep down, that it was because I didn't know him that well and some things are better said to people who don't have a complex, set idea of who we are. Gabriel wasn't a mirror for me, like Jeff or Laurent were. When I talked to him, when I told him about my life and all its little events, all I had to do was lay them out, just as they were, without having to think about the countless bonds between us. It was virgin territory, and I felt infinitely like myself and surprisingly free in that territory. Maybe it was because of the deep self-confidence he exuded, and the strength he inspired, but when I was with him, I wasn't playing a role, I was only myself – and in his green eyes, I saw a simple and imperfect image of myself, and this image actually did resemble me.

We were spending the days together – I was neglecting my father and stupidly rationalizing the way people in love do, I told myself my father wanted me to be happy, that it's impossible to help others unless you're happy yourself.

Still, I was trying to hold back, to harness this irrational bliss that accompanied our every encounter, and the even less logical anxiety that would inhabit me whenever a whole day went by when I didn't hear from him. Together, we'd spent hours under the big wool blanket we tossed on the bed every morning to make it more comfortable, and we felt so good that no amount of willpower could get us to crawl out of there. Intertwined in the gentle warmth of our satisfied bodies, we'd make futile, charming lists, asking each other our top five passions ("the sea, books, walks alone in the city, the moment you realize you're going to be able to save the life of someone in danger, the one when you feel like you're on the brink of falling in love," according to Gabriel. "Being alone, surrendering your body and your heart, people in general, happiness, the mind," in my case. We argued about walking alone, but I let him keep it in exchange for being alone in general).

Our other lists included our favorite flavors, the people we'd like to have at our table in the after-life (he got Brillat-Savarin, Rita Hayworth and Mordecai Richler, but I had Walt Whitman and Proust as dinner guests AND Baudelaire and Nerval as servers), our best drunken stories, passages of books that had moved us the most. It was pretentious, silly and adorable and I knew that when we were apart, we both thought of new lists to make up simply for the pleasure of sharing them with each other and seeing our personalities, our taste and preferences come together and blend.

He'd tell me to meet him in cafés and little bars, and I would literally run to them, my heart feeling light and certainly oversized – I could feel it taking up all the space in my chest, making it a little hard to breathe and stifling my legendary appetite. Then I'd sit down opposite him and get lost in his big eyes, his warm, deep voice, and I wasn't even in a hurry to go back to his place because we felt so good together and because for us, talking was just another way of making love. We'd leave the café or the bar in a state of almost tangible excitement to get back to the wool blanket and our bodies discovering each other with a troubling instinct we were both more than a little proud of.

Then there were periods of absence, when he was working, that didn't bother me at all, and then there were the times he spent doing other things – I don't know, reading, seeing friends, taking walks alone – that stupidly tortured me, because all I wanted to do was be with him.

One night he'd told me about his strong need for independence and freedom – it wasn't a warning, it was just
something that, evidently, was such a deep part of him
that he wanted to share it with me, just like many other
facets of his personality. The other parts had delighted me,
but that one made me feel like I was chained down,
though otherwise, I was ready to joyfully soar.

But all right, as Julien (and Laurent and Fred and Jeff)
regularly reminded me, we'd only been together for two
weeks and if I didn't give it a rest, I was headed straight for
a relationship which would inevitably self-destruct before
it even had a chance to really blossom, as well as earning
me the official status of being fucking crazy, in Gabriel's
mind. And I knew they were right, but my powers of reason were remarkably lacking, which, though regrettable,
still seemed relatively normal to me. I was, after all, completely infatuated with Gabriel – and even though I knew
it wasn't love yet, the two states were strangely similar.
Especially since they shared the same symptoms, in everything exquisite and absurd they have in common.

"Thanks," I said to Flavie when she came and sat down
beside me at Le Lulli.

"Thank YOU," added Andrew, who was already tired
of hearing me coo and ramble on about Gabriel.

"No problem, sweetie!!!" She was wearing a little jean
jacket that was utterly normal, but, beneath it, was a white
dress with big cherries that clung to her thin waist before
it stretched over a crinoline that was about three feet in
diameter. Also, she was wearing high heels (strange, bright
lime green, platform things) which seemed somewhat out
of place to me since, when she was perched up there on
them, she was officially a foot taller than me. "So," she said,
indicating the *Boreal Rousse* tap to Andrew. "What's up?"

"I needed to talk to a girl."

"Excuse me?" She burst out laughing, throwing back

her head and placing one hand on her big green straw hat, so it wouldn't fall off. "You? To a girl?" Then she put her hands on her hips and added, "I know you'd need one of your peers someday, Marine Vandale."

"Okay, okay, okay. It's okay."

"You're in love, right?"

"What?! No!" I must have looked like a kid who got caught with their hand in a cookie jar and was trying to deny it.

"Marine. I know you pretty well. And I know you've always found everything you need with your boys and your brother, and I also know that you're much too proud to admit that, sometimes, girlfriends can offer something that even your best guy friends can't."

"Okay! Okay! That's enough!"

"AND!" A finger with a fire engine red nail popped up just below my nose. "And I know that when a girl needs her girlfriends the most is when she's in love." She seemed to be thinking it over. "Or when it's time for an honest opinion about a new bra. So. Which is it? You don't remember if you wear a B or a C, or are you in love with Gabriel?"

"I don't knoooowwww."

"You wear a C. Now. About Gabriel. Let's go! We don't have all night, after all." She'd already finished her pint of beer, which, in her hand, looked like a very small glass, and was gesturing to Andrew to bring another.

"Okay. Is it normal, after barely two weeks together, to go completely crazy when the guy in question doesn't call for twenty-four hours or gives you a long speech about his need for freedom?"

Flavie raised one finger to her lips and seemed to be thinking hard. "Do you want to know if it's normal meaning 'it's a good idea,' or meaning, 'it happens quite a bit'?"

"Um… both?"

"Wait. You KNOW that's a bad attitude, right?"

"Yes, yes, yes, I know. But is it my fault I can't help it?"

"No. No, we're almost all the same."

"Really?" I was as happy as a dwarf who'd been raised in a land of giants, and had just discovered a whole village full of people just like him.

"Nonetheless," Flavie continued, "most of us know that getting carried away is probably the surest way there is to turn off a guy. Especially if he's already spoken to you so highly of his freedom."

"So I should hold back."

"And relax, sweetie. As much as you can."

"Is that possible?"

She took a big drink of beer. "Honestly? Only a little." We both started laughing and she took me by the shoulder. "Welcome to GirlLand, Love."

"Mmm."

"In any case, it's where you've always lived, I like to point out."

"Okay. I know."

"And your sister Élodie, too."

"My sister Élodie is the mayor of GirlLand."

"At least, she accepts it, darling. You're like a citizen who wants to believe she's always been from BoyCountry, but she's really lived in GirlLand for forty generations. Stop kidding yourself. You're a real girl, Marine."

"Shit…"

She pretended to look insulted. "Easy there! You think I'm going to let you insult my compatriots like that? A bit of respect, please."

"I always laugh at French people in front of you."

She gave me such a shot with her elbow I almost went through the window; then, with her mocking little smile, she added, "You're a real pain in the ass."

"No, but seriously, Flav. Have you ever been like this?"

"Oh, yeah. I've even read my boyfriend in France's emails."

"What?!" I raised a hand to my chest, sincerely horrified. "Flavie! That's awful!"

"And I could introduce you to twenty girls who have done the same thing. And, now that I think of it, twenty guys, too."

I thought of Mathias and nodded my head, I had to accept it was true.

"You never went through this with Laurent," continued Flavie, "because... because it was almost too simple between the two of you. But now... if you want things to work out with Gabriel, you're going to have to let him have a little breathing room."

"You just said most girls are the same way!"

"And now I'm telling you that most girls with a head on their shoulders calm down, Marine. There's not a guy on Earth who wants to be with the village crazy woman."

"Arggh..." I rubbed my eyes. "It's too complicated, Flavie. If I do that, it just means I'm playing a game."

"No. It means you're learning to see, and to breathe. Breathe, Marine, breathe."

I instinctively took a deep breath, and it immediately made me feel better. She was right after all, and I remembered Julien's famous theory that the worse someone's love life is going, the better their advice is.

"What about you, Flav. Everything okay?"

"I'm okay, yeah."

"Flav..."

"I'm okay..."

"Flavie..."

She turned abruptly towards me, and the fire engine red fingernail popped up again just beneath my nose. "If I tell you something, will you promise, I mean, really promise that you'll keep your mouth closed."

"Well, it depends if..."

"Shit, Marine! GirlLand!"

"What?"

"It's one of the laws of GirlLand! Silence and secrecy! No betrayals!"

"I've always found that girls are a lot more prone to betrayal than guys and…"

"Wait, do you want to hear my secret or not?"

"Okay, yes. Tick-a-lock. Promise."

"You swear?"

"Yes."

"You *swear*?"

"Yes."

"You SWEAR?"

"YESS!"

"On your father's head?"

I was about to answer when Andrew banged on the counter in front of Flavie. "Jesus girl, she said she swore!"

Flavie looked at him for an instant, with her eyes squinted like a bad comic book character that was mad, and she was about to turn back to me when I shouted, "I swear, pinky swear, cross my heart, hope to die, on the head of Jeff, Julien, Laurent, Fred and Claude François, my sisters and my parents, on the head of my old blue cashmere sweater, on the head of Gabriel and even Jerry Seinfeld."

"You know it would have been a nice gesture if you'd mentioned my head before Géry Cinnefèlde. But never mind."

"Right, but moving right along! Shoot!"

She opened her mouth, we were both leaning on the bar, our faces close together – then she fell silent and we turned around to see Andrew practically hovering over us, listening eagerly. "DUDE!" I shouted at him, but he'd already taken off towards the other end of the bar, undoubtedly more terrified by Flavie's physical force than by my tone.

"It's Jeff," said Flavie.

"…"

"Don't worry, nothing happened."

"Why would I worry?"

"Because I know what happened between you and him, sweetie, and I know what it can feel like after something like that. And I also know, there's not a chick on Earth who wants to see her good friend fool around with her ex-lover."

I was mortified. "He told you?"

"No, dummy. I figured it out. Honestly, Helen Keller might have been able to figure it out."

"Ohhh… you think Gab…"

"Yes."

"Ohh… But… But wait, what exactly were you just saying?"

"Your housemate, silly!" She was whispering. "Your housemate. He's all I think about."

"…"

"I…"

"You think I stand a chance?"

"…" For the first time in weeks, I wasn't thinking about Gabriel. In my head were idyllic images of Flavie and Jeff, walking hand in hand, laughing together, wrapping their arms passionately around each other on a big bed, a sofa, against a wall. It would be wonderful, I kept saying to myself, trying to convince myself, wonderful. But the effort was futile and I was troubled, terribly troubled. I looked at Flavie, unable to say anything at all and we just sat in silence for a few seconds, looking each other in the eyes, until I could no longer hold back a little smile and we both started to laugh, and Flavie ran a hand along my back.

"We're pretty ridiculous, eh?"

"Oh, sweetie, we certainly are. So?"

"So, yes. I think you stand a chance."

"Does that bug you?"

"It…" I tried to think. "You know what? It'll be fine."

"It does, eh?"

I smiled at her and put my arms around her – or rather, I let Flavie's huge arms wrap around me. "Yeah, but it'll have to be all right. Because the idea of you and Jeff may bug the shit out of me, but I believe in you." I couldn't believe I'd just said that. But it was true, and the simple fact of saying it made me feel good.

Flavie hugged me close. "You know what? It'll be okay."

"Yep, it'll be okay. We'll find our way."

I thought about my colorful little cups. "Flavie?"

"Yes?"

"You really think I wear a C?"

I was trying not to wait. But I was still up at midnight because I knew his flight was coming in at about eleven-thirty and I didn't know how to do anything but wait. At eleven-thirty-five, I'd already started pacing around the apartment, followed by Claude François, who, as a cat, was well versed in the art of aimless walks, with a vague hope of something – a scratch, a treat, prosciutto scraps, a fuzzy toy.

"Little sister…" said Frédéric as he came in. He smelled like cool alcohol and springtime. "Stop."

"Can't. Seriously. I can't!" The absurdity of the situation struck me and I started to laugh. "I swear!" I said giggling. Fred was laughing too. "Stop, it isn't funny!"

"But you're laughing yourself!"

"That I know, but it makes no sense… I mean, I'm completely conscious of how ridiculous I am, but there is nothing, and I mean NOTHING I can do. I am unable to rationalize and I can't even think about anything else. Fred, I even have a hard time following an episode of *Friends*."

"Ouch."

"Shit, like it wasn't bad enough I'd just become unbearable, but, now I'm stupid on top of it!" And I started to laugh again. "Like, really…" I made a moronic noise and an idiotic face.

Fred put his arms around me. "You want a glass of wine?"

"I want a cask of wine, Fred. But I don't want to get drunk in case he does call."

"Well, first of all, I know you well enough to know that it takes more than a glass to get you drunk, and plus, if you start to stop doing certain things *in case* Gabriel calls, that's very, very bad. Do you really want to be the girl who stops calling her friends 'cause she has a new boyfriend?"

"Well, no…" I made a pitiful face and reached for the glass he was offering. "Christ, do you think this will pass?"

"I hope so."

He sat down on the sofa and I came and sat next to him, with my legs stretched out over the top of his. Happy to finally see me sitting still, Claude François came and curled up on the back of the sofa, just next to my head. He was purring so loud, the vibrations could be felt in the cushions.

"Could he purr any louder?" asked Fred.

"No. Really, I don't know why I'm like this and…"

"Okay, you really *can't* talk about anything else, can you?"

"No. Do you think that it's a sign that means I really am in love?"

"Marine, it's been *two weeks*!" He thought for a minute then he added, "Listen, it's surely the sign of something, but I'd wait a bit before I said it was love. Especially if the guy seems to value his freedom and…"

"But that's just it! It's like a vicious circle! He tells me his freedom is important, and he shows it by sometimes letting a day or two go by without any contact, and then, I go more and more crazy and I aggravate him and bug him more and more… it's catastrophic, Fred."

"Stop it…" He was laughing. "Will you? I've met the guy, I've seen him with you, and I've talked to him about you and I can swear he's going to hang around a while. If you don't scare him off."

"How can I not scare him off, Fred, I've become the village crazy woman!"

"Okay…" He gently lifted my legs off him, stood up, and went to stand just behind the La-Z-Boy. "Now, I'm going to share a theory, and I'm going to do it from *here*, for reasons of personal security." I raised one eyebrow. "Did you ever consider that you might be trying on purpose to convince yourself that this relationship won't work out because, well, that's what you always do?" And he finished his sentence by ducking down behind the La-Z-Boy, thereby avoiding getting hit in the face by the pillow I threw at him.

"It's just a theory," said his voice from his hiding place.

"It's a bad theory. Really. I really, really want this to work."

"You sure?"

"If you want to get out of there in time for your flight back to Paris, you'd better believe me, Frédéric Vandale."

"Okay, okay… You want it to work." He added, raising a white hanky over the top of the headrest.

"Come on, you dope," I said with a laugh as my cell phone started to ring.

"Marine! No!" shouted Fred, as I was literally flying over the coffee table to get to the counter where my phone was. "No! He doesn't need to think you spend every second you're apart waiting for him to call!"

"Hmmm?" I was in the middle of the room, practically panting and completely ridiculous, with my eyes riveted on the phone, which finally stopped ringing.

"Bravo," said Fred. "Good job, sis."

"Ohhhh…" I finally grabbed the phone and saw that it

was Gabriel who'd called. I jumped up and down, cooed, shouted joyously, generally acted like a stupid little girl.

"Okay," said Frédéric, trying to calm me down. "Now, can you accomplish the superhuman and not call him back till tomorrow morning?"

"Yeah, but what if he wants to see me tonight?"

"Then he'll want to see you tomorrow, too."

I nodded my head, as I took a deep breath, like Flavie had suggested. Apparently, breathing really was helpful. I smiled at Fred, then I gave him a little punch in the arm. "Thanks for being there, Fred. Thanks for being there, for being you and for not judging me because I'm me."

Oh, hmm hmm," he had a mouth full of wine and was waving his finger back and forth to say no. "No, no," he added, after he'd swallowed. "I am judging you. I don't want there to be any misunderstandings about that."

I gave him another punch, a little harder this time, in the chest, then I wrapped my arms around him. "Don't go away anymore, okay?"

"I have to go."

"You could write anywhere…"

"Maybe. But I'm not done with Paris yet. I don't know if you know what I mean, but I'm still like a kid in love with that city."

"Stupid, seductive Paris."

"Oh, it's seductive all right… but you know I've always been easy, too…"

"Jerk." I leaned against his chest a little longer. "You going to send me the rest of your book?"

"To you and nobody else. You going to come see me?"

"Well, now, that would be…"

There was a little pause and then, as he pushed me backwards by the shoulders, so he could see my face, Fred said, "You're imagining strolling across the Pont des arts with Gabriel, aren't you?"

"Well, now, that would be…"

We both laughed and he asked if I was going to take good care of our father – a strange and almost touching question because we knew it was more a formality than anything else. Of course I was going to take care of *Papa*. And of course, Élodie was going to take even better care of him. And of course because we were so young, we were convinced that *Papa* could only get better – protected by optimism and the naivety of our youth, the smallest shred of hope made us completely incapable of worry. And there was hope in my father's case, lots and lots of hope. He'd already been able to take a few steps, he could say whatever he wanted (slowly, with difficulty, certainly, but the vocabulary was all there) and Gabriel kept telling me that except for the slight damage to his brain, he was as healthy as a thirty year old. Which, for a man who'd smoked three packs a day for fifty years, was something of a miracle.

And above all, above all, he'd gotten his memory back, because it had been affected all this time by the pressure on who-knows-what part of his brain. And the simple fact of remembering everything, especially remembering things that had just happened, made him so happy that he improved day by day.

As for my mother, she was getting over it all almost more slowly than him, and sometimes I felt like she was mad at him for exhausting her like that, for scaring her so badly, and then ending up just comfortably lying in bed, out of all immediate danger.

"He's going to be fine," said Fred.

"I know." And I believed it. I believed it so much that I didn't even feel the need to elaborate and changed the subject without warning. "Hey," I suddenly said to Frédéric, "you'll never guess what Flavie told me." Gabriel had called, I was free, I could finally think about something else. Opposite me, Fred smiled knowingly. It was absurd and childish, but I felt twenty pounds lighter and

I was so happy I wasn't even upset with myself about it.

"What did she tell you?"

"Jeff. She has a crush on Jeff. Or, to be more exact, she 'thinks about Jeff all the time.'"

"You sure she won't be mad you told me that?"

"No, but I know you won't repeat it to anyone at all, so it's okay."

"Interesting logic."

"It's girls' logic."

"So, you're accepting that you're a girl now?"

"No choice really, right?"

We both laughed. "Does it bother you?" Fred asked.

"I don't know. At first, yeah, a little… but whatever. I just tell myself I have no right to be bothered, you know? I'm half-crazy because of Gabriel, and when I'm with him, it's absolute happiness, so I don't see how I could really be upset that two of my best friends have a shot at being happy, too."

"My God… can you imagine that? Flavie and Jeff together?"

"I know… They'd have babies that are already four feet tall."

We were still laughing when Jeff came in. He saw Fred first, and shouted a joyful, "Hey, *l'frère*" at him, then he saw me and his face lit up with a big, happy, spontaneous smile that warmed my heart like a thick blanket. "Hey," I said to him with the same smile, and I thought, I really want you to be happy. And for a moment I saw what a possibility that was and the idea made me so happy, and seemed so right and good that I wanted to go give Jeff a big hug, to hug the whole world really, in an idiotic fit of universal joy and love.

Then his smile faded – not completely, but it was more like he'd adjusted his aim, as if he'd just thought, Okay, don't go overboard. But there was no uncomfortableness between us – at least when we were alone together or just with the boys. We'd learned to talk to each other again like we used to, with the same ease as someone who's sprained an ankle learns to walk again like before the injury. And the few times I'd seen him when I was with Gabriel, he'd been pleasant, but no more. But I was like him – I tried not to touch Gabriel too much, walking on eggshells which, after all, only existed in our heads.

"Wasn't your man coming back today?" Jeff asked as he got himself a glass of wine.

"Yes… but I preferred to spend time with my friends and my brother who's leaving in two days."

"You are so full of crap…" said Fred with a laugh.

"Okay, okay… I'm just trying to give him a little breathing room so I don't terrify him."

"That's a strange idea," said Jeff. "Seems to me if I was in love with a girl, I'd want to spend all my time with her."

"Liar," said Fred. "You, of all people, would go absolutely crazy. Distance holds invaluable virtues."

"Not too much distance, though."

"No, just a safe distance."

"Does anyone know how big a safe distance is?" I asked.

"It depends," answered Jeff. "Especially since guys measure in miles and girls measure in inches, and…"

"God, you're old-fashioned!" He was already laughing his big laugh, with one arm across his face as he waited for the inevitable pillow to be thrown, and he was still behind the La-Z-Boy, so I had to settle for making a face at him.

"Did you talk to Laurent today?" Jeff asked.

"No, why?"

"I ran into him at the store, he looked like he was in a hurry, but he said he had some big news."

"And you didn't ask him what it was?"

"Of course I did, Dopey. But he said he wanted to save it for brunch tomorrow. Apparently, it will be interesting for everyone. He stared at me for an instant then pointed a finger at me. "Hey. You are not allowed to play hooky from brunch if Gabriel calls. Fred is leaving the day after tomorrow."

"Hey!" I put on an indignant look which was completely useless: he had literally read my mind.

"You think he's got an idea for a new documentary?" Fred asked.

"No, he hasn't even finished the last one yet... and at the rate he's been working lately, it won't come out for another ten years, I bet."

"Maybe Carole is pregnant."

"Whoa, *l'frère*! We are talking about Laurent here. Don't expect miracles."

Around the table, Julien, Jeff, Fred and I were staring at Laurent with such astonishment that he began to laugh. Then we all looked at each other, with our mouths wide open, looking flabbergasted. The server was passing by and Jeff, who hadn't even blinked since he'd heard Laurent's news, simply raised his hand and stuttered, "Champagne. We're going to need a bottle of champagne."

"You said 'I love you,'" Julien cooed. "I love you!"

"Seriously," said Fred to no one in particular. "I would have been less surprised to find out Carole was pregnant."

"I can't believe it," I repeated for the hundredth time.

"You think *I* can believe it?" Beside me, Jeff's mouth was still hanging open.

"Okay, okay, that's enough!" said Laurent, as the server, who seemed to be wondering what was going on, opened the bottle.

"He said 'I love you' to his girlfriend!" I told her.

She opened her eyes wide and said, "Noooo way" – apparently, the charming Julie had been listening to our conversations for years and was as surprised by the news as the rest of us. "Well, it's about time!" she added, before she ran away looking sorry, having realized she was talking to a customer she didn't really know all that well.

"Will you all cut it out?" asked Laurent. "I'm already having a hard enough time digesting the information myself; it doesn't help to have all of you staring at me like I just told you I'd won the lottery."

"We'd be *a lot* less surprised if you told us you'd won the lottery," said Julien, causing the rest of us to nod in the affirmative.

"Seriously," I confirmed.

Laurent crossed his arms. "What, what's with you, I bet you're mad 'cause I didn't say it to you when we were together. You know I love you. It's just that…" He kept going, but I wasn't listening anymore. No, I wanted to tell him. I'm not mad. But the idea of you telling someone the words that I can't let myself say right now is like a stab in the heart because I'm jealous of you. It had been so long since I'd said "I love you," at least in the context of a relationship, that the idea literally caused me pain, and filled me with charmless melancholy.

And since Gabriel apparently had a supernatural gift for giving me a shot of hope at the exact moment when I couldn't find one more drop of it in me, he showed up, standing next to our table, and, as he looked me right in the eyes, he said, "I knew I'd find you here." And I could feel a burning wave of joy flood through me, starting in my heart and spreading quickly to my brain, then all the way to my fingers and toes. My heart was beating a mile a minute – it was as if instantly, in the space of two seconds, all my priorities changed focus: he was here, I couldn't be anything but optimistic.

He kissed me discreetly and sat down as he gave all the guys a good slap on the back, and we all tried to cut each other off to share the latest news. I crossed Fred's gaze and I read in his eyes exactly what I was starting to feel in my heart: that this ridiculous joy caused by the presence of a single man was indeed radiant, but it was dangerous, too, and my lack of perspective was almost like an addict's reaction to their drug of choice. "Go back to Paris," I mouthed at him, and he gave me a sad smile.

Less than two months later, that smile was what I missed the most in the world as I told the boys over and over a hundred times a day, "I spoiled everything. I spoiled everything, just like I knew I would."

To: Marine
From: Frédéric Vandale
Subject: Paris is worried

How are you, cutie?

To: Fred
From: Marine Vandale
Subject: Montréal's depressed

You know in the *Road Runner* cartoons how for no reason a bulldozer runs over the coyote and he comes out all flat? Well, I feel pretty much like that. Completely one-dimensional, empty and incapable of any movement at all. No kidding, if it keeps up like this, I'm going to literally disappear into the sofa.

To: Marine
From: Frédéric Vandale
Subject: Man-eating sofa

Yeah, Jeff kind of told me you'd more or less moved into the sofa and that he wouldn't be too surprised if you melted into it. Now are you sure it's a good idea to watch every season of *Grey's Anatomy* non-stop? Because I can kind of see a link with the characters' jobs, and if you see what I mean, I'm starting to wonder if you haven't become a bit of a masochist.

To: Fred
From: Marine Vandale
Subject: Feminine psychology

I don't give a shit what they do. I just want to watch people who are worse at handling relationships than I am, it makes me feel better. And, unfortunately, it only exists on TV, because in real life, no one is as much of a disaster in their love life as I am, so there's no way I'm getting off the sofa.

To: Marine
From: Frédéric Vandale
Subject: Feminine paranoia

Marine. You know he's going to come back. Give him some time, that's all.

To: Fred
From: Marine Vandale
Subject: Facing facts

Listen, I did it to him twice. The first time he let it go, but a little birdie told me that demanding love and commitment a second time, after he'd explained that it was something he wasn't ready to offer just because it was asked for, was a pretty surefire way of making him take off for good.

To: Marine
From: Frédéric Vandale
Subject: Masculine intuition

Why won't you listen to us, when the four of us are telling you that's just it – if he came back once, he'll probably come back again? It's only been a week since you've seen him, and, I'd like to remind you, he's called twice.

To: Fred
From: Marine Vandale
Subject: House of spies

What, did you have a camera installed over the sofa, or do you have a hotline to Jeff?

To: Marine
From: Frédéric Vandale
Subject: Red telephone

It's Jeff. And don't act surprised, you know your friends are as
worried about you as I am. You don't have one brother, Marine,
you have four.

To: Fred
From: Marine Vandale
Subject: Enemy brothers

Yeah, well the three brothers who are left here are flitting
around to the rhythm of their love-filled hearts, and you
wanna know what I think of love-filled hearts?

To: Marine
From: Frédéric Vandale
Subject: Let's be nice

Be kind to the love-filled hearts. And Jeff still hasn't made it to
the summit with Flavie, so don't get carried away.

To: Fred
From: Marine Vandale
Subject: Bernard Voyer

Don't worry, they're climbing steadily. I know he's just being
polite and holding back from pouring his happiness all over
my sadness, but I can see he's fallen like a ton of bricks. And,
me, on my pitiful sofa, in the depth of my unkind soul, I hope
it flops, because if I end up alone in the land of the loveless,
Fred, I'm becoming a Carmelite.

To: Marine
From: Frédéric Vandale
Subject: Those poor Carmelites

....

Marine, Carmelites take vows of silence. And chastity. So, don't kid yourself, that's not the order for you. Still, I understand how you feel. It's not really moral, it's normal.

To: Fred
From: Marine Vandale
Subject: (none)

....

It really feels like I ruined everything, Fred, and, though I've never regretted anything in my life, I have a bitter taste in my whole body and I can't get rid of it. I can't even blame him, you know what I mean?

To: Marine
From: Frédéric Vandale
Subject: Re: (none)

....

I know, I don't want to add insult to injury as they say, but you're right, Marine. He was honest with you. But please, Marinette. Believe me when I say he'll come back. And please, Marine, be cool when he does.

To: Fred
From: Marine Vandale
Subject: Doubt and promises

....

Don't worry. I swear it ever night as I flagellate myself. If by some miracle he comes back... If by some miracle he comes back. But I don't believe it. I really don't believe it.

To: Marine
From: Frédéric Vandale
Subject: Faith

....

You've always believed in miracles. It used to make me laugh
when we were little and it worried me when we were teenagers
because I thought believing in miracles was like having a one-
way ticket for disappointment. So you're not going to convince
me you don't believe anymore, because *I* don't believe *you*.

To: Fred
From: Marine Vandale
Subject: Atheist

....

I told you I don't believe in miracles anymore. And be nice –
don't believe for me. Because I couldn't stand another false
hope.

To: Marine
From: Frédéric Vandale
Subject: Re: Atheist

....

Sorry, Marinette. I'm still a believer. Devoted, even. You just
wait. You'll see.

    :)

Chapter 17

From my permanent spot on the sofa, which was seriously starting to conform to the shape of my body, I could hear Jeff's voice on the phone: "I know... yes, I know, but what about MY mental well-being... I could see you with a woman crying non-stop on your sofa... Yeah well, at our house, the sofa is pretty much in the middle of the room, so I can't really ign... And on top of that, she's my friend, I'm not going to sit on her and pretend she's not there!... I know, but... Okay, okay. Thanks, Élodie."

That's all I need, I thought. Élodie, of all people, had become the righter-of-wrongs for our little group. I sluggishly rolled over onto my stomach and leaned my chin on the armrest. "You aren't really having Élo come over, are you?"

"I'd have Bonhomme Carnaval come over if I thought that was what it would take to get you moving."

"Yeah, but Élodie... Am I in that bad shape?"

Jeff shot me a look that needed no words. "You know what you're doing, Marine? You're wallowing in unhappiness like a teenager 'cause you don't have anything better to do. Shit, not only is it not the end of the world, but I know you know it's not over. It's like some weird part of you *likes* going 'It's ooooover' over and over again in a pathetic voice... What's going on, Marine? Are you really that bored?"

He turned his back and I took it without flinching. It was the truest and most stinging thing anyone had said to me in a week. It was so right it wasn't really even insulting. I suddenly sat up – I hadn't been in that position in a few days and I wasn't used to it anymore – and I rubbed my face vigorously and moaned a little. "Okay," I said. "Okay, you're right."

Standing up behind the bar, Jeff was wearing the stunned, relieved look of a guy who thought he'd been condemned to death and just found out he'd been pardoned. "I'm... right...?" he said in a tone that forced me to laugh.

"You know you are, you big jerk..."

He came and sat down next to me. We sat there for a moment, side by side, in the same position, with our forearms resting on our knees, our hands crossed, our heads angled downwards.

"You're going to have to give yourself a good shake," he said.

"Jeff..." I was cut to the quick as if he'd said something stupid. "Did you ever hear the expression 'easier said than done'? I know I have to give myself a good shake. But right now, I don't even have the energy for a kick in the ass to get things going."

"Marine, *even* if you were head over heels in love..."

"What do you mean, *even*?"

"Because no one falls in love in two weeks, Marine, it just isn't possible."

"What the fuck do you know about it? You don't know fucking anything." I sat up again. I was overly insulted, and unable to control myself. And I didn't want to control myself. I was mad because I'd been convinced for quite a while that no one believed in this sudden infatuation, so much so that I sometimes even doubted it myself, and I would say to myself as I stared at the ceiling from my spot on the sofa, that maybe I'd imagined the love, had blown it all out of proportion, and, thanks to solitude and idleness, I'd unknowingly exaggerated something that was nothing more than a crush. Then I could see Gabriel and his eyes sparkling with joy when I told him something that impressed him, I could hear our endless, rhythmic conversations, I remembered the feeling of his skin, his chest against my back, his fingers intermeshed with mine, his breath on my neck, and I had an almost irresistible desire to hit my head hard against the living-room table so I would feel something other than the emptiness that was invading me and filling my chest. I was, in fact, dumbfounded by the extent of what I'd lost through my own fault.

"How can you say that?" I asked Jeff.

"Listen…" He spoke in a conciliatory way that I knew wasn't really sincere, like when you talk too calmly to someone who's annoying you, just to show you're more in control than they are. "Maybe you're right. If there's one thing I know, it's that everything is possible." I raised my head towards him and we looked at each other for a moment: yes, if we'd paid any attention at all to the last six months, right now, we would know it was true better than anyone else ever could.

"It's just that…" I turned toward the little table so I wouldn't have to look at him as I talked; it was a shy but futile gesture. "It's just that because of what I did, I feel like I missed out on something… Look, I'm not saying I was going to spend the rest of my life with Gabriel. Maybe it would have only lasted a year or two, or maybe it would've gotten screwed up after eight months. But at least I would've had the chance to see through whatever it was going to be. Now, I… I don't know what got into me."

That was true, I didn't know. I had stupid, easy excuses in mind, like "It's 'cause I'm in my thirties," "It's 'cause I really do love him," "It's because all his signals said he was in love and I was stupid enough to believe him" – that's the one I almost believed myself. And when I was "mad" – when I'd stopped being sad, stopped being suddenly filled with new hope, stopped blaming myself, and comforted myself by saying it wasn't my fault, I accused Gabriel of doing everything wrong, of being too good at acting like he was in love, and I asked Claude François, out loud, how a mentally stable man could be so demonstrative and then play innocent.

I saw demonstrations of his love in his eyes, his smiles, the enthusiasm he sometimes showed towards me when we were sitting on a terrace or in a restaurant, as if he was having a hard time holding himself back to keep from hugging me to death right then and there. I could see it in the books he lent me, filled with wild poetry and all marked by an eroticism that was as deep as it was languid. I could see it in his insatiable curiosity about what I liked to eat, to read, to see, to understand, to discover, as if I were the most fascinating creature in the world. In his voice, too when, one night he said, "I always feel so good when I'm with you."

Then I went back to being sad and cynical, and I said to myself maybe he was like that with all his girlfriends, that he'd undoubtedly been like that with the psychologist he was seeing when we met and who he'd never mentioned again, as if she'd simply never existed. Then I'd convince myself that I'd wanted to see love where there was just good company and shared tastes. That's when the images of the last time we were together would resurface like so much proof of his indifference.

We were talking quietly, sitting on the sofa which was about to become my permanent home. I was telling him a story, which I'd been unable to remember since, that made him laugh and, now and then, inspired him to cover my body with his and kiss me, looking radiant and delighted. I must have looked radiant and delighted, too (an easy deduction since I was radiant and delighted). Then, I fell silent, getting lost for an instant in the gaze he always settled on me and that gave me the impression he was trying to swallow me up in it, or completely absorb me with his green eyes, and I'd said, "Gabriel…" I think he'd understood by my tone, he'd known that I was again

going to ask him for something he could only give when
he was ready, and he'd shook his head no, it was one of
those "no's" that came with a sorry and empathetic smile
– and I started crying. It was too much for me. The last
months, the emotional climb our relationship had been
(I'd never felt so close to someone after so little time) had
shaken me up so much that I couldn't muster any critical
distance. I'd been out of my depth for a long time, and I
knew it, but, faced with Gabriel's apologetic "no," I felt like
I'd never be able to regain my balance, that the ground
had permanently slipped away from beneath my feet and
that I would spend the rest of my life floating, with no
attachments, no specific goals. And the fact that he told
me that was exactly what he aspired to – no attachments,
no goals – was almost too much for me to take.

He'd looked at me for an instant, then shook his head
again and got up. "Are you leaving?" I asked him through
my tears, and he said something vaguely incoherent like,
"I can't… You can't…" and he'd left.

"Marine," said Jeff. "Didn't it occur to you that you just
might have scared him?"

"Shit, don't you think it scares me?" I was almost
shouting, and I knew that, within the next two minutes,
there was a good chance I'd start to cry.

"Yes. That, I know. I know you're afraid, too."

"Excuse me?!" I leapt up. "*I'm* afraid?"

"Christ, Marine, we sleep together ONCE and you go
half crazy, you can't talk to me normally and then you 'fall
in love,'" he made air quotes to emphasize that was what
I thought but that he had no intention of subscribing to
such an insane theory – "with the first guy who comes
along."

I opened my mouth, prepared to bury him in insults,
but the words all bumped into each other and I couldn't
actually say anything, there was nothing that could translate how I was feeling, because I really didn't know what I

was feeling. I was mad, insulted, hurt, frustrated, humiliated, so, with all the conviction I had left, I said, "You're
one to talk!" And for the first time, the statement was not
met with a smile. Jeff looked at me almost hatefully and
slowly said, "Ex-cuse me?"

"I said, 'You're one to talk.'"

"Hold on. Are you going to make a scene 'cause I'm
seeing Flavie? Because once in a while I have a drink with
a girl who, by the way, is supercool and brilliant and *normal*?"

I almost screamed at him that Flavie was almost as
crazy as me, that I knew it for a fact because she'd told me
herself and the only difference between her and me was
that she managed to control her passion (unfortunate difference, I had the chance to think to myself. Maybe that's
what separates crazy people and people who go too far
from normal people – the ability to control themselves).
"*I* am not making a scene," I finally said. "*You* are."

"No, no, no. YOU'VE been making a scene on your
fucking sofa for a week."

I didn't know what to say. I thought he was being
mean, and, what's worse, I wanted to be mean, too. I
wanted to shout things that would hurt him and that
weren't true. "You see!" I yelled at him. "You see! You kept
saying, everything's okay between us, Marine, everything's
normal, the fact that we slept together isn't going to
change anything at all, well, take a good look at yourself,
there!"

"You look at *yourself*."

"Okay, you know what?"

"What?"

"Fuck you. Really. Fuck you. You're just pissed off
because you're insulted that I didn't fall hopelessly in love
with you after I slept with you. Christ, get over yourself."

"That's it, that's it. I'm insulted. Boo-hoo. I *really* would
have loved to have a girl who claims to fall in love about

twenty-four seconds after she meets a guy fall in love with me. Your love is so deep, Marine."

I wanted to say something, but the very idea of what I could have said, the very idea of the love I'd felt (and I knew maybe it wasn't deep, maybe it wasn't the kind of love that lasts a lifetime, but it existed and, above all, it was inhabiting me) flooded over me and I started crying. I was standing there, in front of him, in a camisole and a sarong, in the raw, pitiless light of a late June noon, and I was crying, with one hand over my face. The air was almost liquid – no air at all was coming through the open window and I suddenly hated summer, almost viscerally. I would have liked it to snow, for us to be snowed in in the apartment with its golden light, snuggled up in big turtlenecks and protected by the white bubble of our winters. I could see Gabriel in the snow, and I was mad at the sun for spoiling everything, for melting away my good sense and, thereby, melting away the love that may have blossomed one day.

I was still crying when Jeff got up. "You should be happy," he said. "Now you can blame someone besides yourself." And he walked out. In the entryway, I heard him mutter something to Élodie, who came straight towards me, took me in her arms and said, "Hey, you big dummy…"

She rocked me for a minute, as I kept mumbling more or less incoherent things about how mean Jeff was, how disgusting and crazy I was, how I scared men off, how everybody was in love except me, how I was going to end up an old maid, how I'd ruined everything, and my God, how had I gotten to the point where I had to be consoled by my little sister?

"Shit, six months ago, I was wiping your nose 'cause that Félix-Antoine-Frédéric-Beaubien-Dumouchel, or whatever his name was, had dumped you…"

"Yeah, but now you're the one who got dumped…"

"I didn't get dumped!" And there went the waterworks

again. Above my head, I could almost hear Élodie rolling her eyes. But my little sister, smelling like raspberry perfume and hairspray, was making me feel better – I'd seen her cry so often, so many times I'd thought she was being childish, that it didn't bother me at all to fall apart so stupidly in front of her, panting as I cried and spouted the usual stupid remarks we make when we've been disappointed by love, just so the other person can say, "Of course not, of course not." Things like, "Things never work out for me," "I'm repulsive," "I never, never have any good luck," "How could she do that to me," "The bastard, he'll regret it some day," "I'm sure there's somebody else," and the ever popular "Why doesn't he/she love me?"

I'd always enjoyed making fun of those kinds of remarks, in a mischievous kind of way, and of people I thought were weak enough to have to say them. But now, with my head on my little sister's knees, my eyes riveted on the ceiling, I found a kind of pleasure in them. I didn't believe them – not really, not deep down – but they made me feel better, the way a placebo makes a sick person feel like they're in less pain.

After about an hour, Élodie got up and went to open a bottle of wine. "Go get dressed," she said. "We're going to be late."

"Late where?"

"At *Papa* and *Maman's*! It's Ariane's birthday, may I remind you!"

"Argh…" I laid back down in a fetal position. "No, no. Seriously, Élo, I can't."

She put her glass down on the table authoritatively. "Oh, yes, you can. Geez, for TWO months I've been taking care of *Papa* like a full-time nurse and you've been messing around with your doctor."

"Baaah… My doctor left…"

"Hey! I'm not saying I'm not glad to take care of *Papa*, but you owe this family something, for Chrissake."

"Baaah! Even my family hates me!" A part of me, a teeny, tiny part that was currently muzzled by my brain, thought I was so ridiculous, I almost laughed. I'm playing a role, I thought. I sat up again and said to Élo, "Okay. Okay, okay. Fuck, I don't have a present."

"We'll buy her a tree. We'll have a pine planted somewhere up North. As long as the certificate is printed on recycled paper, she'll be happy." I gave a little laugh. "Oh, and while I'm thinking of it," she went on, "Ariane's a lesbian."

"Okay…" For a minute my head hurt. "What?"

"Well, we don't know if it's going to last, but she's been going out with a girl for a couple of weeks."

I looked at Élodie for a second, mouth wide open, then I fell back down on the sofa: "Baaaahh! Even my twenty-four-year-old little sister is in love!"

Behind my mother, the little television that had been enthroned on the kitchen counter forever was spilling out images of a chef who smiled too much and joyously danced around an unnaturally clean kitchen alongside his co-host and partner, a woman who smiled as much as he did and had an unbelievable ability to get excited about, for example, potatoes ("In oil! So shiny! How beautiful!") and filets of sole ("Mmm! It doesn't even taste like fish!"). And, triumphantly, the two of them repeated how "haute cuisine was in everyone's reach," and for proof, they offered the breast of duck ("Rare! With APPLES!") they'd prepared.

Jeff and I would often imitate them, behind *our* counter as we cooked, smiling as wide as possible and getting overexcited about such culinary triumphs as spaghetti with tomatoes: "And, what's really incredible, Jean-François, is that we added a little secret ingredient…"

"… and that makes all the difference, Marine."

Exchange of flirty looks. "Shall we share our secret ingredient with our viewers, Marine?"

"Dig in, Jean-François. It's so good when it's fresh."

"So, for unforgettable spaghetti, at home, diced tomatoes, and…"

"… garlic!"

"Garlic!"

"That's right, Jean-François, a simple clove of garlic,
and voilà! You'll think you're in Italy!"

We exaggerated, but not by much. And, suddenly, in
my mother's kitchen, the memory of Jeff melted my heart,
right when the co-host was going into ecstasy over what
seemed to be, for her, the miracle of caramelized onions.
From the living room, I could hear Ariane enthusiastically
describing the trip she wanted to take to India with Julie,
her girlfriend (Ariane repeated the word *girlfriend* every
thirty seconds and had been careful to point out to our
parents, "This is Julie, my girlfriend." I suspected she was
rather proud of having a girlfriend, of seeing it as a sym-
bol of eccentricity and open-mindedness, and I wondered
if Julie was aware of that, too).

I'd left them in the living room with Élodie, who was
almost too charming, wishing undoubtedly to show that
she was resolutely heterosexual, but didn't have anything
against anyone who wasn't. Our father, more chipper than
he'd been in years, was sitting opposite the three girls,
dead silent, looking back and forth from Ariane to Julie,
seeming to wonder how someone "became a lesbian" from
one day to the next. He'd taken me aside as soon as we'd
arrived to ask if I thought it was "for good."

"I don't know, *Papa*," I said in my tired voice.

"Oh, but I don't have anything against people who are
like that, you know."

"I know, *Papa*."

"Your friend Julien… I like your Julien a lot."

"I know…"

"It's just that, I have a hard time understanding what's going on in their heads…"

I just looked at him for a minute – his hair had already grown back a while ago, and his gaze was as lively as it used to be, and above all, he was no longer wearing a veil of worry caused by the memory losses he'd been having for almost two years. He'd never said so, and I knew he never would, but the specter of Alzheimer's disease had completely terrified him. Knowing he was now beyond it made him almost carefree. He'd escaped something worse than death after all. For an unpolished man like my father, the idea of seeing death approach, of feeling it settle into him with each forgotten name, every lost memory, was worse than anything, and, though I couldn't put myself in his place, I understood.

He shrugged his shoulders disconcertedly. Of course he didn't understand what was going on in their heads. He'd spent forty years of his life in a truck, then in a garage where almost every square centimeter of wall space was covered by pages ripped from *Hustler*, *Penthouse* and other similar quality publications.

"I know…" I'd repeated as I wrapped my arms around him. I knew he wasn't judging Ariane. But the sudden change in sexual orientation had left him in such a perplexed state that it almost made me want to laugh.

"Have you… What about you, have you ever…"

"*Papa!*"

"What? I don't know."

My father was not the kind of man you could answer with "Well, yes, once or twice in university." The very idea of such an answer forced me to grimace and I ran off to the kitchen where my mother, an oven mitt on her hand, had her nose buried in a book of recipes by the smiling chef. She was making vegetarian moussaka for Ariane. "Would you please tell me what kind of person doesn't eat meat… I just don't get it," she'd sighed. Being a lesbian was one thing. But being a vegetarian was too much for my mother. And on THAT, I agreed with her.

The memory of Jeff and I laughing behind the counter was still in my mind and I went towards the fridge to get myself a glass of wine.

"Marine!" my mother said. "It's not even six o'clock!" Item number 35 in my mother's inexplicable guide to good manners: no alcohol before five o'clock. Item 35-B: beer is acceptable after five o'clock. No wine EVER before six o'clock. She didn't see it as a personal opinion, but as a law that was as unquestionable as "No killing your neighbor" or "No burping at the table" (a law my brother and I had already broken a thousand times – burping, not murder – when we would have real burping contests every night, making our little sisters die laughing and our mother go half crazy).

"*Maman*, I've just been dragged through the shit by my best friend, and I superbly managed to scare off a guy who was absolutely extraordinary. It's a miracle I don't start drinking at ten in the morning, okay?" (That was a nasty lie: over the past week, several Bloody Caesars had been consumed before noon.)

My mother just watched me, an oven mitt firmly planted on her left hip. "What did you say to him?"

"Hmmm?"

"What could you possibly have said to Gabriel?" (She called him "Gabriel" now though she'd never met him. He was a doctor and I knew she fully intended to be able to mention her son-in-law the doctor before the end of the year. Now that my father was out of danger, that was her new project.)

"I said… Oh, let it go."

"No! Tell me. I've been married for forty years, little girl. Just because I've spent my life in a kitchen doesn't mean I don't know anything about men, I'll have you know."

I smiled at her. It was true that we underestimated her, like we were the first generation to claim to really understand love and relationships. I smiled and told her, as honestly as I could, what had happened between Gabriel and me.

"Mmm," she said when I'd finished my story. "Not great."

"What?"

"Well, Marine, you need me to explain to you that guys are all scared when the time comes to mention love? Do you think your father was the kind of guy who sang 'La vie en rose' to me when we were twenty-five?" The image of my father singing "La vie en rose" made me giggle. "I know it's not like that anymore nowadays, since now some men are romantic, too…" A little light crossed over her eyes and I thought about how she must have dreamed when she watched soap operas or turned the pages of the Harlequin Romances she used to devour, imaging another life, with men with Latin accents who brought her red roses and would say "I love you" as easily as my father said "I'm hungry."

"Listen," she continued. "I knew your father loved me. And I certainly would have liked to have a man who was more… eloquent, let's say. But we don't choose, do we? We fall in love and that's who it is. We don't choose. I fell in love with my friend Lorraine's brother because he was handsome and he was strong and when I was with him, I was… Oh, Marine, I was so *proud* to be seen with him. No other boys dared come around me. And he made me laugh! Oh, how he made me laugh!"

I imagined them, holding hands somewhere in the middle of the sixties, in front of the Orange Julius, my father wearing a coat and my mother in a miniskirt and the white boots that went up to her knees – the ones she'd saved and that I'd had so much fun wearing when I was little – I had a really blurry image of what Cartierville –

the neighborhood they grew up in – must have been like in 1967. I imagined a mix of old *Archie* comics, the first hippies, something wavering between Elvis and Jimi Hendrix.

"But I knew what he was like," my mother continued. "I knew he wasn't the kind to say 'I love you.' So I didn't try to drag any 'I love you's' he didn't want to say out of him, you see?"

That's exactly what Gabriel had told me: people don't say "I love you" because someone asks them to. They say it because they *want* to. Obviously. An opinion I shared completely, nonetheless. But at the time, I couldn't help it, I didn't know and now it was too late.

"He'll come back," said my mother.

"That's what everyone says."

"Because everyone can see the situation more clearly than you…"

"Hmmmf…"

She shrugged her shoulders, visibly discouraged by my refusal to understand, and went to put her vegetarian moussaka in the oven, though she was looking at it scornfully.

"I can't turn into someone else, *Maman*. I can't pretend to be above my problems and indifferent, it's not me."

"Well, take a page from Gabriel then. Watch what he does. You're an intelligent girl, after all, do you really need it all to be spelled out for you? For two months he didn't give up and he even came back after you went crazy the first time."

"I didn't go crazy!"

"Oh, daughter of mine. Jeff told me."

That damn Jeff was too comfortable with my mother.

"So be happy reading the signs. Let things come at their own rhythm. Breathe a little. Nothing, nothing in life ever works out right because people dive in before they see how deep the water is first."

"What is that, a proverb?"

She smiled at me and rubbed my back (with her oven mitt). "Don't suffocate him, Marine. If he's going to fall in love, you have to leave him the space to do it in. But *don't force him.*"

I was amazed: my mother, the great control freak, the one who managed our universe and governed my father's whole life from the kitchen, was telling me to let go. And she was right.

I went back into the living room as I tried to breathe and to relax. If I didn't want to suffocate Gabriel, I had to give myself room to breathe, too, after all. I was going into the room when Élodie came out in a rush, crashed into me and bumped her forehead against mine – both of us shouted out "Ouch, shit" and we stood there for a minute, rubbing our heads while my father laughed uproariously. Slapstick, now that was something he understood.

"What are you doing running like that?"

All Élodie did was wave my cell phone in my face. I leaned forward, with my hand still on my forehead, to read the list of "Missed Calls," where Gabriel's name was in the top position. "It just rang," said Élodie.

Intense, bright, luminous joy, the desire to stamp my feet, to be alone to greedily enjoy my happiness, or with other people so I could share it. "BREATHE!" shouted my mother from the kitchen as Élodie and I exchanged a smile and I rolled my eyes. Okay, I was going to breathe.

"Are you going to call him back?" asked Julie when I went and sat down beside her. She must have been three or four years older than Ariane, and had the same air of moral certainty. They'd met at a peaceful demonstration against (or was it for?) I don't know what, and shared the same ideals (and their ideals were countless and immense. Together they'd be able to cover the whole world in organic virtue and fair-trade convictions).

"I… I don't know," I answered her. "Not right away, in any case." She looked at me and nodded her head briefly, as if she were thinking of something appropriate to say. She had very wide eyes and their green was almost translucent, like glass, or a Rocky Mountain lake, and she smiled easily.

"Personally, I think I'd call back. If you want to call him back that is. I don't think that kind of game ever works out really well. I spent three years playing games because of a girl who didn't know what she wanted, and then, pfff…" My father, whose discomfort increased with each comment, fidgeted on his chair. "Does your boyfriend even know what he wants?"

"He's not my boyfriend." Had he ever even been my boyfriend? No, I said to myself. Strange thing after all. We'd hardly been apart in two months, but I didn't feel like I had a "boyfriend." Maybe that was a sign.

Julie waved her hand as if to say that was nothing but semantics. "Okay, but does he *know what he wants*?"

"I don't know! I don't know if he knows what he wants. I know what I want."

"You sure about that?"

Listen, I felt like telling her, who do you think you are to talk to me like you were my psychiatrist? She was getting on my nerves, but I didn't want the conversation to stop: it was helping me, and there was something almost sensual about discussing Gabriel with someone who was nearly a total stranger.

"After my three years of spinning around like a weather vane, I decided it was time for me to see things clearly in my own life. Now, I'm not saying I have everything figured out, but at least I know what I want." She smiled broadly at Ariane and ran her hand along her thigh. My father couldn't take any more and got up to join my mother in the kitchen.

I thought for a minute. Yes, in the beginning, I'd been

doubtful, too, about getting carried away so suddenly, about how quickly Gabriel and I started feeling comfortable with each other. I'd wondered myself when I'd noticed he was all I'd been waiting for, in a certain way. He was cultivated, he made me laugh, he was witty and he was an incredible storyteller, he was good in bed (better than good. *We* were good together and we did it twenty times a day, proud and naive), he liked quiet and alone time, he got along well with my friends, he was handsome. He was nice, even. Though I'd never been particularly excited by nice guys, his way of being nice was really attractive – I thought it was sexy. And even then, his desire for independence, his honesty about love and his own feelings, the clear-headed way he made me so much more grown up than I was – even if all these things hurt me, I loved them, I respected them. And there was something almost suspicious about the way he embodied everything I wanted. Maybe it was too good to be true. Maybe that was exactly why it couldn't last. Maybe I'd sabotaged our relationship because some part of me didn't really believe in it.

"You know what?" I said to Julie. "I think you're right. I don't think I know what I want. I have a bit of an idea, but… I'm too irritated to see straight. I mean, he was really, *really* incredible. It blinded me a little, I think. So now, I'm not really sure anymore. It's more mixed up than anything. I have the very distinct feeling that I know what I want, but there again, I only half trust myself."

"Maybe you shouldn't call him," said Ariane.

"You think so?" Julie asked her.

"Well… maybe it would do you some good just to let things ride for a little while, no? Just not to get any more mixed up, just to see what's going to happen and deal with that. Maybe you'd see things more clearly? No? I don't know…" It wasn't like Ariane to give relationship advice, and she seemed almost shy to me.

"Yes," I said. "I think you're right." She gave me a big

smile, completely proud of herself, and Julie stroked her
thigh. At the same time, Élodie came into the living room
shouting "Telephone!" She'd taken my cell into the kitchen
and was again holding it out as far away from her as she
could as if it were a bomb. "Teleph…" She looked at it.
"Oh. It's Julien."

I smiled and took the phone from her.

"Hello?"

"This is the worst night of my life." He was whispering.

"Okay, what's wrong now?"

"We're on a double date with Laurent and Carole."

Damned, damned double dates. I hated double dates
and double daters because they reminded me I couldn't go
on double dates because I wasn't double. And there was
something about the concept in general that seemed
deadly boring and predictable and put it for me in the
same category as suburban bungalows, nude pantyhose,
nine-to-five jobs, people who only go to restaurants on
Friday nights, or serve port and chocolate after a meal.
But about all, I was jealous. Not of beige pantyhose, but of
double dates and people in love.

"And?" I said to Julien.

"I don't know. It's awful. Awful! I don't know if it's
because Mathias and Carole both know that Laurent and
I know everything about them, but I've never seen such a
fucking awful, uncomfortable situation and… Seriously,
come pick me up, do something."

"Didn't we already talk about double dates? That even
with people you like, it's the antithesis of fun?"

"I know… It wasn't supposed to be that. But you
weren't answering at home, and we haven't been able to
get in touch with the big guy since noon."

"Had a fight with him. A big one."

"Really? Tell me about it."

"No, Ju… You're on your date, it's Ariane's birthday…"

"Any news from Gabriel?"

"He just called. I didn't ans… Hang on two seconds." I'd just gotten a text message. I looked at the display, it was Gabriel: "Free tonight? Maybe a drink at Le Lulli around 7?"

"Oh my God," I said to the girls. "He wants me to meet him at Le Lulli." The girls started chattering and giving opposing opinions. I was still looking at the phone and I could hear Julien's voice, and he wasn't murmuring anymore, "Who is it? What is it?"

"It's Gabriel," I said talking into the phone again. "Wants to go to Le Lulli with me. At seven."

"Oh my God, it's quarter to seven."

"I *know* it's quarter to seven. But I can't go. I have to breathe, I have to give him breathing room, I have to appear cool and distant. If I rush over there I'll look like a damn crazy woman." In front of me, Ariane was nodding her head yes.

I heard Julien's voice, and he apparently was no longer listening to me, he was saying, "It's Marine. Looks like Gabriel wants to see her." There were some indistinct noises and then there was Laurent's voice saying, "Well, I hope you're not going to go, are you?"

"No. No, no, no." There was only ONE thing I wanted to do: go. I could hear Carole saying, "Yes, she has to go," and Mathias agreed with her wholeheartedly.

"Marine?" said Laurent.

"What?"

He'd evidently moved away. "If you go, it might do you some good."

"Since when did you become rational?"

"Ohhh, I told Carole I loved her, okay. Against ALL my instincts. But, it was apparently the ONE thing I could do to get her to relax and be relatively cool and pleasant and… well, you know… it's not easy to… to lo…" The word, it seemed, was not going to become old hat from one day to the next. But there was progress. "What I mean is… You know, it's like the Band-Aid you pull off in one shot…"

I started to laugh: "You're very good at talking about love, Loulou."

"In any case, you see what I mean… Go, listen to what he has to say to you, after, you can see. No? If it can stop you from repeating the same things and asking us the same fucking questions all day long, I'm in favor of it."

"You want me to be happy with another man?" I was teasing him, but part of me was sincerely surprised.

"No, I just want you to stop rambling on about it." Silence. "Yes, yes, okay, I want you to be happy because I lo… ve you. Okay, that's enough, I said it, can we move on now?"

"Okay," I said with a big smile on my face. "But anyway, it's Ariane's birthday. I'm in Laval, I really can't go."

"I think you should go." My father was standing between the living room and the entryway and he was watching me. "If you don't go, won't you regret it?" He was talking carefully – it was completely unfamiliar territory for him, and he was moving forward with the thoughtful, polite look people have when they know they're away from home.

I was astonished. "I…"

"You should go, Marine."

Behind him, my mother came out of the kitchen, her oven mitt on her hip. "Raymond…"

"No, don't say no, Monique. She should go. If you want, I can drive you back to Montréal." He looked so decided and it was so exactly what I wanted to do, that I was already convinced. "Do you want me to drive you, Marine?"

I looked at my father, then at Ariane, who was signaling "Go, go, go" before she finally said, "Really, if you're going to regret it…" I was going to accept my father's offer when I suddenly remembered Laurent, on the phone, who was shouting to be heard.

"What did you say, Loulou?"

"I said, we'll come get you."

"What?"

He lowered his voice, "Marine, we are having such an awful time, and we're only on cocktails. I won't last through a meal. We're on our way." I could hear him walking. "I'm going to go pick up Marine in Laval," he said. "You coming?" From a distance, the voices of Carole, Julien and Mathias came to me in a chorus of "Yes, yes" and "Good idea" and "We're like Cupid" and "Yay! An adventure!" (which was followed by "An adventure in Laval? Shut up, you dope").

"You really have no life, do you?" I said.

"None at all," replied Laurent triumphantly.

I hung up. "They're on their way."

"They really have no life, do they?"

"None at all, ma'am!"

My father was looking at me with a big happy smile, and I went and wrapped my arms around him. Over his shoulder, I could see my mother with a gruff smile, murmuring, "Breathe." I blew her a kiss and went back to my cell to send Gabriel a message: "Sure, why not? On my way."

To: Fred
From: Marine Vandale
Subject: The unfathomable heart of men

....

Will you please tell me again, who was the clown that decided one day that women were complicated? Because, I swear, you guys break all the records.

To: Marine
From: Frédéric Vandale
Subject: Brotherhood of clowns

....

I think every man who's lived on Earth since the wonderful hunter-gatherer years in Africa has formulated that thought, Marine.

To: Fred
From: Marine Vandale
Subject: Re: Brotherhood of clowns

....

Yeah, well, your brotherhood of clowns is at least as complicated, if not more complicated than all the girls I've ever met. Can you please explain the true meaning of Gabriel's behavior and why Jeff's doing what he's doing, because neither Flavie nor I can figure out the doctor who's acting like a platonic lover and the housemate who took off for Gaspésie a week and a half ago.

To: Marine
From: Frédéric Vandale
Subject: Men's hearts

....

If I tell you our poor hearts are soft and fragile and we're afraid for them, will you tell me to take a hike?

To: Fred
From: Marine Vandale
Subject: Re: Men's hearts

....

Oh, yeah. You think our hearts aren't fragile? I'm such an idiot
and I'm so afraid of losing Gabriel completely that I see him
twice a week for dinners that are always fantastic, then I get
dropped off at the street corner with a little peck and a smile
that would make statues melt. And *Maman* and the sisters keep
telling me he'll come back, I just can't scare him again. Like
I'm not scared myself, Fred, I'm going to revolt.

To: Marine
From: Frédéric Vandale
Subject: Revolutionary steps

....

Okay, okay. Still no news from Jeff?

To: Fred
From: Marine Vandale
Subject: Exile in Gaspésie

....

No, he took off the day after our fight and just left a cryptic
note about camping in Forillon Park, and necessary distance.
And yesterday I found out he'd bing-bada-bing-ed with Flavie
the night before. So, from here, it looks like he's run away.

To: Marine
From: Frédéric Vandale
Subject: Re: Exile in Gaspésie

....

Bing bada bing bada bing bing bang?

To: Fred
From: Marine Vandale
Subject: RE: Exile in Gaspésie

....

Bada bing bing bang.

To: Marine
From: Frédéric Vandale
Subject: Surprise and dismay

....

Well now. And he didn't even tell me, the jerk. You're right,
Marine. Smells like he's run away. I can smell it from here.
Since when does big, old Jeff get scared?

To: Fred
From: Marine Vandale
Subject: Heart of men, bis

....

Since his soft heart met up with Flavie who is, I'd like to
remind you, quite a bit more substantial than all the Marie-
Bonheurs in this world.

To: Marine
From: Frédéric Vandale
Subject: Not too proud

....

Well, I shouldn't say so, but I'm starting to think those two are
giving us a bad reputation.

To: Fred
From: Marine Vandale
Subject: Look who's talking

....

Um... I wouldn't want to insinuate anything, but let's say as
far as commitment is concerned, you're not a record-holder
either. When and where was the last time you spent more than
six months with a girl?

To: Marine
From: Frédéric Vandale
Subject: Sneak attack

....

It was with Caroline Julien, at CEGEP. I'll grant you it isn't very recent, but I think you're very sneaky to bring that up with all the self-assurance of a girl who's managed to prove her point. It has nothing to do with fear, it's my legendary love of independence.

To: Marine
From: Frédéric Vandale
Subject: Men are blind

....

Yes, I'm sure that Gabriel and that other crank sitting on his rock in Forillon Park are telling themselves it's all about independence, too.

To: Marine
From: Frédéric Vandale
Subject: Men's rights

....

Listen, I'm not saying you're wrong or anything, but don't we have the right to be a little – and I do mean to say "a little," in the virile, self-assured tone you can imagine – scared once in a while?

To: Fred
From: Marine Vandale
Subject: Men's responsibility

....

You can have all the rights you want. But would it rip out your guts to admit it once in a while?

To: Marine
From: Frédéric Vandale
Subject: Re: Men's responsibility

Our guts and our balls, Marine. I don't have to write you a thesis on male pride, do I?

To: Fred
From: Marine Vandale
Subject: Proud animal

No, that's okay, I think I'm familiar with the topic. But, shit,
Fred, if that's the only reason Gabriel's not coming back, then
it's really too stupid. Because if *my* love doesn't get nourished,
the poor thing'll shrivel up. And I don't want it to shrivel up,
'cause I'm fond of the feeling and, no matter what the
Abominable Shick Shocks Man says about it, it really does
exist. And if it is really destined to die a natural death, then
Maman is going to go crazy, lose all hope and sell me to some
Thai pimps because between having a daughter who's a pros-
titute and a daughter who's an old maid, it's no contest for her.

To: Marine
From: Frédéric Vandale
Subject: Maternal mission

Well, she's ready to FedEx me her neighbor from across the
street, she's so sure we're "made for each other." What's the
neighbor from across the street like?

To: Fred
From: Marine Vandale
Subject: Advice

Let's just say if you get a package from FedEx that weighs 200
pounds, don't sign for it and have it returned to sender.

To: Marine
From: Frédéric Vandale
Subject: Re: Advice

....

Got it. Now, if I can give you a piece of advice: don't give up too soon, Marinette. If fear is what's motivating your man, he'll get over it. That's how we are. We're just a little slow.

To: Marine
From: Frédéric Vandale
Subject: Ya bunch of dopes

....

Yeah, I did notice that. Don't worry about it. Even if I wanted to, I couldn't give up hope. I think it's genetic. For the last week and a half the Count of Monte Cristo and I have been fighting the same fight: wait and hope.

:)

Chapter 18

I put the computer down next to me, under the ficus Jeff moved out onto the balcony every summer. It must have been almost seven o'clock, but the sun was still warm and I closed my eyes for a moment. "Wait and hope," I repeated out loud. It was stupid, and a little childish, but I believed myself. And I was almost comfortable in the hollow where I was waiting, I was peaceful and serene – I was passive. Élodie and Julien thought I was wrong for giving in, for finally giving up against the fortress that was Gabriel (and love in general, I always felt like replying), but I saw it as being more aware, being clear-headed once again. If Gabriel was meant to come back, he'd come back. And I didn't know if it was just drowsiness brought on by the July heat or weariness, but I just couldn't get worked up about it anymore, simply because there was nothing I could do about it.

"*Maman* can't do anything about it, can she?" I said to Claude François, who was sensually rolling around in a puddle of sun. "*Maman* can't do anything about it." I took a sip of rosé and closed my eyes and did the only thing I'd been able to do for the past few days: imagine Gabriel's return, the bright, gentle scene that would precede our meeting, the magic, unforgettable words that would follow. I had a thousand versions of it in my head, and I would polish them lovingly, and fine-tune them according to our most recent conversations, and stretch out with a kind of lascivious happiness. I'd linger a little on the clothes we'd be wearing, the exact intonation of his voice and the strict meaning of my words, our glances, the people around us, witnessing the rebirth of our love.

"You've really gotten ridiculous," Laurent would say to me. "I know," I would answer, but it's so much easier than being actively crazy. Just in my head. It's a lot less risky." He would laugh then, and get up to get another glass of white wine, and we'd drink together on the little terrace behind my studio.

They'd shown up in Laval, the night of Ariane's birthday, grinning from ear to ear, with a bottle of convenience-store wine that they'd bought on the way so they wouldn't arrive empty-handed.

"And, we also have…" said Julien rummaging around in a big bag, "plantain chips… guava juice… that seems like your kind of thing, guava juice, no?… a copy of *Adbusters*… a *Marsupilami* piggybank…" One by one, Ariane laughingly took each gift, while next to her, Julie was looking worriedly at the bag, as if she were wondering what useless item would emerge from it next. "… and a copy of lesbian erotic photos." He winked at Ariane and added, "Welcome to the club," which was followed by a groan from my poor father. "Sorry," said Laurent. "It's just that we didn't have much time, so we got everything at Multimag, it was easier… We thought about some Kleenex with little hearts on them, but they were on bleached paper, so…"

He went to sit down when Carole pointed out that the original idea was to get me to Le Lulli for seven-thirty, a feat that was going to be difficult to accomplish since it was already seven-ten. Five minutes later, Laurent was choking himself shouting "Go go go, people, goooooo!" like he was in charge of a battalion in Vietnam, as we ran towards the car where I ended up sandwiched in back between Mathias and Carole, while Julien, triumphant and jubilant, was in the passenger's seat.

"Are you ready?" asked Laurent. "Yes? Well, let's hit the road…"

"Is it just me or is he having way too much fun?" I'd asked Carole.

"He's having *way* too much fun."

Mathias leaned against my shoulder. "If you'd been at the restaurant with us, you'd have fun picking up people in Laval, too. Wowzers."

"Wowzers?"

"WOW-zers."

There followed a cacophony of laughter and stories, each one emphasizing how boring the evening had been, "until we were saved by Laval, for Chrissake!"

"I think it's going to become a new measuring stick," Laurent had said. "From now on when I'm being bored to death somewhere, I'm going to ask myself, 'Would I be better off in Laval?' If the answer is 'yes,' then it's time to get the hell out."

They continued to dissect the evening for quite a while, trying to pinpoint the "source of the boredom torrent" that had flooded over them until Mathias pointed out that, after all, their fun was pretty dark. "We going to eat?" Laurent finally asked.

"Yeah, but what if the boredom suddenly sets in again?"

"We'll go back to Laval."

"Asshole."

"Really, you're hungry?"

"Well, we can eat at Le Lulli."

"Julien!" Mathias and I shouted at the same time.

"Whoa, hang on there... you didn't think we were just going to dump you off without taking advantage of our privileges, did you? We came and got you in Laval! At the risk of our very lives!"

"Yeah, you always have to be on the lookout for an attack by a bungalow or a shopping mall..."

"Excuse me! The Colossus, the Cosmodome, the... the Fuzzy... don't those sound like alien neighborhoods to you?"

"Mathias, can you make him shut up?"

"Oh, I can be quiet, but we ARE eating at Le Lulli. You owe us that much. We have a right to front-row seats."

"Julien. No."

"Come on."

"NO!" we all shouted with one voice.

"All right already! Go eat wherever you want and…"

"I want to see you sitting all alone in a dark corner!"

"Okay! Okay… Shit, nobody understands me…"

Mathias had run a hand through his hair. We were almost there. "Seriously," I'd said. "Do you think I'm doing the right thing? Maybe he'll think I'm pathetic, maybe he'll…"

I'd felt one of Carole's manicured hands on my thigh. "I think you're doing the right thing. You listened to your heart." I'd looked at her, surprised, without saying anything. A long time ago, I'd decided that "Listen to your heart" was one of the most ridiculous things a human being could say in their whole lifetime: it was meant to be deep and daring, but it only meant one thing, really, make the worst decision possible and, if you ever regret it afterwards, justify it by saying you were listening to your heart, noble and magnificently fallible organ that it is. I almost answered Carole that I hadn't listened to my heart, I'd listened to my father, but she was smiling at me with such confidence, and something that looked even like admiration (she had undoubtedly told her heart to be quiet a number of times – unfortunately, that's what it took to live with Laurent), that I smiled back at her and squeezed her hand.

I'd gotten out of the car outside Le Lulli, feeling strangely calm. When I'd turned around, Julien was sort of making a face and signaling for me to call him later and Mathias was shouting, "Patience, Marine! It always pays off." That was as helpful as telling a shopaholic to save money, I'd thought as I'd crossed the street, with my heart light and my head almost empty. I was there, I'd come, all I had to do now was listen to him. The ball was in his court, I was telling myself, and I found that thought utterly soothing.

He was writing in a little notebook when I came into the bar – I stopped in the doorway for a moment to look at him, to take advantage of the fact he hadn't seen me. I'd known him for such a short time – a little less than five months, what was that in terms of an entire life? – but, already, the shape of his shoulders was gentle and familiar to me. I examined his profile, the way he held his pencil, his long legs beneath the table, and I suddenly felt so close to him that I had an urgent desire to hold him tight. What we'd had together had been so good, I thought to myself. Why put the brakes on? The idea that it was over forever, that he might happily consider me just a friend, made me feel more sad than hurt, because all I could see was a terrible waste and I didn't even know who I was madder at over it.

First, he'd noticed my reflection in the window next to him and he'd turned towards me with a happy smile that went straight to my heart. "Come back to me," I felt like saying as I sat opposite him, "Come back to me."

"I'm happy to see you."

"Me, too." I'd placed one hand on his little notebook. "You writing?"

He shook his head and shrugged his shoulders as if to say it was nothing, just an unimportant little pastime. "I don't write very well. But I like it."

And I was in that state of love where everything he did seemed adorable and touching, and I was almost mad at him for writing in a little black notebook because it was another habit that made me love him even more.

There was a period of silence punctuated by stolen looks – his green eyes avoided mine, but when our gazes did cross, his instantly lit up with a smile that both enchanted and disconcerted me. He rested his forearms on the table and leaned the top half of his body towards me a little. "So," he'd said. "How is everybody?"

So we'd started talking. Talking like we always did, wholeheartedly and for a long time, a little too quickly and sometimes a little too loudly when we got carried away, each encouraged by our ideas and our sense of humor. The conversation flitted on nicely, hopping from one topic to another, combining subjects, going back and forth. He'd pushed back his chair and was sitting with his profile towards the table, his back leaning against the big window, which was open up to my head and letting in a warm breeze and the sound of wind in the leaves. He ran a hand through his hair from time to time, leaned his head back when he laughed, did all the insignificant little things that have no meaning except for the people we love, and I didn't even know anymore if I thought he was handsome because he really was or because, for me, he had all the infinite, eternal graces of a loved one.

We'd ordered another bottle of wine and he was sitting opposite me again, with his arms crossed on the table, and he'd finally looked me in the eyes. And then, as I was waiting, almost carefree, to hear the words I'd been dreaming of for weeks, he'd said, "Someone died today on my shift."

I'd instinctively pulled back. I knew death was part of his day-to-day life, but it wasn't common in mine. And its sudden presence between us, in the charming and incredibly lively context of a bar on a summer's evening, left me totally speechless.

"You never get used to that."

"Never?"

"No. I don't know a single doctor who's gotten used to it."

"Was it... was it your fault?"

"No. There was nothing I could do. It was a car accident, the guy had a perforated liver. His whole abdomen was done for – he'd been on the passenger side and the door was smashed in, and I mean, completely smashed in, and everything had slammed right into him… On the other hand, his head was perfect. He was conscious." He'd paused for a second and then said exactly what I was expecting: "He was my age. It's always weird when they're young."

I'd wondered, terribly selfishly, if that was why he'd wanted to see me.

"So thank you for being here," he'd said. "It's really making me feel better to think about something else."

Oh. So he'd wanted to think about something else. So I was the friend to help him think about something else. You think too much, I said to myself, you think too much and you analyze everything. Stop it. Let go. Breathe, as my mother would say.

But my mother and her oven mitt were far away, they were in Laval serving vegetarian moussaka, and I was sitting downtown with a bottle of white wine and a man who made me feel better than I could anywhere else, and I'd added, "Gabriel… I feel like I'm walking on eggshells." And he thought for a minute about I-don't-know-what kind of answer, and I imagined myself walking delicately across a floor of eggshells and I'd thought, "Hmpf. There are some expressions that are even dumber than 'Listen to your heart.'"

Gabriel slowly shifted back to leaning against the window, looked straight ahead for a moment, then turned back towards me – he was obviously choosing his words carefully, and finally, he came up with, "You have… you have plans, Marine."

"What?"

"I can see it. I know it. You want… you have plans."

"What plans? Which plans? I don't understand."

"You imagine the future."

I was completely taken aback. "But of course I imagine the future! That's a good one! Who doesn't imagine the future?"

"I don't imagine the future. I thought we were doing great one day at a time…"

"Are you *kidding* me?"

"What, we weren't doing great?"

"Shit, Gabriel, you're smarter than that."

"No, I don't imagine the future. Because the future I once imagined blew up in my face."

"But I… I'm not imagining the *future*, I…" I what exactly? I'd imagined hundreds of statements, but "You imagine the future," was one I really hadn't expected. "You're too needy," "I'm not ready yet," "I'm in love with another woman," "I don't want to make a commitment," "In fact, I'm a transsexual and I've always preferred men" – any of these would have surprised me less. And there I was, wrapped in the July breeze, being reproached for an imaginary future.

I didn't know what to say. Had I imagined a future? Did I have plans? Suddenly, I regretted telling Julien not to eat at Le Lulli – if he'd been there, at least I could have asked Gabriel to wait a minute while I debriefed and vented a little with him, discussed the situation with someone who spoke my language instead of this strange, adored creature who talked about dying young and feared the future.

"I…" I didn't get angry, I didn't even want to cry, I was simply tired and too disconcerted to formulate a constructive thought. "I don't think I can keep doing this, Gabriel. I'm sorry. I can't keep seeing you like this then…" I'd let the unfinished sentence float between us for a moment and then Gabriel, with a look that broke my heart because I could see more regret than anything else in it, had answered, "Okay, I understand then."

But apparently, he didn't understand, and I was able to keep seeing him like this and then to… There were dinners, coffees, the hope I could never completely squash and the fact that he seemed to need to see me and talk to me regularly. "It's too absurd," I said to Julien. "I'm literally having a platonic love affair with Gabriel. Will you please tell me why we can't just sleep together and have things back the way they were?"

"Because you *can't* get things back the way they were," Julien replied, in an infinitely weary voice, as he studied the combination of his new violet tee-shirt with his green jeans in the mirror. "You can never go back to the way things were, Marine. And I don't mean to turn the knife in the wound, but you're the one who burned the bridges getting back. With what you said. You can't just start screwing again without being sure if you're a couple or just lovers after what you said to him. If you're going anywhere, it should be straight ahead, and that's where the love you mentioned is too, and so is the future he's afraid of and which, by the way, you're afraid of, too."

"Less than he is."

"Now, that's funny. No one rushes like that with predictions and dreams and plans."

"I don't have plans!"

"… and plans after just two months unless they're scared to death. No one makes that kind of demand of a guy – or a girl for that matter – unless they have a secret desire to get dumped right there. You knew he'd choke, Marine."

"No!"

"Yes, you knew it. But it scared you less than living in insecurity."

"You're killing me."

"It always kills you when I'm right."

"You're double killing me."

"Come on, let's go. Let's go see how my new tee-shirt does on the terrace at Unity."

That night, he'd turned around before he'd left and said, "You know, Mathias and I can't go back to the way things were for us, either. Our bridges were blown to hell in that whole mess, too. And there sure are times when I have the cold sweats when I think there's no going back. But it's the best thing that can happen to people like us, Marine. Just one choice: forward! *Adelante*! To infinity and beyond!"

"To infinity and beyond," I said to the cat who was sitting opposite me and looking at me with adoration. Then, more loudly still, with one fist raised in the air, I repeated, "To infinity and beyond!"

"Hey, everything okay up there?"

I leaned over the railing. Two floors down, Flavie's face was looking up towards me, "Have you gone crazy or what?"

"People have gone crazy for less, no?"

"Yeah, you can say that again." She stretched out a hand with a bottle of rosé in it. "Shall I come up?"

A bottle and a half later, we were now on the balcony shouting "To infinity and beyond," towards the sky, so loud that the dog across the way had started yapping.

"Maybe we should give it a rest," I said to Flavie.

"You may be right. Still no news from Jeff?"

We'd avoided that topic since she'd arrived – she didn't mention him to me and I thought that her silence demanded my own.

"No," I answered. "Not a peep."

"What bullshit."

"I agree it's pretty lame. I even agree it's worse than pretty lame."

"You know what's really a pain in the ass? The fact that that pussy asshole has made me doubt myself."

"What? No, no, no, no, no." I wagged a drunken finger under her nose. "No no. Not you. You are forbidden to doubt, is that clear? Geez, he's the one who got scared, he's the one that used the varnishing powder…"

"Vanishing."

"Whatever. He's the one that ran off to Gaspésie like a little girl, so no. I absolutely will not stand for us to start doubting ourselves, just because we fell for two cowards."

"Aren't *you* afraid?"

"Of course I'm afraid, but I'm here, aren't I?"

Flavie shook her head. "I don't know. I don't understand, that's all. We see each other for weeks. We flirt like there's no tomorrow, we end up sleeping together and it was good. It was really good. You believe me, Marine?"

"Well…" It's always a little uncomfortable to talk to a girlfriend about your best friend's sexual prowess. "Yes, yes, sure." Especially since I could imagine the two of them, made for each other, larger than life – you never know, of course, but it seemed to me it could only be magnificent, that there must have been earthquakes, tectonic shifts, tsunamis. "In fact, I'm sure sure," I said, relieved to talk about something other than the act itself. "He wouldn't have left if it had been ordinary. I'm telling you he took off because he's afraid. And there's only one thing Jeff's afraid of. Falling in love."

"Isn't that kind of a simple theory?"

"Why do you think he spent his life with girls who were pretty as anything, even though he thought they were dumb? Because he could have fun with them, with no risk of falling for them. He'll never admit it, but…"

"Or maybe he left because of your fight. Maybe you're the one he's afraid of falling in love with."

"What? No. That's crap…"

"You see what I mean when I say he makes me doubt myself? What bullshit…"

"I'll drink to that." We clinked glasses in the setting sun.

There wasn't much to add after all: we'd asked for the impossible for fear of seeing the possible materialize too quickly, and they were afraid of our demands. What a wonderful mess, I thought, emptying my glass.

"It's absolutely fantastic," I said as I put Fred's manuscript down on the table. "Absolutely fucking fantastic."

"Don't you think you're a little biased," Julien asked.

"Of course I'm biased, Dopey, but that doesn't mean I can't read... If it was crap, I'd just *pretend* to like it because I love Fred, but I wouldn't say it was fantastic."

Beside me, Laurent was sipping his mimosa as he flipped through the pages. "What's it about?"

"It's a little weird, if you just say it out, but it's the story of a writer who one day decides to wr..."

Laurent let his head drop down onto the manuscript and imitated a loud snore.

"Okay, that's enough, you lowbrow jerk. Just because you've never read a book in your life..."

"I'll have you know, I devour *Le Guide de l'auto*, every year."

Julien and I exchanged an amused glance. It was a running gag between us – Laurent had raised his allergy to books to the status of a phobia, and he was always sure to remind us of it by yawning and snoring loudly, unless he just grabbed himself by the throat and made croaking noises like he was being strangled.

"Anyways," I said to Julien. "I'm telling you it's great. You should read it."

"I'd love to! Oooh! A preview of a future Goncourt Prize winner!"

"Okay, don't go overboard just yet, eh? But you'll see, it's... I don't know, I was talking to Fred the other night and I was almost intimidated. It's like I just discovered that this person I know better than I know myself was... I don't know how to put it... like, if you suddenly discovered a huge extra room in a house where you'd lived all your life…"

"I'd like to say that for the sister of a supposedly great novelist, you're having an unusually hard time expressing yourself…"

"That's enough from you, Mr. I-get-pimples-if-I-see-a-book."

Laurent smiled at me and gave me a little bump with his shoulder. He'd almost finished his documentary on the *Main* and the first scenes I'd seen where more than conclusive. As complex and hard to follow as he was, his films were simple and to-the-point, intelligent, without excessive ornamentation. I gave him a little kiss on the cheek.

"Do you think I should have the smoked salmon or the grilled salmon?" Julien asked.

"Hey now, you on a diet or what?"

"Well, if I want to be a pretty boy on the beaches at Christmas, I'd better start now."

"Are we renting the house again this year?" Laurent asked. Every year, for the past five years, we'd gone to a huge house in the Dominican Republic that one of Julien's clients let him have for peanuts. The geometry varied – some years, there had been no partners, and there had been others when we were with someone, but the base was the same: Jeff, Julien, Laurent and I. At the mention of the house, the three of us looked at each other: if we went, would Jeff come with us? And most of all, could we go without him? There was something sacrilegious about the idea and suddenly images of the sea and white sand, the parrot fish that Jeff would grill on the big barbecue, the little trails that criss-crossed the mountain behind the house and led to sleepy little villages where children played with hoops and deflated balls, country taverns where we'd drink a mix of rum and condensed milk, the fluorescent green that surrounded the house – all these memories that

I'd held preciously inside me between visits now seemed heavy and almost empty.

"Still no news, eh?" asked Julien.

"Nope. You guys neither?"

"No."

"It's really weird. It's really, really weird. It's really, really, real…"

"That's enough, Marine. We get it."

"He'd been dreaming about Flavie for months. Flavie comes into his life and he buggers off. Still, it's exactly what we said this winter, remember? We were at our place, drinking Bloody Caesars and we said we had to stop acting like kids and take responsibility for our love life… Shit, you guys did it! Even *Laurent* did it!"

"Well, you don't really have to say it like I was mentally challenged or something…"

"Um… as far as emotional commitment is concerned, you're about as evolved as an amoeba, Loulou. So if even you managed to take the plunge, everyone should be able to do it."

"And if Julien has managed to not cheat on his boyfriend for three months…"

"Exactly."

"What are you waiting for then?"

I turned towards Laurent. Opposite us, Julien was observing the situation with the cautious, ready air of any man who had just spotted a grenade. "I'm waiting for…" What was I waiting for exactly? Gabriel, of course. But it was more than that. I was waiting to be able to not have plans, I was waiting to be able to be in love day by day, I was waiting to stop waiting.

"I don't know," I said. "I really don't know." I was about to add something else, when I saw Julien's eyes open wide – and before I even had the chance to turn around, Jeff sat down opposite me.

Two minutes later, despite my protests, Laurent and

Julien were on their feet, fleeing the table as fast as they could: Laurent claimed he'd forgotten a meeting with his film editor and Julien suddenly remembered he was supposed to meet Mathias all the way across town. As for Jeff, he had a strange five-day-old beard that looked pretty good on him and he was signaling to the server to bring him a glass of red wine. He looked tired.

"Did you sleep in Forillon?"

"Didn't go to Forillon."

"Where'd you go?"

"Québec City."

"Québec City?"

"Yep."

"You spent two weeks alone in Québec City?"

"Is that really harder to believe than Forillon?"

"Um… yes? Because, it's only two hours away and because you know very well that Julien and I went to Québec City last week and… Who spends two weeks in Québec City for the fun of it, anyway?"

"Someone who needs a break?"

"A break from what? What could you possibly need a break from?"

"What do you think?"

"From Flavie? Already?"

"You really think it was Flavie?"

"Do you really want me to believe it was something else?"

"Do you…"

"Okay, that's enough!" interrupted the server as he set down a tomato salad in front of me. "You've been talking in question for ten minutes, how do you feel about saying something else, instead?"

Jeff and I didn't say anything for a moment, watching the server as he took his time, setting the plate down just so, pouring a bit more wine into my glass. Then we exchanged a glance and, despite or because of our current problems, there was a hint of complicity – a half-smile, a dim spark, and we looked down, him at his glass, me at my tomatoes.

"What you did to Flavie…"

"I know…"

"But…"

"But what…"

"You know… Do you…?"

"Finish your sentences!" the waiter shouted from the next table.

"Hey!" said Jeff, pointing a finger at him. "Don't press your luck, you!"

I laughed, a little. "Jeff, seriously. I'm in no position to talk, but Flavie doesn't really understand, if you see what I mean. And personally, I don't really see why you fucked up something you'd wanted for so long and why you left after a little fight and why you didn't say anything to us… to Lo or Ju, or me, or even Fred, and why…"

"Okay, whoa! That's enough! I… That's too much. I needed some space to think, that's all. Didn't you ever just need a little… break?"

A break? I felt like saying. I'd needed a break for at least five years; I'd needed a break since my late teens, even. But that's just what we had to do, right? Tough it out, like the English say. You had to learn to swim in troubled waters when you were young before you could drop anchor, and take the famous break.

"Jeff…"

"I'm sorry I took off."

"No, no… it's for Flavie… I mean, she *really* doesn't understand and, honestly, in her shoes, I wouldn't understand either."

"I know, I know…" He took a drink of wine then looked me right in the eye, with one eyebrow raised. "You think I still have a chance?"

I choked into my glass. "Whoa, you've got some nerve

there, Jean-François Murphy. I don't know if you still have a chance, but if you do, you're going to have to work your ass off… Flavie's not exactly happy now…"

"But yeah, but no…"

"No no no!" I put one hand up in front of him. "Zero excuses, little man. You literally fled all the way to 'Gaspésie,' but you were really just hiding in Québec City and you never called the girl after you slept with her? There's no excuse for it, Jeff."

He put his head in his hands.

"Listen," I said. "Do you… do you really want things to work out?"

"What? I don't know, I…"

"Christ, Jeff, you had two weeks to think about it, and…"

"I don't know, okay?! I think so. I think so, but I can't be sure because, I'd like to remind you, I've never been in this situation, okay? I never…" He hesitated for a moment, choosing his words carefully. "Shit, I'm not good at this. What I mean is, it's that… I'm thirty-six years old. I can't screw around anymore. I don't *want* to screw around anymore, but I… I don't know how, okay?"

He looked so lost, so sincerely lost that I couldn't keep from laughing. It was a tender, sincere laugh and I took his hand. He laughed a little at himself, too, and added, "Christ, even Laurent's managed to quit fooling around…"

"I know! I know…"

"Your doctor…"

"Oh, forget it… It's absurd. We're in a sea of absurdity. We see each other twice a week, he calls me almost every night, but apparently he doesn't want anything serious with me. I think he just wants to be friends. To tell the truth, I don't know what to think anymore."

"I'm pretty sure he doesn't just want to be your friend. Believe me."

We smiled at each other. Then Jeff said, "I wasn't very

cool the other day. I... I know you... In fact, I don't know if you love him, but I do know it's what you thought. Sincerely."

I thought for a second – I could have gotten mad again, I could have screamed at Jeff that I really did love Gabriel, but I had neither the strength nor the desire to be stubborn. And there was a strong chance he was right – lately there was a strong chance anyone but me was right.

"Jeff?"

"Mmmm?"

"Do you think I have plans?"

"Plans?"

Then I explained Gabriel's theory to him. I told him about the plans he thought I had and that I wasn't sure I had, about the future I had already filled in, despite myself, about the waiting I couldn't take anymore because it had been going on too long. Opposite me, Jeff listened, only looking up from time to time to order another glass of wine.

"Marine," he finally said. "Do you think you can imagine things with Gabriel without projecting into the future?"

"Yes!"

"I'm not so sure..."

"Okay, Jeff? Don't start that again, okay? Because you are in no – I mean NO – position to talk. Because if anyone is projecting into the future, it's you. If you weren't projecting, you wouldn't have choked like that after you slept with Flavie."

He looked at me for a minute, vaguely insulted, then he shook his head. "Maybe it would be better if you and I didn't talk about this, eh?"

"Maybe, yeah."

"What do we do then?"

"I don't know... Ask for the check?"

"Ask for the check," repeated Élodie as she filed a nail. "That's quite an original statement."

"Well, what did you expect me to say to him? Let's go to couples therapy? It's been three days anyway and he's still acting like nothing was said."

"Yeah… really."

I crossed the studio, trying not to drop any of the ten rolls of paper I was holding against myself. Drawings that had accumulated since the beginning of the year, posters, two or three sketches. "Still," Élodie said, "he's not completely wrong."

"Hmm?" One of the rolls that was on the top started sliding to the right – I tried to catch it by leaning to the left, but, of course, the result was that all the rolls fell in a crash of crumpled paper, bumping boxes and echoing metal covers.

"OH!" said Élodie, covering her ears with her hands.

"Hey! That's enough. I'd like to remind you that you get paid for helping me around here and, for some reason I don't quite get, *I'm* the one lugging rolls of paper around while you file your nails." I looked at her with my hands on my hips and we both started to laugh.

"You are the worst, and I mean the *worst* employee in history. And if I thought for a single second that you'd changed your attitude with *Papa*, then I'm sorry."

"Hey! Don't laugh at me. You should know I have an interview for a job as an assistant at *Chérie*."

"What the hell is *Chérie*?"

"Um… just the best magazine for girls on the market?" She brandished a magazine whose cover was adorned with a model who must have been about fourteen, surrounded by pink and mauve headlines: "Your autumn horoscope," "How to drive him crazy in bed," and "Star quality make-up at low prices."

"Really?" I asked, very eagerly.

"Yes!"

"Like, you'll have a real job and I'll be rid of you as an employee?"

"Yessss!"

"Oh my Godddd!" I put my arms around her and we both hopped up and down, arms around each other, in the middle of the studio, until the phone started ringing. "Élodie," I said after five rings. "Unless I'm wrong, you haven't been hired by *Chérie* yet, right? So maybe you could answer the phone?" But it was too late, and of course, she settled for a little shrug of her shoulders. A few weeks before, she'd chosen to go back to the single life and it suited her remarkably well. Without having to worry about men who were never what she needed and always seemed contraindicated from the get-go, she was finally blossoming, and this could be read on her pretty face, which now was free of some of that make-up. But she was still the little princess she'd always been, and this was something I found reassuring and surprising – I realized that if she'd really changed, I would have had some serious mourning to do.

"Hello?" I said into my cell phone.

"It's me," said Julien.

"Did you just call the studio?"

"No, it was Jeff. Call him back. Call him back right now."

"I can't explain it on the phone," Jeff had said. "Just come home, okay?" And because it was Jeff and, despite what we'd been going through for the last few months, because I trusted him more than anybody, I jumped in a taxi and headed for home, wondering what he could have to tell me that was so urgent, what kind of words could only be spoken face to face. Laurent had called, too, and since I didn't answer, he'd left a message: "Um… It's me… Listen, I don't want to stick my nose in where it doesn't belong, but… I think Jeff just called you and uh… Just, go, okay?"

When I got to the door of the condo, I stopped for a minute. There was something somber about all these calls and this sudden, impromptu invitation that wasn't like Jeff at all, and I had an absurd inclination to knock on the door, as if I didn't have the key. After a few seconds, Jeff came and opened it. He stood in front of me, just looking at me without saying anything, as rain began to fall.

"Come on," I said. "What's going on?"

Jeff looked at me for another few seconds, then gently stepped aside – until, behind his wide shoulders, I could see Gabriel standing there.

I stood on the doorstep quite a while, looking back and forth from Gabriel to Jeff, occasionally muttering "Um," and sounding completely stupid, until Jeff said, "Okay, then… I have to go, I have… I have my thing… my… thing to do."

And since unexpected situations always make me a little stupid, I said, "What thing? What thing do you have to do?" and I saw Jeff turn back towards Gabriel with a look that clearly said, "Can you believe how thick she can be sometimes?" – and I immediately dispelled any doubt by triumphantly declaring, "Oh yeah! Your *thing*! Of course…" Opposite me, Gabriel, who was still standing there, with his arms crossed, burst out laughing.

I looked up towards Jeff – I wanted to say something, ask him fifty questions, but he gave me a little wink and pointed towards the door before he left. I turned around to say something to him (what, I have no idea). When I turned back towards Gabriel, he was still looking at me, with his arms still crossed, and he had a huge smile on his face.

"Wow," he said. "That was… How can I put it? Some performance!"

Now it was my turn to cross my arms and I tilted my

head to one side and gave him a nasty stare that made him laugh.

"I'm sorry, it's just that…" He was laughing whole-heartedly.

"Okay," I finally said. "What… Why…"

Gabriel, who was visibly enjoying the whole thing, was making big, encouraging movements with his head as he repeated after me, "What… "Why…"

"What the hell?" I finally shouted.

"What what?"

"Can you please stop teasing me?"

"I don't know, it's kind of fun."

He was wearing the old white tee-shirt that was too tight and that I loved 'cause it perfectly hugged that body that I'd adored, and I'd simply wanted to cross the few feet between us and wrap my arms around him, feel his arms around me and his lips on my face, but I was paralyzed and, I realized, I was actually scared to death.

"Jeff called me," Gabriel finally said.

"Jeff called you?"

"Yup." He nodded his head in an exaggerated way, as if to say he was as surprised as I was.

"Oh… I…" I almost asked him what Jeff had said exactly, but I was too afraid to hear the reply. "I… you want a glass of something?"

"I thought you'd never ask."

Relieved by having something to do, I walked overly quickly towards the kitchen and opened the liquor cabinet. The bottle of gin had been prominently placed and in front of it were two little cucumbers. I looked down with a smile – it wouldn't take much more to make me cry.

"What?" asked Gabriel.

I picked up the cucumbers in one hand and the bottle in the other and I showed him – and he had the exact same reaction as I had.

"Listen," I said.

"No. No, you listen."

"Okay." And while I got our drinks ready, Gabriel started to talk.

"I don't want to have any plans. I don't want to think that YOU have plans because the last thing I want to do in this world is disappoint you. I've disappointed a lot of girls, Marine. Since I got divorced, that's kind of who I've become – the guy who disappoints girls. Sometimes I didn't act right. I lied. But I can't lie to you and I don't want…"

"I don't have plans, Gabriel." I handed him his drink. "I know that's what you think, and I've really thought hard about it myself… Shit, it's all I've thought about for a damn long time, but I don't have any plans, it's just not true. But, I do have dreams. I have dreams."

"It's the same thing."

"No, it's not the same thing since… Hang on two seconds, are you telling me you don't have any dreams? What kind of person has no dreams?"

"I'm not talking about that kind of dream. I'm talking about the kind of dream…"

"Okay, you didn't come here to give me a lesson in semantics, did you?"

Obviously, we were getting off to a bad start. Outside it was now raining cats and dogs and the hammering of the raindrops on the skylight was almost deafening.

"Sorry," I said. "Sorry. But just listen to me for a second. I have dreams. I've always had dreams. I'm Joe Dreamer. That's what I do with my life, Gabriel, I dream. I dream when I'm walking down the street, when I'm reading, when I'm drawing, when I'm looking outside, before I go to sleep and when I wake up. That's just how I am."

"I know, Marine, but I…"

"Let me finish. They're just dreams, okay? They're not plans. Moving dreams that change and are transformed… Sometimes you're in them and sometimes I'm all alone on a beach in Tasmania, sometimes… Shit, they're just dreams, get it? Why do you think you feel alone like you do, Gabriel? Why do you think you were so attracted to us? Maybe just because we don't hold back from dreaming, just out of fear of falling on our face."

It was a little melodramatic, and certainly a low blow. Gabriel had told me, just once, about the solitude that inhabited him, despite his family, his co-workers, his friends. But I was hurting and I was weak when I was around him – and because of that, I wanted him to suffer, too.

As usual when he was angry, Gabriel spoke in an even calmer tone: "I just don't want... I just don't want you to ask me for anything, okay? Because if I'm going to give you anything, I want it..."

"Oh, stop saying that! That's just bullshit! If you're that fucking scared, Gabriel, it means you're not interested in me, okay? And it would be sincerely appreciated if you'd just have the guts to say so clearly for once."

"HEY! WHOA!"

I stepped back – I'd never heard Gabriel raise his voice. He was facing me, on the other side of the bar and was pointing a finger at me. "Can you just stop accusing other people for two seconds?"

"I'm not accusing you of anything!"

"Um, excuse me? You just told me, one, I was fucking scared and, two, had no guts."

"Do you have any? Do you have any guts?"

He opened his mouth to say something then he was quiet – I started talking, serving myself another drink, my head stubbornly pointed towards the counter because I figured as long as I didn't look at him, there was no risk I'd start crying.

"I don't know what you're doing here, Gabriel."

"Sorry?"

"I said: 'I don't know what you're doing here.'"

"I don't think I know either."

We were silent for a moment, with the counter between

us. I was convinced he was going to turn and walk out and I know that, if he did, I wouldn't have the strength to stop him.

"What did Jeff tell you?" I asked him, concentrating on everything except him, our glasses, a book that was sitting there next to the stove, Claude François purring at my feet.

"He let me have it, if you must know. He told me I was a fucking clown if I missed out on a girl like you and I'd better quit screwing around if I didn't want to lose you."

"You don't want to lose me?"

"No. No, I don't want to lose you."

"What do you want, then? To be my nice doctor friend? To be my…?"

"Stop it! Stop it, Marine! Do we really need to spell it out? Do you need a life plan before…"

"… I DON'T HAVE PLANS!"

"Oh give me a break, okay? I'm still here, Marine, and I don't want to be mean, but there are a lot of guys who would have split a long time ago."

"That's a surprise."

"Okay, you see? You *see*?" He was pointing his finger at me again. Mechanically, I refilled his glass. "You see, that's just it. Every time we had a conversation that got a little close to that, I felt like you were lecturing me because I wasn't enough of a knight in shining armor. He's not coming, Marine. Your knight in shining armor isn't coming. Just me. But you're going to have to take me as I am."

"How can you ask me to do that? YOU don't take me as I am. You don't even want to deal with the fact that I have dreams, in life."

"Stop lecturing me, Marine. Stop lecturing me, because, for your information, that's something I've already done in my life. I accepted someone for who she was. And I know what kind of risk and sacrifice it takes, and I know the price you might have to pay. So don't tell me I'M afraid. I've already been where you want to go."

"Okay, could you be any MORE condescending?"

He almost starting shouting, "I have other things to do than be condescending, Marine, you're not listening! The *second* I say something you don't want to hear, you stop listening! It's a game for two, Marine, I'll have you know. It's a dialogue!"

"What is?"

"Love."

There was a period of silence. I could only hear the rain and that last word echoing in me: love. Gabriel slowly came around the counter and stood in front of me. I looked up at that face which was all I desired – towards what was behind it, too, his mind, his heart, this imperfect man who I wouldn't want any other way.

"I'm not going to stop dreaming, Gabriel."

"Okay."

"Okay?"

"Okay."

I put both my hands in front of my mouth. I don't think, at any time in my life, that I've ever looked into someone's eyes so intensely. He gently took each of my wrists and spread my hands apart, then he kissed me. When he finally let go of my hands, we were still kissing and I could finally put my arms around him – my hands were grasping his hair, I was sighing in his ear and I could feel his mouth on my neck when he said, "Give me another chance, okay?"

Afterward

"I'm too hot. I'm really too hot."

"Get under the umbrella, dummy."

"What about my tan?"

"If I hear another word about anybody's tan, I'm impaling them with the umbrella," said Laurent.

Julien smiled lecherously: "Hmm… impaled on an umbrella."

"Barf!" shouted Laurent, without even bothering to remove the tee-shirt he was using to protect his face from the sun. "Bar-arf!"

"Seriously," I said to Julien, "maybe you should sit in the shade. You're going to roast."

"Oh, no no. The pretty boy of the beaches doesn't fear the sun. *El minetto de la playa no tiene miedo del sol.*" He flexed his bicep in the light. "Something else, eh? For a forty-year-old guy, it's not bad…"

"Gabriel is forty," mumbled Laurent. "Does he spend the whole day trying to make us look at his biceps?"

"Well, I notice them anyway," said Julien. "Oh, I notice them… Look at that… Meow…"

"Cut it out already," I said, while next to me, Laurent was shouting, "BARF! You're never interested in any guy over thirty!"

"Hmpf… maybe I'm willing to make a little exception."

"Shut up!"

I took off my dark glasses to look at Gabriel as he came towards us. The sparkling, blinding ocean unfolded behind him – the beach was almost empty and stretched out on each side in a long, light croissant, bordered by the uneven, thought-provoking shapes of mountains, a blessed virgin on the left and a Greek profile on the right.

"Hey," he said as he sat down on the end of my chair.

"Hey," I answered, blinking my eyes in the sun.

"Is the water nice?" asked Laurent, though he would have preferred to die rather than stick a toe in the ocean.

"The water is perfect." Gabriel took my left leg and raised it towards him for a kiss, then he pulled me towards him, making me flop down suddenly onto the end of the chair.

"HEY!" I was laughing like a little girl, giving in to the stupid, simple pleasure of pretending to fight. Then he stretched out on top of me, while I pretended to struggle, shouting he was all wet, that he was going to rumple my book, all those silly things we say in those situations even though the ocean is made for people to get wet, and the books we read on the beach never come home intact.

"I love you," Gabriel whispered as he kissed me. His tongue tasted like salt.

"I lov…" I hadn't even finished my sentence when Jeff and Flavie's voices reached us from the house, although it was more than fifteen meters from the beach. The words were unclear, but one thing was clear, they were fighting, and not just a little, more like cats and dogs, like a whole pack of cats and dogs.

Being careful of me, Gabriel sat back up and extended a hand towards Julien. "Three hundred pesos. You owe me three hundred pesos."

"Okay, okay. I'll pay the next round at the bar on the hill." The bar on the hill consisted of a sheet metal roof held up by four cement pillars, and we went almost every night because the family that ran it was adorable and from it's location on the mountain, you could see the ocean and the sun as it slowly died over the waves in a burst of flame that left us as silent and as thoughtful as we would have been in a divine presence. "Man," Julien went on. "I would have thought we could get at least one day without…"

From the house, a strident, "Fuck you!" reached our ears. Gabriel looked at me and we both laughed.

"Give me a chance," he'd said to me five months earlier, and I'd wondered if it wasn't more like he was giving me one. And after the caution of the first few weeks, there came a gradual abandon until one morning in September, which still seemed like the middle of summer, when, as we looked into each other's eyes, lying side-by-side between the sheets Gabriel said, "I love you." I'd put one hand on his face and he'd taken me in his arms, and we stayed motionless for a long time. With my chin on his shoulder, through the window, I was watching the sun dancing on the leaves of the tree across the way and I smiled till my cheeks hurt.

"Weren't you supposed to go get some drinks?" Laurent asked me, raising the tee-shirt just enough to look at me.

"Oh, no. I'm not going in there. Really. They scare me. Ju?"

"No! I'm always the one who has to… No! I protest. I went yesterday and I'd like to remind you she had her boobs hanging out and…"

"She's French, that's normal."

"They're still boobs!" shouted Julien.

"We can always wait till Carole and Mathias get home," I suggested.

"Are you kidding me?" Julien said. "Every time they do the shopping, they take three hours." Recently, Carole and Mathias had discovered they enjoyed each other's company and they especially enjoyed what they called their gastronomic outings. Armed with Carole's little motorbike and Mathias' Spanish, they'd criss-cross the region looking for fishermen, produce growers and little farmers, and they'd come back laden with shining fish, conches, and whole octopi, fruit we didn't even know the name of in French, and chickens that hadn't even been plucked yet. Our meals were grandiose and stretched on late into the night – until we climbed onto the roof of the house to count the stars and finish our wine singing old French ballads while Flavie, looking splendid in her long summer dresses, spun in place, with her profile outlined against the dark night.

"Okay then," said Gabriel, in a surly tone. "I'll go."

"Are you sure, my love? Are you sure?"

"Somebody has to…"

He stood up, pretending to be somber and I kissed him. "My hero…"

"In any case," said Laurent, who was now sitting up on his chair, "if you don't come back, don't worry, we'll remember you."

"I know," said Gabriel.

Then Julien got up, just in time to give Gabriel a military salut. "He's really got a lot of guts," he said as he watched him walk away.

"I know…"

Five minutes later, Jeff was down at the beach, flopping down on the end of my chair, shouting, "Fucking crazy woman! She's a fucking crazy woman!" I could have said something, but since his weight was about double mine, the end of the chair had sunk into the sand and I had literally flown into him, while Laurent and Julien applauded.

"Christ, Jeff!"

"Nice bikini," he answered – my breasts were in his face.

"Jeff!"

"Fucking crazy woman. I'm telling you, she's a fucking crazy woman. She's gonna drive me crazy."

"Um… did it ever occur to you that it's too late for

that?" Laurent suggested.

"You two are really made for each other," I said as I adjusted my bikini top.

After Jeff got back, he and Flavie didn't talk for a month. But I knew he was obsessed with her, and she was making such efforts to convince me she didn't give a shit about him, that I was sure he was at the heart of every thought she had. So I pulled a Jeff myself and arranged for them to meet, supposedly by chance. Since then, they hadn't left each other's side, fought eight hours a day, and adored each other the rest of the time.

In the big white house by the sea, we heard them make love every night – and some afternoons – and we'd exchanged surprised, amused looks when we witnessed the depth of their passion. "You think it'll work out okay?" Carole, always the practical one, sometimes asked. One night, Julien answered, "Even if it doesn't work out, it'll be splendid."

"Geez, it's taking a long time," said Jeff after twenty minutes. "What are they doing in there?"

"They're talking, you big dope."

He made a face. Jeff had become another man with Flavie, he was just a little more human, and it only made me love him all the more. The two of us had spent an evening together, after I'd gotten back together with Gabriel. He'd spoken with a vulnerability that knocked me off balance at first, then it moved me, then it made me love him still more. "When I was in Québec City," he'd said, "I could only think of one thing: I wanted to be happy. And I couldn't be happy if you weren't happy."

"If you're not happy, I can't be happy either."

"I was so afraid you'd be mad at me for calling Gabriel."

"It's the most generous thing anybody's ever done for

me."

I heard Carole's motorbike as she parked it in the alley next to the house.

The four of us were stretched out on our lounge chairs, facing the ocean.

"My mother called this morning," I said.

"And?"

"Oh, same old, same old. My sisters are fine – Élodie has fallen in love with a guy who has two first names and three last names. Ariane dumped Julie and started going out with someone called Mathilde… My parents have put the house on the market."

"What?"

"Yup. They want to move to Florida."

The boys started to laugh. Opposite us, three little boys and a little girl passed by, at the end of his arm, the oldest was holding a kite that had risen thirty meters in the air. We watched them go by, then I got up.

"Too hot," I said. "I'm going in the water."

Slowly, I crossed the space separating me from the ocean, savoring the bite of the burning sand on my feet and the sun on my shoulders. When I turned back, I saw Jeff, Laurent and Julien, still stretched out on their lounges, laughing together. Gabriel was on his way down to the beach with a bottle of rosé and he waved at me. "I love you," I said, more or less to myself.

Then I advanced into the blinding, turquoise waves, letting their waters envelope me, as I slowly lost my footing, and I realized I'd finally regained my balance, I wasn't afraid anymore.

To: Fred
From: Marine Vandale
Subject: Test

....

Is this working?

To: Marine
From: Frédéric Vandale
Subject: Obviously

....

Of course it's working, why?

To: Fred
From: Marine Vandale
Subject: Nagging doubt

....

If you could see the size of the thing I'm emailing you on, you
wouldn't believe it, and besides, you never know, apparently,
after some authors get published, they become a little bit distant.

To: Marine
From: Frédérique Vandale
Subject: Short distance

....

And what if I replied that some people, when their hearts are
satisfied, become a little bit distant themselves?

To: Fred
From: Marine Vandale
Subject: Mini distance

....

I'd suggest you look out your window. You didn't tell me the
chestnut trees were already flowering in Paris.

To: Marine
From: Frédéric Vandale
Subject: Re: Mini distance

....

Hang on, where are you?

To: Fred
From: Marine Vandale
Subject: Open your window

....

We're at the café downstairs from you. The tall dark-haired guy
in the turtleneck, and the little blond girl in the gray toque,
can you guess who? Come down, Fred. We're not going anywhere. We're waiting for you.